T0283551

FREEDOM'S
GHOST

FREEDOM'S GHOST

A MYSTERY *of the*
AMERICAN REVOLUTION

ELIOT
PATTISON

COUNTERPOINT
Berkeley, California

Freedom's Ghost

This is a work of fiction. All of the characters, organizations, and events portrayed in this novel are either products of the author's imagination or are used fictitiously.

First Counterpoint edition: 2023

Library of Congress Cataloging-in-Publication Data
Names: Pattison, Eliot, author.
Title: Freedom's ghost : a mystery of the American Revolution / Eliot Pattison.
Identifiers: LCCN 2023019117 | ISBN 9781640093201 (hardcover) | ISBN 9781640093218 (ebook)
Subjects: LCSH: United States—History—Revolution, 1775-1783—Fiction. | LCGFT: Historical fiction. | Detective and mystery fiction. | Thrillers (Fiction)
Classification: LCC PS3566.A82497 F74 2023 | DDC 813/.54—dc23/eng/20230501
LC record available at https://lccn.loc.gov/2023019117

Jacket design by Farjana Yasmin
Jacket art © Science and Society Picture Library / Bridgeman Images
Series design by Jordan Koluch
Book design by tracy danes

COUNTERPOINT
2560 Ninth Street, Suite 318
Berkeley, CA 94710
www.counterpointpress.com

Printed in the United States of America

1 3 5 7 9 10 8 6 4 2

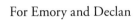

For Emory and Declan

But what do we mean by the American Revolution? Do we mean the American war? The Revolution was effected before the war commenced. The Revolution was in the minds and hearts of the people, a change in their religious sentiments, of their duties and obligations . . . This radical change in the principles, opinions, sentiments and affections of the people was the real American Revolution.

—JOHN ADAMS, *writing in 1818 on the founding of the United States*

FREEDOM'S
GHOST

Chapter 1

"DEAR LORD, NO! NOT THE GRINDERS!" yelled the elegantly dressed man at Duncan McCallum's side. "Veer away, for the love of God, or all is lost!" Duncan could not recall if he had ever heard his companion so frantic, but the blood was rising among all the spectators of the race, and John Hancock's desperate cries could be forgiven. It was his cherished personal yacht that was about to lose its keel to the notorious bed of submerged rocks and sandbars at the edge of Marblehead Harbor. "Too close, I say! Too close!"

Duncan, not sharing Hancock's anxiety, watched through his pocket telescope as the women on board scurried on the deck and in the rigging, tightening one line, loosening another, while Sarah Ramsey kept her steady hand on the wheel of the sloop. Sailing had become a passion for Sarah ever since the day Hancock had taken them for an afternoon cruise months earlier. Duncan had commanded Hancock's commercial ships on short runs to Bermuda and Newfoundland, and as their friendship blossomed the Boston merchant had generously offered the yacht with its crewmen for Duncan and Sarah to use on their own rare days of leisure. Knowing his fiancée's questing ways, Duncan had not been surprised when she had asked if she might take the helm on their first such day, then asked him to name for her the sails and each element of the rigging. "A fair return," she had quipped, reminding him of how she had once taught him the Iroquois words of her youth. Since that day she had become an adept sailor, and on the last harbor cruise with Hancock she had astounded Boston's merchant prince by taking the yacht's helm to thread a course through the outer islands.

No one, however, had expected Sarah to speak up days later at a dinner at Hancock's regal Beacon Hill home to challenge the commander of the local revenue cutter to a competition. Duncan had often revisited that conversation, trying to navigate its many subcurrents. Sarah had no love for the British navy, especially the patrol vessels that enforced Britain's onerous trade laws. Until that point she had adroitly guided the discussion among Hancock's guests, avoiding the traps that seemed inevitable in Boston when the dinner company included both officers of the occupation troops and leaders of the Sons of Liberty.

Duncan did not recollect how, but the discussion had veered from the weather to the advantages of American-built ships in being able to sail closer to the wind than those from British shipyards. When the officers—at first surprised, then amused, that a woman could hold her own in such a conversation—had good-naturedly defended their shipwrights, Sarah had offered to prove her point.

"We must have a competition!" she ebulliently declared. "A match between boats of similar burden. Say the navy's fast revenue cutter and one of the sloops crafted in Marblehead, ending of course in Marblehead Harbor." The officers and Hancock had laughed but then leaned forward as she persisted. Sarah had turned to the youngest officer, who was well-known and largely reviled in Marblehead. "Why, come to think of it, Lieutenant Oakes, isn't that vessel under your command? Named for some archaic god, I recollect." She knew perfectly well the name of the boat.

The lieutenant's cool smile was close to a sneer. "I indeed have the honor to command the king's revenue cutter *Neptune*. Bristol built, and she can outsail any vessel she meets. But surely no captain of a comparable vessel would meet me, Miss Ramsey, since my nimble *Neptune* has already overtaken so many of them as they sought to evade the king's customs duties."

Duncan had suspected that Sarah had some hidden motive in openly taunting the arrogant Oakes, and her next words had removed all doubt. "Why, doesn't Mr. Hancock have just such a Marblehead boat? Suppose we Americans give you an advantage. I will take the helm of the Hancock yacht myself and crew her with the doddering females of Marblehead. Shall we say Sunday, a week?" She fixed Hancock with a pointed gaze, and then the merchant's face lit with understanding. Sarah wasn't taunting the navy; she was trying to calm troubled waters. The tension between the occupation troops and civilians was near the breaking point, and they desperately needed to find common ground, if only for an afternoon's distraction.

Several of the officers had been aghast, but when Hancock had vigorously exclaimed "Brava! Brava!" and raised his glass to Sarah, they had joined in his gleeful toast, their vigor growing when he proposed to host one of his famous teas at the race's end.

Captain Lawford, commodore of the navy's inshore fleet, likewise embraced Sarah's apparent intentions. "Why, that would be capital!" he exclaimed. "What say you, Oakes? I've no doubt we can arrange to have your cutter in those waters for a Sunday frolic with our American friends. What better way to celebrate the approach of spring!"

Sarah had shot a victorious glance at Duncan before raising her own glass. The women, he knew, would be from what she called her Nightingale Club, all from Marblehead sailing families. They would have cut their teeth on backstays, and all were secretly dedicated to Sarah's increasingly bold efforts in support of the nonimportation cause, aimed at cutting off trade with Britain.

"But sir," Oakes had protested, "we've had fresh intelligence that somewhere in the bay the traitor is at last going to—"

"Lieutenant! Have a care!" Lawford interrupted, then put on a more genteel expression. "Of course we shall defend the honor of His Majesty's navy." The commander of the inshore fleet raised his glass. "And fear not, Lieutenant. Surely you know the navy relies on the Heart of Oakes, eh?" he added, laughing at his wordplay with the familiar maritime fighting song.

Now, as Sarah guided Hancock's boat through the maze of rocky shoals and sandbars, Duncan began to worry not about her motive but whether her rash decision was going to destroy Hancock's elegant vessel.

"Thank God!" Hancock shouted with glee a moment later. "She's cleared it!" Oakes's *Neptune* was close behind, the lieutenant having decided to preempt Sarah's advantage by following her into the narrow passage between rocks and shore for the final sprint to the end of the harbor.

"It is not over, sir!" Lawford crowed. "My man has decided that two can play at this game! I shall soon have your guinea in my pocket, John!"

"Damnation, Duncan," Hancock quietly muttered. "He's right. Look at how the cutter's sails fill with the breeze. That foolhardy Oakes has laid on extra canvas."

"But the *Neptune*'s keel—" Duncan began. He had no need to finish his sentence as groans shot through the group of gathered officers. The sound of shuddering masts echoed across the harbor. The yard of the added topsail Oakes had hoisted snapped, tumbling to the deck in a tangle of lines. The cutter had cleared the rocks only to have one of the sandbars seize her keel. She lost all headway, and the furious shouts of her commander could be heard above the chaos. For a moment Duncan thought she would move no more until the tide came in; then, long seconds later, she inched forward. But as she finally cleared the bar, the signal gun at the finish line fired. A cheer broke farther down the harbor, where townspeople had gathered in dinghies and on the town wharf. Sarah was victorious.

With a gleeful laugh Hancock extended his palm toward the captain. Lawford good-naturedly dropped a heavy coin into it and looked over the assembly of officers. "Our redcoat has missed all the fun," he added, referring to Lieutenant Hicks, head of the small army contingent temporarily stationed in Marblehead. "I fear I owe him as well, for the scoundrel had the nerve to wager against the navy."

Lawford grinned as Hancock hurried down the dock to congratulate the crew of his mooring sloop. "The Boston papers will love this story. I will get no end of ribbing, I am sure. Oh my," the commodore added as the winning crew assembled on the dock. Two of the women had stripped to their petticoats during the competition, and the others, including Sarah, wore sailor's breeches. All had been saturated by the bow spray.

Sarah was shaking the water from her auburn curls as Duncan reached her. "I'm soaked!" she protested as he spread his arms to embrace her, then laughed as he ignored her warning.

"You laid a trap for Oakes," he whispered as he held her close. "You knew he would scrape."

"I seem to recall the very first advice I received from my sailing master," she said with an impish smile, "was to always know the lay of my keel. Can I help it if the lieutenant doesn't know the cut of his own boat?" Then, she added after a moment, "That's good of John."

Duncan pulled away to watch as Hancock distributed coins to each of her crew members. The jubilant merchant then led them toward the long brick building that was his Marblehead warehouse. At the far end, men stood at trestle tables, serving ale, fresh loaves, and boiled mussels to the townspeople who had gathered for the finish of the race. In the yard paved with crushed oyster shell at the near end of the building were other tables, draped with linens, where more robust offerings of lobster, oysters, pies, cakes, and wine awaited Hancock's invited guests.

"Where is that scrub Hicks?" Lawford asked one of his subordinates as he heaped oysters onto his plate. "Not like him to miss a taste of the famous Hancock larder." The aide leaned into the commodore's ear with an apparent explanation. "Oh that," Lawford said with a wince. "Damn the deserters," he groused. "They should swing just for keeping a zealous officer from our frolic."

Duncan caught the anxious glance Sarah aimed at the ridge that jutted into the harbor entrance. She had been so insistent on the place and time of her little competition that he could not shake the suspicion that she had other reasons in mind. But if she had intended to distract all the officers in the town to divert them from one of her smuggling operations, her plan had not been entirely successful. She turned to the captain. "I must beg your leave," she announced to Lawford. "Allow us a few moments in the sloop's privacy before we catch our death," she said, indicating her wet clothing. The sun had begun its descent, and what had been a providentially mild day was cooling.

"Of course, my dear," Lawford replied. "But make haste, for we can hardly celebrate these heroics without our heroine."

Hancock's guests energetically attacked the stacks of food. Only Hancock and Duncan noticed that Sarah paused at the foot of the wharf to speak with one of her crew, sending the woman up the street at a run. Hancock's gaze shifted to the town's two magistrates sitting farther down the table, and then he cast a worried glance at Duncan, who shrugged. Sarah did not share all her secrets with Duncan and fewer still with Hancock, who engaged in the delicate balancing act of maintaining close relations with the government despite being a leader in the Sons of Liberty.

The secret that most troubled Hancock, Duncan knew, was not one of Sarah's but that of the dead infantry officer they had found floating off Marblehead ten days earlier, killed by a stab wound in the back. He and Duncan knew the presence of so many high-ranking officers from Castle William, the island headquarters of the military, was unprecedented. They, too, he suspected, had come for more than the sailing match. There had been no official reaction to or even notice of the officer's murder, which made Duncan all the more uneasy. If they had kept the killing secret, so, too, might they conceal their retribution.

Hancock collected himself and turned to the table. "Gentlemen," he announced as he reached into a case of wine and extracted a dusty bottle, "I give you the claret of sixty-four, I daresay the first case to arrive on American shores. Best of the decade, I've been told."

"Have you the duty slip?" the port commissioner asked playfully. Hancock, who had had a ship seized by the government for failure to pay duties less than two years earlier, winced but then pushed a smile onto his face.

The guests enthusiastically gathered around the case as Hancock filled and distributed glasses, not looking up until Sarah reappeared, wearing a hunter-green dress that set off her auburn hair. That at least two of the officers reacted coolly toward her did not surprise Duncan, though he could not tell if it was because she had bested the navy's cutter or simply because they resented a woman who presumed to command a sailing vessel. But the others at the table cheerfully joined in when Captain Lawford raised his glass for a toast to "Miss Ramsey and the distaff navy of Marblehead!"

They ate with a camaraderie unusual for such an assembly of officials and citizens, and although the good humor of Lawford and his officers was sometimes forced, Duncan concluded it was because of Oakes's defeat. Halfway through the meal, however, Hancock came up behind Duncan and gripped his arm, directing his gaze to Lawford. The commodore had gone silent and was staring at one of the larger fishing boats anchored across the harbor. The boat was painted a distinctive mustard with green trim, her net raised to dry along her backstays.

Hancock bent low to top off Duncan's glass. "Good God!" he whispered. "He recognizes it!"

"Marblehead has the colony's largest fishing fleet," Duncan murmured. "It should come as no surprise that the boat would be here. It just triggered an unpleasant memory."

"Unpleasant?" Hancock rejoined. "A nightmare!"

Duncan saw now that the color had drained from Lawford's face. He wasn't seeing a fishing boat; he was seeing a ghost. Only the week before, that vessel had arrived at Castle William with the waterlogged, bloodless body of a British officer hanging in that very net.

Ten days earlier Hancock had invited Duncan and John Glover, one of the town's leading shipowners and an able mariner, to join him on his coastal packet boat to help inspect the decrepit channel markers leading into the harbors of Lynn, Marblehead, and Salem. The governor was not shy about asking Hancock, as a prominent member of the legislature, to perform such duties, knowing his appetite for asserting authority and his willingness to personally pay for improvements to public property. It had been mere coincidence that they had spied the desperate waving of the crew of the mustard-colored boat. They had eased the packet close and accepted the line tossed to bring the boats alongside each other.

The fishermen's net had been pulled to the opposite side of the boat. At first Duncan saw only the densely packed herring, but then a crew member shook the net and the silver flickers began to alternate with snatches of scarlet. The mate in command of the boat called for the crew to pull the net higher, and the body surfaced, shedding the crabs and eels that had been nibbling at its flesh.

They had laid the pale soldier out on the deck. He had been dead only a few hours, his flesh largely intact, not yet found by the larger predators of the bay. No one spoke, no one moved, aghast not simply at the gruesome death but also at who, or rather what, the man was. Judging by his once elegant uniform, he was a captain in the Twenty-Ninth Regiment of Foot, one of the hated regiments occupying Boston.

"Toss him back in, I say," the mate suggested. "No one the wiser. Marblehead don't need it."

Hancock stared at the dead man, clearly confused, and then his eyes went round. "Captain Mallory! Dear God, he has dined at my own table! A most genteel officer! He and his fiancée were expected at the governor's ball and never made an appearance." Duncan took a deep breath and knelt beside the corpse. The officer had been a handsome, fit man in his forties and had been wearing his dress uniform as if planning to attend an official function. Duncan quickly examined the limbs, then unbuttoned the tunic. Finding nothing suspicious, and fervently hoping he could declare the death a drowning accident, he straightened, then shook his head, knowing he had not completed the task. He bent and pressed down on the dead man's abdomen. Only air escaped from his lungs. "Help me turn him over," he asked with foreboding.

No one stepped forward until finally Glover bent and lifted the man's feet. The compact, muscular mariner helped Duncan twist the man onto his stomach, then muttered a low curse. The back of the officer's waistcoat had a slit in it, just to the left of his spine and over his heart. The blood had not been entirely washed away.

"Murder?" Hancock gasped. "My God, a senior officer murdered? No, Duncan, we can't . . ." His voice trailed off.

Glover wore a grim but more collected expression. "If he was out of Marblehead we'll feel the wrath of the governor. He already lends an ear to those who say our town has become a den of murderers and thieves since last year. This will be their excuse to square accounts with us."

"Marblehead don't need it," the mate repeated. Now Hancock understood his words.

The people of Marblehead hated the customs duties and other trade restrictions imposed by London but reserved a special loathing for the navy's press gangs, which often detained their vessels at sea to seize men for involuntary service on their warships. The year before, a Marblehead man had been charged with harpooning the officer leading a gang that had cornered him on his own ship with drawn weapons. Although the court had ultimately ruled the killing justified as self-defense, rancor over the incident still simmered on both sides. Since then, when a naval vessel sailed close to a Marblehead boat, crew members usually taunted it with raised harpoons.

"No," Duncan said as he contemplated the body. "The senior officer in Marblehead is a lieutenant. And he was going to the ball in Boston. The tide will have brought him from the inner harbor." He looked up at the merchant. "Meaning they will think the Boston radicals are behind it." Duncan glanced at Glover, and the men gathered around the body with new worry. He knew Glover was fiercely committed to the Sons of Liberty but did not know the political leanings of the others.

Glover instantly understood. "Committed patriots to the man here," he said of the fishing crew.

"As are my lads," Hancock murmured.

Duncan surveyed the men standing around him, then gazed at the steeples of Boston, just visible across the bay. "He goes back in the water," he said, "back in the net. And the boat goes to Castle William."

"Like hell!" the mate growled. "I'm not offering myself up to some mob of angry lobsterbacks!"

"I'll go," Glover said and turned to the mate. "Duncan's got the measure of it. I'll tell them it's my boat, that as soon as we snagged the poor soldier we knew we had to take him to his comrades at the Castle. We never touched him, never raised him out of the water. They'll identify him and know that he was from Boston. As a top officer he will have been missed by now. We'll just be doing our duty to the king, ye see," he said to the crew, who answered with mocking grins.

Duncan saw that Hancock was not convinced. "Otherwise, John, they'll be turning Boston inside out to find him. The magistrates will give the army leave to search the house of every radical. Especially the leaders of the Sons," he added.

"They wouldn't dare!" Hancock exclaimed. "There's such things as bonds of honor!"

"In Boston?" Duncan rejoined. "Where there's an angry soldier for every four citizens, half of whom are equally on edge? I daresay we are beyond bonds and honor. Massachusetts is an uncharted land these days. And there are those on both sides who would be happy to transform it into a bloody battlefield. We can't give them an excuse for doing so. You never saw the body, know only that Mallory missed the ball."

Hancock grimaced, then slowly nodded.

Duncan turned to Glover. "Fix this as the position of the discovery, mark your chart, note the time. The navy well understands the flow of the tides here, knows that if he had been killed on the north shore he would have been swept far out to sea. Meanwhile," he added to the crew, "bring in the herring. And this is a fishing boat. She's too tidy. Cut up some fish and scatter the remains. Let some seagulls follow you in to soil the Castle's wharf. Do what you can to make her stink so the Castle won't want you to linger."

The crew looked to their mate for direction. After several heartbeats he nodded, then kicked over a basket of fish. "Stink it up, boys."

As the crew worked to fill the oversized baskets on deck with their catch,

Duncan more fully examined the dead officer, finding no other signs of injury but also no sign of a purse or personal effects. Glover and the mate then restored the dead man's tunic, placed him back into the now-empty net, and lowered him into the sea. As the boats drifted apart, Hancock stood at Duncan's side. "Once again, Duncan, we may need you to protect us."

Duncan gave no voice to the question on his tongue. Was Hancock referring to Duncan's skills as a physician or as, in words Hancock sometimes whispered, the "master of secrets" for the Sons of Liberty?

While Sarah's freshly attired crew mingled with the officers, Hancock lived up to his repute as a generous and attentive host. Duncan suspected his other guests would ascribe his nervousness to his compulsion to keep every cup filled and every empty platter quickly replenished. The merchant prince had warned all in advance that given the exceptional weather the tea was to be alfresco, in North Shore picnic style, meaning he had brought only one servant and, at Sarah's urging, had attired the man in a simple brown waistcoat and breeches instead of his usual brocaded livery.

The company was turning its attention to the stack of cakes and pastries at the end of the table when the gaze of the port's senior customs official fixed on the point of rock Sarah had been watching.

"The infernal savage is lighting up again," the commissioner muttered.

Heads turned toward the solitary figure who tended a smoky fire on the tongue of land that jutted into the mouth of the harbor. They were not close enough for Duncan to make out details, but he recognized the man's slow, methodical dance and shoulder-length gray hair.

"Every few days we must suffer the aged fool, sir," the customs man explained to Lawford. "One of those pathetic old natives, no doubt reliving some memory conjured from his barbaric youth."

Duncan noticed the smile that flickered on Sarah's face. The figure was their close friend Conawago, and the fire, Duncan knew, was a signal.

"Not at all," Duncan quickly countered. "He is performing a blessing for the harbor and the town. The fishing fleet leaves soon for the Grand Banks on its first sailing of the year, what they call First Fare. He asks the favors of his gods for the First Fare mariners."

"His gods?" one of the younger officers snorted. "Surely they are all deaf and dumb by now!"

As the words brought a round of guffaws, Duncan shot a worried glance at Sarah, who stared down into her plate without expression and, he suspected, was biting her tongue.

The commodore stifled the laughter with a raised hand. "You can recognize this as a tribal blessing?" Lawford observed with a lift of inquiry in his voice, then contemplated Duncan a moment. "Ah, I forgot. You and Miss Ramsey have a settlement adjoining the native lands, in the New York wilderness. That must breed certain"—the captain searched for a polite word—"certain awareness."

"The Iroquois," Sarah replied in a careful voice, "have generously accepted us as neighbors, yes. And you may be surprised, Captain, at how many natives live in this very town. Responsible citizens, mostly employed on the sailing vessels. Valued seaman, every one."

"I have several on my own ships," Hancock confirmed. "Fearless fellows. Always the first to scramble up the shrouds in a storm. I'm surprised the navy hasn't—" Hancock caught himself, glancing awkwardly at the naval officers who sat across from him, many of whom would have commanded impressment parties. "Surprised they haven't fully recognized the skills of such men," he awkwardly amended.

One of the officers, well-known for commanding bullying impressment squads, responded with a bitter expression. "Our coppery friends may hate what the Americans have done to their people," he haughtily observed, "but put them in earshot of one of my press gangs and they become the most loyal of colonial residents, damn their eyes."

Impressment had become such a source of friction that the navy had agreed not to seize any man who could prove an established Massachusetts residence. That proof could be hard to come by for the native mariners, many of whom lived wandering lives, but Marbleheaders were quick to support the natives, if just to spite the navy.

Out of the corner of his eye Duncan caught movement on the hill above the warehouses. A man was walking at a fast, determined pace toward the harbor. Sarah, too, took notice, studying him for a moment, then glancing uneasily at Conawago, who raised and lowered his arms through the thick, fragrant smoke of the burning juniper.

"One of your tidesmen, I believe," Hancock observed to the customs commissioner as the port inspector approached their table. Sarah cast a nervous glance at the approaching tidesman. She had made a point of inviting all the local customs officers to the tea, but apparently at least one had declined. The commissioner rose and turned to receive a whispered report. Hancock offered the man a glass of claret, which he gulped down before departing. It was, Duncan knew, the merchant's ploy to pry loose the news delivered by the man. "I daresay one of yours, Mr. Hancock," was all the tidesman offered before leaving.

The commissioner, however, was all too happy to share the report. "Brig from the West Indies has dropped anchor," he announced to the table. "Sugar and molasses. In the outer harbor beyond the Neck. A bit odd given that we have ample berthing closer to shore."

Hancock did a creditable job of hiding his surprise, but Duncan could see he had not expected the ship, at least not at Marblehead. His larger ships all ended their ocean voyages at Hancock Wharf in Boston. "Her captain is a God-fearing man who no doubt does not wish to disturb the Sabbath," the merchant offered.

"But is he a king-fearing man?" the customs commissioner shot back with a thin, needling smile. "We shall see at first light tomorrow." He would reap a rich bounty if he could prove another Hancock ship was engaged in smuggling.

Sarah, sensing the tension between the two men, lifted her glass. "Our noble competition arrives!" she announced, indicating the sullen file of sailors who had finally cleared the wreckage from the cutter's deck and were now approaching their table. The face of Lieutenant Oakes reflected the ignominy of his defeat, but then he spotted Sarah and her crew and halted. He collected himself, straightening his uniform and ordering his men into a less ragged line. They advanced at a jaunty pace and upon reaching Sarah, the young lieutenant removed his hat and bowed to her.

"'Tis far better to have raced you and lost, Miss Ramsey," the lieutenant declared, "than to have never raced you at all."

"Hear, hear! Well done!" Lawford exclaimed. "A noble sentiment!"

The cutter's men did not entirely share their skipper's graciousness, for Duncan heard one mutter something about "the vixen leading us into a trap," but the tension melted as Sarah's crew approached the sailors, holding mugs of ale. Fifty paces down the waterfront, where the townspeople were gathered, someone started playing a fiddle.

Duncan grinned as the women stepped into the open yard and began dancing a jig to the distant tune, pulling the chagrined sailors out of their line to join them. He felt Sarah tug at his arm and turned, thinking she was inviting him to dance, then followed her gaze toward a man stumbling down one of the side streets, running at a gasping, uneven pace in the direction of their table. His face was so pale, his long hair so disheveled, that Duncan did not recognize him at first. The man staggered to Hancock's chair, bracing himself on its back as he struggled to catch his breath.

It was Simon Pollard, a retired schoolteacher who watched over Hancock's operations in the port. His mouth opened and shut, but only a stuttering groan came out. Hancock hastily poured his deputy a glass of water. Pollard's hand shook so badly that half the glass's contents were lost before reaching his mouth.

"The belfry, sir! It's . . . it's . . ." Pollard glanced at the military men who lined the table and lowered his voice. "That lieutenant who runs the army patrols, he . . . Oh dear God . . ." His voice trailed away, and his head slumped. One more word escaped his lips, in a frantic whisper. "Crucifixion!"

Hancock leapt to his feet. Duncan was out of his chair an instant later and followed Hancock toward the long building that was fronted by the belfry, the name given to the tall structure at the end of the long rope walk Hancock had built to supply his merchant fleet. The tower's latticework of timbers was used to suspend shrouds and special rigging in their finishing stages. Duncan last visited the belfry just three days earlier. He had watched in admiration as workers scrambled over the scaffolding, twisting and knotting fibers into a heavy backstay for a ship that was being refitted in the harbor.

As they reached the building's door, Hancock halted Duncan. "There is trickery afoot, Duncan! They somehow know we were with that dead officer, I swear it! Did you not see the knowing gazes, the slippery glances? And now they surprise me with one of my own ships! They weren't here for the race; they were here to beat down the leaders of the Sons of Liberty! It's a plot to seize another of my ships! I'll be ruined!"

"Steady on, John," Duncan cautioned. "Something is afoot, but it's still unfolding. Don't indulge them by overreacting." Duncan looked over Hancock's shoulder. Lawford was bent over Pollard, and as Duncan watched, the captain spun about and hurried up the hill, followed by several of his officers. He took a deep breath and put a hand on the door, which was ajar. "Let us see what new trouble Lieutenant Hicks has brewed for us." He stepped inside and froze. The timber scaffolding had not been used for its usual maritime magic this day.

"Blessed Jesus!" Hancock gasped as he entered the chamber, then retreated a step, stricken by the sight before them. Moments later Lawford and his companions arrived. One of the young officers made a croaking sound and doubled over, staggering to a corner as he retched onto the stone flags.

Duncan had taken Pollard's muttered "Crucifixion!" to be just the expletive of a pious man, but now he saw the terrible truth.

Ropes had been tied to Hicks's wrists, then strung through the pulley blocks fastened eight feet high on the side walls and fed through the overhead center block used to raise heavy rigging. The lieutenant had been hoisted six feet into the air, his arms stretched tight toward the opposite walls so that he was splayed against the scaffold. His face was drained of blood, his open eyes unseeing. His mouth and nostrils were sewn shut.

Chapter 2

"**Y**OUR SWORD!" LAWFORD SNAPPED TO the officer at his side, who had added his weapon to his dress uniform. When the stunned aide did not respond, Lawford reached out, drew it from its scabbard, and with a deft swing of the blade severed the line that suspended Hicks's left arm. Duncan darted forward to support the body as the captain cut the second line, then lowered Hicks to the ground.

"The stitches, Duncan!" Hancock cried and thrust out the silver folding knife he used for sharpening writing quills.

Duncan choked down his reply, opened the blade, and quickly cut through the stitches that sealed Hicks's nose. He looked up to see if Hancock now understood what had been obvious to him: Hicks would never breathe again. With more measured strokes he opened the stitches that clamped the mouth.

The officer remained bent over in the corner. "Ensign, collect yourself," Lawford ordered. "Outside the door. No one else enters."

"No," Duncan protested. Seeing anger flash in the captain's eyes, he added, "I mean, sir, an officer will attract attention, advertise that there is a military matter inside. Half the town is gathered down the street. Surely we do not want to invite a few hundred onlookers. Perhaps there is a bolt on the door? We must consider what is before us first."

"Blackhearted murder, sir!" Lawford barked. "Any fool can see that!"

Duncan remained on his knees by the body. "And I read recently a letter to Parliament from General Gage published in the Boston papers," he stated in a steady voice. "I recollect the supreme commander in America reported that Massachusetts towns were like powder kegs waiting for a spark."

Lawford, clearly not used to being contradicted, smoldered for a moment, then gestured the ensign away from the door.

"No bolt," Pollard reported. "But I can block the latch so it can't be opened from outside." He cast a glance at Hancock, who nodded his assent.

Duncan had started to untie the collar of Hicks's linen shirt when the flat of the sword blade pressed against his arm.

"McCallum!" Lawford warned. "He is a king's officer!"

"We should consider what is before us," Duncan repeated.

"No! Just shut his eyes, the poor soul. By all that's holy, shut his eyes!"

"Sir?"

"His eyes! Do you not speak English?"

Duncan gestured to the dead man's face. "And do you not see that his eyes have been stitched open?"

Lawford seemed unable to contain his emotion. His confusion gave way to fury. "By God, this town shall feel our wrath!"

Duncan fixed the captain with a level gaze. "We need to understand."

Lawford raised the sword in frustration and was about to erupt, when Hancock spoke a single word.

"Deathspeaker," the merchant said.

The captain hesitated, lowering the sword. "Sir?"

"Mr. McCallum has assisted in resolving other deaths, in Massachusetts and on the frontier. The tribes say he can make the dead tell him how they died, sometimes even who killed them. The Iroquois call him Deathspeaker."

Lawford's eyes went round as he stared at Duncan as if seeing him for the first time. He retreated a step.

"The tribes are fond of colorful titles," Duncan explained. "There are no black arts involved in what I do, just the arts I learned at the University of Edinburgh."

Lawford studied him for several long breaths, then slowly nodded. "What do you require?"

Duncan stood and surveyed the chamber, his gaze lingering for a moment on a stool that lay on its side near the wall. "When you entered," he asked Pollard, "was the scene just as we find it?"

The manager considered the question and nodded. "Except the stool was sitting in the center of the flagstones. I tipped it over as I backed away from the horrid sight, then kicked it aside."

"I need the crates pushed together," Duncan replied to Lawford, indicating two heavy, waist-high crates. "Some canvas stretched over them. Lanterns, whale oil if possible. And," he added, gesturing toward the one officer in a scarlet uniform, "advice from the army."

Soon they had Hicks laid out over a clean piece of sailcloth. On either side of Duncan, two of the young naval officers held spermaceti lamps provided by Pollard. Duncan silently studied the bruising along Hicks's jaw and the bloody lumps above his right ear and on his crown, then cut the stitches holding up the dead man's eyelids and closed the eyes before turning to the threads that had sealed the mouth and nose. They were neatly uniform, done with a tidy, experienced hand. He extracted a segment of thread and held it to a lamp flame, watching the end burn before blowing it out.

"Linen," he announced, "but waxed."

"The kind sailors use for rain tunics and such," Hancock observed.

"Please, sir," Lawford spoke in a whisper now, "the remaining threads." Duncan hesitated, then understood as the captain repeated, "A king's officer."

He extracted the remaining bits of threads from the lips and nostrils and then straightened and addressed the senior officer. "He was assaulted with something round and very hard. Knocked unconscious. Perhaps he came round, for he was struck again, accounting for two such blows. The weapon may still be here," he suggested, motioning toward the shadows. "A club, a cudgel, perhaps a pry bar."

Lawford quickly sent the idle officers into the shadows for the search as Duncan unbuttoned Hicks's uniform tunic. He would have preferred to have stripped away the clothing from the torso but restrained himself, lifting the flaps of the scarlet coat and the linen shirt to expose the chest. Seeing nothing unusual, he ran his hand over the ribs, pausing on the left side to feel the bones, then lightly running his fingers along the rib cage. They came away sticky, with a blush of pink.

"This killer was shrewd, a careful planner," he declared to Hancock and Lawford, "but carried a deep resentment he could not entirely control." As he spoke, an exclamation of surprise came from the shadows, and the young ensign approached, carrying what appeared to be a metal bar as long as his arm.

"Not serviceable anymore," the officer announced as he handed the bar to Captain Lawford. "Looks to be an old Land Pattern, sir."

The ensign had discovered the discarded barrel of a Brown Bess musket, a type used extensively by the British military. It was well-worn, and the muzzle end was deliberately pounded shut and shaped into a spike.

"Aye," came Pollard's strained voice from behind Duncan. "Salvaged by our smith. We use it to pry knots out of heavy lines and such."

"And crush bone," Duncan added in an absent voice as he continued examining the torso. The company had gone silent again. Duncan looked up to see them staring uneasily at him. He straightened and cleared his throat. "Judging from the temperature of the body and stage of rigor, I would say that Hicks died over twelve hours ago, probably before midnight. On Saturdays the rope walk closes—" He turned with a questioning glance toward Pollard.

"Just before the supper hour," Hancock's manager said. "Then I reopen on Monday morning."

"So say after five of the evening but before the end of the day," Duncan continued as he retrieved the musket barrel for a quick examination. "His assailant surprised him from the rear, hitting him with this musket barrel, which shows a few drops of blood." He indicated tiny flecks of red near the end. "He was rendered unconscious, then his killer went to work with the ropes. A strong man, an agile man, who could climb the tower to set the pulley and then heave up the rope. But first he used needle and sailor's thread." Duncan pointed to the dead man's mouth. "At the third stitch the lip is torn. I suspect because Hicks was stirring, accounting for the second blow to his head. But he had already passed from lack of breath when the Brown Bess barrel was used a third time."

"Third?"

Duncan lifted the flap of the jacket. "His killer's anger was not fully sated. He hit Hicks again, breaking the third and fourth ribs. The blows ripped open the skin but there was almost no blood." He glanced back at the pointed barrel. The killer could have ended his victim with a thrust of the sharp point but did not. He wanted to prolong Hicks's suffering.

"Meaning?" Hancock asked.

"By the time of the last blow his heart was no longer pumping. The ribs were broken after death."

"Jesus wept!" Lawford muttered.

"What were the lieutenant's responsibilities here?" Duncan asked no one in particular.

One of the men behind them cleared his throat. Lawford turned and acknowledged the army officer. "Ensign?"

"Lieutenant Hicks leads the unit of the Twenty-Ninth, assigned to bringing in deserters, sir, especially naval deserters, who seem rather fond of the North Shore. He was proud of his rate of return, as he called it. Unblemished. Always got his man, so to speak. Sometimes he would work in his off-duty hours, to pick up the scent, you might say. He was on the trail of one yesterday. A man named Jacob Book."

"You may call them deserters," Duncan said and instantly knew his words were too sharp. The officers glared at him. "I mean, the people of Marblehead do not consider a man who escapes illegal servitude to be a deserter." He did not know Jacob Book but recognized the name as one assigned to a Christian convert. "Including those of the tribes."

"People," Lawford repeated with a chill. "You mean the Whigs of Marblehead."

Hancock shot Duncan a censuring glance. "The view is not universally held," the merchant prince confirmed.

"And," the army officer inserted, "a member of the tribes who cannot prove residence in the colony is eligible to be pressed. It is the law."

"My point," Duncan continued, "is simply that the views are strongly held on both sides."

"Meaning?" Lawford asked.

"Meaning, Captain, that if you announce without proof that an infantry officer has been murdered by a deserter, the Loyalists and soldiers will be furious. And if you announce that you seek a Marblehead sailor as a killer without clear evidence, then the Whigs will be doubly so. The sailors and harbor men of this town are almost all Whigs. Need I remind you that one killed a naval officer only months ago and was excused by the court?"

"His Majesty's soldiers will not be intimidated by riffraff!" the infantry officer snapped.

Lawford held up a hand for quiet. "I believe you are saying, Mr. McCallum, that the real muscle of this town, so to speak, will not be sympathetic to a search for this deserter."

"And they are very proud of their militia. Marblehead is one of those powder kegs General Gage refers to."

The words brought a troubled silence. A voice from the shadows broke it.

"His regimental badge," someone said.

Lawford turned. "Ensign?"

"Yes, sir. It's only that Mr. Hicks's regimental badge is missing. He would not have gone out without it. He was very proud of his service in the Twenty-Ninth. He always kept it pinned to his lapel in the regimental custom."

Lawford ordered another search. As the officers thrust the lanterns into the shadows the captain's mournful expression shifted to one of worry.

"Forgive me," Duncan said, as much to the dead man as to the captain. He leaned over Hicks and pressed on the dead man's chest. One of the junior officers gasped in fright as air rushed out, making it appear as if the dead man were breathing. The jaw slightly parted and Duncan gently pulled it wider, exposing a glint of metal. "It never left him," he stated in a grim tone and stepped aside.

"Bloody hell," Lawford murmured as he bent over the mouth. Hicks's regimental badge was in his mouth, its long pin having been jabbed into his palate before his mouth was sewn shut.

"Could he—did he regain consciousness before he died?" Lawford asked in a tight voice.

"I don't know," Duncan replied. It was a lie, for he had seen the bloody rope cuts on the wrists and the burst capillaries in the eyes that were evidence of a violent struggle at the end.

Lawford gestured Hancock and Duncan into the shadows as the others gazed upon the corpse. "When I report this to General Gage," the commodore said in a despairing whisper, "he will turn this town into a military camp and start stringing up Whigs just to send a message."

Hancock gazed at the tall rigging tower with a contemplative expression. "Others have died here," he observed.

"I don't follow," the captain said.

"Suicides," Hancock explained. "By the noose."

"I will not dishonor Hicks by declaring him a lowly suicide!"

"No," Duncan said, now grasping Hancock's suggestion. "We will just let it be known that another body has been recovered from the belfry. Let the townspeople reach their own conclusion."

"Why would I—"

"Because we need time to find the truth."

"What are you suggesting?"

"It will be dark soon. The crowd will disperse. Go about your business. We will prepare the body, get it in a pine box. Dispatch an honor guard in the morning to escort it to Castle William," Duncan said, referring to the army's island fortress. "His comrades will expect internment at the burial ground there. Tell them what you will. An accident perhaps. Hicks was diligently inspecting the tower because it was to be used to make equipment for the military. He fell and tragically suffered a mortal blow to the head when striking the stone floor."

Lawford frowned. "I have to report this to Colonel Dalrymple, the commander of the land units. He will send men to investigate. Provosts."

The word sent a chill down Duncan's spine. "You must slow them down. Provosts run their investigations like the Inquisition. How do you think the proud people of Marblehead will react? I can smell the fuse burning already."

Lawford frowned but did not argue. "Let us find out what happened here, Captain," Hancock urged.

"The army must have the killer."

Hancock and Duncan exchanged a worried glance. "The army will have the killer," Hancock agreed.

Lawford sighed and gazed at the body on the crates. "There should be a guard. A military vigil from his unit. I will leave an officer. He can get a room and mind things until the honor guard comes from Castle William in the morning."

Duncan, knowing he needed more time with the body, was about to argue, when Hancock laid a hand on his shoulder. "Very appropriate, sir. I know an innkeeper we can trust. Let your officer come with me and we will make the arrangements. Then he can help me locate a coffin. Two hours or so," Hancock said with a pointed glance at Duncan. "Mr. McCallum will stand vigil until then. He is, I have heard, a good friend of the dead."

Friend of the Dead and Deathspeaker were only two of the names Duncan had attracted in trying to decipher mysterious deaths. The tribes also called him Spirit-walker, Blood Teacher, and Last Talker. The labels disturbed him when he first heard them. The feeling was compounded by the frightened way people looked at him when he touched, and sometimes whispered to, the dead. He no longer paid heed to such labels, or such fears, and had to admit he now found a strange kind of peace when sitting alone with the dead. The dead were dependable. The dead had no pretense, no argument. If one only knew how to ask, the dead were always willing to share their dying secrets, their last link to the mortal world. They always told the truth.

His gaze fell on the outer door. Hancock would struggle to find a coffin on a Sabbath night. Although the merchant often lived up to his reputation as an arrogant aristocrat, Duncan and Hancock had developed a certain bond. When alone, they often spoke of their work for the Sons of Liberty. While Hancock was something of a public representative of the Sons before the government, Duncan's work was often clandestine and increasingly treacherous. Hancock was more sensitive than most of the Sons' leaders, particularly the fiery Samuel Adams, to the danger of antagonizing the British military. There were those among both the Loyalists and the patriots who favored an outbreak of violence, which both Hancock and Duncan sought to avoid. The militias, lacking sufficient muskets, cannons, and gunpowder, were no match for the British military.

Hancock's quick thinking had cooled Lawford's anger and bought Duncan valuable time to confer with Lieutenant Hicks. He now worked methodically, with smooth, efficient motions accompanied by the low, comforting whispers he would use with a skittish horse, pausing for moments of intense study as he slipped off Hicks's scarlet tunic and linen shirt. He recalled seeing Hicks with a squad of soldiers at least twice in recent weeks, moving briskly down Marblehead streets. On one occasion, the lieutenant had brandished his sword, clearing his way through imaginary enemies, to the great amusement of his men. Duncan had watched with his friend John Glover. "Arrogant popinjay," Glover had muttered. "Acts like he is lord of the manor and the rest of us his serfs. Brags about how he always finds the man he seeks. Half the deserters he nabs were never legally pressed in the first place, and after he returns them to the navy most are never seen again."

Along Hicks's right side was a long straight scar, years old, that appeared made by a sword or perhaps a pike or spear. Considering Hicks's age, he decided that the lieutenant had been old enough to have seen action during the war with the French and their Indian allies. With gruesome effort he replaced Hicks's shirt and tunic and did what he could to make the officer presentable. He found his gaze drifting toward the open space in front of the rigging tower. His instincts told him that the killer had sewn Hicks's eyes open to assure he would witness something as he slowly suffocated. What had the killer staged there on the stone flags?

Duncan paced slowly along the space, back and forth, dropping to his knees twice to study the dirt in the cracks between the stone flags, then gave up. Too many boots had trampled the floor since the killing for him to find evidence of the prior night's performance. He stepped into the shadows, gazing at the empty flagstones, visualizing now the stool placed in the center as Pollard had found it. The killer sat there, but for what purpose? Just to watch Hicks die? He retrieved the tall stool and settled at the lieutenant's side.

The officer had been the most resented of all the soldiers serving in the small Marblehead detachment. Yet death was a great leveler. Duncan felt neither bile nor compassion toward the infantryman. Hicks was just one more soul who had been denied a full life and was otherwise a great enigma. What he was saying to the Deathspeaker seemed to be in a foreign tongue.

"What was it, Lieutenant, that your killer forced you to watch as you died?" Duncan asked. He tried to think more objectively about the dead man. To Duncan's friends, Hicks was a bullying thug, but to others he may have been a hero, a mentor, and perhaps even, among the free-thinking women of Marblehead, a lover. Finally Duncan asked the question he had first heard from a Mohawk matriarch sitting with the body of her dead grandson: "Which are the spirits who will welcome you on the other side?"

"Gaoh."

The soft, disembodied reply, name of the wind spirit, seemed to float down from the darkness. Duncan's heart leapt into his throat. He found himself off the stool, backing away from the corpse.

"Surely not Hemo, the warrior spirit," the gentle voice continued, growing louder. "This man was a bully, not a noble warrior."

Duncan spread out his arms and Sarah Ramsey stepped out of the shadows and into his embrace. "How did you find me?" he whispered into her ear.

"John told me of a death in the belfry, so I knew where you would be."

"But you came from up there," he said in confusion, gesturing toward the dark, upward-sloping hall, over a hundred paces long, where most of the rope production was performed.

"The door at the far end, yes. I couldn't wait. I need you. We need you."

"We?"

"Please, Duncan, no questions," Sarah said in an insistent tone, then turned to gaze at the dead officer.

"You knew Lieutenant Hicks?" Duncan asked.

"We knew him."

We again. The *we* that did not include him. Ever since his return from London with Conawago weeks earlier, that *we* had been building like a wall between him and Sarah. They each reserved parts of their lives from the other. It was a necessity of their shared work. Like Duncan, Sarah would sometimes be urgently called away. The bond between them had to yield to that secret enterprise, but he took comfort in knowing that Sarah was working in her own way for the cause of liberty.

"The people of Marblehead care not for king's men watching over their shoulders," Sarah reminded him. "The lieutenant applied his writ too large, entering the homes of honest citizens without so much as a by-your-leave. Why should the army even concern itself with naval deserters? Do you not recall that we came to Marblehead to avoid such soldiers?"

The words stung. In London, Duncan had learned that secret operatives of the secretary of war were stalking patriots who smuggled manufacturing secrets out of Britain to help build American production. They had the code name of the leader, Hephaestus, but little else. Less than two weeks earlier, at Hancock's dining table, he had heard an officer remind Captain Lawford of new intelligence about a traitor lurking in Massachusetts. Duncan choked down his warning, for he knew it would only anger Sarah. On his return from London he had begged her to retreat with him to the safety of Edentown, their settlement on the New York frontier, but she refused, saying it was not yet time. They compromised by moving from Boston to Marblehead. He could not shake the feeling that she had agreed because it facilitated her own surreptitious plans.

"I am here, *ma lucidh*, not for the army's sake but because his death could bring more uniforms to the town," Duncan said. Sarah hesitated over the soft Gaelic words, *my heart*, and sighed, then wrapped a hand around his arm and listened as he explained his discoveries. "A man named Jacob Book was being sought by Hicks. There was bad blood between them. I fear they will try to seize him for the murder."

"From one of the tribes north of the big waters." It was an Iroquois way of referring to the great inland seas of Erie and Ontario.

"You know Book?"

"I know that two nights ago Lieutenant Hicks and his men burst into the home of the cooper and his wife as they were putting their children to bed, demanding to know where Book was. Terrified the children."

"Why the cooper?"

"His wife is Wampanoag." She stared at the dead man. "I know who will summon him on the other side. Those of his own kind. The Otkan." She spat the word with the fierceness of the Mohawks who raised her, then pulled him into the shadows of the long rope shed. He looked back at the dead man with foreboding. The Iroquois would have left Hicks's mouth sewn shut for fear of what would come out. The Otkan were evil spirits. It seemed more likely that the Otkan would be released into this world by the vengeful Lieutenant Hicks.

He assumed Sarah was leading him to the yellow-painted clapboard house above the waterfront that they shared with Conawago, but when they reached the end of the long building, she turned in the opposite direction. In the dim light of a half-moon, she led him down alleys toward the edge of town. After a few minutes she paused, hitched up her skirt, and leapt over a ditch, then took him over a snake rail fence. She ignored the bleat of the pasture's startled sheep and headed toward the darker shadows of structures on the far side of the field.

Duncan saw water through the trees and realized they had circled around nearly to the base of the narrow causeway that led to the Neck, the long tongue of land that cradled the east side of the harbor. The group of rundown buildings once housed waterfront craftsmen but now was mostly used for storage by the boatwright who operated a busy shop at the water's edge. Sarah did not hesitate as she reached the first building. She unlatched the rear door and entered. Duncan was chagrined at her melodramatic air. Several times before, she had taken him to meet down-on-their-luck colonists looking to make a fresh start on the frontier. She would want him to explain life on the Edentown lands, so that they would understand the hard work ahead of them if they accepted Sarah's invitation. Indeed, some did abandon their plans after hearing of the brutal winters and the tribes, and others, he suspected, pocketed her coins for the journey to the Catskills but never made the trip. He braced himself, deciding he would mince no words, and followed her into the shadows.

Lifting a candle lantern she led him past stacks of fragrant oak and cedar planks and into a storeroom filled with kegs and barrels. She squeezed past a stack of casks that obscured the rear wall, then opened another door that led down a narrow set of stairs.

Sarah reached the bottom and rushed into the shadows, but Duncan halted on the last stair. Two lanterns hung from the cellar's ceiling, illuminating the upturned faces of people sitting along the side walls, all fixed on him with expressions of fear. He made out three men and a woman who appeared to be African, a mulatto boy nestled close to the woman, and three more who were tribesmen. They were all emaciated and looked exhausted. They pressed against the wall as he stepped down onto the packed-earth floor, as if expecting him to assault them. He studied them, trying to decide if he had seen any of them on the streets of Marblehead.

"Oh, 'tis only Mr. McCallum," came a deep, comforting voice from the other side of the room. "Miss Ramsey's intended and always a friend in the hour of need. He be a great healer, knows the original ways. Yer gonna be fine now, just fine."

The speaker was a broad-shouldered man of powerful build who had been among the crew who yielded Hancock's yacht to Sarah that morning. Duncan acknowledged him with a nod. "Crispus." The brawny man returned his greeting with a smile, then turned toward one of the Africans with a ladle from the bucket of water he carried. Duncan stepped across the chamber to Sarah, who now knelt beside a prostrate middle-aged tribesman who was shivering violently despite the blankets heaped on him.

"How long has he been like this?" Duncan asked as he examined the man.

One of the strangers answered, the oldest of the Africans. "The shakes come and go every few weeks. Bad chills, then bad fever. The first time, poor Henri could barely walk. That was nigh two years ago."

Duncan bent closer to his patient. "A lantern," he said, as he took the man's pulse. He put his hand inside the man's tattered shirt to feel his liver, but the brighter light of the lantern Sarah now held told him all he needed to know.

"Someone needs to go to Dr. Bond's house," he declared, referring to the town's leading physician. "Ask if he has any extract of Peruvian bark. Otherwise there is some bark in the flour bag in my medicine box. We'll have to boil it into a tea."

Sarah considered his words, then looked for a long breath at the burly man who was ladling out the water. "I'll have to go. Dr. Bond doesn't know Crispus, and a stranger calling late on the Sabbath might not be welcomed."

Duncan surveyed the other sickly men and the woman and pushed back his fatigue, wondering where Sarah had found such an assembly of invalids. "I'll be here," he said, "but take Crispus," he added, refraining from reminding her that a killer was loose in the town. As the two climbed the stairs, he spied a basin of water and lifted one of the wet rags draped over its side to wipe the sick man's yellow-tinged face, then dropped the rag into the basin. The man's chills would shift to fever soon, and he would need cold compresses. His patient was lying at an awkward angle, his back partially wedged against the wall. He seemed not to notice, or was too weak to resist, when Duncan gently pulled at his shoulder.

"Let me look. I want to help," he said in a low voice. He could not be sure of the man's tribe, but he whispered the same words in Mohawk, getting no reply. Duncan had never seen the man before but well knew the lined, weary features of his countenance. He had been battered by a world that had turned against the tribes. Many lost their homes and families, some their entire villages. Finally he rolled the man over and lifted the rags of his shirt, thinking he might bend close and listen to his lungs. He froze.

The man's back was nothing but crisscrossed scar tissue. There were scars on scars and deep ruts where shredded flesh had not healed before being shredded again.

Suddenly the man came to life, groaning and twisting away from Duncan. "*Non! Non! Non!*" he moaned, half rising. With surprising strength, he shoved Duncan away before collapsing against the wall.

The African woman pushed past Duncan and knelt beside the man, pulling his head and shoulders into her lap and patting him as she might a frightened child. "*N'ai pas peur, n'ai pas peur*, Henri," she murmured. The woman spoke to the battered tribesman in French, which must mean he was of one of the northern tribes that had allied with the losing side in the last war. Abenaki perhaps, or Ottawa, even Ojibway. Duncan longed to speak with the man named Henri, but his eyes fixed Duncan with a wild, desperate expression, whether from fear or from malarial delirium Duncan could not tell. He stood, backing away, and turned to the others in the cellar.

The other Africans remained silent as he examined them, not replying to his questions, which he tried in both French and English. Their eyes were bright, their bodies frail. Only the one with gray in his hair cooperated when Duncan asked them to show their teeth and tongues. The man beside him, a big-boned man in his forties, resentfully jerked his arm away when Duncan tried to lift it. In his other hand he tightly clutched a stone with a sharp edge.

The two other tribesmen seemed in better health. One seemed to sleep, and the other was defiant at his approach but quickly calmed when he addressed him in Mohawk. "Haudenosaunee?" Duncan asked, referring to the Iroquois confederation.

The man pounded his chest. "Oneida," he declared proudly, then pointed to his companion. "Mohawk," he said, then pointed to Henri. "Ottawa."

Duncan looked up at the sound of the door latch. Sarah appeared, followed not by Crispus but by Duncan's friend Conawago.

Before Duncan could speak, she extracted a green bottle with a cork in it labeled *Cinchona*, another name for the healing bark.

"A clean cup, half-filled with water," Duncan said. Sarah stepped to the keg on a trestle behind the stairs and returned with the cup. Duncan poured a dose into the water and took it to his malaria patient, still cradled by the woman. "*Il doit boire ça, tout ça*," he instructed. She accepted it with a nod and coaxed the man to sip the medicine.

Duncan stepped to Sarah's side. "Except for Henri, there is nothing ailing your friends but malnutrition. They need fruit and bread and meat, vegetables if we can find some. Milk and water to drink for now."

Sarah nodded. "Crispus had loaves and milk waiting when they arrived. And Conawago has sent him for something more substantial."

"And the cellar is too damp," he said, lowering his voice. "We can find people to take them in. There's work aplenty to be had in the fish-drying sheds."

"No. There's work waiting for them on the west slopes of the Catskills."

"They will not be fit to travel to Edentown for weeks." Duncan choked off the rest of his protest. Had Sarah gathered up such a crew of outcasts just to ship them off to her tract on the frontier? And what was so urgent about his introduction to them that she had to interrupt his examination of the dead lieutenant? It made no sense.

Conawago spoke with the tribesmen. The African woman was whispering to Henri again, the empty cup at her side.

The entire day had been a puzzle. Following Sarah's unlikely victory, he assumed they would spend the evening at home celebrating or perhaps at a tavern with Hancock. He never understood her unexpected challenge to the captain of the cutter and had wanted to dismiss it as whimsy, but he had seen little whimsy in Sarah since his return from London. He remembered now Conawago's signal fire, and her apprehensiveness when the tidesman rushed to report the arrival of Hancock's West Indies brig to his commissioner.

He thought back to the day she made her unexpected sailing challenge. Why had the challenge suddenly become so important? What else happened that day? The only event he could recall was the dawn arrival of Hancock's swift packet, the courier boat that carried information about expected port arrivals so warehousemen and chandlers could stand ready. Later that day as they sailed on that same packet to Boston, she had grown very interested in details of the revenue cutter and the name of its master. She meant to attract all the senior officers, manipulating Hancock to offer his personal yacht and knowing that the beguiling event would mean the staging of one of his famous alfresco teas. Had the entire spectacle been a carefully orchestrated decoy, to distract the navy from the West Indies ship?

Henri shifted in his blankets, his shivering subsiding, and his nurse repositioned herself as the boy shifted closer to take Henri's hand. The woman acknowledged the boy with a tender smile as she put her arm around Henri. Her repetitive whisper changed. She now comforted him with a chant of "*nous sommes libres, nous sommes libres.*"

Suddenly the pieces slid into place: the sailing race, the unusual anchoring of the West Indies brig outside the Neck, the signal fire, the starved condition of those before him, the ruin of Henri's back.

"My God, Sarah!" Duncan gasped. "You've smuggled in escaped slaves!"

Chapter 3

"I'VE PROVIDED A NEW LIFE to eight tormented souls!" Sarah shot back, her eyes flaring as Duncan pushed her into the corner under the stairs.

"That remains to be seen," he whispered. "A new life or a more rapid death. And punishment for the rest of us. Does John know?"

"Of course not. But Hancock's captain is both a patriot and a resolute abolitionist who abhors the lash and chain. The opportunity to save them arose unexpectedly in Barbados, and he took it."

"The opportunity arose? You mean you made no provision for them?" Sarah stared at him in mute defiance. "Alarms will have gone out, Sarah! They will know what ships left around the time of the escape. Inquiries will be made. Anyone harboring them will be brought to court for punishment."

"Marblehead is far from the West Indies, and Edentown a world away. And no Massachusetts judge is going to rule against someone doing their Christian duty."

"Except for those who have slaves themselves. And the army seems convinced this man Book killed Hicks. They will soon be ripping the town apart to find him."

"Let them try," Sarah stubbornly asserted. "I understand he has many friends."

"But who else might they find? The soldiers will be in hot temper, quick to punish whatever they find. And won't they think old storehouses a prime hiding place for a deserter?" Duncan glanced at the company, all of whom seemed to be listening, and choked down the other questions that leapt to his tongue. He had not the time, and this was obviously not the place. He had to rejoin the dead lieutenant before the soldiers returned.

Sarah gave a shrug and turned to the man nearest the stair, an African of about thirty years who seemed slightly more fit than the others. "This is Solomon, who knows the skills of ironwork," she said in introduction, then moved to the man with graying hair. "Tobias, well acquainted with milk cows and oxen. And this gentleman," she said, indicating the surly man who had seemed poised to pound Duncan with a rock, "is Cuff?" She let the word hang like a question, as if inviting the man to offer more than a nickname.

"Cuff," the man spat. "Jist Cuff. And we nay need yer help."

Sarah refused to be goaded. "Thank you, Mr. Cuff. You look like a man who enjoys the company of animals. A teamster perhaps?" Her words brought guffaws from Solomon and Tobias and a snarl to Cuff's face. "We can always use teamsters," she added with a smile.

She moved on, indicating now the mixed-blood boy and the woman holding the ailing Henri. "Young Josiah, as agile as a cat, and his mother Esther and father Henri." She nodded to the two remaining tribesmen. "Tall George," she said, indicating the Oneida who had spoken with Duncan, "and Silent Louis beside him, though I daresay we shall not preserve names conjured by some overseer."

"You truly mean to take them to Edentown," Duncan murmured, still shocked that Sarah would so vastly multiply the dangers they faced. They well understood how to navigate the risks of smuggling, but now she was creating a whole new layer of enemies.

"I *will* take them to Edentown. And please, Duncan, stop speaking of my new friends as if they were not right here in front of us. They will journey to Edentown, and they will be given land if they want it or jobs in town. I think Josiah would enjoy helping Conawago in the printshop after school."

Thankfully, before Duncan could respond, the door above them opened and Crispus appeared, carrying an oversized basket. "Sunday dinner," he announced with a laugh as Conawago retrieved a long bench from under the stairs, set it in the middle of the floor, and then with a cheerful bow bid good night to his new acquaintances and hurried up the stairs.

From the top of the basket Crispus extracted a piece of sailcloth, which he used to cover the wide bench, then began arranging dishes of food. Some of it still lay on expensive porcelain platters. He had taken the leftovers from Hancock's tea, much of which appeared untouched after the summons to the belfry. There was one small cake with sugar icing left, which Crispus handed to young Josiah. The boy accepted it with wide, awestruck eyes, then promptly divided it into thirds, sharing with his parents.

Duncan stepped back from the bench, and the escaped slaves warily advanced to the makeshift table, in awe of the feast before them. "Not too much at once," he cautioned, but no one was listening. Sarah, handing out servings of meat pie, laughed as an entire piece disappeared into Solomon's mouth, followed by a groan of pleasure. Duncan tried, and failed, to get her attention, then turned and climbed the stairs. At the top he tried once more. She studiously ignored him.

Duncan settled once more onto the stool beside the dead lieutenant. Above him, a soft croaking sound emanated from the ventilation openings in the steeplelike structure atop the belfry. In the moonlight that filtered inside he made out a shape on the crosspiece inside the steeple that twisted its head downward, as if responding to his gaze. An owl had taken up the vigil.

When his comrades returned they would want Hicks as presentable as possible. Duncan straightened the sleeves of the scarlet tunic, then arranged the lieutenant's arms at his side in a final posture of attention. He hesitated at the tunic buttons. The top three were not fastened, even though he was certain he had left only the topmost loose. As he raised his hand toward the buttons the door behind him opened.

"Jesus, Mary, and Joseph!" a tenor voice called out. "Never woulda believed it without laying me own eyes on his earthly remains, him being such a stubborn fighter and all." A slender soldier appeared at Duncan's side, removed his hat, and bowed his head with a whispered prayer. Duncan puzzled over the man's soft, singsong accent.

"Corporal Rhys," came a deeper, impatient Yorkshire voice. A burly infantry sergeant stepped into the light. "You be here to guard the door."

As the sergeant spoke, the owl sounded and the corporal's head snapped up. He made the sign of the cross and then with a muttered curse shook his fist at the bird. "Be gone, ye blaggard! We ain't said words or even spilt whisky on 'im!" Rhys caught himself and offered an apologetic nod to his sergeant. "Beg pardon, Robbie. It's come to gather his soul, ye see. But words must be spoken first."

Duncan had not often heard the accent, but now he marked the way the man's voice dipped and rose in the midst of a syllable. *Rhys.* He was Welsh.

"Peter, collect yourself, man!" the soldier beside Duncan snapped. Duncan assessed the two more closely. The men sent to watch over the dead were non-commissioned officers from the local infantry unit and obviously friends. "The door!" The sergeant turned to Duncan and announced himself with a sharp salute. "Sergeant Briggs of the Twenty-Ninth. And ye must be Mr. McCallum. Prithee, forgive the corporal, sir. The old ways run deep with him even after twenty-five years in the army."

"Twenty-six!" the corporal corrected. "One score and six, and don't I deserve the king's best medal for putting up with you for most of 'em."

The sergeant rolled his eyes. "The door?"

"Aye, sir, of course, sir. Excepting his tunic needs closing. Lieutenant Hicks took pride in his appearance, Sarge."

Briggs hesitated, looking at Duncan, then the dead man. Duncan moved his hand toward the open buttons, but the sergeant pushed it away. "I should do it, sir. Soldier to soldier." The sergeant touched a button and paused. Duncan, too, noticed a protrusion under the tunic. Briggs unfastened the next button and spread the tunic, then paused again. The linen shirt underneath had been sliced open, as had the flesh over Hicks's heart, in three separate, deep cuts. A metal disc had been driven into each slice.

"I thought . . ." Briggs began, then collected himself. "Beg pardon, sir, but I was told you had already examined him. Readied him."

Duncan stared at the discs, trying to understand. "You can see that there is no bleeding from these wounds," he finally said. "These were not here earlier." Duncan leaned over Hicks's exposed chest and answered the question rising on the sergeant's countenance. "There was a sound in the distance," he explained, motioning toward the end of the long shed. "I went to investigate, stepping out the back door, and so was away for a short time." It was not entirely a lie.

"But why—" Briggs began, then Rhys pushed in at his side.

"May the hounds of hell rip the bastard limb from limb!" the corporal spat.

"Corporal?" Duncan asked.

"Dinna ye see what they be? The navy's tokens for a month's pay, given to pressed men while their early pay is held back. It's Book, God rot his soul! Jacob Book, sure as stones! The damned savage served three months before swimming away. So three tokens. It's his message, his alone. Debt paid in full."

"A traitor to our blessed George and a sneak assassin to boot," Briggs growled.

"Lowest vermin of all!" Rhys put in. "If we was in London that damned Book be drawn and quartered," he added, then turned to Duncan as if he needed to explain. "Hang 'im first, ye see, but before he dies ye cut him down, slice out his guts as he lives, and chop off all his limbs. That's the justice for enemies of the king, sir."

"You act as though Book were already tried and convicted," Duncan pointed out.

"Oh, he be the one right enough. Playing cat and mouse with Hicks these past weeks, and the lieutenant getting more and more furious. And Book knows well enou' how Massachusetts magistrates protect the killers of His Majesty's officers. That murdering knave who harpooned the naval officer last year be from this very town. Probably celebrating with Book as we speak."

The corporal's bitter words contained a kernel of truth. The Marblehead sailor who had been found innocent on grounds of self-defense after killing an impressment officer would be an obvious source of comfort for a fugitive sailor. Duncan would try to find the man in the morning in the hope of locating Book. If Book were not quickly captured, the town would be torn asunder by the army. But if Book *were* captured, he might try to trade his life for information of interest to the government, and some Marblehead deserters were familiar with the town's smugglers, including Sarah's new network of nightingales.

"Just wait till the provosts come," Rhys added in a dark whisper. "They'll teach the town a blood-soaked lesson. Make us look like the gentlest of lambs."

The yellow clapboard house on the hill was unusually quiet. A solitary candle lamp burned on the table by the stairs. Their taciturn landlady, the widow Godwin, would have long since retreated with her knitting to her rooms in the east wing of the house. Duncan could hear Moll, the Scottish cook, humming as she moved about her room behind the kitchen. Duncan's body was exhausted, but his mind was racing. He was deeply troubled by Sarah's recklessness in smuggling escaped slaves into the town, compounding the risks they already faced in their secret work, but even more so by his exchange with the soldiers in the belfry. Why would someone secretly, horribly, kill Hicks? And why return to further mutilate the body?

Before climbing the stairs Duncan replenished the dying candle in the lamp by the stairs so that it would be lit when Sarah eventually returned, as she often did for him. He paused at the door of the first bedroom, grinning at the faint whiff of cedar and cherry-scented tobacco, then gently pushed it open. Finding it empty, he stepped to the narrow door at the end of the corridor, which was slightly ajar. At the back of the linen cupboard was a ladder fastened to the wall.

He climbed up to the widow's walk, the railed platform built into the peak of the roof. The figure sitting on the rail greeted Duncan with a nod, then with a foot pushed toward him a pewter bowl, which contained a familiar deerskin pouch and a smoldering rush. Duncan extracted the clay pipe he carried in his waistcoat pocket, filled it from the pouch, and lit the fragrant tobacco. He took his first puff and then swept the pipe in a slow arc over his head.

"*Yoyanere,*" the silhouetted figure whispered after repeating Duncan's motion.

"*Yoyanere,*" Duncan echoed.

Like many Mohawk words, it conveyed much. Its direct meaning was simply *it is good,* but it was used both as a warm greeting and a blessing. His aged Nipmuc friend also used it as a way of cutting through worldly cares. Conawago was reminding Duncan that despite the facts that Sarah, smuggler of British manufacturing secrets, was the target of a ruthless hunt that spanned the Atlantic, that her aristocratic father had repeatedly tried to have Duncan killed, that Duncan was undertaking the nearly impossible task of setting up a network of clandestine operatives for the Sons across colonial borders, and that Sarah had escalated their dangers by harboring escaped slaves, Duncan and Conawago were here, on the top of the town, with the stars glistening and the moon gilding the vessels in the harbor. They had smoked their pipes on wilderness mountaintops, on deck in the middle of the Atlantic, even in canoes gliding along Lake Ontario shorelines. Such nights were filled with miracles, Conawago was saying, and if Duncan was foolish enough not to see them, it was because he was letting himself be blinded by worldly troubles.

"We were speaking of the great white bears of the north," the Nipmuc abruptly said. "He encountered many as a youngster. The wise women of his tribe told him they guarded the edge of the spirit world. He says on his last voyage they touched the shores of Greenland, and his captain shot a white bear, then brought the pelt on board. They had nothing but bad luck afterward. Empty nets, storms, the captain died of a sudden fever, and then a press crew boarded. He says the pelt is still on the ship, in the captain's trunk, because everyone is frightened of it. She sits in Gloucester Harbor to this day. Can't find a new captain. Becoming something of a ghost ship, you might say. Someone has to take her north again, return the bear to Greenland, to plug the hole in the spirit world."

In his fatigue Duncan had only half listened. Now the words registered. "He?"

Conawago chuckled, took a puff of his pipe, then extended his foot into a darker shadow below the railing of the widow's walk. The shadow moved, and a face emerged out of the darkness. "Jacob," the old Nipmuc said, "wake up and meet my particular friend Duncan."

A sinewy hand rose up into the moonlight, and Duncan clasped it, feeling its calloused strength. "Jacob," he repeated, with new foreboding. "A man named Jacob has been sought by Lieutenant Hicks of the town garrison." Duncan recalled now how Sarah said the soldiers would not find Jacob Book. She knew where he was.

The man stretched and rose, lifting his weathered face into the moonlight. He was a tribesman in his fifties. Conawago handed him a spare pipe, and Book spoke as he lit it. "Oh, just a little misunderstanding, that. I've signed on to a schooner sailing with the First Fare fleet for the Banks. That pestilent hound will be left far behind." The fish tattooed on his cheeks seemed to swim as he spoke.

"You were taken by the press gang that boarded you on the Greenland voyage," Duncan suggested.

"Like Conawago said, bad luck all around. Had no papers to show I lived in Marblehead, because I mostly live on Marblehead boats. I said I have no paper to prove I am breathing, but here I stand before ye. Lost a tooth when that ensign hit me with his cudgel. Three months on a navy transport, back and forth from Halifax bringing more of the lobsterbacks who plague Boston. Then at the end of my watch one day, we anchored alongside a cod hauler sailed by friends from Marblehead. The gods had clearly sent her for my deliverance. As soon as it was dark, I dropped over the side and swam across to my old shipmates."

"And the navy branded you a deserter."

"They hold the pay of pressed men for the first six months. I never took a shilling from the king, though I gave him three months' hard labor. Figure he owes me, not t'other way. If I ever get to London, I'll take the matter up with old George," Book added with a hearty laugh.

"You're of a Canada tribe," Duncan suggested.

"Born Cree, though when I was twelve my mother moved us to Quebec City so she could find regular work to keep us fed. Two years later I shipped out to work the Gulf of Saint Lawrence. Been at sea ever since, these past ten years out of Marblehead."

"So you are familiar with Lieutenant Hicks," Duncan stated.

"Sure, I know 'im. One more devil in the employ of the king. America would be well rid of such. He nigh trapped me twice, the weasel, but I slipped away."

"He was murdered last night."

Jacob was genuinely surprised. "My God," he said after a moment, gazing out over the harbor. "That'll go bad for the town."

"Worse for you. Can you leave any sooner?" Duncan asked. "Tonight?"

"Can't. Signed on to that Grand Banks schooner. My signature is my word. Leaves after the First Fare celebration," he explained, referring to the traditional opening of the Grand Banks season. Book gestured to Conawago with his pipe. "Except my Nipmuc friend be trying to steer me toward a new life on the New York frontier."

Duncan saw his old friend's pleased nod and realized the two were growing close. Book was another careworn tribesman who managed to remain jovial and, like Conawago, unusually articulate. Duncan suspected that he, too, had been educated by Jesuits.

"You need to catch a boat right away," Duncan pressed. "The army—"

"Duncan, no," Conawago interrupted. "We have plans."

"The army thinks Jacob killed Hicks."

His words silenced his companions. Duncan became aware of a low wheezing sound coming from Book that grew into a soft laugh. "My mates will be buying me ale in every tavern in town."

"Jacob, it's the army. They are ruthless."

"Pups with guns. The infantry ain't yet truly grappled with a Marblehead sea wolf."

"Who would have had a grievance with Hicks?" Duncan asked.

"Who wouldn't? He and his men have no business in this town. Bursting into homes unannounced. Poking into the holds of honest boats. Demanding to see papers they know don't exist. Not to mention the crude comments and gestures to womenfolk. Plenty of folks would stove in his head if given the chance."

But who, Duncan asked himself, would want to see him strung up with his mouth sewn shut?

"Sky streaker," Conawago abruptly said and pointed to the tail of a brilliant meteor. It was his way of saying they had spoken enough of worldly matters. "Tell me, Jacob," he asked, "in any of your voyages have you ever witnessed a whale communing with the moon?"

Duncan and Conawago had voyaged back from London together, experiencing two full moons at sea. Conawago, fascinated by the mysteries of the sea, had insisted on staying on deck on those nights, and each time they witnessed whales frolicking in the silvered waters. The old Nipmuc, having previously declared the whales possessed of a higher level of intelligence than humans, had decided they were seeing some sort of communication between these sage creatures and the moon.

"Ah, leviathan," Book sighed. "I was on a whaler in my youth, the best harpooner on the ship. But one day we was chasing a great trophy, biggest spermaceti we had seen on the voyage. I sunk one harpoon in her flank and she sounded. We thought it would be long minutes to wait, but suddenly she breached just a hundred feet from us and fixed me with that big soulful eye. So wise. So like my mother. I lowered my spear and tipped my cap to her. The captain was furious and asked why I lost him the great prize. 'Because,' I said, 'she asked me with great dignity to spare her life.' He raged and declared that I needed to change my line of work, then abandoned me in the next port."

Had the tale been told in a tavern, it would have raised boisterous laughter and offers of a tankard to the jokester who spun such a yarn. But here the words were spoken with great solemnity, and Conawago listened with an equal air. Duncan had learned long ago that his friend had a link to the natural world beyond that of ordinary humans. He heard and saw things in nature that no one else did. As if in confirmation the old man turned and nodded into the darkness, toward the chimney that rose at the side of the house. With a skip of his heart Duncan saw that a great owl sat there, as if listening.

"I know a Micmac woman up on the Bay of Fundy," Book continued. "She calls in whales with her songs, seen it with my own eyes. They swim right up to her canoe, and she rubs their backs. I can take you up there this summer during their season," he offered, a glimmer of joy in his voice. "We will go out with her and sing the whales under the full moon!"

Conawago had many congenial acquaintances but very few close friends. Jacob Book was reaching the old man's heart. The Nipmuc clasped his hands and raised them in salute to Book. "I should like that above all things, Jacob! We shall bring Duncan so he can learn about those who touch the earth."

Duncan raised his pipe in acknowledgment. He wished indeed that he lived in a world where he could join the old men in a quest to find those who touched the earth. But his world was populated by crucified army officers, secret killers, vengeful soldiers, and overzealous patriots, all of whom seemed blind to the threat that haunted Duncan ever since his return to occupied Massachusetts. One more violent incident could push the colony into open warfare.

The official name of what the locals called the Triple Fish was the Three Cods Tavern, its identity proclaimed by the large sign extending over the entrance that depicted a trio of the sleek creatures. They were painted gold, not because it was the natural color of the species but because cod was the age-old source of Marblehead's wealth.

The early afternoon hour was a popular one for the crews of the inshore fishing boats, who were usually out of the harbor long before sunrise and had put in a day's work by midday. Several greeted Duncan by name, and he paused to chat while searching for his friend John Glover. He spied him at a corner table with three other mariners. Duncan greeted Winifred the barmaid and ordered a tankard of winter ale, then slipped into the empty side chamber, where he took a seat overlooking the harbor.

He had expected to find a sleepy fishing village when John Hancock and Sam Adams suggested moving to Marblehead, charging him with the impossible dual task of keeping the patriots' secrets far from the government's sight while simultaneously keeping the angry population of Marblehead from starting a war. Instead, he was surprised by the town's bustling commerce. While cod still supplied the livelihood of most, Marblehead's merchants had built a lively trade with the West Indies, Britain, and the ports of Portugal and northern Spain. Although Parliament's Sugar Act required all sugar and molasses to be imported from British colonies and all imports of many manufactured items to be only from Britain, there was still ample latitude in commerce, legal or otherwise, for the merchants to turn respectable profits. Marblehead, Glover once quipped, only rendered unto Caesar what Caesar earned, "and most consider that to be damned little."

The compact, red-haired man who joined Duncan a few minutes later was of venerable Marblehead stock. The quick-thinking, no-nonsense Glover became one of Duncan's first friends after the two of them crewed one of Glover's inshore fishing boats for three days after half its seamen had abruptly taken up the offer of speculative riches from a whaling captain. Their relationship grew closer when the two men revealed their respective involvements in the cause of liberty.

Glover sat across from Duncan and sipped at his tankard while making admiring comments about a big schooner that was taking on stores at the nearest wharf for a voyage to the Azores. Duncan nodded, then lifted one of the little birch slats with a burnt image of three fish that was a token of the tavern to sample the pickled herring brought by Winifred. He waited to speak until Winifred had closed the door behind her.

"I never heard the details of your unpleasant errand to Castle William," Duncan said.

Glover shrugged. "I stuck to the tale we agreed, close enough to the truth, and they said the proper things. Too shocked to do much else. 'Cept that Commodore Lawford came out and stood on the wharf with another man, the colonel in charge of the soldiers, I suspect. They watched, solemn as priests, as we raised the net with the body up. The corpse was caught up in the lines, and we had to lift him up higher to untangle it. An ugly sight to be sure, him hanging there in the shrouds with crabs clinging to his flesh and kelp wrapped around his head. The commodore ordered linen to cover him, and a stretcher. One of those provosts came out and took my name, then marked on a map where we found him and what time, just like you expected. Lawford was shaken, knew the dead man, told me he was Captain Mallory, one of the best-liked officers in his regiment. Once he was one of those fancy Horse Guards in London, the commodore told me, but bought a commission in the infantry because he yearned for something other than desk work and soirees.

"I said I reckon Mallory didn't know how to swim, and the provost just said he was an infantryman, not a damned fish, and that was that. I was given permission to unmoor and return home."

They sat in silence for several breaths. Ever since that day Duncan could not shake his foreboding, a feeling that the dead man would come back to haunt them. Now that foreboding was doubled. Two dead infantry officers in two weeks was not something the army could ignore. "I never explained the full tale of why Sarah and I moved here," he finally said.

"To get away from the lobsterbacks. You can't take three steps in Boston without bumping into one."

"Yes, but I had just come from London, where I discovered that not all our enemies wear uniforms."

Glover sipped his ale. "I don't follow."

"The War Council has a small company of men who work in the shadows. Officers of those Horse Guards you mention, though they seldom wear their uniforms. They disguise their appearance and their missions."

"I've heard tales of such subterfuge in Europe, in the intrigue between France and Britain."

"Benjamin Franklin and I learned they have been deployed across the Atlantic. In the intrigues between the king and his colonies."

Glover chewed on the words, and his herring, before lifting his square, windburned face to Duncan. "Surely not, McCallum. Such artificers are used in war, against the real enemies of the king."

Duncan fixed Glover with a meaningful gaze. "Exactly," he said, letting the word hang for a few heartbeats. "These men are merciless, John, and *they* decide who the king's enemies are." Duncan pressed on, hoping to win the argument he had lost before the leaders of the Sons of Liberty in Boston weeks before. Despite the entreaties of both Duncan and Franklin, secretly writing from London, Hancock and Samuel Adams refused to believe the king would set clandestine agents against them.

"No, no. Surely we would have heard of such thugs."

"They act with impunity, John. They invoke the warrant of the king to commit murder and mayhem. I have seen their work in London, where they cut the throat of an innocent boy just as a warning against Franklin and me. They don't waste their efforts on those who merely evade the sugar duties. They play for higher stakes. Against those who would smuggle in secrets of British manufacturing. Against the vital organs of the Sons of Liberty." They both knew that the most important manufacturing processes were all banned in America and that secret efforts were under way to defy the ban.

Glover frowned. "You mean like looms and spinning jennies and such. Such things might touch Marblehead shores, sure enough, but our people are stealthy practitioners of the smuggling arts. They will ne'er attract the attention of your cloaked strangers, even if they were on this side of the Atlantic."

"They are on these shores as we speak, John. On these streets, I fear."

Glover frowned, obviously not convinced. "We don't jump at shadows in Marblehead." The sturdy waterman turned his attention to the herring. Winifred stepped into the doorway with an inquiring gaze. Duncan nodded and she disappeared into the kitchen.

"The magistrate visited me," Glover announced. "He heard about Lieutenant Hicks, went to the belfry to see the body before the soldiers took it away. Pompously declares it to be his honor-bound duty to investigate any mortal crime committed in Marblehead. I daresay the army doesn't agree, for they wouldn't surrender the body to him. One of my mates builds coffins in the winter months and had gone with Mr. Hancock to deliver the box, was there in the belfry when one of the soldiers talked about how Hicks was furious with someone, had heard him say just the day before something about 'that damned meddler, thinks he can just sail in from London and disrupt our work. The Twenty-Ninth is a fighting unit, and he'll damned well learn that soon enough.'"

"Why would the magistrate visit you?"

"It was the Loyalist one." Marblehead had two magistrates, one who always supported the government and the other, who was a militia officer and more skeptical about the benefits of a king.

Duncan hesitated. "I don't understand."

"He has marked the Sons of Liberty as no friends of the king. Official view in Boston may be that the Sons must be tolerated, but this isn't Boston, and he is eager to make an impression on the governor. You are an outsider with no tie to a church or any enterprise here, so easier for him to prosecute."

"Being an outsider violates no law."

"No, even though he may wish it so. He wanted to know if it was true what he heard, that you were recently arrived from London."

Duncan contemplated the words a moment, then his eyes flashed with understanding. "He can't possibly think I am the meddler Hicks complained about! I didn't even know Hicks."

"He wanted to know what it is you do to afford the lodgings of the widow Godwin. I told him you were a doctor and a shipmaster. He asked who are your patients and where is your ship."

Duncan frowned. "He wants me out of Marblehead."

"Magistrates consult with their counterparts in Boston and take orders from the governor. They know you are close to John Hancock and Sam Adams. Now you have settled in Marblehead and are visited by Hancock."

"You mean they think I am trying to stir up the population."

"Worse, I fear. He sees you as an opportunity. A murder charge would be a convenient way to eliminate you and win favor with the governor."

"Ridiculous! On the basis of some soldier's memory of a vague complaint about someone from London?"

"Steady on. It would never succeed but it would give them leverage over you. Meaning us. We are in uncharted waters here, my friend. The murder and mutilation of a king's officer is a grave matter. Pray they don't discover we didn't tell all about our discovery of Captain Mallory's body."

Duncan had no time to respond, for the kitchen door opened and the owner of the Triple Fish appeared, carrying fresh tankards. He presented two to Glover and Duncan, then sat down with the third. "Opened a keg of last year's cider," he declared, then raised his cup. "Peace and liberty," he toasted and took a long swallow. Gabriel's involvement with the Sons was a well-guarded secret, though not to the two men at his table.

"You've encountered the soldiers who hunt deserters," Duncan said to the innkeeper.

"Who hasn't?" Gabriel snorted. "The blaggards roar into my establishment at least once a week, as they do with every sizable tavern in town. They seem to think their fugitives just lounge about with a tankard waiting to be dragged away."

"Both the navy and the army?"

"'Twas only the navy, an officer with marines, until that company from the Twenty-Ninth Foot arrived. Since then it's mostly been that wretched Hicks and his men." Gabriel paused. "Pardon, it's ill to speak so of the departed. I hear the lieutenant will no longer plague us."

"Did he sometimes find his quarry here?"

"Not often, but yes, and don't I feel low when they drag off one of my customers, for I know he's bound for misery. They say our pressed men are treated little better than dogs on the king's ships. Not many survive the first year. And if they've deserted, they know they may hang, though the ships are so shorthanded none have had their neck stretched yet, just a hundred lashes, God preserve them."

"Never anyone else with the soldiers? A civilian?"

"Nay—" Gabriel hesitated. "Well, the last time was different. Hicks came in, placing a private to block the entry. No one in or out until Hicks examines the customers. A sailor named Yates leaps up and dashes into this very room, slamming the door behind him. No doubt hoped to flee out the back," the innkeeper reported, indicating the kitchen door. "Except another gentleman had come in through my kitchen. Winifred was in there, and my cook, and they remember because the blaggard helped himself to the leg of a roasted chicken without a by-your-leave. That was clearly the end of poor Yates, who had already deserted once. I recall him crying out 'tell my daughter,' like the words of a dying man. That be his twelve-year-old daughter, who has no one else, seeing how her mother died of consumption last year."

"A gentleman, you said," Duncan pointed out. "Not a soldier, not a marine."

"No uniform, and he carried himself like a gentleman of leisure. Slender fellow of maybe thirty-five or so years. Smudges of snuff on his waistcoat collar. A gristle-hard face with pox marks on the cheeks. Long black hair tied at the back, no wig. Tied with a yellow ribbon, which struck me as odd. I had seen Hicks with deserters before. Always shouting and damning their souls to hell. He liked to mark the men he caught with his dagger. Used to be a slice on the arm or hand till the navy complained that the men had to be serviceable, so he took to doing it on their cheeks. Two short slices right across the jawbone, deep enough to leave scars. To mark them as one of his trophies, he would say."

"But something different happened that day," Duncan suggested.

"Aye. Curious. Yates shouted sure enough, but only for a few moments. Then all went quiet. No screaming, no beating, no slicing."

"You mean Yates gave himself up and went peaceably."

"That's the curious thing. After a quarter hour they went their way. The stranger slipped out through the kitchen, quiet as an Indian, though pausing to snatch a fresh loaf, the scrub. There was some shouting at the end, come to think of it, but it was Hicks shouting at that stranger. He was furious when he came out of the chamber, just yelled 'wrong man' to his soldiers in a very hot voice and marched them away. Though I knew for a fact that Yates had been pressed and jumped ship."

"But Gabriel, that makes no sense," Glover said, then reconsidered. "Ah. Yates paid a bribe."

"A man who ain't paid a debt in months, owing every merchant and innkeeper in town who give him credit to keep his poor little girl out of the workhouse? I doubt he had more than a ha'penny to his name."

Duncan stared out at the harbor, his foreboding mounting as he watched the *Neptune* emerge from around the Neck. Yates couldn't offer money, but he could offer something more valuable. "Have you seen the stranger since?" he asked, keeping his eyes on the revenue cutter.

"Nay, 'cept Winifred says she saw him at the market, asking how he might find a seaman from that Hancock brig that anchored off the Neck yesterday during the race. He seemed right pleased with the answer he got, that none of the crew be in Marblehead because the brig weighed and sailed off that very night, on to Boston. Made the tidesmen right suspicious. Why stop in Marblehead with no cargo to unload?"

"And Yates?"

"Wandering around the waterfront, swapping tales and ales with old mates."

"Not hiding anymore?"

The innkeeper pursed his lips, considering the question. "True enough, Mc-Callum," he said with a slow nod. "He's no longer skittish about the patrols." Gabriel lowered his tankard and shook his head. "Hellfire," he muttered, then looked up. "But if he turned coat, he would give up some of the other deserters. Probably five or six of 'em on the loose in these parts, and I wager he knows nigh all of them, and their hidey-holes. I ain't heard of even one being nabbed." He turned his gaze to Glover. "Lieutenant?" Glover was one of the senior officers of the local militia.

"None," Glover confirmed. "Word of captures spreads fast, and everyone knows the militia does what it can for the families."

Duncan gazed into his cider. There was indeed a meddler recently arrived from London, one of the ruthless members of the Black Office of the War Council. The very powerful, very devious, members of the Council who had planted a spy in Franklin's household in London, and tried to kill Duncan the year before, had an agent lurking in Marblehead.

"And here, Gabriel," Glover said, raising his cup to Duncan, "is when I apologize to my Scottish friend for disbelieving that the king might be engaging in subterfuge. I fear you have proved his point."

Duncan acknowledged his friend with a grateful nod. His companions may at least have glimpsed the threat, but they had no inkling of the evil such men could inflict. "Say nothing of this," he said to them. "But if you see this stranger with the poxed face, Gabriel, send word immediately. I want to know where he lives. I want to know whom he speaks with. And send a message with the night coach to Boston. These men don't work alone. Let our friends know that demons lurk among us."

The condition of most of the refugees from the Indies had improved significantly since Duncan's first encounter with them. The grayness, and the fear, on their faces had largely disappeared. He laid a flour sack full of apples on the bench that had served as a table the night before and surveyed the company. At first he could not understand why several had oak barrel staves close at hand, but then he saw the nervous way they watched the stairs and realized the staves were makeshift weapons. The surly African called Cuff was in the shadows under the stairs, methodically rubbing a stone along the edge of an old sickle. The expected fever had overtaken Henri the Ottawa, who now lay stretched out on a straw pallet as his wife Esther dabbed at his face with a rag. She accepted the new dose of cinchona from Duncan with a weary smile. He suspected she had gotten little sleep since he had last seen her.

Duncan knelt by the Oneida tribesman, who sat alone in a corner warily watching his companions. When he declined the muslin-wrapped bundle Duncan extended, Duncan set it before him and opened its folds. A glimmer of surprise crossed the man's coppery countenance. Slowly he reached out for the clay pipe and pouch of tobacco. Duncan dropped a flint, striker, and tinder beside them.

"We mix crushed cherry and cedar bark with the tobacco," he explained.

"We?" the Oneida asked.

"My particular friend Conawago, who was here last night. We have sat at many council fires in Onondago sharing such pipes," he added, referring to the Iroquois town that served as the capital of the six-tribe confederation.

The Oneida opened the pouch, held it close to his nose, and closed his eyes a moment. When they opened again, all apprehension had left his face. Duncan had brought him a fragment of a life that he thought lost forever.

"How long has it been?" Duncan was about to rephrase his question to make it less ambiguous, when the tribesman replied.

"The last year of the big war, when Montreal fell."

"Nearly ten years then," Duncan concluded. "I was there, with Mohawk rangers."

The Oneida stared intensely at Duncan, as if gauging his truth, then rolled up the threadbare sleeve of his shirt. He pushed it past the ugly brand of an *S*, for *slave*, to expose a tattoo just above his elbow, of a hawk clutching an arrow. Duncan gazed at the image in surprise. It was the sign of an elite unit of rangers from the French war. "I had friends who wore that bird," Duncan said in a low voice. "Many died in the final battles."

A distant look settled on the Oneida's face. "A British officer came one day," he began. "He selected six of us, the strongest, for a special mission, he said. He told us how brave we were, how the great generals valued us so. We were too proud to decline and too thirsty for blood to avenge our fallen friends. We were to report before dawn to a landing by the river, across from the great fortress. No firearms, he said, which we thought meant it would be a mission of stealth, perhaps raiding and firing a French depot as we had done before. But when we arrived we were ringed by men with muskets, the crew of a French privateer that had tricked its way up the Saint Lawrence by flying a British flag. The privateer captain handed the British officer a purse of coins, and we were put in chains for the voyage to the Indies. We were sold to a Barbados sugar plantation." He pointed to his ankles, which Duncan now saw were ringed with heavy scars. "I kept trying to escape, so they left my chains on for three years. By then all the others who were taken with me had died, and I had learned that there was no point to escape unless it was on a ship back to America."

Duncan acknowledged his tale with a sober nod, then lit a spark as the Oneida packed the pipe. He didn't speak until the Oneida had taken several puffs. "I am not going to call you Tall George, not even George. You have nothing in common with the king."

The tribesman studied Duncan for several silent breaths. *"Ikhnenyehs ohneh-ta'kowa,"* he said.

"You are called Tall Pine," Duncan translated. "Call me Duncan." He turned to the older tribesman, the Mohawk Sarah had called Silent Louis, who was listening. Rummaging in his pockets, he produced another pipe.

The man grinned as he accepted the pipe. *"A'nowara. Oronya a'nowara."*

They were the first words Duncan had heard him speak. "Blue Turtle," Duncan translated. "And also a ranger?"

The Mohawk leaned toward Duncan, rolling up his own sleeve. Above the branded *S* on his forearm was the tattoo of a wolf. "War chief," he declared with sudden fierceness. Then the fire seemed to dim. "Long ago," he sighed.

"I can get you both work on a fishing boat. You could leave tomorrow." Sarah might want to take her refugees to Edentown, but Duncan just wanted them safely provided for. Lessening the number of escaped slaves gathered together lessened the danger.

It was Blue Turtle who replied. "The forest is our home."

Tall Pine solemnly nodded his agreement.

The simple eloquence of the words, and the determined glint with which they were delivered, was all Duncan needed to hear. The Iroquois would not be fleeing into the ocean, no matter the risk they faced on land. He studied the two for a long moment, seeing now the warriors emerging anew from the shells of former slaves.

He turned to the Mohawk. "Do you know the war chief Sir William Johnson?" he asked, referring to his friend, the superintendent of Indian affairs, who lived west of Albany. He then added Johnson's Mohawk name: "Warraghiyagey."

Blue Turtle reacted with surprise. "I was at the council fire when he was adopted into the tribe. I fought alongside him at Lake George and at Niagara."

"Can you find his home on the Mohawk River?"

Blue Turtle grinned. "Follow the sunset to the waters of the Hudson. Once I am on the great river I can find Warraghiyagey. And my people," he added, with a touching hunger in his voice.

The words pinched at Duncan's heart. He knew too many tribesmen separated from their homelands for years, only to return to find no trace of their families. Conawago, taken by Jesuits for a European education, had vainly searched for his family for decades. He traveled thousands of miles and endured unspeakable hardships. The long years of torment had created an emptiness in his heart that could never be filled.

"I mean to take Henri and his family to our house so I can care for him better. Help me with that," he said to the two Iroquois. "Then Tall Pine—"

"Just Pine," the Oneida said.

"Pine," Duncan continued, "I need you as a ranger at my side." He turned to the war chief. "And Blue Turtle, I will give you coin for travel, and letters for some along the western road who will shelter you without asking questions. I need you to deliver two messages, one to Sir William and another to a friend who once led Oneida and Mohawk rangers. You can ask at Johnson Hall where to find him. His name is Patrick Woolford."

"Captain Woolford," the Mohawk repeated. "He ran with Rogers along Lake Champlain for a time," he stated, speaking of the famed ranger leader. "He ran with me on the Saint Lawrence."

"He married a Mohawk woman," Duncan added.

A smile slowly rose on Blue Turtle's face. "And how many child gifts should I take to my old friend?"

"Two, the last I heard."

Blue Turtle puffed on his pipe with a look of deep satisfaction.

Pine studied Duncan with a new intensity. He switched to his native tongue. "The big man who helped us, the one called Crispus, says you are a secret warrior. Against the king."

Duncan replied in the same careful tone. "I am against what the king's men do in the colonies."

The Oneida slowly chewed on his words as he puffed on his pipe. "Your king makes slaves. Free men have no need of kings."

For a moment Duncan was transported to the council fires of Onondago, where orators, usually the oldest men and women of the tribes, shared pipes as they reduced complex conundrums to such simple, profound truths.

"You mean the colonies have no need for a king," he said.

A conspiratorial grin rose on Pine's face. For a moment Duncan sensed he was back at the fire ring of a ranger camp, making plans for war. "I mean there is no longer a place in my life for a king," Pine replied. "Ever again. A man who loves freedom must hate the king."

Duncan studied him in silence, wondering who was testing whom in this conversation.

The Oneida inhaled and let the smoke drift out his nose. "I will trust Duncan," he concluded, separating the two syllables, "though others do not." Duncan followed his gaze toward the far side of the cellar. Cuff continued to sharpen the edge of his sickle but had moved. He now sat on the stairs, as if intending to block Duncan's departure. The two other Africans, Solomon and Tobias, had joined him, standing like dutiful soldiers, barrel staves in hand.

Duncan, ignoring Cuff's taunting gaze, moved back to Esther and Henri, laying a hand on his patient's forehead, then taking his pulse. The medicine was working but not as quickly as it should, because his body was so frail. In a low voice Duncan explained that he and the Iroquois were going to take them to the house where Sarah and he lived, so he could tend more closely to Henri. Esther cast a worried glance at Cuff. "He'll cut you," she whispered, "for no good reason other than men like you used to do it to him. He would take a hundred lashes for defying the overseers and laugh, so they began slicing him instead."

Duncan rose and took a step toward the stairs. "I have to remove Henri," he declared in a level voice.

Cuff stood and turned to Solomon at his side. "What you suppose the bounty be for a returned sugar slave?" he loudly asked. "Five pounds? More for some." Duncan did not understand why his gaze lingered for a moment on Esther. "Mr. University of Edinburgh has salvaged hisself a treasure of human cargo, eh? Take us piecemeal, that's his plan. Less danger to him that way. Just another puppet of the king!"

Duncan tried to choke down his temper. He and Sarah were taking profound risks because of these escapees. He exchanged a long glance with Pine, who rose onto his haunches. Duncan spoke slowly, heat rising in his voice. "Men of my clan died fighting the king's forces at Culloden. Those who survived the battle were tortured and hanged by the king's men at Inverness. It was the king's men who bayoneted my younger brother in our Highlands home and raped and slayed my mother and sisters. It was the king's men who dragged me from my university to imprison me, then transported me for indenture in America. I am no one's puppet and no friend of the king."

For a moment Duncan thought his words had reached Cuff, who lowered his sickle and stepped off the stairs, but then he saw it was because Sarah and Crispus were descending into the cellar.

"Cuff!" Sarah cried as she saw the weapon in his hands. "Duncan is helping you! You must not—"

"He ain't one of us!" Cuff interrupted. "Look at 'im, putting on airs with his fancy gold watch!"

Duncan looked down at the nearly forgotten watch, which he hadn't wound in days. He wondered if it would matter if he explained that it had been a gift from Benjamin Franklin, whom Duncan had saved from the horrors of the Bedlam asylum months earlier.

"He is very much one of you!" Sarah cried as she reached Duncan's side.

"We be better on our own," interjected Solomon.

"The army is patrolling this town," Duncan explained in a simmering voice and batted away Sarah's hand as she tugged at his shirt. "They are searching the streets and alleys for a murderer. You can't just—"

"We know well enough how to deal with soldiers!" barked Cuff as he raised his sickle higher. "And you'd just keep us in this pit. I'd sooner die a free man fighting in the open air than wait in this trap while you strike the bargain for yer bounty!"

Sarah pulled again at Duncan's shirt. "No!" He pushed her away. He kept his gaze on Cuff, the man with the most dangerous weapon, but sensed new movement behind him. "Do not be enslaved by your hatred," he stated.

The words seemed to quiet Solomon, who lowered his stave, but Cuff gave something of a war cry and bent his knees to spring at Duncan. As Duncan pushed Sarah away again, there was a blur of movement at his side and a figure flung itself at Cuff. The two men were instantly wrestling on the packed dirt floor and as Esther cried out, darting into the tangle of limbs, Duncan realized it was the still feverish Henri who had thrown himself at Cuff.

The fight was quickly over when Crispus entered the fray, using his foot to pin the hand with the sickle. Pine pulled the weapon away, then helped Esther and her husband off the furious Cuff.

Tears welled in Sarah's eyes. She seemed about to speak, once, then twice, but each time emotion overcame her. Finally she pulled at Duncan's shirt again. This time he did not resist and let her pull it over his head, then turn his bare back toward Cuff and his makeshift gang.

It had been years, but the long scars of the overseer's lash still crisscrossed Duncan's back in ugly ridges. "Duncan was helping the friends of liberty when he was captured and enslaved on a Virginia tobacco plantation." She spoke in a pleading whisper. "He could have escaped, saved himself, but he didn't. He stayed to find freedom for all those chained on his plantation. Africans and tribesmen alike. He wants to get you away, to Edentown. Away from the king."

"Your Edentown is just another hiding place," Cuff growled. "I am done hiding. The king didn't make us slaves, but he kept us slaves. Now that I have the chance I will not walk away from the fight."

"I don't understand," Sarah confessed.

Cuff pounded the end of his sickle handle into his palm as he replied. "My freedom ain't yers to give." His voice was fierce. "I have to earn it." With that the fugitive slave turned and sprinted up the stairs.

Chapter 4

"HANCOCK PENNANT IN THE HARBOR, Mr. Duncan!" Moll's announcement carried down into the cellar, where Duncan was administering another dose of cinchona to his malaria patient. Sarah and the two Iroquois had helped move Henri and his family into their house the night before. Now Esther took the pewter cup from Duncan and promised that her husband would drink the entire draught as she motioned Duncan toward the stairs. He hurried up to the kitchen, threw on his coat, and darted out into the street, dodging the reeking cart that collected Marblehead's night soil each morning.

Pollard, the local manager, was supervising the unloading of the broad, sturdy sloop the merchant used for his coastal trade when Duncan arrived. "Six cases of porcelain, eight crates of woolens for First Fare sailors, a dozen kegs of nails, and one slightly green lawyer," Pollard reported, as if reading from a manifest.

Duncan nodded at the diminutive, scholarly-looking man who waited by the ship's wheel until the cargo was unloaded, then with one hand on his belly stepped unsteadily down the gangplank. He accepted Duncan's hand, though not before straightening his wig. "You seem to exercise an unnatural sway over the estimable Mr. Hancock," the man said. "When he came personally with your note, I told him I was engaged today with two clients. He asked their names and within an hour both sent messages apologizing for having to reschedule their engagements to later in the week." He extracted the message Duncan sent him and impassively read it: "I need you for an urgent matter of liberty." He lowered the note. "Intriguing. Are you sure this wasn't meant for my cousin Samuel?"

"I feared that if I had said an urgent matter of murder you might flee all the way back to Braintree."

"The Marblehead murder of the infantry officer, I take it," John Adams replied in the same level voice. "Forgive me for not being surprised, my friend, but that was the tale that monopolized all conversation on our voyage across the bay this morning," he added, gesturing toward the men offloading the cargo. "What's that quaint expression for rumors on a vessel? Oh yes, *scuttlebutt*. What a curious word." He took a step closer to Duncan. "I must admit that particular scuttlebutt intrigued me. It would seem further discourse is in order."

Duncan had learned not to be put off by Adams's stiffness, for he knew that it concealed a fervent and compassionate intellect. "When I left the house I smelled scones in the oven," Duncan said. "Our cook is not one to be trifled with, but I expect I can cajole her into sharing some, with her famous currant preserves. After a quiet talk along Fore Street," he added with a motion toward the thoroughfare that ran along the waterfront.

Duncan asked how John's wife, Abigail, fared in her latest pregnancy and about their new house off Brattle Street. Adams's responses were curt but polite. He had recently lost a daughter to illness and even in a more affable mood was never a man for small talk. They had not gone a hundred paces when the lawyer halted and settled onto an empty crate. "A quiet talk," he repeated. "Meaning out of earshot and before we reach your abode." He surveyed their surroundings. "This seems a particularly quiet section of the street." Duncan saw his gaze settle on the nearest structure, a decrepit house with a tattered red cloth hanging from its portico. Adams stiffened. "A quarantine flag?"

"From long ago. Everyone inside died. They call it the ghost house, home to undead demons. Locals won't go near it."

Adams cocked his head. "Fascinating how the human mind creates monsters out of thin air." He shrugged and settled back on his crate. "I have learned that you are a man of extraordinary interests, McCallum. So now tell me how the cause of liberty is wrapped around the unfortunate demise of this officer. An abjectly cruel man, if my Marblehead crew is to be believed."

"I think you and I, John, prefer the colonies to find a path to liberty without violence," Duncan began. "There are wise men on both sides of the Atlantic who seek that peaceful path, one that lifts our servitude while keeping us in the king's fold. But with Boston and the shore towns being treated like enemy outposts, that seems less and less the likely outcome. And you are well aware that there are also those on both sides who look to turn the colony into a battleground."

"Even the Sons of Liberty would prefer to secure liberty without bloodshed," Adams replied, then reconsidered. "Or nearly all the Sons." His own cousin Samuel, Duncan knew, was one of those who pressed relentlessly for overt resistance to the soldiers occupying Boston.

"If the troops stay much longer, violence is inevitable. Honest citizens are challenged on their own streets. Soldiers are pelted with snowballs and worse from alleys. We need to calm people, to show them that a balance can be struck, if there is to be any hope of the army's withdrawal. The people of Massachusetts need to see that the government will treat them fairly. Everyone. All men of this land."

Adams was considered by many to be unduly taciturn, but Duncan knew his silent, absent expressions often just meant the wheels of his formidable intellect were engaging. "As words spoken by a man who usually resides among the aborigines of the forest, I take them to refer to those who are not European." A half dozen seamen passed by, two of whom had coppery skin and heavily tattooed faces.

"The army is convinced their Lieutenant Hicks was murdered by a native named Jacob Book. He was illegally pressed into the navy and later jumped ship. Hicks, who was loathed by the townspeople, was rabid in his search for Book, who has many friends here. The army is outraged over the death, and when the crime is reported to General Gage in New York he will likely order the town to be put under the boot of martial law and pour more troops into our streets. I am convinced that Book is not the killer. But if they capture him and take him to Castle William for trial he will be hanged, whatever the evidence says."

"But you have an alternative to propose," Adams stated.

"Suppose you go to the government as Book's counsel. Offer to surrender him here in Marblehead on condition that he be tried here as well. The people here trust you. They are well aware that the last time a Marbleheader was accused of killing an officer, you were able to find a solution that avoided new riots."

Adams offered a slow nod. "We accepted the charge that my client did indeed kill the impressment officer in question with his harpoon, and the court accepted our claim that it was in self-defense."

"Had he hanged, this town would have exploded, with Boston not far behind. People have been collecting weapons all over the colony, waiting for that first spark. Now two more officers are dead and the fuse on that powder keg is smoldering."

"Two more? You suggest there is another?"

Duncan ignored the question. "The chance to avoid the detonation is rapidly diminishing."

Adams frowned as he ruminated on Duncan's words. "I am aware that you perform secret errands for the Sons of Liberty." He raised a restraining hand. "I do not want to know details. But I know you went to London for them and almost died protecting Benjamin Franklin. That seemed more like a mission of war. Is this a change of heart?"

"Not at all. I work for liberty and against those in London who oppose it. But I have seen the horrors of war, John. We have to find another way. Each of us must work for liberty according to our particular talents," he added with a pointed glance at the lawyer.

Adams sighed, then rose and fixed Duncan with one of his rare smiles as he self-consciously adjusted his wig again. "I suppose we will be sharing scones with this icon of freedom named Book?"

The warmth of Moll's welcome matched that of the hearth as Duncan escorted Adams into the kitchen, although she protested that such a fine gentleman from Boston should be seated in the parlor. Adams settled the matter by taking a seat at the broad oak table, saying he was a man of simple pleasures and preferred to linger by the oven to drink in the intoxicating scents of her baking.

"Would that be a Scottish burr I detect in your dulcet tones?" Adams asked the cook as Duncan stepped away. He heard Moll's laughter as he climbed the stairs.

Book's little attic room was empty. Duncan concluded that he must be with Conawago, but the old Nipmuc was alone, snoring in his bed. The two had likely passed the night watching meteors. Duncan laid a comforter over his friend before climbing the ladder to the roof. The widow's walk, too, was empty. Perhaps the

Cree mariner had learned there was a fugitive tribesman of the north in the cellar, but there Duncan found only Henri and Esther, laughing as their son played with the house cat.

"Our upstairs guest," he said to Moll when he returned to the kitchen. "I asked him to stay in the house."

"Don't reckon he's much inclined to be taking orders from any man," the Scottish cook declared. "I found 'im washing up at the well last night. I said it's a chill air to be out with no shirt, let me put some water on to heat by the hearth, and he just laughed, said he wasn't going to trouble anyone over his ablutions. I had the impression he meant to go out."

The news tied a knot in Duncan's stomach. He recalled how Book declared that his mates would be buying him drinks in every tavern. "But he's not returned," Duncan pointed out.

"Jacob's a Marblehead sailor. Ye ken how they will drink into the wee hours, then just curl up in some warm corner in a tavern. He'll be wandering up by midday."

Adams, finishing a bite, took another swallow of Moll's herbal concoction before speaking. "My boat returns to Boston when the tide shifts. Perhaps we should undertake a search for this intriguing gentleman?" he suggested, then grinned at the new plate of pastries that Moll pushed toward him. "In due course," he added and reached for another scone.

They had already checked two taverns when a boy ran up and pointed to the nearby wharf. "Mr. Glover says come quick, sir. One of his men took a bad blow when some rigging fell on him."

Duncan hurried to Glover's side, Adams a step behind, and found the ship-owner beside a man on a crate, clutching his side. "Pint of rum and I'll be good as new, sir," the sailor gasped as Duncan bent over him.

"You'll perhaps feel fine while the rum lasts," Duncan rejoined, "but rum won't heal your cracked rib. You need to wrap your ribs with a length of linen, tied tight but not so much as to impede your breathing."

"Well, 'tis the end of your wife's petticoat," a nearby sailor quipped to the injured man. "Just pray you don't bust another rib getting it off her."

His patient's laugh ended in a grimace of pain.

"Much obliged," John Glover said as Duncan turned to go. "I'll send up a fresh cod when—" He was interrupted by angry calls from the end of the wharf.

"Some damn fool's dropped a trap off the wharf," a sailor explained as Glover and Duncan approached, pointing to a line that stretched out from a piling, threatening to foul a nearby fishing boat's rudder. "If he's landed a lobster in that pot, then by God it's going to the boys in that boat!"

The man hauling the line was clearly having trouble. A second man joined him, struggling against the weight. They pulled in twenty feet of line when a chain broke the surface, tied to the end of the line, raising confused exclamations. Another man joined in, and another, until the grisly catch was exposed.

The chain was wrapped around a dead man's torso several times and knotted at his back. The corpse floated just below the surface now, facedown, until Glover broke the stunned silence. "Prithee, boys, fetch the poor soul back to us." With another tug the corpse cleared the water, then was heaved onto the wharf and rolled onto its back, exposing the tattooed face.

Duncan's heart turned to ice. There would be no singing of the whales that summer, no new companion for Conawago in Edentown.

"God's blood!" a sailor cried. "It's dear old Jacob! Jacob Book!"

The Hancock boat that spirited Adams away passed the revenue cutter as she entered, looking like a brightly colored bird among the dull plumage of the fishing fleet. Troops from Castle William lined her deck, their scarlet uniforms brilliant in the late winter sunlight. Spit-and-polish elites filed down the gangway and formed ranks along Fore Street. Someone behind Duncan muttered unhappily, then stepped to Duncan's side.

"The high and mighty have arrived," John Glover said. "See that braid on their shoulders? The commander's personal guard, not from the Twenty-Ninth, and probably with a warrant as provosts. The lads from the garrison," he said, indicating several soldiers hurrying out of the waterfront barracks, straightening their uniforms, "will not be well pleased. Outsiders coming to meddle in the murder of their lieutenant."

An officer appeared out of the barracks, formed up his men, then advanced to the elite guard unit. He halted his small formation ten paces from the officer who led the newcomers, whose sour expression deepened as the garrison officer marched forward, extending a paper. Duncan and Glover eased closer, trying to get within earshot. The newly arrived officer was clearly disappointed with what he read and seemed inclined to challenge it. He was beginning to complain, when the local officer made a gesture toward his men. The ranks split to allow two soldiers through, towing a civilian between them.

"It's him!" Glover spat. "Yates!"

Only Yates's loud, frightened voice could be made out over the distance. "Aye, sir," he said twice in answers to less audible questions from the provost officer, who then held up the paper. "I did indeed, Yer Honor, sir," he added in an obsequious voice, and finally, as the officer pointed to the bottom of the paper, he said, "Oh aye, sir, sworn to, each and every word sacred as the gospel. No need to trouble yerselves."

With a chill Duncan realized the little drama was about dissuading the provosts from their task. They were talking about Jacob Book, who now lay in a pine box in the stable behind the yellow house, a devastated Conawago standing vigil. The instincts that grew with Duncan's role as Deathspeaker were sometimes a blessing, but today they felt like a terrible curse. They told him that Book had been killed simply to keep the provosts out of Marblehead.

Duncan was administering Henri's evening dose when he heard anxious voices from the kitchen, which were abruptly extinguished by the scolding tones of the landlady. He reached the top of the stairs just as Mrs. Godwin raised a broom as if to sweep Tobias and Solomon out the door. Sarah darted in front of the runaways. A familiar Mohawk heat rose in her eyes. Duncan stepped to Mrs. Godwin and gently pushed down the broom.

"I do not run a public inn!" the landlady barked. "This is a respectable house, not open to any vagabond who wanders in!" She was not a woman who used her voice often, but when she did, it was easy to recognize the no-nonsense schoolmarm she had once been.

Duncan kept one hand on the broom and pushed his other into the pocket of his waistcoat. He extended a bright coin and held it in front of the widow. "One guinea," he declared. "One guinea more a month to include our new friends. And we will provide their food, of course."

The landlady relinquished her grip on her weapon but did not accept the coin.

"And," Duncan said with a glance at the new arrivals, "they will start replacing the leaking roof on the stable tomorrow."

Mrs. Godwin touched the coin. "And the privy?"

"And the privy roof," Duncan agreed. "New shingles all round."

The landlady tucked the coin into her apron and retreated victoriously back into her rooms.

Moll, unlike her employer, seemed pleased to have new mouths to feed. "I have a duck stew in the pot," she announced, "with fresh wild onions I pulled this very morn."

Duncan waited until the nervous men from Barbados were safely tucked in at the big trestle table, with Solomon eagerly slicing a fresh loaf, then slipped out into the cool moonlit night.

In the barn a candle burned at either end of the plank table that held the simple coffin. Conawago sat on a keg, gripping one of the coffin's rope handles as if he feared Book would slip away again. His voice was weak, his eyes closed. He was murmuring a Nipmuc mourning chant. Pine stood at one end of the table, Blue Turtle at the other. Duncan gestured for the two men to join him in the shadows.

"Soldiers were searching warehouses by the water," Pine reported.

Duncan realized he was explaining why he brought Solomon and Tobias to the house. There was still one runaway unaccounted for. "Cuff?"

"He watched from the trees, then followed us, is keeping watch behind the barn now."

"Why were the soldiers searching? The man they sought is accounted for," Duncan said, gesturing to the coffin.

"I saw them waving papers. Moll said it must be some of those writs they use against smuggled goods. Excuses to enter houses and break heads, she said."

The soldiers of the Twenty-Ninth were restless and infuriated by the murder of their lieutenant. Book's death had been too abrupt and, Duncan suspected, not of their doing. It had not slaked their appetite for vengeance on the people of Marblehead.

Duncan turned to Blue Turtle. "Can you ride a horse?"

The aging Mohawk didn't answer. He was gazing at Conawago. "Seldom have I seen such sorrow. He has winter in his blood."

Duncan studied his Nipmuc friend, who had suffered loss after loss for years. His once energetic spirit was gasping.

"He may never come back," Blue Turtle declared. "I saw such on the plantations. The bones of his soul are broken."

The words were a fist that closed around Duncan's heart. He found it difficult to speak, and when he did his voice was choked. "Can you ride a horse?" he asked again.

Blue Turtle shrugged. "I usually don't fall off."

"I want you away tomorrow, riding for the Hudson. There's food in the house. Eat and rest today. I will arrange a horse and have it here before dawn. Sleep in my room."

A quarter hour later he approached a solitary tree near the water's edge, known by the watermen as the anchor oak, for the many boats that fixed mooring lines to its thick trunk. He didn't speak at first to the man who sat against the oak, just followed his gaze toward the Triple Fish, directly across the crushed oyster shells of Fore Street.

"'Tis a fine evening for a pipe or two," John Glover observed, waving his smoldering pipe toward the bright moon.

"I expected one of your mates or bosuns," Duncan said. "You're a busy family man."

The sturdy waterman chuckled. "The instant I lift my pipe, my wife herds me out the door, saying, 'If you insist on behaving like a chimney, then go offer your fumes up to the sky.'" He nodded at the tavern. "Been in there nigh two hours. Winifred's been taking the air from time to time to report. Says he's only drinking sassafras punch. No ale, no spirits. And before ye say he could have slipped out the back, let me remind you that the kitchen door opens to the alley, not the rear, for deliveries and such. So by mooring myself here I have an eye on all comings and goings. I can put a name to every man I've seen go in, and our man hasn't budged."

"I can take the watch now, John," Duncan offered.

Glover seemed not to hear. "I've been thinking on what you said, McCallum, about men in the shadows working for the secretary of war, as if honest citizens were his enemies. If it's true, the king has truly gone too far. The government tidesmen searching our boats and homes is bad enough, but at least they do their work in plain daylight." Customs officers, when applying the writs of assistance that authorized their searches, were only permitted to search between dawn and dusk. "The men you describe be nothing but sneak thieves in the night, come to steal our liberty." As he spoke, a figure emerged from the tavern. "At last," Glover whispered.

Yates wore a white sailor's smock that made him easily visible even as he stepped away from the lamp hanging at the tavern's entrance. He was a short man with the thick shoulders of a seaman. As he pulled a wool cap over his head, he looked in both directions, then set off along the waterfront.

"My watch, John," Duncan reminded Glover, then slipped into the shadows.

Yates passed four intersecting streets before turning up a twisting, sloping road lined with shops and homes. Duncan tightened the gap, moving always in shadow, and was about to follow his quarry around a corner when a hand seized his arm and held him back.

"Pine!" he whispered. "What are you doing here?"

The Oneida offered no reply, only pointed to a new figure who materialized out of a shadowed doorway behind Yates. The man, clad in a dark cloak and a large tricorn, walked with a steady, fast gait that in moments put him alongside Yates. Duncan and Pine watched for several silent breaths. When the men ahead of them turned at the next corner, they followed.

The stealthy Oneida stepped forward at the corner for a quick look. His whispered "Gone!" instantly brought Duncan to his side. The two men had vanished.

"I'm not traveling to church services," Blue Turtle protested when he met Duncan in the stable at dawn. The clothes Duncan procured for him were somber black.

"That's exactly what you're doing," Duncan said as he handed the aging war chief the reins to a sturdy bay horse. He lifted a pouch from a nearby barrel. "There's a Bible in here. You're bound for the Indian mission north of Albany if anyone asks. If they press, raise the Bible and offer a blessing. Folks don't know what to do with native pilgrims, but they know they are no threat, so they back away. In the Bible is a paper with the names of several farmers and how to find their houses, all on the western road. All friends of mine, and all friends of liberty. There's a note from me you can show them. They will help." He extracted two folded letters from his waistcoat. "One for William Johnson, one for Captain Woolford, his deputy."

Blue Turtle hesitated. "You need me here. There's trouble. I no longer run from trouble."

"I would welcome you at my side, and that day will come. We're seeing only the rising tide of trouble. If my instincts speak true, greater trouble will hound us as we make our way home, and in our voyage up the Hudson we will be at our most vulnerable. I know these enemies. They wield great power, and once on a scent they do not give up. When you give my messages to Johnson and Woolford, tell them we are trying to save tribal slaves and others. Tell them to watch for our flag. Woolford knows it. Afterward you can join me in Edentown. We will have need of a wise war chief in the months to come." Duncan extended his hand. He did not mention, sensed no need to mention, that traveling tribesmen frequently encountered hatred, and even assault, from colonists. "I am not sending you to keep you safe. I am sending you because I need a warrior on this mission. Our lives may depend on it."

Blue Turtle straightened, his eyes brightening as Duncan's words sank in. Years seemed to drop away from his leathery countenance. He vigorously shook Duncan's hand, accepted the letters, and hid them inside the Bible. He took the reins and mounted, then fixed Duncan with a somber gaze. "Bear Walker. My mother, used to tell me of a mighty bear who sometimes walked on two legs. He would touch the dying, and they would come back to life." A smile lifted the tattoos on his face. "I was gone, but you touched me and now I am alive again." He nudged the big bay with his heels and, with the cry of an eager warrior, set off on his long, treacherous journey.

Duncan was waiting in the small storeroom for John Glover to arrive with Yates. He spent his time wisely, probing its rafters and even the crates stacked in one corner, each half-filled with sawdust that would have cushioned a shipment of porcelain or other fragile goods. The only evidence that the room may have been used by the mysterious man in the black cloak was a line of spilled powder on a crate. Duncan moistened a finger and tasted the powder. It was an expensive snuff, subtly flavored with spices, the kind sold in exclusive shops along Piccadilly in London.

Pine and Duncan discovered the chamber before dawn after investigating the alley where Yates and the stranger had disappeared. It was hidden behind a curtain wall built to shield the entrance from the harsh harbor winds, a wall that cast the doorway in deep shadow at night. Duncan had warily ventured through the inner door, which led into an empty shop that fronted the adjoining street. The storage room was the perfect lair for clandestine meetings, hidden in plain sight and accessible from two sides. Footsteps sounded on the floor above. Duncan smiled. The shopkeeper's widow, though a well-known Loyalist, posed no threat to them. He confirmed as much when he had paid her a visit earlier, after first consulting his landlady's encyclopedic knowledge of Marblehead gossip.

"I know the shop and knew its deceased owner as well," Mrs. Godwin said when Duncan asked about the vacant building. "The old Huguenot was a dear man, twice a widower, and most say Pierre took a wife thirty years younger to avoid that heartbreak a third time. Some say she just wore him out, gentle soul that he was, but he left her well provided for. She keeps a rather lavish residence on the second floor. Black curly hair, very pale complexion, fond of rouge, and dresses more like a maiden than is proper for a widow, if you get my meaning."

He had some idea. The attractive woman wearing a close-fitting dress with heavy red smudges on her cheeks clearly welcomed Duncan's interest as he intercepted her at the door, explaining that he had a few questions on behalf of the selectmen. He was prepared to invoke the name of John Glover, prominent among both selectmen and merchants, but after examining him for a few heartbeats she smiled and gestured him inside, saying, "But only if you join me in a hot beverage to banish this chill and damp."

After her stove was stoked and the kettle put on to boil, they sat in her opulently furnished sitting room and engaged in banter about the weather and the First Fare ball that would launch the fleet. After Duncan disclosed he sometimes served on Hancock's ships as something of an auxiliary captain, her face lit with excitement and she eagerly inquired about the merchant's fabled mansion.

"Prithee, sir, you must tell me all when I return!" she exclaimed as she rose to go to the kitchen. "Is it true he imported wallpaper all the way from Paris, France?"

"Printed with scenes of French châteaus," Duncan confirmed to her back.

As she disappeared, he sprang up and paced a quick perimeter around the room. On a small stand by the hearth a pewter saucer held a half-smoked cheroot. On a table under the window were lengths of cloth and what looked like an old dress. Each was a different color—blue, green, gold, and cream—and each had a square about ten inches to the side cut out of it. He was staring at them when she returned carrying a tray with a dainty china tea service. Duncan quickly picked up the conversation as he returned to his chair. "You might say that Mr. Hancock is why I am here. You see, John and the governor keep a delicate balance in their relations with the army. There's much tension about the housing of troops."

She hesitated, but only for an instant. "But housing of troops is a Boston issue." She filled his cup, leaning much closer than she needed to. "Do you truly address the great man by his Christian name?"

Duncan nodded and pressed his point. "The provincial government insists that the army has no right to force its soldiers upon private households. If that happens, the governor wants to hear of it, for he will not be shy about complaining to Castle William."

"I'm not sure why—"

"Nothing to fret over, I'm sure. It's just that there have been reports that an officer has taken up residence here."

The widow's eyes flashed for an instant, and she looked away as if to hide her reaction. "I have no . . ." she said slowly, searching for words.

"Of course, a flash officer arriving from London might exaggerate his authority, especially to win over an attractive widow."

The rouge on her cheeks seemed to deepen in color, then she collected herself. "Lieutenant Vaughn is an old friend of the family, who arrived unexpectedly on errands for the king. I am doing him a favor, nothing more. He could catch his death in that drafty old warehouse they use as a barracks."

Duncan spoke in a tentative, inquiring tone. "That would be your dead French husband's family?" he asked, then hurried on. "So we might call the lieutenant a guest? A tenant? There's some confusion because the local garrison disavows any knowledge of him. Peculiar. Must be some foul-up in paperwork. But of course the Horse Guards always know best."

He had clearly given the woman much to contemplate. Her face grew paler, and she began chewing on her lip. "I don't want any trouble," she said at last.

"Exactly. That's why I am here. I can now assure the governor that Lieutenant Vaughn of the Horse Guards is an invited guest. As long as nothing happens here to attract further attention, there's no need for more questions. No need for anyone to know about your India tea," he added with a gesture to his cup. "And such a good Darjeeling at that."

She blushed again, and he wondered if serving the India tea had been an oversight. They both knew that Marbleheaders were adamant in opposing its use.

The widow grew subdued. "No further attention," she whispered, staring into her cup.

Duncan rose, forcing himself to praise her taste in furnishings so he might survey the room once more. On the broad windowsill was a bottle of London gin, a rare sight in a town whose tastes ran to rum and ale, and two lengths of yellow ribbon.

"So you are a friend of Mr. Hancock's," she said, recovering as he stepped to the door. "Prithee, is it true that he is not yet married?"

Now, hours later, Duncan stood at the outer door of the storage chamber and listened for approaching footsteps. Glover had agreed to entice Yates with a day's work in his warehouse, sweetening the offer by indicating in confidence that he tried to provide work for deserters from the navy whenever possible. Glover asked Yates to pause in the windbreak of the enclosed doorway so that he may light his pipe. On that cue Duncan opened the door and grabbed Yates's arm, pulling him inside. His cry for help was muffled as Glover stepped in and closed the door.

Glover pointed to the crate beside Duncan. "Sit," he commanded the sailor.

Duncan offered no explanation, and abruptly recited half a dozen names. "Marblehead and Salem men who were impressed, then deserted, like you, Yates. Six all told. Two were found by Lieutenant Hicks in the week before his death and delivered to the navy, in bruised but serviceable condition with slices on their jaws."

Yates gave a low growl and lurched to the door. Glover seized his shoulder and pushed him onto the crate.

"Then," Duncan continued, "there was Book, who mocked Hicks and went about his business. The others disappeared, assumed to have gone to ground, probably to New Hampshire or some relative's farm far from the coast. But you linger, wandering about without a care in the world, and you even have coin in your long-empty purse. Word is that you paid off your creditors. That was a bit reckless, Yates. Better to have given them just a few shillings since no one can cipher out how you suddenly came into so much coin."

Yates lunged for the door. Glover seized his collar and roughly shoved him onto the crate.

"You used to run scared when you heard the rhythm of army boots," Duncan continued. "But then you were cornered in the Triple Fish, and a gentleman from London made an offer. Not long afterward Book, the one deserter who couldn't be tamed, was pulled up from the bottom of the harbor, wrapped in a chain."

"Ye got no right!" Yates snapped. He leapt up, only to be shoved back down by Glover.

The door opened and Pine appeared, followed, to Duncan's surprise, by Cuff. Pine upended a sack on a crate near Yates, dropping three freshly killed rabbits. Cuff lifted one of the rabbits, clamped two fingers around its neck and began swinging it from side to side, like a corpse on a gibbet, to a low mournful whistle. It was unsettling, even to Duncan. Pine produced a thin skinning blade, and as Cuff steadied the body, the Oneida deftly slit the pelt, then began peeling away the skin. Cuff kept up his whistle. Duncan had asked Pine to come and help persuade the informer to talk, but Pine had obviously recruited Cuff and devised a bit of drama for the informer's sake. Yates glanced nervously at Duncan, then inched away from Pine. "We are pressed for time," Duncan stated. "Tell us about this Lieutenant Vaughn. From London. What have you shared with him?"

Yates, though uneasy, kept his chin up. "Ye've got me confused with some other fella," he shot back. "Release me or—" His words died on his tongue.

"Or what?" Duncan asked. "Please continue. Or you'll call your friends the soldiers? I'm afraid they won't hear you."

For a moment Yates seemed about to argue, then Pine dropped the skinned carcass beside him. Cuff extended another rabbit, holding the hind feet as Pine's blade circuited the body.

"You signed a statement that Book killed Lieutenant Hicks. Why?"

Yates spoke toward the stone flags at his feet. "Can't tolerate the fools from the Castle, can we? Provosts stir things up, push our quarry into cover."

Duncan tried to keep his voice level. "Vaughn said that? Where is he?"

When Yates did not reply, Glover grabbed the front of his shirt and shook him. "Did you kill old Jacob?" he demanded. "Did you wrap that chain around that gentle old soul and toss him into the harbor?"

Yates glanced fearfully at Glover, then pursed his lips, remaining mute.

"Speak now," Duncan suggested, "and it can stay among us." Glover released his grip. "Otherwise, what we know will spread through every tavern in town. It won't go easy when people learn you betrayed their friend."

"The shipyard always has fresh tar," Glover added, "and the butcher's yard abounds with the feathers of chickens and ducks." Yates winced, clearly understanding that Glover was referring to a Marblehead robe, the seaport's version of tar and feathering. "That's if folks be in a generous mood. Otherwise they know the wharf always has more rope and chain lying about."

"Prithee, mercy! A man's gotta pay his debts!" Yates whined. "A man's gotta look to hisself."

Glover gave Duncan a shrug as if to say he had tried and was finished. Pine dropped the bloody skinned carcass of the second rabbit beside Yates, who gazed at it with new apprehension.

"What does Lieutenant Vaughn seek in Marblehead?" Duncan asked.

Yates spoke into his hands, which he had clasped tightly together. "He's a cold, cruel one. If he found I talked, he'd thrust his steel into my liver and laugh as he twisted it."

"Only if he finds out," Duncan observed and gestured to Pine. "Did I mention my friend is an Iroquois? They do so love toying with captives. It's a blood sport, you might say, testing how many ways and how many days they can make a prisoner suffer before he dies. 'Arm or leg?' he asked me earlier," Duncan continued, leaning closer. "I said, 'Poor Yates, he'll need to walk, so just start with an arm.'"

As he spoke, Pine raised the third rabbit before Yates's face and with a quick jerking motion peeled away the skin, exposing the mass of raw flesh and blood vessels. The color drained from Yates's face. His eyes went round. Cuff's laugh sounded maniacal.

"Your sleeve," Duncan said. "Roll up your sleeve. We'll just start at the forearm for now. It won't take long. Scream all you want. No one will hear. These walls are thick. My friend will no doubt make a pouch out of what he peels off your arm. He has an impressive collection of pouches."

Pine dipped his finger into the bloody carcass, then with a hungry expression drew two red stripes on his cheek.

Yates's voice was as pallid as his countenance. "Blessed Jesus! He's a savage!" he gasped. "Prithee, don't—" he began, then suddenly Cuff was behind him, his powerful hands around Yates's neck. The informer froze. Pine began rolling up Yates's sleeve.

"The prince!" Yates cried, his eyes bulging as Cuff squeezed. "They call him the prince, 'cause he came special all the way from the Horse Guards palace in London! He says a Horse Guards lieutenant is as good as a prince on this side of the Atlantic. Most of the soldiers are right eager to please him since he's generous with his coin."

Duncan held up a hand to restrain his companions. "What did he ask?"

"Call them off! I beg you!" Duncan nodded at Pine, who straightened, still extending his knife. Cuff released his grip. Yates gasped for breath. Once he recovered, he continued. "Destroy all traitors, root and branch, says he! First he asked where the other deserters were. He had names—not just the pressed men but deserters from the army. Sure, I gave him some suggestions, ye might say. And he was that hot when Lieutenant Hicks nabbed two of them. Stole 'em, Vaughn said, as good as picked his pocket. He has one of those long Italian knives, razor sharp, and he makes two slices in the air, like he was slicing Hicks's cheek. He was so blind with anger I thought he would cut me."

"You didn't run," Duncan observed.

"I got a daughter, barely twelve. When I take ship, she has to be looked after. Sure, I paid my debts to the butcher and baker so she could get meat and bread next time I sail."

"Why the deserters?" Duncan asked. "Why is Vaughn so interested in deserters?"

"Birds, looking for little birds. Oh, he nabs deserters fair enough. My job is to see he gets to them first, and there's more all the time. He talks with them, offers 'em coin. Building his own secret brigade, he boasts. Lieutenant Hicks was that furious with him, said he was going to complain to Castle William. 'Spoiling my record,' Hicks shouted at him once, 'good as stealing from the king.'

"Vaughn just laughed, said he *was* the king as far as Marblehead was concerned."

"What birds?" Glover pressed.

Yates clenched his jaw, then flinched as he looked at his bared arm. Cuff had lifted one of the carcasses and was dripping blood onto the forearm. "Nightingales! He asks the deserters about nightingales, orders them to go out and find nightingales. Great George—that's what he calls the king—wants to learn all about Marblehead's nightingales, where they live and where they fly at night. Vaughn says they be a rare breed, but he knows now they roost in Marblehead, maybe married to friends of ours. I said no man here be married to a bird and he laughed, said keep looking. They probably know their way around a boat and about secret coves along the coast. Onc't I mentioned a skiff offloading illegal Madeira, and he says Great George ain't so interested in the common trade of smugglers, not mere sugar and molasses and wine. Great George wants to know about machines and such."

"Machines?" Glover asked.

"Looms was one. Watch for any smugglers bringing in looms, or talking with weavers, or bearing plans for making looms and spinning devices and the like. And extra-heavy crates with certain markings, which I figured meant lead, 'cause they always watch for lead. They don't like the militias getting their hands on more lead. I told 'em the lead don't matter when there's no gunpowder, and there is no powder to be had 'cause the army is so jealous of the supply. That's why the militias make do with silent practice, just aiming their muskets and pretending to fire, looking like boys at play, the fools. The patriots have no chance if they have no powder."

"What markings?" Duncan pressed. "What did the others report to you?"

Yates knitted his brows, as if struggling to recall. "Crowley, I remember that one. He wrote them down. My daughter helped with that," he added for no apparent reason, tapping a waistcoat pocket from which scraps of paper extended. "And didn't get much in the way of reports, not yet. Some of the fellas took their money and bolted or signed onto merchant ships for Europe or the Indies. There was a report of a loom coming off a ship in Salem in the middle of the night, and a small boat that took away four crates from a Thames ship, back out into the bay. Someone said they thought they recognized the boat, one of those squat coastal shallops, maybe out of Quincy or Scituate. Oh, and Vaughn's hot to nab some old Greek fella running the smuggling. Haparaus, Heferus, something like that."

"Hephaestus," Duncan said in a tight voice.

"Sure, could be. And didn't I tell him, do I look like a fella who passes time with some rich Greek merchant, and when did anyone see a Greek on the North Shore anyways?

"'Try harder,' he said, 'if you expect more coin the next time.'"

"Captain Mallory," Glover inserted unexpectedly. "Did he speak of the dead Captain Mallory of the Twenty-Ninth?"

"Not a word. Dead?" Yates looked down into his hands. "Poacher, I reckon. Vaughn says the king's huntsmen know how to deal with poachers on the royal hunting ground."

Duncan paused over the words, then pressed harder. "Next time. When you meet here next, he meant."

"Sure. But I ain't got much. Lucky to get half a crown. And I'll drink through that in a night."

"Payment for what?"

"All I got is about that curious ship of Hancock's, what came in on the Sabbath and anchored outside the harbor even though there was plenty of space in the harbor, then sailed off in the night without unloading so much as a cask. You know, the day of that sailing match with Hancock and his friends. Behaving like some phantom, though we all knew well enough whose ship it was. There had to be some secret cargo, Vaughn insisted, but I told him no one knows, 'cause everyone was down watching that red-haired wench and her unlikely crew."

Duncan clenched his jaw, trying not to react, then saw how Cuff clenched his fists and heard Pine's sharp intake of breath. They were well aware of what cargo that ship had brought to Marblehead and all knew the red-haired wench. The women who had sailed Hancock's yacht that day were the very nightingales Vaughn so desperately sought, all of them steadfast wives and daughters of Marblehead.

"But that is no secret," Glover pointed out. "Hardly worth a ha'penny."

Yates shrugged. Duncan nodded to Pine, who straightened, then with lightning speed threw his blade so that it quivered in the crate barely an inch from Yates's leg.

"Bloody Christ!" Yates moaned. "There weren't nothing else, I tell ye! 'Cepting talk of how some women were asking who could cook dinner for the vicar on the last Wednesday of the month. Like he needed to steer clear that night."

Duncan and Glover exchanged a worried glance. "What church?"

"St. Michael's, the one with the old cemetery down along the water. Vaughn laughed when he heard that. How very convenient, says he, that these nightingales like to roost in cemeteries."

The words silenced Yates's interrogators for several heartbeats. Glover was one of the few who knew of Sarah's particular club, as she called the nightingales. Yates's report stoked his anger.

"Did you kill Book?" Glover demanded again. When Yates did not reply he slapped him, hard. When he swung back for a second blow, Duncan restrained his arm. "McCallum!" Glover snapped. "He's not telling us everything!"

Yates shook off the pain of the blow. "Just that Vaughn had a visitor from Boston one evening when he was meeting with me. Dressed like a dandy, but a face like a chunk of bone, put me in mind of those on a boat who always press forward with a club so they can kill the cod. Major, Vaughn called him, though he wore no uniform. He wouldn't even speak with me, just asks Vaughn, 'Does your dog know Boston? We need to pick up the scent of the grenadier woman.' Then Vaughn just pushed me out the door."

Duncan felt a knot tying itself in his belly. "This major, did he have a scar? A blade cut through his eyebrow?"

"Aye, and eyes like blue ice."

Duncan stared at the informer, not wanting to believe what he heard. "What grenadier woman?" he managed to ask.

"Never said. The Twenty-Ninth has a grenadier company with the garrison on Boston Common. Figured he meant one of their camp followers. Washerwomen, seamstresses, and such." Glover pried away Pine's blade and impatiently pressed the point against Yates's exposed forearm. "What did you swear to in that statement for the army?"

Yates swallowed hard. "They said it was about Lieutenant Hicks."

Glover hesitated. "You didn't read it?"

"Can't read, sir," Yates replied defiantly. "Nary a word. Like I said, my little girl helps me, clever as she is. But I can sign my name, can't I? That's all a man like me needs. Sign the ship's book to get its coin."

Glover glared at the man but pulled away the knife. "What did you swear to, Yates?" he demanded.

"Vaughn had the other officer from the Twenty-Ninth write it all down. He signed it, too, after me, said it meant he witnessed me take an oath to its truth.

Jacob Book confessed to me that he had killed Hicks, but his soul was tormented by the sin and so killed himself."

"By wrapping himself in a chain and tying it in a knot at his spine?" Glover growled.

"Army don't know that, now do they? The chain was off by the time the soldiers saw the body. Worked fine. Provosts filed onto their boat and sailed back to the Castle, didn't they? Report sent to regimental headquarters. Another Marblehead man kills another officer. But this one realized his mortal sin and sought his penance. Account settled. No provosts needed, take yer damned gold lace back to Castle William, growls Vaughn."

"But Book wasn't the killer of Lieutenant Hicks," Duncan stated.

"Sure he was. The army says so. It's official, in writing."

A rumbling sound rose in Glover's throat, and he seized Yates's shirt, ripping it this time and lifting him off the crate. "Did you kill Book?" he demanded.

"Nay, nay, nay!" Yates gasped. "I was well and truly in my cups by the time he gave up the ghost. All I did was give a nod."

"A nod?"

"Mr. Vaughn said if Book came into the tavern, I was to point him out with a nod. That's all. Just a nod. Vaughn just wanted a quiet conversation, I figured."

Duncan and Glover exchanged a painful glance. The drunken nod had killed the gentle old tribesman.

The silence was broken by a tap on the inner door. "Vaughn?" came a woman's voice. "Lieutenant? Vaughn? I had a visitor. We must talk."

Duncan had more questions, but he couldn't let the widow from upstairs see him with Yates. "Breathe a word of this and it's a Marblehead robe for you!" he whispered to the informer. With a quick motion he snatched the scraps of paper from Yates's pocket and motioned his companions out into the alley.

They had reached the street when Cuff halted, his brow twisting as he seemed to recall something. "Nightingales," he suddenly declared. "I know where nightingales sing," he said and darted away without another word.

Duncan lost track of the time as he sat on the hill overlooking the harbor, contemplating the words of the deserter turned spy. Yates had confirmed all his worst suspicions. Not only were the Horse Guards in Massachusetts, but they were led by the man with the scar though his eyebrow, the major who had plagued Duncan and Franklin in London the year before. Major Hastings, a favorite of the Black Office, had learned of Sarah's nightingales. There were no more than a dozen women who secretly helped Sarah, and they were all as tight-lipped and reliable as Iroquois warriors. But they were facing the most ruthless of enemies, an enemy unencumbered by truth or morality, skilled in the black arts, and callous when it came to human life.

Their enemies would, at least, search in vain for the smuggling ringleader Hephaestus, for immediately upon returning from London Duncan saw to it that Sarah abandoned the use of the code name. They still sought the ringleader bringing in banned equipment, and that troubled Duncan. Sarah would not be dissuaded from her efforts to build up American industry.

Each scrap of paper he had taken from Yates had a drawing, done in a surprisingly artful hand. There was a crow and a ship, with arrows pointing at one side of the vessel; a drawing of a heart and club as if from a deck of playing cards; the image of a squat nail; and what looked like a clockwork gear beside an acorn.

It was nonsense. They made as much sense as the other pieces of his puzzle. Mallory, Hicks, and Book were dead; the Horse Guards had loosed their beasts onto the Massachusetts colony; and he was spending his time looking at nonsensical scrawls made by an adolescent girl.

He gazed out over the dusk-lit waters, drifting into a vision of Book, Conawago, and himself surrounded by playful whales as a native matriarch sang. We did not live in one world, Conawago had once declared to him under a shower of falling stars, but at the juncture of many worlds. The challenge of a successful life was knowing how to balance those worlds.

He watched the sun until it disappeared, then looked back at the paper scraps. Yates and his daughter inhabited a different world. Yates couldn't read but his daughter helped him. He had been charged with ferreting out some very specific smuggled goods, had been given a list he couldn't read. Duncan lifted the drawing of the bird and the ship. The arrows might indicate wind. A mariner looking at it wouldn't see wind but rather the lee, the side of the ship that defined so much in navigation. Duncan cocked his head. He was looking at pictograms. A crow and lee. Yates had spoken the name of Crowley, the premier English maker of tool steel, the manufacture of which was banned in America. He was looking at Yates's makeshift guide to his quarry. He quickly lifted the other scraps. The squat nail was a rivet, vital for assembling steel parts. He lingered over the last drawing, of the gear and the acorn. Then, as sudden as a spark from one of Franklin's Leyden jars, realization struck. With an excited whoop he cried out the answer to the puzzle. "Cog nut!"

His hand, as if of its own accord, gripped the gold watch that Benjamin Franklin had given to him.

The drawing the inventor had pushed toward Duncan across his workshop table on a rainy London day was in a French newspaper. It was of a bizarre, monstrous-looking contraption with a kettle-like vessel suspended in front of a large wheel over which a man sat holding levers as if to steer the wheel. At the rear of the machine were two heavier wheels, separated from the front by a long frame holding something like a wagon bed.

"Steam, Duncan!" Franklin exclaimed, removing his spectacles. "It moves on its own power, lad! It can transport four tons! The Cugnot machine, they call it. The French army expects to replace its artillery teams with them. It will change the whole balance of modern warfare! No need for hundreds of horses and the tons of feed needed to maintain them during campaigns. One man at those levers can do it all! Cannons can be mounted on them. The article says it doesn't even need roads!"

"I don't quite follow, Dr. Franklin," Duncan admitted to his new friend and looked back to confirm that the door to the room was closed. "I thought we were going to talk about the War Council."

"But we are, we are! Brace yourself, lad," Franklin said and straightened, growing more solemn. "As we have discussed again and again, what the patriots need is time. Time to prepare for the worst, time to build resources, time to develop more cooperation across colonies. Imagine, Duncan, if the War Council thought the patriots were equipped with such machines!"

Duncan examined the drawing again and read some of the accompanying article. Monsieur Cugnot had already built a working version of his machine. "But we don't have them. And it would take a small army of smugglers to transport them."

Franklin's eyes twinkled with excitement. "The army we need numbers two. You and me. And a handful of trusted souls in America."

"But Dr. Franklin—" No matter how often Franklin insisted that Duncan use his Christian name, Duncan was still sufficiently in awe of the man that he found it difficult to do so. "I don't see how we could obtain—"

"If the War Council *thought* the patriots were equipped with such machines," Franklin pointedly repeated. "You've seen my collection of anomalous mirrors. With the right mirrors I can make even the War Council perceive themselves differently. Have you never read of Alexander's brilliant deceptive maneuver at the Hydaspes or Hannibal's at Lake Trasimene? In the right hands subterfuge can be one of the greatest weapons of war."

"My God," Duncan murmured. Realization struck him like lightning on the famous kite. "Is it possible?"

Thus was hatched a very private scheme shaped equally by Franklin and Duncan, always in the private workshop with the door closed, involving intricate lists of parts and even specifications of high-grade steel derived from hematite ore. Franklin contributed a detailed, but fanciful, drawing of what he called his "land frigate," with three of the machines connected together, mounting thirty-two-pound guns, with specifications of the materials and number of men required to operate one, including the estimated coal or wood it would consume.

The challenge wasn't so much in designing convincing drawings but rather in how to convincingly bury them, deep enough to make them seem a carefully protected secret yet not so deep as to be never discovered by War Council spies. Although they had formulated plans for an elaborate structure of intrigue, the abrupt and terrifying turn of events at the end of Duncan's stay in London meant he left only with detailed plans for communicating in code and never directly, only through trusted contacts that included Franklin's married sister in Boston. Franklin finally declared the scheme complete and launched it over the winter by sending the drawings over in his own name in pieces, like a literal puzzle, in separate letters to a fictitious Mr. Currier, General Delivery Boston. He was well aware that the Black Office read all his mail. As deputy postmaster of the colonies

Franklin could assure that Mr. Currier's mail was forwarded to fictitious addresses in other colonies.

Now in his hand Duncan held proof that the War Council had taken the bait. Yates had been given notes by his Horse Guards handlers but could not read. His daughter, not knowing French, had translated the French inventor's name into literal English, cleverly depicting it as a cog and a nut. His conclusion was confirmed by the inclusion of Crowley steel on Yates's list, the only steel that could be used to make the high-pressure vessels at the heart of the French war machine.

He lay back on the dry, brown grass and watched the stars emerge. The intelligence from Yates excited him but also deeply frightened him. He could not reconcile all he knew with the murders but was seized by the thought that the treachery that arrived in Marblehead may have been caused by what he and Franklin had launched. He was again at the intersection of several worlds, and most of them could be fatally dangerous. At least he knew someone whose long life had consisted of constantly navigating treacherous terrain.

By the time Duncan reached the rooftop widow's walk Conawago was gone with only the rich scent of his tobacco left behind. He worried terribly about his closest friend. Book's murder had devastated him. On hearing the news the old Nipmuc had collapsed into Duncan's arms, sobbing and looking frailer than Duncan had ever seen him. He realized with a heavy heart that he could no longer rely on his friend for his usual support. Here, in the still of the night with only the stars for company, he could also no longer hold back the fear that had been gnawing at him since he heard Yates's report. He was back in another battle with Major Hastings of the Horse Guards. The last one had left blood on the streets of London and taken Duncan to within an inch of his life. There at least he had possessed allies who understood the danger. Here he alone grasped the threat.

Unbidden, scenes of his last encounter with the Horse Guards assassin flashed through his mind. Duncan encountered Hastings along a trail of death that had stretched from the Ohio country across the Atlantic to London. Hastings worked directly for the most ruthless faction of the War Council, including Sarah's own father, the Earl of Milbridge. Hastings had tried repeatedly to kill Duncan as he engaged in his secret mission for Benjamin Franklin. Duncan left Hastings's partner at the bottom of the river Thames, but Hastings slipped away, bound for America to find and eliminate the leaders of the secret cartel who were smuggling secrets of English manufacturing. Duncan took at least small comfort from the realization that Hastings's departure for America predated the launch of the Cugnot conspiracy. He had been in the colonies already, ferreting out smugglers of industrial goods, before the War Council would have sent urgent word of the war machines. But he was not a predator who gave up on scents. He was still trying to find the elusive leader of the smugglers, trying to find the woman Duncan loved. Her secrecy had protected her until now, but here in Marblehead the spies had somehow learned of her nightingales.

John Hancock, who was broadly aware of Sarah's clandestine activities, did not share his concern that Sarah was in mortal danger. "Her very name protects her, Duncan!" Hancock had insisted when, weeks earlier, Duncan argued that for her own safety Sarah should no longer be invited to his soirees. "If word leaked that Earl Milbridge's daughter was leading the smuggling, the earl would be shamed out of London. If she were arrested he would be booted off the War Council and cut off from the king. And even if I were to accept your notion that assassins lurk among us, they would never dare kill the daughter of their protector on the Council."

"All you are saying, John," Duncan replied, "is that once they identify her they just have to find a way to eliminate her without arresting or killing her."

Hancock winced as if biting something sour. "Not even your fanciful spies could perform that magic. She is indestructible!"

Duncan desperately wished he could share in Hancock's confidence. Even if the merchant prince was right, those seeking her in Marblehead did not know her aristocratic connections. They were rabidly scouring the town for the head of the nightingales, the smuggling mastermind. They might eliminate her without ever asking her name. And if they did discover her identity, they could inflict lifelong torment by killing those in her network.

He lingered a long while, struggling to push down his foreboding, and watched absently as a figure wearing a dark cloak stepped out of the kitchen door and into the moonlight. She lifted her long tresses and tucked them under a large tricorn hat.

Suddenly his senses were afire. It was Sarah. He hurried down the ladder into the kitchen and was thrusting his arms into his overcoat when he called out to Moll, who sat by the hearth. "What day is this, Moll?"

"Why, 'tis Wednesday, last of the month," the cook replied.

Sarah was walking toward the edge of town. For a moment he wanted to run to her side but held back, staying in the shadows.

The twisting street and dim light made it difficult to keep her in sight, and for an agonizing moment after she turned down an alley, he thought he lost her. She reappeared in a patch of moonlight on the lane that led to the old church at the edge of the harbor. The tide was ebbing, and he recalled a low tide line path that led to the fish-drying sheds on the other side of the church. He ran along it with the stealth of a Mohawk and reached the low stone wall of the adjoining cemetery as she approached the churchyard gate. Assuming she was meeting someone in the sanctuary, he edged along the gravestones, keeping in shadow, then halted as a flock of gulls burst from their resting place just offshore. He could just make out a dinghy being rowed by a solitary man on a course for the shingle beach below the graveyard.

Duncan retreated to the deeper shadows of an oak, watching as the stranger beached the boat and began climbing toward the graveyard. As Sarah, too, turned toward the rows of graves, someone sneezed. The sound was low and muffled yet unmistakable and came from the darkness beyond a grouping of tall headstones. He bent and stole through the shadows to another tree, then froze as he caught a glint of polished metal in the moonlight. On feathered feet he advanced until he was certain of the shapes beyond the headstones. At least four red-coated soldiers were huddled against the stones, watching Sarah. They held muskets with fixed bayonets. It was an ambush. They likely did not know it was Sarah they sought, only that an important meeting of the smugglers was taking place. When the stranger reached Sarah, they would spring their trap, capturing both.

Duncan's only weapon was his belt knife. He dared not shout out, for he expected Sarah would move toward his voice, directly into the hands of the soldiers. The man from the harbor was about to enter the cemetery. He desperately cast about for anything that might help him deal with the soldiers, and his gaze fell on the steeple with its open belfry, only thirty paces away. He knelt, groping about, and found two walnut-sized stones.

The first stone he threw bounced off the belfry roof. The second hit the bell, the bronze London-made bell that echoed throughout the town on Sunday mornings. He bent and found another stone.

The first peal stopped Sarah. The next stopped the approaching figure at the cemetery wall. A window opened in a nearby house. "What's afoot?" called the man who leaned out. "By Jehovah, are those muskets I see?" At the next house, a door opened and a man ventured out, raising a lantern.

"Damnation!" someone in the shadows spat. The soldiers began rising from their hiding places, looking not at the church but at the speaker, hidden in shadow. "Stand down!" the man barked. "Stand down and withdraw!" The inquisitive man with the lantern began approaching the churchyard. "On the double!" the officer snapped.

Sarah stared in silence as the running soldiers revealed themselves in the moonlight. After a long moment she continued, but now toward the church, not the graveyard. The phantom from the harbor had disappeared.

Duncan fought an intense urge to run to Sarah, to join her in the sanctuary, but then faded back, deeper into the night. Revealing himself would alert her that he had been stalking her, prying into her secrets. The danger was past. He turned, hesitated, then ran toward the sound of boots pounding on the packed road. He caught up with the soldiers just as they reached their Fore Street barracks. As they began filing through the doorway, a figure in a cloak peeled away from the group and disappeared into the night.

As he stepped into the house, Moll was serving out hot cider to a gathering by the hearth. He gratefully accepted a mug and listened as Solomon and Tobias reported on their progress on the stable roof while Josiah, Sarah kneeling at his side, stroked the calico house cat. Moll muttered a good-natured complaint at a muffled knocking on the door, then gasped as she opened it.

The woman in Cuff's arms was barely conscious. Blood seeped from blows to her face. One eye was swollen shut.

"Amanda!" Sarah cried, rushing to the injured woman.

Cuff followed Duncan into the sitting room and laid the woman on the divan as Moll hurried for hot water and towels.

"Please, Duncan!" Sarah cried as she bent over the divan. "She has two young children!"

Amanda had been viciously beaten about her head. The rest of her body seemed untouched, though she moaned as Duncan moved her arms and shoulders. He rolled up her sleeves and found more bruises. She had raised her arms to fend off her attacker. As Sarah began washing away the blood, Duncan recognized Amanda as one of Sarah's crew on the day of the sailing race. "A nightingale," he murmured, then looked up inquiringly at Cuff.

"That storeroom," Cuff explained. "I went back this morning to make sure nothing had been left behind. Feathers were stuck in the door. Seven feathers."

When Sarah would not meet his gaze Duncan asked the others to leave, saying he had to conduct a more thorough examination of his patient. Moll closed the door behind her as she herded the onlookers into the kitchen.

"Seven feathers," he said. "Seven o'clock? A seven o'clock meeting of your nightingales?"

Sarah kept her eyes on her friend. "She's fearless on the water. Goes out in a sailing dinghy to meet ships in the night. Why would . . . who . . . I don't understand."

"I told you about the War Council's secret soldiers I fought in London. They call themselves the king's huntsmen. They are here. They have been trying to sniff out the trail of Hephaestus." Sarah grimaced as he spoke the former code name but remained silent as he explained what he had learned from Yates.

"But no one knows. My nightingales would never—"

"A deserter knows," Duncan said as he examined Amanda's scalp. "And they have recruited deserters as spies."

He heard her sharp intake of breath.

Amanda stirred, then with a groan sat up. "I must go," she said through a split lip. "My children . . ." She tried to rise but collapsed back onto the divan.

"Who, Amanda? Who did this?" Sarah asked.

Amanda clenched her eyes shut, collecting herself before speaking. "He had the eyes of a serpent. Demanded to know where the Hargreaves machine is and what ship carried it. When I would not reply, he began striking me. Harder and harder. I ne'er cried out, mind. If someone had come, there would be questions about what I was doing in the shadows with a strange man in the first place."

"Hargreaves," Duncan said. "You mean the spinning jenny."

Amanda glanced at Sarah and nodded. "I would never tell, Sarah, you know I would ne'er say a word."

"Of course not. Why were you there? Our meeting is tomorrow."

"Just checking the time. Seven feathers. Seven of the evening then. I had to be sure, 'cause I would need to find someone to watch the children. He was waiting, expecting to trap someone."

"You must stay the night," Sarah said, "let Duncan tend to you. Later you can help me cut down the dress we discussed."

"Never in life! Bless you, Sarah, but I must be off to my children." Amanda clutched Duncan's arm for support as she made it to her feet, then paused. "But what do I tell my husband? If my Tug knew, he would kill the man, not caring if he hanged for it."

"You were helping us unload barrels of dried fish from a wagon," Duncan suggested, "when the horses were spooked by a rabbit. You took a bad tumble as the wagon lurched. Hit your head on a crate. I will walk with you and explain to him."

"Thank you kindly, Dr. McCallum, but nay trouble yerself." Amanda straightened her dress. Her one open eye was defiant. "Next time I'll have my fillet knife," she declared, then bravely raised her head and marched away.

Sarah followed her and watched from the room's entry as Amanda stepped outside. She closed the door but did not turn, just rested her brow on the door, eyes shut.

"They already knew last year about the smuggling of looms and spinning jennies," Duncan said to her back, "no doubt from the spy who was discovered in Dr. Franklin's household. By the time Major Hastings, the leader of the War Council's spies, left London, he knew to look in New England. I don't know how many layers of secrecy have been protecting you, but they have reached the last one. The next woman they beat may not have Amanda's fortitude."

Sarah pushed herself from the wall but did not turn, did not speak. Was it anger or embarrassment, Duncan wondered, that accounted for her silence?

"You have four squares of cloth," Duncan ventured. "Blue, green, gold, and cream colored."

The words startled Sarah. She spoke toward the wall. "How could you know that?"

"Because they were cut of dresses and fabric by the woman who gives shelter to the man who beat Amanda. Lieutenant Vaughn of the Horse Guards, who has a nest with the one they call the Huguenot widow."

Sarah seemed to have lost her strength as she stumbled to the divan and sat. "No, no. They are from a textile works in Virginia. The owner gave them to us himself. A model gentleman who is a secret patriot."

"Us?"

"There is no point to bringing in spinning jennies if there is no one to fund their installation and operate them. We plan to duplicate them and set them in a works, a factory, some call it. It's known throughout the colonies that New England ports engage in the most smuggling. Inquiries have been made, very discreetly, by this gentleman, who said he could offer the avenue for establishing the American industry we seek."

"Inquiries made to whom?"

"Patriot friends. Innkeepers. Barmaids. Merchants. John Hancock helps sometimes. He even gave me a list of known weavers in New England. No one but John knows my name, and no one else knows the nightingales. John has been willing to help further, but he does not understand the need for skilled hands to be involved."

"But then a new friend from Virginia appeared. Who calls himself a patriot."

"The nightingales are not all mariners. Winifred at the Triple Fish helps, even speaks with the servers at other taverns. One of them said she had an interesting discussion with a man with a weaving concern in Virginia, and he gave her swaths of his cloth as his bona fides. He's asked for a meeting."

"Ask about him. I wager he is very lean, with a gaunt face bearing pox marks. I doubt he has ever been in Virginia. He is setting traps, even using soldiers from the local garrison like highwaymen. He reports to Major Hastings, and they are desperate to snare the smuggling ringleaders and haul them back to London to face charges of treason. There are more than a few in the king's court and Parliament whose fortunes have been built on textile works and other factories. They will cheer as the gallows fill with those who would undermine their wealth."

Sarah's face darkened. At first he thought it was fear that seized her, but then he saw the fire in her eyes. "You know nothing of what we do! It's not . . . it's much bigger," she sputtered, then thought better. "Just stay out of it, Duncan!" When she rose, a pewter porringer was in her hand, snatched from the table at her side.

For a moment he was certain she was going to throw it at him, then her gaze fixed on a stain of blood Amanda had left on the divan and it softened. She dropped the porringer on the divan and stormed out of the room.

Sarah was right. He knew nothing.

Duncan was on the Hancock supply sloop when it sailed for Boston the next morning. He watched the town behind him with an unfamiliar fear. The evil spirits, the Otkan, had indeed been released, and he had no idea where they would strike next. How little he knew of Sarah's secrets and the risks she faced. Like Duncan, she was zealous in her ambitions to serve the patriot cause, but she was blind to the predators London had unleashed to crush such ambitions.

As Marblehead faded from view, Duncan found the largest of the sloop's crewmen sitting against the rail amidships, intensely studying a tattered letter. The muscular mulatto acknowledged Duncan with a nod as he sat beside him but kept his gaze on the paper.

"I could write out a copy for you," Duncan suggested. The paper seemed about to disintegrate from being folded and unfolded so often since Duncan had delivered it upon his return from London.

His companion considered Duncan's offer for several heartbeats then shook his head. "A kind offer, to be sure. But then, ye see, it wouldn't be in his hand." He pointed to the name at the top of the letter. "Ain't it just the finest hand ye ever did see? *Crispus*, he writes at the top. *Dear Crispus*, it says, plain as can be." Duncan knew his friend couldn't read, but he had memorized the letter. The big man indicated the name at the bottom of the closely packed words. "My brother," he said in a voice choked with emotion. "Miss Sarah says if I come with you to your settlement on the frontier she can teach me my letters so I could write back to him." He repeated his brother's name. "The only family I have in the entire world. Tell me again, Duncan. Tell me about the grand house he lives in."

Duncan grinned. He had lost count of the times Crispus asked with childlike fascination for him to describe the London mansion where his well-spoken half brother served as a groom and handyman. "In Mayfair, Crispus, the neighborhood of dukes and princes, and no house in Boston is its equal, not even Mr. Hancock's fine mansion. The stable itself is filled with gilded carriages and harnesses with brass fittings, and eight magnificent Friesian horses, and your brother is master of the stable and the one they call if ever there is some difficulty in the house. And he lends a hand to the cause of liberty when he can. He helped me save Benjamin Franklin last year." Duncan never added that his very versatile brother was in fact a key operative for the clandestine smuggling ring run by the aristocratic mistress of the house, who had been raised alongside Sarah in a Mohawk village. Duncan did not, however, spare any detail about the elegant mansion, including its sweeping mahogany stairway lined with oil portraits and the remarkable library, ending as usual with a declaration that Crispus's brother had given generous support to Conawago while the Nipmuc visited London. He refrained from revealing that for most of that visit Conawago was confined to the Bedlam Hospital on secret orders of the War Council.

Duncan shifted the subject. "Did you know the sailor Jacob Book?"

Crispus's smile evaporated. He carefully folded the letter and stuffed it in a pocket before answering. "Sailed with 'im to Portugal once. Best voyage I ever made, 'cause of him. Talked with me most every night about the old ways, teaching me, said it was how we kept them alive."

"You mean tribal ways."

"Aye. He was of a far north tribe. My ma's tribe was Natick. When he found out I was a whaling man once, Jacob wanted to know all about the waters I sailed and if any whales had ever spoken with me. He was convinced that there is a remote sea somewhere where the whales ruled, and the ones we saw were just scouts and messengers who go back and forth to report the events of the world. I liked those great fish, I told him, and grew sadder and sadder the more we slayed them. When he paid out my share the captain said he'd be glad to have me back for another Pacific voyage as bosun, but my heart was too heavy over the dead leviathans."

"Who killed Book, Crispus?"

"Ah well, Mr. Duncan, ye know a tribesman's life come cheap. Jacob liked his ale and had many friends in the taverns. Wouldn't be the first time a Marblehead man drank hisself blind and walked off a wharf."

"After wrapping a chain around his body?"

Crispus sighed. "I heard it was a chain. I heard it was a lobster line that snagged his foot. I heard one of those shooting stars fell and knocked out his brains. And I heard he didn't have his pay tokens from the navy 'cause he pounded 'em into the heart of that officer he killed."

"I helped pull in his body, Crispus. I helped remove the chain. Book killed no one. He was murdered. Conawago is taking it very hard. He hasn't spoken to anyone since he heard the news."

Crispus took several breaths before speaking. "The lobsterbacks was looking for Book. They was about to rip the town apart to arrest him."

"The army wanted him alive, to send a message about the king's justice." Duncan paused. "Tell me something, have you seen a stranger hovering about the waterfront in Marblehead or Boston? A man about my height but slight of built. Likes to stay in shadows. Pox marks across his cheek."

Crispus gave a mocking grunt. "In a busy port every other man is a stranger. And if he's spent much of his life at sea he's had one pox or t'other."

"This one conceals the fact that he is an army officer. He'd have soft hands, no sign of hard labor. He's the kind whose work involves lifting blades in the night and wrapping gentle old men in chains."

Crispus took long moments to grasp Duncan's meaning. Heat rose in his words when he replied, though he made an effort to keep his voice low. "You mean a two-faced coward then. The army's got no business with honest fellas. 'Twas the king who decided to treat us like enemies, sending his troops among us without so much as a by-your-leave, and damn his eyes for doing so! Give me a blade in the night and I'll gladly even the score. The lobsterbacks shall have their comeuppance soon enough, and pray Jesus I can be there."

"Save such words for shore, my friend," Duncan whispered as he surveyed the crew on deck. "We don't know all these men, and this spy passes out coin like candy."

Crispus seemed not to hear. He ground a fist into his palm. "Damn them, damn them all!" he growled. "We need to shove every lobsterback into the sea. Wilkes and Liberty!" he growled, loud enough to turn several heads.

Suddenly their vessel veered sharply to the port and backed sail. Duncan looked up to see a small, fast launch sprinting toward them, a spray of white water off her bow, only fifty yards past their stern. Half a mile behind, the revenue cutter was on a course to catch up. The sight of her Union Jack filled Duncan with dread.

Two men in scarlet uniforms stood in the bow, meaning the navy was doing the army's bidding.

He stayed seated with Crispus as the two officers boarded, in no small part because he saw the fire build on his companion's face upon catching sight of the uniforms, and he feared that Crispus might decide that at least here were two redcoats he could shove into the bay. Crispus's fists began to clench and unclench. The mulatto's heart and physical strength were outsized, but his temper was even bigger.

The master of the Hancock sloop clearly did not welcome the news brought by the officers, but his protest was short-lived, cut off when one of the officers motioned to the cutter, which was in pistol range now. Her gun crew was standing by a swivel gun. Duncan avoided looking at the master as he made his way down the deck but finally rose when he stopped before him.

"We are summoned to Castle William," Hancock's captain announced with a scowl. "To deliver you, McCallum, to the commander."

Duncan recognized the infantry officer left on board the sloop as they tacked toward the castle-like fortress. The ensign, who days earlier retched at the sight of Lieutenant Hicks's mutilated body, was now stern and collected.

"Mr. McCallum," the ensign said with a stiff salute as Duncan approached.

"What business are we about, Ensign?"

"Orders to fetch you as swiftly as possible."

"The commander doesn't even know me."

The ensign hesitated, then spoke in a lower voice. "He was with the commodore Captain Lawford. The Command Council, they call themselves, along with the commanders of the Boston regiments."

"And how, pray tell, did you know how to find me?"

"We left before dawn. The tide and wind were with us. When I arrived in Marblehead I asked for your residence and the wharfmen reported that you left an hour earlier on the Hancock sloop for Boston. It's not hard to pick out the Hancock colors among the inbound vessels," he added with a gesture toward the colorful banner flying off the sternpost.

The Castle William fortress was far larger than Duncan expected, its armaments more threatening. As he followed the young ensign down the wharf and onto the gravel path leading up to the fort's gate, he counted the guns visible in the nearest bastion and did a quick calculation. The castle easily mounted a hundred guns, many of them heavy enough to reach far out into the harbor or just as easily to the buildings of Boston.

Fear seeped into his blood as they advanced through the gate and toward the large building that sat on the far side of the parade ground, the fears that had been building finally seizing him. Despite Glover's threats, Yates must have identified Duncan as an enemy of the king. Someone reported Duncan as the man who spoiled the ambush at the Marblehead church. Duncan had been seen with the escaped slaves. As he passed the fixed bayonets of the two sentries at the entry to the headquarters building, the worst possibility of all stabbed him like a blade of ice: the Horse Guards spy was waiting inside to clamp him in irons. They were looking to cage some traitors for trial, and fatal punishment, in London.

Duncan looked about for anything that might be used as a weapon and now wished he had accepted Crispus's offer to accompany him. As they entered an outer office his gaze settled on a long, spear-like spontoon hanging over the fireplace. He slowed. If he could surprise and disarm his captors, he might be able to reach the water again. Once he dove into the harbor no one could overtake him.

"Dr. McCallum!" a familiar voice called out from the adjoining office. Captain Lawford hurried through the doorway to shake his hand. "Thank God we were able to find you! Pray there is still time!"

Lawford led a confused Duncan into the office and quickly introduced him to Lieutenant Colonel Dalrymple, commander of the army units deployed in the Boston region. Dalrymple had no time for small talk. "Your peculiar—" He paused and began again. "Word of your extraordinary talents has reached me," he said with a glance at Lawford. "Our surgeon is in the encampment of the Twenty-Ninth on the Common, where there has been an outbreak of camp fever. I beg your assistance," he declared and, without waiting for a response, motioned Duncan through an inner door into a corridor connecting with an adjoining building. They stepped into a long chamber with rows of cots along the walls, all occupied by soldiers, several wearing bandages and splints.

"Our infirmary is small," the colonel explained, "but we do have a separate examination room." He led Duncan through the ward, into a short hallway, and opened another door.

The man on the table was comatose.

"Sergeant Briggs collapsed last night in his barracks, with violent seizures," the colonel explained. "He's not been conscious since." Dalrymple fixed a worried gaze on the sergeant. "I am deathly afraid of a new contagion. Our troops are packed into close quarters. At our West Indies garrisons, we've had regiments reduced to half strength in days from fever." He sighed. "And the sergeant is one of our veterans, the most seasoned noncommissioned officer in his regiment, one who earns both respect and affection from his men, a rare combination. Just the kind of man we need to hold the army together. The perfect soldier, in a way. Been with the Twenty-Ninth for over a quarter century, I'm told. Prithee, save him, Doctor."

Duncan choked down his response, choosing not to mention that the soldiers were closely packed only because of the military's rash decision to deploy four thousand troops in a city of only sixteen thousand residents, without adequate housing or sanitation. He bent and lifted the sergeant's eyelids, laid a palm on his clammy forehead, then touched his carotid and held his wrist. Only then did he realize he had met Briggs in Marblehead. He was the sergeant with the rich Yorkshire voice who had come for the vigil over Hicks. Duncan had liked the man.

"His pulse was hammering most of the night," came a squeaky voice. A short, middle-aged man wearing a soiled apron over green overalls stepped out of the shadows. "The sergeant's a big bear of a man, but I don't know how his poor heart can take it. And now, well—" The orderly gestured to Duncan's fingers, still on the wrist. The pulse was light as a feather. "Color all sapped away. Pale as suet."

"Saliva?" Duncan asked.

"Foaming like a mad dog the first hour," the orderly reported. "And every hour or so through the night a grievous twitching. His whole body in spasm, like it was fighting some demon within."

Duncan straightened and faced Dalrymple, the blue-jacketed Captain Lawford now at his side. "Not a contagion," he grimly announced.

"Thank the Lord," the colonel declared with a sigh. "You can suggest a dose?"

"There's little a physic can do for him. Maybe in the first hour but no longer. I'm sorry. He has but little time left."

The colonel closed his eyes a moment, then his face hardened. "What did this? How do I know the cause is not still among my men?"

"I need to speak with someone in his unit, someone close to him. About where he's been recently. I recall meeting Sergeant Briggs just days ago, in Marblehead. How long has he been at the Castle?"

"He's been on detached duties there with his company, just came into the Castle yesterday before heading over to his garrison on the Common. Transferred because of—" Dalrymple glanced at Lawford.

"McCallum was there, with Hicks," the commodore confirmed.

"Because of the difficulties surrounding that death," the colonel continued. "Why does it matter where he was if this was not a contagion?"

"He was exposed to a severe nerve toxin. Not a contagion, but we do need to know the cause is not still among the men. The toxin is fatal."

"My God, sir!" Dalrymple protested. "Be not so callous. The sergeant lies before us, still breathing! Surely you must try something! An antidote! A purging! Leeches!"

"I doubt he can hear us, or even swallow at this point."

The colonel dropped into a chair and sank his head into his hands. "Lord, cut down when I need such men the most."

"I believe, Colonel, that we must let Dr. McCallum learn more about the circumstances." Lawford turned to Duncan. "Certainly there are secrets you can yet discern. There's a reason the heathens call you the—"

Duncan interrupted. "He is not yet gone to the other side. And surely this is a military matter. There will be time when your own surgeon returns. I have business in Boston." He glanced out the window toward the parade ground, painfully aware that he would indeed be clamped in irons if these officers glimpsed the truth about him.

"Give us an hour, I beg you," Lawford said. "We will leave you to your work," he added, gesturing the colonel to the door. "And I'll have a fast launch with my best oarsmen standing by to deliver you to the Long Wharf."

Duncan gazed at the dying man. "A brighter light will help, a spermaceti lamp if possible," he said to the orderly. "And a magnifying lens wouldn't go amiss."

He turned back to Sergeant Briggs, loathing his inability to help the man. In the Marblehead belfry the sergeant had seemed as healthy as a bull, well primed to reap the reward of a half-pay pension for a career that must have spanned back to the 1740s. He could not bear to perform his usual work as Deathspeaker on a living man, would not strip off the sergeant's clothing to examine his body as if he were already dead. But still he might find telltale signs.

The sergeant's knuckles were scarred, evidence of many brawls, and his neck bore the long-ago mark of a saber strike. The rolled shirt that served as a makeshift pillow was damp.

"Like I said, he was frothing at the mouth something awful," the orderly reminded Duncan as he reappeared, carrying a bright whale-oil lamp. "Soaked through two pillows."

As he spoke, another soldier appeared at the door. "They said to report here," the man said in a low, hesitant voice. He stared at the floor then slowly forced his gaze to the figure on the examination table and crossed himself. "I'm his corporal. I was hoping the sarge needed help getting back to his cot." He looked up at Duncan. "Why it's you, sir!" he said in surprise. "From the belfry in Marblehead."

Duncan now recognized the Welsh corporal who accompanied Briggs that night. "Corporal Rhys, I recollect."

"Aye, sir, 'tis me right enough," Rhys said and gazed back at the table. With a pang in his heart Duncan recalled the friendly banter between the two. They had served many years together.

"He's not going back, Corporal," Duncan said.

The Welshman stared at the sergeant with a stricken expression. "Nay, nay! Can't be!" he cried, his voice breaking. "Robbie's the one who binds us together. Oh, Mother Mary, the lads will be devastated!"

"Binds you together?" Duncan asked.

"Patrolling Boston ain't proper soldier's work. The Twenty-Ninth is a proud unit. But the posting is right hellish on morale. Not a proper duty for a fighting man." The corporal cast a nervous glance at Duncan, as if suddenly worried he had said too much.

"I'm not a soldier, Corporal, just a civilian physician," Duncan reassured him. "You may speak openly."

"Desertion, drunkenness, fornication like never before. The Irish lads pick fights with the English lads, and the London lads pick fights with the Yorkshire lads. The sergeant was our conscience, ye see, keeping us steady, tamping down the boys who wanted fisticuffs with the locals. These people of Boston ain't our enemies, he would say, just some stubborn folks who need the king's reminder. We'll be transferred soon enough, hang on just a little longer. Too many hot tempers on the streets, he would say. 'So when ye charge yer muskets I want no balls loaded,' he would tell us. 'We ain't here to kill English citizens.'"

"How long were you in Marblehead?"

"Six weeks, give or take, assigned to Lieutenant Hicks, the one they buried two days ago. Such a run of infernal luck. Glad to be rid of the place."

"When did you leave? I recall seeing soldiers there just this morning."

"They would be our replacements from the Fourteenth. We marched overland to Ipswich and caught a boat from there yesterday."

"So you ate together yesterday?"

"Field rations on the march. Bread and cold sausage with navy grog on the sloop that brought us here. Then the barracks mess last night. Cod stew and soda bread."

"And no one else was sick?"

"No one. Just the sarge, just as we was getting into our cots. It was awful, sir. He suddenly clutches his gut, then starts shaking and vomiting, then collapses and flops about on the floor like a fish out of water. It took three of us to get him here, with him twitching and groaning and foaming at the mouth the whole time." The corporal looked back at Briggs. "Perhaps he just needs a good sleep? I can stay with him through the night, I don't mind."

"Did you pass through a marsh yesterday? Drink from a river? Get offered some of the strange new teas being brewed these days?" All over the colony people were experimenting with roots and dried leaves to find a substitute to their boycotted though beloved tea from the East India Company.

The corporal stepped closer to the dying man. As he gazed at the pallid, wasting countenance of his friend, his eyes welled with moisture. "Oh, Robbie, lad," he murmured before looking up. "No, sir, nothing like that."

"Later in the day," Duncan suggested, "perhaps he ate something just before settling onto his cot."

"No, sir," the corporal said, then hesitated. "Except a girl up the shore was sweet on one of the lads, on account of he was a good talker and had straight teeth and such. Went to university in Dublin, he told me, but had to leave after a spot of trouble with his landlord's daughter. Anyway, this lass in Marblehead runs up as we was marching away and says to 'im, 'Don't forget to write me,' and hands 'im a sack of pork pasties. The sarge saw him trying to sneak one out as he reached his cot. 'No eating in the barracks,' he says. 'Brings in the rats.' So he took the sack, saying he'd give it back when we returned to the regiment. But . . ." the corporal seemed reluctant to continue.

"But?"

"Robbie said he'd had his fill of fish stew in Marblehead, never touched his bowl last night. I reckon he was still peckish."

"You mean he ate a pasty."

The corporal nodded.

"And then the seizures started."

Rhys nodded again.

"You say this girl lived in Marblehead?"

"Aye. Don't recall I ever heard her family name, just Priscilla. Hair the color of straw. Right pleasing to gaze on. Too young for our man."

"Go to the barracks, Corporal," Duncan said. "Find that sack of pasties and bring it here. Do not touch them."

"Sir? They ain't mine."

"Retrieve the sack, Corporal!" a sharp voice snapped behind them. "Now!"

The corporal spun about and gasped. Lieutenant Colonel Dalrymple stood in the doorway. "Double time!"

As the corporal darted away, the colonel stepped inside and shut the door. "Are you suggesting someone is poisoning my troops, Doctor?"

"All we know is that the sergeant ingested a fatal substance. If no one else has fallen ill, then it was not something of general exposure. It may well have been those pasties."

"A Cornish dish, I recall," Dalrymple observed.

"But popular in the port towns. Wives and mothers pack baskets of them for their fishermen to eat at sea. Flour is in short supply, so roots are often ground up to extend it. Someone harvesting roots by a marsh might mistakenly pull up a cowbane root. The tribes call it beaver poison. There are tests I might do to confirm the substance and its concentration. If even a small amount was introduced to some flour, it could be enough. A larger amount would indicate a deliberate action. Give me a day or two, Colonel, and I will report a more definite answer."

"Deliberate. Meaning if this was not an accident, then someone was trying to kill another of my men. And if that were the case, Doctor, you would be the one civilian with particular knowledge of murders among my troops."

Duncan, hearing the challenge in the colonel's voice, returned Dalrymple's steady gaze. Was the colonel speaking of two deaths or three? "I have no reason to share my knowledge with others, sir. And we must not leap to conclusions about Sergeant Briggs. I will study the substance and circumstances further and send you a report."

Dalrymple nodded and fixed another mournful gaze on the sergeant. "Is there anything I can do?"

Duncan bent and listened to Briggs's breathing. "I think he is in no discomfort, sir. Not long now."

The colonel laid a hand on the sergeant's forehead. "He deserved better."

"He deserved better," Duncan agreed.

"Clean him up afterward," the colonel instructed the orderly. "Dress uniform."

The orderly silently saluted the colonel. The colonel returned the gesture, then saluted the dying sergeant. "I am indebted, sir," he offered as he was leaving. "Your boat is standing by."

Duncan, however, felt an odd bond with Briggs. He would not leave while the sergeant still breathed. His lungs were rattling now, each breath more shallow than the one before. The corporal arrived with the sack of pasties. "Destroy them," Duncan said after removing one from the sack and wrapping it in a bandage from the orderly's table. "Burn them." The corporal nodded, his eyes brimming with tears again as he gazed at his comatose friend. "Oh, Robbie," he forlornly whispered.

Duncan stood solemnly before the sergeant, hands clasped in front of him. "The embrace of Saint Michael awaits you, Sergeant Briggs," he said in a prayerful voice.

The corporal, obviously recognizing the name of the patron saint of warriors, offered his own soft *amen*. He lowered himself onto a stool at the other side of the table, clasped one of the sergeant's hands in his own, and began singing in a soft, surprisingly melodious voice. The perfect soldier died to the sound of a Welsh lullaby.

Chapter 5

A S HE WALKED ALONG THE streets of Boston, Duncan was haunted by the vision of the sergeant as his chest rose in one final, desperate grasp at life, then collapsed. The terrible image clung to him, as if Briggs had been pleading for an answer to his ignoble ending. Nothing made sense about the wrenching death. Poison was a targeted weapon planted with a specific victim in mind. Yet the sergeant appeared to be a random victim, had only by horrible luck ingested it. Duncan longed to speak with the young soldier who had received the pasties, to inquire among his comrades whether the sergeant made enemies while in Marblehead or if the young beau could have broken the heart of his Priscilla and become the target of a vengeful maiden. But he could not bear to linger in the army headquarters and hoped never to return.

The Twenty-Ninth was encamped on the Common, below Hancock's palatial home. Duncan considered whether he could chance visiting the garrison to speak to some of the soldiers. His instincts told him that the deaths of Lieutenant Hicks, Sergeant Briggs, and the army captain retrieved from the bay were not coincidences, and because of them Jacob Book had died. There must be a common thread, one he could not yet grasp. He had been certain that the first deaths were the work of the London provocateurs, but poisoned flour was an unlikely weapon for such assassins.

The first time he had visited the apothecary off Brattle Square he took it for a bookshop, for all he could see through the few panes of glass not covered with ivy were stacks of heavy volumes. He had stepped inside the unoccupied shop and had grown so absorbed in a book on the herbal gardens of European monasteries that he did not notice he had company until an adolescent girl tugged on his sleeve.

"Father will be out directly after he finishes his formulation," she announced in a precocious voice. "He says install yourself in the chair by the fire and I'm to fetch another log."

Only then did Duncan become aware of the shelves packed with jars and small wooden boxes, flanked by pegs on which bundles of drying herbs hung. The proprietor, a Huguenot from Flanders named DeVries, greeted Duncan enthusiastically, his welcome growing still warmer when he learned that Duncan had studied medicine at Europe's premier medical college.

Now, after half a dozen visits, DeVries stepped from his workroom and greeted him as an old friend. He accepted Duncan's list with a studious expression. "Cinchona," he observed and winced. "You may have to settle for bark. Supplies are short in the winter months and the cries for nonimportation are scaring off some captains. Both hellebore and laudanum I have in abundance. Glauber's salts, I will have to check. As for tragacanth, don't I just wish."

"I came from Castle William," Duncan declared, "where I had to watch a sergeant slowly die. I think one of these may have killed him," he said as he unwrapped the bundle he had carried in his pocket.

DeVries raised an eyebrow at the object Duncan set on the counter. "I have heard of meat pies causing dyspepsia, but a cause of death?"

"I suspect this one has special qualities. I thought we might test it."

DeVries frowned. "Are you suggesting I do work for the British army?" The Dutchman was an avid supporter of the cause of liberty.

"I am suggesting you help me find the truth about an untimely death. What I share with the British army is an entirely different matter."

DeVries shot him a conspiratorial grin, then motioned Duncan toward his workroom at the back of the shop. Its shelves were packed with jars of chemical solutions and glass beakers. Demijohns of vinegar and various salts filled the space under a workbench. "I can stop back before sunset," Duncan suggested. He knew it could take hours to obtain results from the tests he had in mind.

The pharmacologist did not reply, just broke off a corner of the pasty, lifted a lid on a basket sitting on the workbench, and dropped it inside. "Join me in some of that local tea," the Dutchman said. "*Labradore*, they call it. I'm actually acquiring a taste for the vile stuff."

They sat in the adjoining kitchen and spoke cordially over the brew made of winter herbs, which DeVries was beginning to sell as more residents of Boston subscribed to the nonimportation pledge. The Dutchman asked after Sarah and Conawago, with whom he had spent a memorable afternoon wandering the hills of Marblehead Neck to gather plants used in tribal medicines, followed by a delightful evening during which DeVries took copious notes as the Nipmuc described the proper preparation of the medicines. At last DeVries drained his cup and stood. "Shall we go see if I still need to get my beakers out?" he asked.

With a confused Duncan a step behind, DeVries returned to his workbench, then lifted the lid of the basket and reached down, extracting a small brown-gray body. He cupped his hand and whispered what Duncan took to be a grateful prayer in Dutch, then with touching gentleness laid the dead mouse on the bench. He broke off a straw from a nearby broom and used it to straighten the tiny corpse. "Forgive me, little one," he said, "but your hours were numbered. Your suffering was noble." He glanced up and explained. "I grabbed him this morning an instant before the cat snatched him. Mice have very short life spans in this abode." He cleared his throat, adopting a scholarly demeanor, and used his makeshift probe and a lens to examine the mouth, then uncurled the front feet, which were tightly contracted from spasm.

"Hypersalivation," DeVries announced. "Muscular convulsions. And," he added after examining the basket, "prodigious vomiting for such a small stomach. It was fast acting. Severe reaction of the digestive tract, and then it attacked the nervous system." He straightened and reflected on the body. "The honey of mountain laurel could do this," he suggested.

"Not likely to be found this time of year," Duncan observed. "And laurel is seldom seen so close to the coast."

"Baneberry? Snakeroot?"

"Strong tastes that might rouse suspicion. I was thinking of the root of cowbane, ground into the flour."

DeVries slowly nodded, then added, "If only I had sampled his breath at the end, I would have known." He shrugged, then stuck his straw probe into the remains of the pasty. "But either way, we know you have a fatal pie."

"The pie that started a war," Duncan said in a near whisper.

"Sorry?"

"It seems unlikely such an extreme dose was accidental. There are those on both sides of the Atlantic who fervently want hostilities to break out. The radicals think the redcoats need to be punished for all but enslaving the people of Boston. Many aligned with the king, and most in the army, would relish a fight, since they are confident of crushing all opponents. The troops are desperate for action. They sit about and sharpen their bayonets all day, then at night roam about and trade taunts with the citizens. And now the colonel awaits my report." As he rose to leave, Duncan finally gave voice to the fear gnawing at him since leaving Castle William. "Reporting that one of those citizens sent a basket of poison pies into the ranks will mean that those bayonets start piercing civilian bellies. Or if the zealots learn that someone finally had the courage to act against their oppressors, it will be a sure sign to start using the axes and clubs they parade with." He looked down at the mouse, which seemed strangely heroic in its death. "It's as if I have been handed a lit grenade and am expected to lob it either into army headquarters or at the radicals."

Duncan hesitated as he reached the door of the compact clapboard house on Brattle Street. The entry was draped in black crepe. He realized that although John Adams was going about his business, the household was still in mourning over the death of the young Adams daughter only weeks earlier. He was weighing whether to knock when the door opened.

"I cannot waste my afternoon waiting for you to announce yourself," quipped a weary John Adams as he gestured Duncan inside. "Abigail's pregnancy fatigues her," he explained in a low voice. "She will be sorry to have missed you, but she is abed with instructions not to be awakened for anything short of the Second Coming."

The lawyer led Duncan into the parlor that served as his office, then awkwardly excused himself, leaving Duncan to peruse the collection of volumes on law, religion, and natural philosophy haphazardly stacked on the mantel and adjoining shelves. Adams returned carrying a tray with a teapot and two cups. "A hectic day. One of my clients is a customer of a warehouse in Quincy that burned down last night. The owner, Mr. Bradford, is missing, and my client fears he has fled with his customers' funds after hiring men to burn his warehouse. He demands I proceed with a petition in the general court seeking compensation. He insists men were seen rolling barrels of turpentine into the building just before the conflagration. I advised him that those are rather strong charges to be raised in these volatile times, that we would need some credible evidence."

Duncan cocked his head at the report. "And magistrates would need to be informed if arson were committed."

"As I told him. I asked if he could provide a witness statement. He says he was not present, but neighbors ran out at the first sign of smoke and were forced away by several large brutes who had come with a heavy wagon pulled by mules that conveyed the barrels of turpentine. The barrels were rolled into the warehouse and ignited. If there had been a wind from the sea half the town would have burned."

"Big brutes with a wagon hitched with mules," Duncan repeated pointedly, exchanging a worried gaze with Adams. Neither would put into words the obvious conclusion. Big brutes, and mule wagons, were favored by the army.

Adams shrugged. "Nothing can be done until this Bradford is located." He paused and looked into his cup. "Difficult times, Duncan. I am sorry about your man Book. The horror of seeing his body bound in those chains will haunt me forever."

Duncan was grateful that he did not have to broach the painful subject. "The word in the taverns is that his trouble started with his impressment, which itself was illegal. People are suggesting that the governor needs to remind the navy of its duty to keep its hands off our residents."

Adams shrugged. "The governor has little sway over His Majesty's navy. They are a prideful lot."

"The governor has no military authority. The military has no civil authority. The entire colony could be lost in that gap."

Adams fixed Duncan with a sober gaze, then rose to close the two doors that led into the chamber and silently refilled their cups before settling back into his chair. "I am acquainted well enough with you to know you do not waste your time over philosophical riddles. Tell me the reason you are here."

"Slavery, John. Where do you stand?"

"Must you ask? It is an abominable practice, a stain on humanity. I have never owned a slave nor ever shall I."

"More than a few of the most able seamen out of Massachusetts ports are Africans. Many were born into servitude but escaped. Not to mention the tribesmen who freed themselves from the chains of southern plantations by finding work on Massachusetts boats."

"Divine Providence is on their side."

"But not the law."

Adams sighed. "A complicated matter, Duncan. The courts are loath to abrogate property rights, even those established under the laws of another province."

"But if they begin to uphold such rights, they would surely become the targets of fiery sermons on the Sabbath."

Adams studied Duncan in silence, then rose and rummaged on his desk, returning with a copy of *The Boston Chronicle*, which he dropped on the side table at Duncan's elbow. "The edition is two days old."

Duncan's gaze quickly fixed on the story that took up an entire front page column. "West Indies escapees in New England," he read with a sudden chill. The article began with the report of a letter received by magistrates in Rhode Island and Massachusetts from the governor of Barbados. The story pointed out that the governor previously was head of the much-hated vice-admiralty court in Halifax, created to prosecute smugglers and other customs offenders in the American colonies. This meant, Duncan knew, that he would have a deep animus against New Englanders. Not only were they deemed to be the most frequent offenders, but their protests and resistance had rendered the court impotent. The governor, William Spry, now had written to report that nine slaves ran away from their servitude on two adjoining sugar plantations. One led them on quite a chase and was eventually recovered, drowned. His investigations showed that the others departed on one of five ships that sailed the night of the escape, one bound for Rhode Island and the others for Massachusetts ports. He reminded the magistrates of their solemn and sworn duty to return the property of the plantation owners, both of whom had great influence in London, and to severely punish all who assisted in their escape and flight.

Duncan looked up. He had spent altogether too long digesting the article.

"Give me a ha'penny, Duncan," Adams declared in an earnest tone.

"John?"

"A ha'penny, man, and be quick about it. If you can't muster a ha'penny then a peppercorn, a groat, a handkerchief even."

Duncan was confused but extracted the coin and handed it to Adams.

"Excellent," Adams said as he made a show of depositing it in his purse. "You are now a client, and I shall register you as such in my office ledger." He returned Duncan's still perplexed gaze. "A client! I am bound by strict obligations to preserve the confidences of my clients."

A relieved grin rose on Duncan's face. He doubted there was anyone else in the colony who would have so quickly grasped his predicament.

"So, speaking only theoretically," Adams asked, "what would a compassionate soul do to help troubled souls seeking to cast off the yoke of servitude?"

"I have heard of petitions being filed in courts to declare a slave's freedom."

"You speak of manumission. It is not impossible, but that's for those with ties to Massachusetts when no owner elsewhere is asserting a claim. There are at least two cases I can recall, both involving respected, well-known citizens—repenting owners, as it were—who provided affidavits of good character and support from clergy. Runaways are a different kettle of fish. The slaves and those who aid them are considered to have stolen property from the owner as surely as if they had broken into his home and purloined his valuables. Those who help can suffer greatly. I recall one poor soul who sailed from Boston to Jamaica to pay for the freedom of an escapee he had befriended only to be clapped in chains and made to replace the escapee in servitude. Friends made efforts to rescue him, but the wretched man died of the yellow jack a few months later. It's a brutal business, Duncan, and those who pursue escapees are merciless. Governor Spry is offering a rich reward to magistrates who find the runaways, so expect no help from the courts. And no doubt large bounties are being offered to those pernicious hunters who specialize in human prey. The bounties are high, because the plantation owners are obsessed with assuring no escape can ever be successful. I hear there are slave hunters who have grown quite wealthy by hunting down escapees, and they are none too gentle with their captives. More than a few use cages to hold them for journeys that can take weeks."

"Good Christians should be haunted by guilt if they sit back and do nothing," Duncan observed.

Adams rose and paced along the window that faced the street. "Perhaps some are taking actions. A judge whose name will remain unspoken made a request of me last week to review a writ of manumission for completeness." He saw the inquiry in Duncan's eyes. "A writ declaring a slave's freedom is seen perhaps once a year or so, but three were issued in recent weeks."

"I've heard of a slave buying his freedom."

"Which is a transaction between the slave and his master. In these cases, no master was involved."

"I don't understand. How could the master not be involved?"

"Exactly what I asked. But no answer was given. I know nothing more except that the judge in question is a great friend of the army."

"The army has no slaves."

"It nags me," Adams said. "I keep trying to puzzle it out. I always come back to the possibility that an officer has confidentially requested the writs."

Duncan sipped his tea. "Freedom in exchange for services. Secret services," he said with a chill. "Turning against their owners."

Adams offered a solemn nod. "A dark stratagem, but very clever."

"How many, John?" asked Duncan. "How many of these hypocrites do you suppose there are?"

"How many?"

"How many of those engaged in the cause of liberty still have slaves or bond servants? And if we are correct in our conclusion, we are faced with a conundrum, John. Who do we help, the slave seeking freedom from his master or the master seeking freedom from his king?"

The silence that followed was fractured by the sound of a shattering dish from the kitchen. Adams hurried out of the room, Duncan a step behind. A slender woman of about thirty with curly brown hair was bracing herself with both hands on the table and seemed about to weep.

"I'm so sorry, John," she said as Adams appeared. "I can't seem to get a grip on anything these days."

"Think nothing of it, Rebecca," Adams said as he surveyed the shards of a dish scattered across the floor. "Just an old porridge bowl. My son and I can share until we find another." He introduced Duncan as an old friend who was visiting from Marblehead and named the woman as Rebecca Prescott, "a friend of Abigail's, staying with us a few days." The lawyer paused, clearly seized by a new thought as he looked back and forth from Duncan to Rebecca. "Mr. McCallum is rather adept at dealing with delicate problems," he said awkwardly. "Secret problems, you might say. For patriots," he added.

Duncan had no idea where the odd conversation was going and apparently neither did Rebecca, who gazed at Adams in obvious confusion.

"Rebecca, dear," Adams said, "we need to find a better solution. You can't hide here indefinitely. Mr. McCallum," he stated as he cast a tentative glance at Duncan, "has a commodious residence in Marblehead. My client Mr. McCallum," he added.

The woman was clearly embarrassed. She glanced at Duncan, then quickly looked away. "John?" Duncan pressed.

"A very proper household, I assure you," Adams continued.

"Prithee, John, enough," the woman said. She sat at the table, taking a chair that offered a view of the rear door, which she gazed at with a hollow expression. She was frightened. "I have only just met Mr. McCallum, and I will not burden him with my dilemma."

"Dilemma, ma'am?" Duncan asked. He was confused but could plainly see that the woman was under a great strain of mind. "I collect dilemmas," he added with an ironic grin, "like some people collect pewterware."

Adams's guest offered a thin, uncertain smile. "I think perhaps there was an old feud involved. Nathan had been in the famous Horse Guards regiment but transferred out because, as he said, he wanted to be a real soldier."

"I'm not sure I follow," Duncan admitted.

Adams sighed. "We have not time to be so indirect. Someone is trying to kill Rebecca."

Duncan stepped to the rear window, looking outside but seeing no one. "There are authorities who can deal with such things," he observed.

"No," Adams countered. "Not these things."

"You see, Mr. McCallum," Rebecca Prescott said. "I witnessed the murder of my fiancé, Captain Mallory of the Twenty-Ninth grenadiers."

"Impossible, McCallum! The king does not resort to lowly subterfuge!"

Duncan stood before the hearth in the chamber John Hancock used as an office in his elegant Beacon Hill home, the largest in Boston. He had been trying to explain his conclusion that secret operatives from London were in the colony, trying to foment hostilities through murder and arson. "Men who work for the king do so already in London. I have shared some of what happened there last year when I was assisting Benjamin Franklin. They sought to kill me and bury him in the Bedlam asylum."

"Yes, well, I recall you saying so. Odd that Benjamin has never reported any of that to us," Hancock observed. "He writes to me frequently as official agent of the colony."

"Because, as I have explained, he is well aware that these same men intercept and read all his correspondence. In this game of shadows, we do not expose our knowledge or plans to the other side." Duncan chose not to reveal to the overly talkative Hancock that Franklin had many allies in London and many siblings in Boston, who saw to it that more sensitive communications were maintained indirectly between Duncan and the famed inventor-statesman.

"It just strikes me as very convenient to say that you can't prove subterfuge here because of subterfuge there. What you suggest is dishonorable. The governor would never abide it."

"The governor, I assure you, is not apprised of such activity. The War Council has contempt for provincial governments, believes their laxness has caused all the problems with the colonies. Most of its members seek to advance the confrontation they believe is inevitable. Some will grow quite wealthy from a new war, and others just want the upstart colonists put down once and for all."

Hancock stepped to the window. "Confrontation," he muttered. "You have no doubt heard of the boy who was killed in the course of one of the riots last week? His funeral was the largest ever seen in this city, more of a rallying cry for action than a mourning ceremony. The patience of Boston is paper thin. The next incident won't be a confrontation, it will be a volcanic eruption, an explosion that will shake the continent all the way to Carolina."

The man in the soft chair by the hearth broke the awkward silence. Samuel Adams, cousin to John, needed no convincing. Few men in Boston loathed the occupation troops more than the portly Samuel, and still fewer had firsthand experience with the army's trickery in ferreting out resisters. Adams lifted the newspaper that lay beside him and held it out toward Hancock. "And do you forget the

Quincy fire, John? Eruptions begin with minor flare-ups. We've already had the first conflagration."

Hancock turned, frowned, and stepped to the sideboard to refill his glass with sherry. "Samuel, we know little beyond what the papers say. How many times must I repeat it? Our biggest danger is overreaction. This is not the time." He looked to Duncan, as if for help. Hancock was not aware of the details of much of Duncan's work but knew that much of what he did was buy time for the independence movement.

"We must not overreact," Duncan agreed. "But we must be dogged in exposing the truth. Elsewise we will be shoved into a war we cannot win. The Quincy fire makes my point. Do the papers mention the men who came with a mule wagon carrying barrels of turpentine, clearly intent on arson? Why that warehouse?" he asked his friends.

Hancock seemed to take a great interest in his glass. "Every successful merchant has his secrets," he lamely suggested.

Adams sighed. "Because every large merchant house has to evade the burden of duties to be successful. Bradford no doubt did his share of smuggling."

Duncan did not miss the nervous glance exchanged by the two men. They knew more. "Do not mince words with me. Bradford was engaged in something especially offensive to the king." He recalled now Yates's mention of a boat coming in the night from across the bay, perhaps from Quincy. "Why was his warehouse important to the patriot cause?"

"The government is cracking down, increasing its enforcement patrols," Hancock replied. "It wants to raise the stakes, create unmistakable warnings to smugglers. The walls of the warehouse were brick, so they partially survive. I hear that a slogan was chalked on one. *Death to Smugglers*, no doubt the work of one those more extreme Loyalist groups. Loyalist vigilantes, people are calling them."

"Or to make it seem so. A ruse too tempting for the arsonists to resist," Duncan said. "What was in the building?"

Adams and Hancock exchanged another worried glance and remained silent.

"Was I not," Duncan asked, heat rising in his voice, "entrusted by the leaders of the Sons in Philadelphia and New York, and yourselves, to do the secret work of the Sons and see that its secrets remain protected? Have I not risked my life many times over to protect those secrets?"

Hancock winced. "Duncan, sit down. Allow me to pour you some sherry."

Duncan remained standing. Hancock went to his sideboard and filled a wine-glass. Duncan accepted the glass but set it down on the side table and kept staring at Hancock, who finally sighed. "I understand Mr. Bradford has been helpful in bringing in a weaving machine that the Crown might have preferred stayed in England."

"A Hargreaves spinning jenny," Duncan stated. Sarah's friend Amanda had been beaten just the night before because of the machine. "Protected by a flock of nightingales." An awkward glance passed between his companions. To Hancock's obvious relief, a great clatter rose from the kitchen. The merchant darted toward the door at the back of the chamber. "The export of which would be strictly pro-hibited," Duncan observed to Adams. He choked down the rest of his thought as he recalled the drawing of a gear and an acorn. It was not just weaving machinery the government sought.

Adams spoke in a lower voice. "Bradford has been a zealous patriot and lover of freedom for all. We dined together not long after the new year. He said he embraced our cause but could ill afford to openly associate with the Sons. He implied the Boston Sons were getting too cozy with the governor," Adams added with a gesture toward the door behind which Hancock had disappeared. "He's a very self-reliant man, so he may have pursued plans without involving us. He spoke of a new alliance in Marblehead. It took me weeks to discover that he made no connection with our customary supporters there. That's when I recalled him speaking very highly of Miss Ramsey. Later still I recalled he had mentioned how he was glad to have made use of his contacts in Barbados. I had assumed he meant the sugar and molasses trade but—" Adams gestured toward the newspaper article about the warehouse fire. "Now I cannot be sure."

Duncan nodded. "Looms don't come from Barbados. And London's spies don't trouble themselves over sugar and molasses." He quieted, ambushed by new worries. He did know what had come from Barbados: eight runaways. Sarah had said the opportunity unexpectedly arose to save them, and they had seized it, as if her original interests lay elsewhere. She had had other plans for a shipment from Barbados that had apparently fallen through.

"But we don't know anything for certain, Duncan," Adams cautioned. "We don't know the exact nature of Bradford's secrets or how the government would have learned of them. And no matter what, the governor will have to officially maintain that the fire was just a tragic accident. Such fires are the stuff of nightmares. If the warehouse had been in Boston, the entire city could have been lost. He can ill afford rumors of arsonists. His first priority is to avoid a public panic."

As Adams spoke, Hancock returned, followed by a servant carrying a tray of small cakes. Duncan could not help gazing at the middle-aged African man in formal livery. Once when Duncan brought up the subject of slavery, Hancock had been quick to deny he owned any slaves. "There's only a couple left in the house," he had declared, "and they belong to my aunt."

"Bradford was a known smuggler of molasses and sometimes cordage from Iberia," Hancock put in. "You know how impatient Castle William is for smugglers to be more severely punished. You mustn't read more trouble into the fire than that. God knows it's trouble enough. I'm already moving some of my Boston goods to warehouses outside the city."

"So impatient that they send soldiers in disguise with barrels of burning turpentine? Do not be so blind," Duncan pressed. "It was not Castle William. As I have been telling you, London has been building networks of assassins and secret informers. I can recite to you exactly who on the War Council instructs them, even tell you the chamber they operate out of at the Horse Guards Palace. They are the ones who tried to kill me last year, the ones who attacked Franklin. The provocateurs have expanded into Massachusetts. And if these men were at Quincy, Bradford will not be found alive."

"No! You succumb to irrational fears!" Hancock insisted. "I have no doubt such operatives exist in Europe. We have all heard rumors of secret operations against the French. But never in America. Forgive me, Duncan, but the only one we have heard speak of such things is you. I tell you, the men on the War Council would not trouble so over our little town on the bay. We are barely sixteen thousand souls, while the great metropolis of the king counts seven hundred thousand."

"Our distant little town, John, is the biggest thorn in the king's backside. Name another British town occupied by the king's troops."

Adams concurred with a guffaw. "Name another that pays such high taxes. None other in the kingdom, I assure you."

"Right," Duncan answered. "It's all about duties and taxes, shillings and guineas. Maintaining the troops here is a massive expense. And the way these men on the Council justify their spies to the king is by claiming to save the Exchequer more expense. Let us either eviscerate the resistance by the act of a few stealthy agents or be ready to bear the cost of two more regiments, then four, then eight and ten. You'll be licking porridge off a cheap tin plate, Your Majesty, if you don't rein in these traitors now.

"And I've already discovered the trail of one of those spies in Marblehead, who reports to another in Boston, the very man I fought in London. No matter the lie they tell the king, what they want is war. You saw the body of Lieutenant Hicks, John. The army was rabid, about to tear the town apart to find the man they assumed to be his killer. The London provocateur killed him instead."

"Surely not," Adams said. "He would have no reason. The army was going to find the culprit."

"The army's rampage in Marblehead was going to frighten away the spy's quarry. He believes he is closing in on those who are extracting British manufacturing secrets. He has already dealt with one, in Quincy."

"I simply will not credit that a king's officer would stoop to arson and murder!" Hancock insisted. He dropped heavily into the empty chair by the hearth.

"Three army officers have died in the past two weeks, all from the hated Twenty-Ninth. Disbelieve at your own risk, John."

"Surely," Hancock replied, "if the army believed the rebels were engaged in murder, they would be involving the civil authorities." He paused. "Three?"

Duncan relayed what he knew of the death of Sergeant Briggs and reminded him of the murder of Captain Mallory. "You saw his body, John. You were there when we plucked it from the bay." Duncan pushed down the impulse to reveal that he had met a witness to the officer's death. "Mallory served in the Horse Guards but spurned a career with them, which meant he may have been a threat to these secret killers, for he could expose them. They aren't here just to eliminate smugglers of manufacturing secrets. Eventually they will be finding ways to eliminate the leaders of the Sons. It won't be outright murder. It will be accidents. A tumble into the harbor off an icy wharf. A late-night fall onto the broken cobblestones of an alley. Or," Duncan continued, addressing Hancock, "just arranging for seizure of another ship. And another, and another, until you are broken and penniless."

The color slowly drained from Hancock's face. Samuel Adams muttered under his breath and drained his glass of sherry. Duncan looked at Adams with new worry. He had not intended to reveal their involvement with Mallory's body. The corpulent legislator made a low rumbling sound and stood to rummage among the papers piled at the end of the sideboard. He extracted a gazette, laid it on the desk, and ran a finger along its columns, then read aloud. "Yesterday's *Chronicle*. Very brief. 'Beloved Officer Dies in Accident' is the headline, then just half a dozen lines. 'Captain Nathan Mallory of the Twenty-Ninth Grenadier Company was laid to rest with honors at Castle William after having drowned in a tragic accident. He was highly esteemed by his men and a credit to his regiment. May he find eternal peace.'"

Adams let the words sink in. "Which is more disturbing," he asked, "that Mallory was murdered or that the army is lying about his death?"

At last his friends were willing to hear Duncan's detailed explanation of his encounters with Hastings and the War Council, then of his discoveries about Lieutenant Vaughn in Marblehead.

Hancock sighed when Duncan finished. "We will help in any way we can." He collected himself and fixed Duncan with a worried expression. "I almost forgot. I had a very odd visit from a magistrate, acting on a note from one of the magistrates in Marblehead, both avid Loyalists. He was asking about you, Duncan: Was it true you recently returned from London? Were you known to be sympathetic to deserters? Had you been invited to the governor's ball? All seemed rather disjointed. I paid little heed."

Duncan chewed on the announcement for a few breaths. "The dead lieutenant was angrily complaining about meddling from someone recently from London. Hicks was about to complain to Castle William. And Captain Mallory died of a very precise stab wound, placed perfectly by the spine to pierce the heart. He was stabbed on the day of the ball."

"Dear God, Duncan!" Hancock exclaimed. "They seek to hold you accountable for the deaths?" He looked from Duncan to Adams and knew no answer was needed. He poured three glasses of whisky. "A dangerous game," he observed as he distributed the glasses.

"The hand we have been dealt," Duncan said.

"But Duncan, your life could hang in the balance!" Adams exclaimed. When Duncan offered no reply, he sighed. "What do we do?"

"A distraction. Soldiers sometimes fire random cannonballs across a battlefield to befuddle their enemy. If you receive more inquiries, let them know I had no knowledge of Hicks until we discovered his body. I was in Marblehead the night of the governor's ball. My arrest would raise difficult questions, especially when I have your cousin John to defend me. They mean to intimidate me, not arrest me."

"Intimidate?" Adams asked. "I thought you said this Hastings wanted you dead."

"Major Hastings," Duncan replied, pushing more confidence into his voice than he felt, "doesn't know I am involved yet. His sights are set elsewhere. Give me a chance to stop this in Marblehead. I know that terrain better than they do. The arrogance of such men is their biggest weakness. I shall use it against them." He looked up into the merchant's worried face. "Let New York and Philadelphia know. And I may need favors from you and your men."

"Pollard and my men in Marblehead are at your disposal. I shall write him, tell him you are engaged in some special, and secret, transaction for me. He is used to commercial mysteries." Hancock sipped at his whisky. "And how are the wind and tide tonight?"

"Favorable. Fair skies."

"My packet crew is from Portsmouth. They sleep on board when in Boston. They will be glad to start home earlier than expected, even if it means a short stop in Marblehead, especially when I give them a pouch of shillings to share. I will send a note immediately. And I shall provide you with a strong ox of a man to watch your back." Hancock stood and drained his glass. "But first I have more pleasant matters to speak of with you."

"Evening spoil! Bring out to Boyle!" The cry was so vigorous that it woke Duncan, who had not reached his bed until long after midnight. "Night soil, night soil, bring your sweets to Boyle!" Duncan sat up, rubbing his eyes. He had spent much of the night composing his report on Sergeant Briggs's death. A familiar laugh brought him to his feet. He stepped to the window as Sarah appeared outside, carrying a chamber pot, followed by Moll and Josiah with two more.

The raggedy Irishman named Boyle doffed his cap and bowed as Sarah emptied her pot into the open barrel on his cart, which always had fresh pine boughs on its sides to mitigate the stench. Sarah handed Boyle the loaf of bread she had tucked under her arm, then extracted an apple from her apron and offered it to the weary horse in the harness as Moll and Josiah dumped their pots. More than once, Sarah had expressed sympathy for the middle-aged Irishman who persevered on his daily retrievals despite being mocked, and sometimes assaulted with snowballs, by youngsters on the way to school. It was a grueling, demeaning labor but of great service to the town, one not often found in the colonies, and Boyle could support himself on the coins paid by tanners for the chemical-rich contents of his barrels.

Sarah always brought a smile to Boyle's grizzled countenance and a quickening of his horse's gait. Duncan grinned as he thought of how this ritual lifted Boyle's spirits. The Irishman had no way of knowing that Sarah was one of the largest landowners on New York's frontier, the head of a thriving community and born to the British aristocracy. He only knew of the joyful auburn-haired woman who ran out to greet him most mornings, always to offer a fresh loaf and an apple. Her instinctively generous heart was one of the reasons she had captured Duncan's own and also one of the reasons he feared for her. That same generosity had embraced runaway slaves and turned their landlady's home into a criminal hideaway.

When he reached the kitchen Moll was alone, stirring a pot of breakfast porridge. "I have a favor to ask," Duncan said. The cook nodded in reply. "A woman is coming on the morning coach from Boston. She suffered a recent tragedy and needs to get away from the city for a spell. Rebecca Prescott is her name. Might you meet her, Moll? Crispus can go to carry her baggage, but he doesn't know the tavern where the coach stops."

Moll smiled, nodding again. "I met Crispus. He seems a man who will know where all the taverns are soon enough. Of course we'll fetch her, not to worry."

"And tell Mrs. Godwin to let me know what additional rent we owe, since I expect Miss Prescott will be with us for a while." He choked off the next words that came to mind. *Keep her safe.* In the little time he had spent with her, he had been impressed with Abigail Adams's friend. She had been married at an early age to a ship's captain who had been lost at sea, then opened a small bookshop where Captain Mallory, a lover of poetry and Shakespeare, called regularly. The young widow and Mallory had recently become engaged and had been on the way to the governor's ball, taking the sea air along the Long Wharf, when a "military man" in a cloak assaulted them. Mallory told Rebecca to flee, but she turned in her flight just as Mallory was stabbed and shoved off the pier. The next day two men with the demeanor of soldiers tried to corner her in an alley, calling her "Mallory's bitch."

They had drawn knives with, she was certain, lethal intent. She screamed, and as bystanders approached, the men fled. Duncan needed to learn more from the woman but for now knew enough. They were facing the same enemy.

He found Sarah in the sitting room, taking up the hem of a dress she was giving to Esther. He dropped the copy of the prior day's *Boston Gazette* on the table beside her. "Everyone in Boston is talking about the big fire," he observed, watching her carefully.

Sarah slowly put down her work. "Fire?" She pulled up the newspaper. "Oh my, a Quincy warehouse. What misery for the owner. What was his name? Here it is—Bradford, it says. Poor Mr. Bradford must be most distraught. I'm so glad we left the troubles of Boston and its neighbors behind us, Duncan. And I so pray we can return to Edentown soon." She glanced toward the kitchen where a chorus of laughter rose, a boyish voice joined by a deep bass one. "Crispus is playing with Josiah and the cat. What is it about big men and small animals?" she whimsically asked.

Duncan returned her uncertain gaze a moment, trying to decide if he was going to embrace her or force her to tell him the truth. The report in the paper was not news to her. "I was with John Hancock yesterday, at his house. He said last fall he and his aunt planted five hundred tulips in his garden, which no doubt means he and his aunt sat and drank some expensive wine as they supervised the planting of five hundred bulbs. He says when they start showing buds, he will send an invitation. 'So my beautiful Dutch blooms may be graced for an afternoon with Miss Ramsey, the most beautiful of English flowers,' he said."

Sarah lifted her sewing. "He was drunk, I take it."

"Only a little. He says you and he have much to do in that garden."

She worked her needle for a few stitches. "Much to do?"

Duncan withdrew a folded letter from his waistcoat pocket and dropped it in her lap. "Hancock has a lawyer in Albany. The lawyer's brother is a magistrate."

With a rush of breath Sarah opened the letter, scanned its contents, and leapt to her feet, spilling her sewing and throwing her arms around Duncan. "We have it at last!"

While they had been pledged to each other for years, the fates, or at least the government and Sarah's ruthless father, had conspired against their marriage. They had endured the completion of Duncan's indenture, the kidnapping of Sarah, the enslavement of Duncan, and the repeated bureaucratic rejections of their plans, the most recent being the requirement that Duncan provide official attestation that his indenture was fulfilled, since a bonded servant possessed no legal capacity and no right to marry. The attestation had to be based on a filing in Albany, which Sarah had previously ignored, but which their friend Sir William Johnson had expedited.

Duncan pressed her close, his resentment of her secrets melting away. "John says we must be wed in his garden," he whispered in her ear. "He mentioned casks of new claret and cases of champagne. I said we were more of the cider and ale sort, and he laughed and said it shall be the best cider and ale his money can buy. And it won't be that much longer until his tulips are in bloom."

Her soft, amused murmur was muffled in his shoulder. He squeezed her again. "There it is," he said. "At last."

"It?"

"Your laugh, Sarah." The sound was a tonic that cured his despair. "I hear it too seldom. We need to go back to Edentown so I can hear it every day."

She slowly relaxed her arms. Her smile grew distracted and he realized she was looking at the newspaper again. "And no more visits to Boston without an escort," he said. "Not when they are burning down your warehouses."

Sarah pulled away, casting a wary glance at Duncan, then walked to the front window. "My warehouses?" she spoke toward the harbor.

"You and I know Mr. Bradford was smuggling in looms and such. I visited the textile works with Dr. Franklin where they were using the new spinning jennies. I recall the plans were later sewn up in the linings of petticoats that crossed the Atlantic. But there is no substitute for having the actual machine to serve as a model for others. Is that why he was targeted? Or perhaps because of his business with Barbados?" He could not shake the sense that the original mission of the ship from the most wealthy of all British colonies was the linchpin for connecting the puzzle before him.

Sarah kept staring toward the fishing wharves, offering no reply.

"Please don't deny it. Not to me, Sarah. You already knew of the fire. What you don't know is that it was done by soldiers. Soldiers wearing civilian clothing. They came well supplied, with clear intentions. How did they know? You have already lost the secrecy that protected you and your nightingales. I do hope your spinning jenny is well hidden because they are building their forces against you.

And a leak in your network means all of you are in danger." She still ignored him, so he continued. "They rolled barrels of flaming turpentine into the building. And no one has seen Bradford or his man since. I fear when they sift through the ashes they will find charred bones."

Sarah's hand reached out and clutched the back of a chair, as if she suddenly needed support. When she finally spoke her voice was hoarse. "Not possible."

"The protesters in Boston are a nuisance to the army. But those who steal the secrets of British wealth are true enemies. That conflict was launched by the War Council months ago. It has nothing to do with liberty. It is about capital and mines and factories. But it can never be a public war for the damage it might do to British financiers and the embarrassment caused to the dukes and earls who own those factories and mines. I've told you, they call it the Black Office, and the officers assigned to it are merciless. Burning a warehouse is exactly the kind of thing they do, and they won't hesitate to throw its owner into the flames if it serves their purpose. If you had been there, your role revealed, they would have tossed you into the inferno."

Sarah dropped into the chair, staring into her folded hands as she spoke. "Mr. Bradford has a wife and daughter. And his clerk. He is very fond of his clerk. They probably fled together."

"I pray it is so, but I wager his bones will be found amid the ashes. We owe him the truth, Sarah, and justice."

She looked up as his words sank in. "You can't, Duncan! Don't you see? You mustn't go to Quincy!"

"Mustn't?"

"Mustn't get involved. If what you say is true, then these people from the War Council know your face."

"Only one of them knows me, and I have eluded him more than once." He did not mention that the one time Hastings had actually captured Duncan, he had found himself in an iron cage being readied for slow torture at her father's pleasure.

"But perhaps not the next time. If they have targeted me, you should stay away from me. You should flee to Edentown."

"No. I am the only one familiar with these games of shadows and mirrors."

"You must go, I beg you!" Sarah pleaded. "I can finish in a few weeks and join you."

Duncan knelt in front of her and lifted her head toward him. "One thing I know for certain, *mo chride*, is that I can't stay away from you."

Moisture welled in her green eyes. "It's too dangerous!"

"As a boy I lost everyone I loved to the king's soldiers," Duncan said, reaching for her hand. "I won't let it happen again. And we have a date to keep in Hancock's garden."

Tears flowed down Sarah's cheeks. "You've been pushed to the brink of death too many times by soldiers or my father's butchers. Your luck can't hold forever."

He rose, lifting her with him. She fell back into his arms and buried her head in his shoulder again, so that he barely made out her whisper. "Damn you, Duncan McCallum, you have to flee because I love you too much, don't you see!"

As he held her, unable to find a way out of their pain, she raised her head. He followed her gaze as it drifted out the window toward the hill by the harbor, then fixed on a solitary figure sitting by a smoky fire.

The old Nipmuc's face was gaunt and expressionless as Duncan sat down beside him. Conawago did not greet him, did not acknowledge his presence, and Duncan realized he was transported elsewhere, withdrawn into one of his past worlds or perhaps, as many tribesmen believed he did, wandering in the spirit world.

For long moments Duncan sat silently, painfully studying the weathered countenance of the man who for years had been as close to him as a father. He had not seen Conawago's usual vibrancy for weeks, except for the brief time with Jacob Book on the rooftop. The discovery of a kindred spirit in Book, and the promise of shared adventures to come, had brought a brightness to his eyes and an energy in his step. Now that brightness and energy were gone, perhaps never to return. What had Blue Turtle said? The bones of his soul were broken. Book had kindled something in Conawago long missing, and his death had devastated the old Nipmuc so deeply that Duncan had at first feared he would disappear into one of his weeks-long retreats into the nearest wilderness. But soon he realized that Conawago, born in the last century, no longer had the strength for such escapes. The old tribesman found another way to mourn and assure Book's safe passage to the other side. Book was buried in the churchyard of St. Michael's, but this was his real funeral.

Duncan had heard his friend speaking to the sky as he climbed the hill, and for a moment had worried that he had stopped his conversation with the spirits because of Duncan, but then he saw the patient way Conawago now studied the embers and knew that it was because the fragrant smoke that attracted those on the other side had died away. He was about to tell the Nipmuc that he would fetch more cedar, when he heard a soft step behind him. Pine approached, carrying an armful of boughs. The Oneida dropped them near the fire and looked at Conawago, who nodded. He laid a bough over the embers and instantly a dense, fragrant column of smoke rose toward the heavens.

"*Jiyathontek! Jiyathontek!*" Conawago called, his arms extended again toward the sky as he summoned the spirits.

Duncan did not know all the words of the death passage song but joined with Pine in the singsong chorus, to Conawago's obvious satisfaction, and helped Pine replenish the fire so the smoke remained constant. At last Pine seemed to sense that the end of the lament was approaching and piled extra boughs on the flames. The smoke increased. By a strange twist of the wind, it swirled about them, enveloping them. For a moment it was so dense Duncan could barely make out Conawago, but he detected an unexpected relief in the old man's voice. The spirits had heard.

As the smoke cleared Conawago rose, gesturing Duncan and Pine to also stand. "*Yoyanere! Yoyanere!*" he called out to the sky with surprising vigor. It had been a propitious offering, and the old Nipmuc seemed satisfied that Book had joined the ranks of the warrior spirits. He watched the dense cloud of smoke reach higher and higher, ever northward, until it was lost in the distant clouds, then gestured for Duncan and Pine to sit again with him. He reached out with a cupped hand to wipe his face with the smoke, then waited as his companions followed suit. When he spoke again it was in a more relaxed, conversational tone. The old Nipmuc could not be called strong, but he was no longer frail.

"It was that big ice storm we had in December," Conawago began. "I was walking with Moll up from the butcher, steadying her on the icy street, when I saw a boy of six or seven on the steep hill below the customhouse. That slope was naught but a sheet of ice all the way to the water, but the poor lad bounded out the back door and started down the hill, calling out to a woman behind him and pointing to a fishing boat coming into harbor. It was his father's, we discovered later, whom the boy had not seen for weeks. But that hill was like glass. His mother screamed, for the boy lost his footing and was sliding straight for the open water. It was high tide, and all bundled as he was the lad would have sunk like a stone.

"Suddenly someone broke away from a band of sailors down the wharf and quick-grabbed a bundle of straw waiting to be loaded and slid it across the ice. The bundle struck the boy with perfect timing, and he veered off along the road where he was snatched up by the sailor. Then Moll and I helped the frantic mother down the hill. She was already offering a prayer of gratitude, saying we had witnessed a divine intervention. I figured it was one of those spry lads you see flying about the rigging of tall ships. But when she was finally able to pry her son loose from his savior she gasped, 'cause the man's face was covered with tattoos of little fish. 'I declare,' she said, 'it's an angel in coppery skin.' Old Jacob just laughed and doffed his cap to her. He declined the shilling she offered him, saying his reward was her smile and knowing the lad had learned a hard lesson about the ways of winter. Then the man's mates caught up with him and pulled him away. ''Twill be a hot buttered rum for you, Jacob Book,' one called out."

"I should have kept him from leaving the house," Duncan said.

Conawago, surprisingly, laughed. "Nonsense. It was his nature. His mates in the taverns had become his tribe."

"They needed him on the other side," Pine offered.

"Exactly," Conawago said with a vigorous nod, and they all went silent.

"Jacob Book!" Duncan abruptly shouted, his own hands lifted toward the sky. "Hear me now! My name is Duncan of Clan McCallum and brother of the Iroquois! I make two vows to you, here before the gods. I will find your killer and see he pays the price. And this, too, I say. I shall take your friend Conawago to the northern waters, and we shall find the woman who sings the whales. She shall know that you have reached the other side, and she will teach us a mourning song to share with the leviathans."

Conawago gazed at Duncan, surprise and joy lighting his countenance. "You would do this for an old man?"

"I will do it for my father, a chieftain of the Nipmuc tribe. I have always wanted to see the great bay called Fundy. I will swim with the whales and speak to them of their old friend Jacob. And," he added, "they will take word to their king in their faraway kingdom that Conawago of the Nipmuc pays his respects."

Conawago's eyes filled with moisture. He gave Duncan a solemn nod, then reached for a worn leather carrying bag sitting beside him. From it he extracted a linen sailor's smock. As Pine laid on another bough, he waved the smock in the smoke, then dropped it into the flames. Next came a tattered pair of moccasins, a handkerchief, and a threadbare pair of the loose trousers worn by sailors, each of which he raised and washed in the smoke before dropping it into the fire. Book would need his belongings on the other side.

As Conawago reached deeper into the bag, Duncan extended his hand. "Please," he said. "Jacob died in this world." The Nipmuc somehow understood and handed the pack to Duncan as Pine tended the fire.

Duncan examined each of the remaining items before handing them to Conawago for the fire. First was a wooden sailor's spike, used for loosening knots, next a leather lanyard that held a beaver carved of wood, and then a pair of woolen socks, some of their holes darned not with yarn but with twine.

The necklace he extracted had a look of great age. Some of the beads were of copper, others of red and blue glass, all arranged on either side of four small fish carved of bone. The lowest pendant on it was a small, tarnished silver cross. Conawago leaned closer. He pointed to the copper, saying, "Huron," then to the glass beads, declaring, "French fur traders," then to the fish, saying, "Cree." Finally he came to the cross, gazing at it with a sad smile. "Jesuit," he said with a twist of emotion. It dated from the long-ago days when French missionaries roamed the northern forests, changing the lives of young tribesmen with a grand and futile vision of a new world to be gained by a Jesuit education.

"I think," Duncan suggested, "that we shall take this north. Give it as a present from Jacob to the whales."

Conawago gave another solemn nod, then took the necklace and draped it around his own neck.

Next came a well-used belt knife, its handle of old ivory, probably a walrus tusk, carved into the likeness of a bear's head. Conawago hefted it, examining it with great curiosity, then raised it to the sky, cocking his head as if listening. He did not drop it into the fire but instead extended it to Pine. "Book says use it in a noble cause," he declared.

The last item was a small, worn leather pouch, once adorned with leaping fish in elegant quillwork, now in tatters. Duncan emptied it into his palm. The contents included several half crowns and shillings, adding up to nearly five pounds sterling. It represented three or four months' wages at sea. He handed the coins to Conawago, who did not examine them and only passed them to Pine.

Left in Duncan's hand were three unfamiliar bronze coins. One side of each was adorned with a broad arrow, the sign used for the king's property. On the other was an anchor. With a chill he read the words inscribed around the edge: His Majesty's Royal Navy. They were Book's pay tokens.

Duncan had surrendered Conawago, still unsteady, to Moll and Esther, when Josiah burst through the kitchen door. "It's Miss Sarah! Miss Sarah and so many soldiers!" Duncan was out the door in an instant.

He followed the slow, steady rhythm of an army drummer, the cadence used to warn civilians away during a military task. Onlookers had begun to gather along Fore Street, some lifting stones as they angrily watched the infantrymen who had marched to the derelict house with the tattered red flag. Duncan slowed as he spotted Sarah, standing on a small knoll that gave her an elevated view over the crowd. Four other women crowded around her, those at her sides each gripping an arm as though to restrain her.

The last smallpox epidemic had subsided years earlier, but no one ever ventured near the house. The entire family inside had died and their bodies decayed until, weeks later, an intrepid John Glover had led a squad of militiamen, splashed with vinegar, to bring out the remains. A rumor persisted that there had been bodies in the cellar that had never been recovered because the stairs had rotted away.

Whether because of ghosts, hideous remains, or lingering contagion, the citizens of Marblehead gave the house a wide berth. When the moon was full, neighbors insisted they could hear moaning and muffled screams from the building. A rite of passage for adolescent boys was to venture onto the portico long enough to recite the Lord's Prayer. Even the infantry who now approached did so with obvious trepidation, eyes cast downward as if trying to ignore the officer who chastised them. He snapped at a young private, who carried an axe instead of a Brown Bess on his shoulder, ordering the soldier to attack the weather-beaten door.

Duncan stepped to Sarah's side as the door splintered and the officer disappeared inside, then shouted for his men to follow. He was about to ask why she seemed so upset, but one of the women, a sturdy mariner who had sailed with

Sarah, elbowed him aside with a resentful expression. He stayed close enough to study the storm of emotion on his fiancée's countenance. Fear flickered on her face, then anger and dismay, all melting into obvious despair as the soldiers reappeared, lugging a large, cumbersome object covered by a sailcloth. As they set it on the ground, the officer threw off the cloth and a gasp of surprise rippled through the crowd. The polished wooden frame had a large wheel mounted at one side and several spindles arranged in a row along the front. The ghost house had been protecting one of London's new spinning jennies.

Duncan watched in confusion as the lieutenant ordered soldiers to pour their powder flasks upon the loom, and others to break apart nearby bales of straw to scatter over the machine. Then the officer blew the primer from his pistol and, holding it close, cocked and pulled the trigger. The powder caught and in moments, to the cheers of the soldiers, the machine was engulfed in flames.

Chapter 6

THE MILITIA OF MARBLEHEAD HAD been formed decades earlier during the bloody wars with the tribes, when raiding parties visited death and destruction on many Massachusetts communities. Over the years it evolved into something akin to a fraternal association, and its current membership even included half a dozen men of the very tribes that generations earlier had wreaked havoc on the colony. Since the arrival of the occupation troops in 1768, however, the militia began taking itself more seriously and, under the leadership of John Glover and like-minded officers, was receiving lessons on warfare and staging practice drills, although many of its members carried shovel or axe handles instead of muskets. At Glover's request, Duncan had joined as resident ranger, a role that chiefly consisted of recounting tales of wilderness fighting at the militia's periodic assemblies.

The position did afford Duncan a degree of influence. When he suggested that a night maneuver might be prudent, Glover readily accepted, having listened with rapt attention, then amusement, as Duncan described the foray he had in mind. Enthusiasm among the corps followed. Duncan and ten others, including all the tribesmen, would simulate a raiding party, which the remaining militia members would pursue through town. If successfully tracked to their unnamed destination, a keg of the Triple Fish's best hard cider would be waiting at the militia hall as their reward.

"No striking of blows," came Glover's gravelly voice as they prepared for the chase, "and no swearing."

Dressed the part, Duncan led his men with loud whoops, joined even by the quiet Unitarian corporal who had volunteered for a tribesman role. They burst out of the militia yard and ran down alleys and streets, hollering all the time, pausing only long enough for Duncan to use the smoldering slow match he carried to ignite previously positioned buckets of tar meant to symbolize burning houses. When the pursuers grew near, Duncan gave hand signals to Pine. The Oneida faded into the shadows with the corporal. Duncan was still close enough to hear the curses as the rope Pine and the corporal stretched ankle high across the alley behind them tripped the front-runners, causing many behind to stumble onto them.

Pine's whoop of joy confirmed their success. The Oneida and the corporal appeared out of the shadows, and Duncan turned his band down another alley. After half an hour of sprinting across pastures, vaulting over fences, snaking back through the town's alleys, and lighting half a dozen more prearranged tar buckets, they arrived at a substantial shed alongside a cow pasture where one of the ship-wrights racked his wood to season before using it in his yard.

Duncan quieted his band. Pine faded into the shadows, circling the structure, then reappeared on the other side of the doors and nodded. Duncan lit the bucket of tar by the shed's double entrance doors and unfastened the latch. With a groan, they swung inward a few inches. Duncan motioned his men into the shadows of a nearby spruce.

Moments later the band of pursuing militia arrived, breathless but exalted that they had cornered their quarry in the shed. Captain Glover let one of his ensigns lead the victorious capture.

"We have you, you heathens!" the ensign announced in a loud, authoritative voice that reflected his work as part of the town watch. "Lay down your arms and accept your fate!" One of the men beside him noticed a pile of unlit torches conveniently left by the entry. He lit one from the burning tar and ventured into the building.

"Halt in the name of—" The ensign's words died away.

"Halt in the name of King George, damn your eyes!" countered an angry voice from the shadows. Two men appeared, both aiming bayoneted muskets at the militiamen, more of whom poured into the building with lit torches. Duncan found Yates, who had been brought with the main body of militia, and clamped his hand around the informer's arm. He stayed in the middle of the throng as John Glover pushed through.

"State your business here!" Glover demanded, unsheathing his sword. "And be not so careless with your firearms before the soldiers of this town!"

"Soldiers?" one of the men with a musket muttered in surprise.

"The militia of Marblehead. And by Jehovah, lower that weapon before I run you through for the brigand you are! Little better than sneak thieves in the night!" Glover motioned his men forward. Two appeared at his side, their own muskets leveled at the strangers. "Tidesmen!" Glover spat as the torches lit a line of opened crates that obviously were in the process of being searched.

The men with the bayonets lowered their weapons. One turned toward the deeper shadows, his open overcoat revealing a scarlet uniform underneath. "Sir?"

Duncan heard a muttered curse. Yates cocked an ear, nodded at Duncan, then lowered his head as if worried about being recognized.

"No writ of assistance will protect you!" the ensign barked. "By God, you've crossed the line!" he declared with outrage.

Two more men with muskets were shoved out of the darkness by the militia-men. "Lieutenant?" one of them asked toward the shadows.

"Do not pretend to be excused as soldiers!" Glover hissed. "It is against army rules and the morals of honest men to skulk about with coats hiding your uniform! If you are not on the business of the customs, which would be illegal enough, then you are but common thieves!" As he spoke, two of his biggest men seized the figure lurking in the shadows, dragging him to Glover, who was clearly enjoying the little drama he and Duncan had arranged by feeding false information to Yates. "State your business, sir!"

The man did not speak. He twisted his head away when a lantern was held up to his face. The militiamen at his side roughly forced him into the light. The pockmarks on his thin, nearly gaunt face were clearly visible.

"Lieutenant Vaughn of the Horse Guards, I believe," Duncan announced. "Are you aware, Lieutenant, that the Horse Guards have no mandate in this town?"

"The Horse Guards have a mandate wherever the king's business takes us!" Vaughn hissed.

"Sergeant," Glover called over his shoulder, and the throng of militia parted to admit a man carrying a bulging burlap sack. "We look forward to learning more about a mandate that excuses you from the laws of decent men. But first, sir, you shall learn that the people of Marblehead shall not be treated so shabbily, be it by you or the king. Ever hear of a Marblehead robe?"

Their captive's eyes flared, and he fixed Duncan with a malevolent glare. "You!" he growled. "You are the one who frightened my landlady!"

"Jacob Book had friends among the militia," Glover continued, "who have questions for you about his untimely death."

The lieutenant went very still. His lips curled into something like a snarl.

The confusion on the faces of their other prisoners changed to fear as another militiaman appeared with the bucket of hot tar, its flames now extinguished, a ladle hanging on its side. Glover dipped the ladle in the bucket and then, holding it high for all to see its pungent contents, emptied it back into the bucket. He kicked the sack and feathers flew out of it. "In Boston they would strip you bare first, but here we let you stay clothed if you wish, although we will have those overcoats off."

As Glover bent to fill the ladle again, Vaughn went limp, becoming a deadweight to those holding him. As he collapsed onto the floor, Duncan leapt forward and jerked Glover back. An instant later Vaughn was up, flinging his cloak over the two men who held him. He swung a long thin blade at Glover. The dagger missed Glover's neck by a hair. Vaughn grabbed the open sack of feathers and flung it into the air, then shoved one of his own soldiers into the militia ranks. The militiamen were distracted by the cloud of feathers long enough for their prisoner to slip through them.

Duncan struggled against the press of bodies, but in the moment it took him to reach the doorway, Vaughn advanced a dozen steps and was about to lose himself in the shadows. A shape hurtled out of the darkness and crashed into him. Pine seemed to have the upper hand as the two wrestled, but as Duncan darted to his side, the stiletto gleamed in the moonlight and sliced into Pine's arm. As the Oneida clamped a hand around the wound, the spy rolled away and sprang to his feet. He was at the tree line when he staggered. Book's ivory-hilted knife, thrown by Pine, was embedded in his shoulder. Vaughn turned with a thin laugh, removed the knife, and with surprising accuracy hurled it at Duncan, who threw himself on the ground to avoid the blade. He quickly regained his feet, though not quickly enough. The provocateur from London was gone.

———

"Gone, Duncan, gone these three days past." Pollard, Hancock's man in Marblehead, had investigated the identity of the fair-haired girl who had swooned over a young soldier of the Twenty-Ninth Regiment. The task proved quite easy, Pollard reported, for her neighborhood was abuzz with talk of her scandalous behavior. With her father at sea and her mother caring for two younger boys, the girl had repeatedly used the excuse of running errands to walk along the waterfront with the off-duty infantryman, sometimes even waiting outside a tavern for him to bring ale out for them to share. "The very morning those lobsterbacks marched away, her mother sent her off in a northbound coach to stay with her aunt in Portsmouth. Elsewise her ma suspected she would steal away on one of the boats taking supplies to the army. Ah," Pollard said after a moment, "it just rends the heart, don't it?"

Duncan followed his gaze toward a limping woman leading a file of three children, two young boys and an adolescent girl. It was Amanda, the injured nightingale out with her family. The children's clothing was little more than rags.

"They walk along the wharves when the night traps are brought up, hoping to catch some of the little crabs and periwinkles that drop out. God knows it's a despairing task to make a meal of such, but the Brewster family be down on its luck, a hair's breadth from the workhouse. Her husband's in debt and about to lose his boat."

He watched the forlorn file, wondering if he should at least check Amanda's injuries, until Pollard touched his arm. A new drama was unfolding on the dock below where they stood. Soldiers in stiff dress uniforms were marching out of their waterfront barracks on a course for the militiamen arranged in a square around four cowed prisoners. Following the altercation, Duncan had taken Pine back to their house to treat his wound. He hadn't had time to seek out Glover for a report but now needed none.

The tar and feathers brought to the ambush scene had clearly been used, although sparingly. The soldiers had been stripped of their overcoats, and each wore a broad band of feathers down the back of their uniform waistcoats, affixed by a heavy streak of tar. Each, too, had a patch of feathers on the crowns of their heads, stuck with a dollop of tar, and one hand covered with tar, with feathers made fast so it seemed each had a feathery paw. They had shamed themselves and their uniforms.

Duncan studied the crowd gathering by the square of militiamen, searching for the lean, pocked face of Lieutenant Vaughn. Not finding him, he ventured closer to the militiamen and saw now how they were struggling to restrain grins, if not outright laughter. Their amusement only increased as John Glover appeared in his dress militia uniform. They were making a pageant out of the army's embarrassment, and the town was clearly enjoying the spectacle.

"My father says to let you know we interviewed each of them at the armory," came a low voice at Duncan's side. "All proper, with our magistrate in his robe and all," the voice added, referring to the judge whom Glover had appointed as his adjutant. He turned to see a youth in his late teens in the uniform of a militia corporal, one of Glover's sons. "The magistrate informed them they were being charged with trespass and burglary unless they could explain why they were in that shed, hiding their uniforms and wielding military weapons while engaged in an illegal search on private property. They were right eager to tell the truth, especially after my father ordered more tar to be set to boil over a fire.

"Seems like they knew little, only that the officer named Vaughn is from a grand palace in London and sometimes offers a half crown apiece for special tasks on behalf of the king hisself. Although he comes in and out of the barracks at all hours, he seems to have quarters elsewhere, and he warns them not to use his name, though we already had it. Once, to make his point, he produced his long dagger, and in a blur of motion skewered a rat walking ten paces away. No one had his Christian name, and no one knew what mission he was on, except that he secretly watched people and had infuriated their Lieutenant Hicks by frustrating his capture of deserters, and he sometimes gave sealed letters to be delivered to a tavern in Boston." The young militia corporal glanced over Duncan's shoulder. "Here we go. Should be a grand entertainment."

The soldiers from the barracks stood at attention twenty paces from the militia square, which now parted to allow the prisoners to egress in single file to hoots and guffaws from the townspeople. The infantry responded with their own taunts, prompting their officer to angrily order silence. The night before, while Duncan and his companions were busy seizing Vaughn, the watch broke up a melee started by local citizens throwing snowballs and rotten vegetables at soldiers on patrol. Duncan learned the news from Josiah. The boy had slipped out of the house with his new friend Crispus, who became the hero of the skirmish by pelting the soldiers with the most snowballs, finishing with an egg smashed against the forehead of an infantryman.

Now, to his surprise, the soldiers' rank split in two, half escorting their four befeathered comrades back to the barracks and the remainder pivoting to march down the long town wharf. The sleek cutter *Neptune* had entered the harbor.

Glover discharged his men, who patted each other on the back before dispersing. Several paused to shake Duncan's hand, thanking him for the most entertaining night in months. Their commander, removing his sword belt and laying it over his shoulder, added his own gratitude and promised that his men would be on the lookout for the wounded provocateur. "And Yates," he added in a lower voice, "is due to be put on a boat bound for Newfoundland at tomorrow's ebb. Gone three months and lucky he didn't get a Marblehead robe before—" His words died away as he gazed toward the dock where the cutter was mooring. Three officers in elegant gold-trimmed uniforms were saluted as they descended the gangplank. Glover muttered a seaman's curse. "Lord, we're about to be blinded by gold lace," he declared as he buckled his sword belt back around his waist. Lieutenant Colonel Dalrymple, commander of His Majesty's land forces in the colony, had arrived in Marblehead. "Think he has authority to court-martial me?" Glover quipped, then turned and whistled, bringing back several of his dispersing militiamen.

The colonel's frown was evident from a hundred feet away. He spoke with the officer commanding his local escort, who seemed to sputter some reply, then nervously saluted as he retreated from the colonel, stepping backward before marching his men, double time, back to the barracks, followed by the colonel's two aides.

Dalrymple, left standing alone, turned and approached Glover with a stern expression. His face lifted as he recognized Duncan, and he offered a sober nod.

"Sir," Dalrymple said in a restrained voice to Glover, then saluted him. Glover awkwardly returned the salute. "Can I take it you command these Yank—" Dalrymple caught himself. *Yankee-Doodles* was the disparaging term most redcoats used for the militia. "The community troops?"

Glover grinned. "Aye, sir, 'tis my honor to command this company of Marblehead warriors."

"Then prithee, accept my apology. I was at breakfast when a courier reached me with news of last night's difficulties. No one under my command was authorized to engage in such conduct, I assure you. Although you went too far, sir," the colonel chastised, "in applying tar to men in the king's uniform." When Glover offered no reply, the colonel turned to Duncan, pushing the scowl from his countenance. "At least you are readily at hand, Doctor." He extended his hand. Duncan accepted it, wondering if it would be more prudent to flee. "I am indebted to you, sir. The supply boat delivered your report on Sergeant Briggs's demise. A rare but sudden reaction, you said, to an ingredient inadvertently used in his food, attributable to the substitutions caused by the flour shortage. Death by misfortune. Poor man. As you so aptly wrote, an indirect victim of the colony's food deficits. As a sign of good faith, I have directed the quartermaster to deliver two dozen barrels of good wheat flour to the town dock—perhaps the militia can distribute it?"

The colonel's gaze lingered on the ghost house, where a pile of ashes marked the end of the smuggled spinning jenny. He sighed. "At least your certification of accidental death lets us put it behind us. The Twenty-Ninth has had its share of calamity these past months. It's one of the reasons I decided to come today, to be sure we eliminate opportunities for more. There are too many uncertainties in unfamiliar seaports."

"Sir?" Duncan asked.

"I have recalled my troops from Marblehead. In fact, no more army patrols for navy runaways. The navy can send marines if they wish, but no more of my lads." As he spoke, soldiers began streaming out of the barracks carrying knapsacks and trunks.

"There is such a thing as rule of law, McCallum," the colonel declared as he watched the retreat.

Duncan straightened, preparing to be admonished.

"I could tell you were an honorable man at the Castle, especially from the way you stayed with the sergeant until he passed despite your pressing business. As I'm sure the militia commander is," he added with a nod to Glover. "We may have our differences with certain noisome citizens of Boston, but we all acknowledge standards of fair play and decency."

"Fair play?" Glover echoed, turning it into a query.

"Yes, well. Damn it, I suppose a full confession is in order. Those men were not on an official mission last night."

"They were commanded by an officer, sir," Glover pointed out. "A Lieutenant Vaughn of the Horse Guards."

The report brought not surprise but worry to Dalrymple's face. He gestured Duncan and Glover away from the bystanders. "You are mistaken, sir. There are no Horse Guards deployed in America." His expression became stern. "Do you understand?"

Duncan and Glover exchanged a glance. "We understand," Duncan said, "that he is not officially here. Just as the militia did not officially tar and feather your soldiers."

The colonel frowned, then slowly nodded. When he spoke again, it was in a whisper. "Not my officer. Not under my command. Not even acknowledged to me. Not a bloody word! Acting as though my infantry is at his beck and call!" He hesitated, seeming to sense he had gone too far.

"A secret officer then," Glover said in a wry tone, "who pays bounty silver to soldiers as if they were private mercenaries."

Dalrymple winced. "Bounty." He spat the word like a curse. "It's the other reason I came. I could not officially transmit a message. But I feel beholden and deemed a warning to be my duty. A schooner with the name *Indigo Queen* arrived from Charleston last week. Captain Lawford intercepted it, since it was weaving among the islands in a most suspicious way. It was brought to the Castle on suspicion of smuggling. Its master was furious, saying he was on official business of the governor. I asked what governor. 'Why, the honorable governor of the most important of all British colonies,' he says, 'and old friend of the king.' Barbados, of course. In search of eight runaways."

The words were like ice on Duncan's spine.

"I fear they are here for bounty as well, and you may well encounter them before long. I discovered that after leaving Castle William, they took a berth at the Long Wharf and have spent much of their time at the Custom House reviewing records, bribing tidesmen, and checking the names and ports of call for the ships that left Barbados the night of that mass escape reported in the papers. I am afraid it means they will soon be here. I fear I am switching out one source of trouble for Marblehead just to let in another. I am powerless to stop it. I don't want the army to be blamed."

"I don't follow your drift, Colonel," Glover admitted.

"Bounties. These men claim to be from Charleston, but they have authority from the governor of the colony that accounts for the greatest revenue to the Crown. They have warrants and bounty contracts funded by some very rich, very angry plantation owners who brook no escapes. Slaves may flee, but they are always found by one bounty hunter or another and returned broken, bloody, or dead. Now they know where those five ships landed. Some tidesman entered Marblehead as the first port of call for a recent Hancock vessel. Port of call, but with no cargo listed as unloaded or received."

"We be not fond of slavery in this town," Glover observed. "Nor of bounty men."

"I share your sentiments. But the law protects them. And one of those furious plantation owners is the governor himself, which might complicate affairs."

"Not complicated for us," Glover declared. "If they make trouble in our town, my militia knows how to split their heads."

A flicker of a smile passed across Dalrymple's face. "Duly warned is duly armed," the colonel said and turned as a soldier approached carrying an object wrapped in sailcloth. Dalrymple directed him to set it on a nearby crate. "For you, Dr. McCallum. A token of my gratitude for the town physician of Marblehead."

Duncan and Glover exchanged a glance but neither corrected the colonel, who now unwrapped the cloth.

The small mahogany chest showed signs of use, but its elegant workmanship was readily apparent. Duncan's heart leapt as the colonel opened the hinged lid. "A regimental medical chest. We had an extra in stores."

"Sir!" Duncan gasped in genuine surprise as he leaned over the chest, one side of which held finely worked scalpels, clamps, scissors, and saws fixed in cleverly fashioned mountings, the other side two compartments holding medicine flasks and bottles. It rivaled the chest he had left in Edentown over a year earlier, a chest he dearly missed. "I am stunned. You are far too generous, Colonel."

"Nonsense. And well deserved. Never once did you ask for payment for your services. A gentleman of honor. His Majesty's army salutes you. For what you did for Sergeant Briggs and, I understand, for Lieutenant Hicks."

Duncan, who had carefully not shared all the truths he knew about the two deaths, felt a flush of guilt. "It will be put to good use, I assure you, sir. And Colonel," he added, straightening, "prithee, you spoke of other mishaps suffered by the Twenty-Ninth. Might I ask of them?"

Dalrymple chewed on the question a moment, then shrugged. "I don't know much, since I was not in direct command. But I did happen to be in Halifax at the time. The regiment has a company of dragoons, not deployed here. An officer died in a terrible fire. Their barn burned one winter night. A dozen mounts perished and a lieutenant, who was quite devoted to his horses." He gathered his thoughts for several heartbeats. "I recall there were allegations but nothing proven. An accident caused by an overturned lantern, probably carried by the officer himself and kicked over by a horse. That was the verdict of the inquest."

"Allegations?"

"There was a claim that the barn doors were barred from the outside. But that was just the confused recollection of the man who first arrived at the scene, then ran for help. By the time anyone else arrived, the building had collapsed. And there was some suggestion that the lieutenant had been bound to a post but, again, no real evidence. There was burnt cordage by his remains, but it could have been a coil that dropped from a peg overhead. Terrible accident." The colonel sighed. "The army prefers accidents." He put his fingers to his temple. "Good day, gentlemen."

Glover stayed at Duncan's side until the colonel had reboarded the cutter.

"You need to be sure they are all gone," Duncan said. "No soldiers quietly left behind. No wounded officer of the Horse Guards lurking in the shadows."

"I was of the same mind. And it wouldn't hurt if I called for militia muster twice a week for a while. Perhaps I'll send out a couple corporals on scouting practice, looking for a traveler with a wounded shoulder. And in case our man lingers in hiding, it occurs to me we might send a couple of Sarah's nightingales on a visit to a certain widow," he added with a meaningful gaze. "A neighborly call during which they can spy out any bloody bandages or fresh cheroots."

Duncan grinned, then motioned toward the physician's chest. "Can you see this delivered to my house, John?" He wanted to check the storeroom that Vaughn and Yates used and perhaps watch the widow's home himself for an hour.

Glover confirmed he would, then restrained Duncan with a hand as he stepped away. He extracted a folded set of papers. "As you asked," he said. Then he added with a slight grin, "My wife has the better hand. She thanks you for the opportunity to help and asks how many more you might need. Shall I tell her seven?"

Duncan's pace grew slower the closer he got to the yellow house as he weighed whether to tell the runaways about the bounty hunters. They would not believe him and probably suspect he was setting a trap for them as Cuff had warned.

The dreadful possibilities gnawed at him as he climbed the hill: The runaways had been discovered and arrested. The runaways had fled and were now being led by the vengeful Cuff. The runaways had divided and fled separately, each becoming a new risk for the others and those who helped them. Perhaps the hunters from Charleston had found one and tortured him to reveal the name of the person who arranged their escape. He recalled John Adams's tale of a do-gooder, seeking to help a runaway, who went to Jamaica only to be enslaved himself.

In confirmation of his worst fears, as he reached the big yellow house someone behind it screamed. He unsheathed his knife and with the fury of a Mohawk warrior sprang around the corner. He froze.

Pine and the boy Josiah were squared off against Cuff, all three raising heavy forked sticks with what seemed murderous intent. Pine seemed to be dancing aimlessly, shifting left and right, back and forth. He whispered something to Josiah, who darted toward the trees at the back of the yard, waving his stick in the air. The boy's high-pitched laughter was what Duncan had taken for a scream.

The tall Oneida suddenly noticed him. He straightened and held his stick high as if to show Duncan. It was cut from a branch nearly five feet long and ended in a fork, into which a small lattice of twine was woven. Duncan saw now that all the sticks were similar, and that the basket on Pine's held a wad of leather bound up with waxed sailmaker's thread to approximate a ball. They were playing *attsihkwa'e*, the Iroquois game of lacrosse.

They were all grinning at him now, and he realized he still held his knife. He sheathed it, gave a wave to the players, and climbed the kitchen steps. He paused to look back at the yard. It was the first time he had seen Pine and Cuff smile.

His new medicine chest was on the kitchen table, some of its contents laid out beside it.

"Oh, Mr. McCallum," Moll said, "one of the young militiamen brought this. It's fine, so fine! I'm just wiping the dust for you." With a linen towel she was cleaning a small, sealed bottle. The glass containers were indeed caked with dust.

"I was looking for—" He hesitated. "Is everyone here?" he asked awkwardly.

"Everyone?" Moll asked. "They were, I guess. Esther and Henri are in the cellar. But two of Miss Sarah's new friends hopped onto Mr. Boyle's stink wagon when he passed by."

Duncan did a mental tally. Blue Turtle had departed for the Hudson Valley two days earlier. If Solomon and Tobias were with Boyle, all the remaining runaways were accounted for. "And Miss Sarah?"

"Gone these two hours and more. Gave those two over to Mr. Boyle and hurried off to the harbor. My sense was that she aimed to catch the Hancock boat on its afternoon run to Boston, said don't hold supper since she couldn't predict the wind. And your friend Mr. Attucks, when I told him a few minutes later, he shot off like a hound after a fox."

Duncan smiled. After the brawny seaman arrived from Boston, Duncan tasked him with keeping Sarah safe, and he had jumped back on a boat to Boston to do so. "Keep him from the rum," Hancock had advised, "and you'll not find a more steadfast worker. Too close to the rum and he'll be shouting his contempt for the lobsterbacks, which can be a dangerous thing these days."

Duncan proceeded to the cellar, where he found Henri sleeping and for the first time without a fever. Esther sat beside him, sewing a patch onto a shirt that already appeared to bear more patches than original cloth.

"I don't recollect when he has had such a long and peaceful sleep," she said in a low voice. "They drove him so hard in the sugar fields. His best friend at the plantation was from my own tribe in Guinea. Jonko was smaller than Henri and often had the bloody flux, which kept him weak. But if you didn't make your quota in the cane fields, the overseer put you in the mill, where they made men push the grinding stones when the wind faded. S'posed to be work for the mules, but they used it as a punishment. If they decided to keep you in the mill, you'd be dead in weeks. So Henri always worked harder when Jonko was sickly, so as he could make his quota and Jonko's, too."

Duncan was scared to ask the question. "Did Jonko get away?"

"Last year. He made it to Cuba, but those cursed bonemen caught up with him."

"Bonemen?"

"What folks in the Indies call the slave catchers, because of what they say of them they catch. Instead of three strong men, they'll say they got three bags of bones for sale, or a cargo of bones to be returned to their owners. They caught Jonko and brought him back with so many broken bones he was no good for work. So the overseer hanged him as an example to the others. Henri was so furious he vowed to 'scape just to find them bounty men and kill them. But I said, 'Ye can't, 'cause ye got a wife and son. Jonko be dead but Josiah and me ain't. We gotta keep going, gotta keep hoping.'"

Duncan lightly laid a finger on Henri's pulse and nodded his approval. "Between rest and the bark, we may be able to keep the fevers away. If you come up, I'll show you and Moll how to mix the cinchona into Moll's herb tea and leave you some in case I'm not here. Twice a day, until I say otherwise."

Suddenly there was pleading in Esther's voice. "Please don't."

"Don't?"

"Please don't go off. If Miss Sarah's gone, then who's to guard us? Miss Moll is a fine, good-hearted soul, but she don't move too fast. I have nightmares. Last night it was Henri being hanged from the yard of a ship. Night before he was having his eye cut out with one of the sharpened spoons those wicked bonemen keep. They do that. The owners don't pay if an arm or leg is maimed, but one eye, that's okay. It's how those hunters quiet their captives. Cut out an eye. Cut out a tongue. Cut off a breast. Cut a man's stones. I've seen it all. All the same to them hunters, they still get their silver."

"Abi-sh-ii?" Pine asked, stumbling over the syllables of the first word on the papers Duncan handed him. His reading skills were rudimentary, and Duncan had to admit the name was a difficult one.

"Abishai," Duncan confirmed. He, too, had questioned the name when Glover handed him the papers. "Mrs. Glover, Captain Glover's wife, prepared the papers. She deeply embraces her Bible. She heard you were a warrior and she exclaimed, 'Abishai, the great warrior of the Holy Book!' Apparently he killed a giant." They reached a fork in the track they were taking. He motioned Pine to continue on the path that led over a wooden knoll.

Pine slowly nodded. "A giant," he repeated with a nod. "Abishai Pine," he added, proudly pronouncing his new identity.

"You have been a resident of Marblehead for two years, as attested by John Glover, officer of the militia and captain of ships. His wife threw in a receipt for a set of clothes she made for you last year."

Pine halted. "Where are those clothes? How did she know they would fit?"

"She didn't actually make the clothes. Just a white lie."

Pine gave a confused shake of his head. "One of those lies of whites."

"It's a fiction, Pine. A tale told to make it seem you were never a slave."

Pine chewed on his words, then halted and rolled up his sleeve to expose the large *S* branded on his forearm. "That says otherwise."

"So until we get to Edentown keep your sleeve down, Abishai," Duncan said, then pointed him toward the grove of trees. A thin column of smoke was rising from the far side. "Now let's go see how your friends are faring."

Fortunately the compound was built on a finger of land that jutted out toward the Salem channel so that the sea breeze dispersed its stench. People in Marblehead sometimes referred to it as Boyle's "works," but all Duncan could see as they crested the knoll was a series of long, rundown buildings that had seen long service as fish-drying sheds in a distant decade. The only structures Duncan would have trusted in a high wind were a sturdy-looking cottage built near a ramshackle wharf and a small stable by a paddock that housed not only the swaybacked nag that pulled the collector's wagon but also a surprisingly sound-looking riding horse, now being brushed by Tobias.

Despite the breeze, the fetor hit them at the bottom of the hill. They could hear Tobias's laugh as Pine's hand shot to his nose. "Go speak with him," Duncan said when Pine returned the man's wave. "Find out what arrangements have been made for them here."

Pine hesitated. "Not my business."

"If they are taken, they will be tortured to give up the rest of you. You are only safe if they are safe."

Pine clearly didn't like the answer. He made a rumbling sound but lowered his hand and stepped toward the paddock.

Duncan did not try to hide but stayed in shadows where he could, studying the compound more closely as he approached the cottage, trying to convince himself that the runaways were not at risk. If Sarah trusted Boyle to watch over them, she was better acquainted with the man than he had thought. He found himself gazing back in the direction of town. She had been despondent at first over the loss of the spinning jenny, but gradually the gloom in her eyes had shifted to something like defiance. Was there another thread of Sarah's mysteries here in Boyle's works?

A long row of barrels filled with waste stood ripening in one of the old fish sheds, so many barrels that Duncan wondered how Boyle could afford them all.

Perhaps his tannery customers supplied them, or perhaps some were left from the days when the dried and salted fish had been packed at the sheds. The long iron troughs that probably once held salt brine were filled with a brown ooze that Duncan had no interest in examining more closely.

He paused in the shadow of the fish house closest to the water as he spotted Boyle. The Irishman wore a soiled leather apron and was stirring one of his odorous barrels with a long wooden paddle. A hound lying at his feet leapt up with a bark as Duncan stepped into the sunlight but then wagged his tail as Duncan knelt and let the dog sniff him.

"My ferocious guard dog," Boyle declared with a grin as he wiped his hands on his apron, "is only fierce in her affection." The Irishman cocked his head at Duncan. "You're from Miss Ramsey's household."

"I am," Duncan confirmed. "Wanted to see how your new workers fare."

"Tobias on the horses, Solomon is working the kettles. Any work is noble if done with noble intent," he added as if anticipating a sharp reply.

"Kettles?"

"My raw material contains much water. More valuable and easier to transport if some of that is boiled off. Lighten the load, get more shillings." The breeze shifted, momentarily washing them with a stench that left Duncan feeling nauseous. Boyle grinned as he saw Duncan grimace. "My very raw material. Ain't for the weak belly, eh lad?" Duncan hesitated, wondering about the very articulate way Boyle had started speaking, then seemed to catch himself, making his language more coarse. The Irishman had somewhat refined features, but his clothes were stained, his hands calloused. Duncan flushed, realizing he had been staring at Boyle.

"Ye be wondering how a man gits in this trade, like most I meet. Spent all my funds on my passage across from Cork. It was either that or earn passage by indenturing myself for seven years, and I am too old and ornery for that. So I started in a new profession, ye might say, one that I had encountered in some English towns. A sanitary improvement for the community. No competition. And in what other business do people pay ye to take the raw material and others pay ye for taking the product ye make from it?"

Someone called Boyle's name, and Duncan saw a man standing on the wharf near a vessel tied close to the steep bank, one of the small flat-bottomed barges used on the rivers to bring cargo to the seaports. It was heaped with charcoal, no doubt for the fires under Boyle's kettles. He studied the Irishman again, trying to understand what about his grizzled countenance struck him as odd. His eyes burned with a strange intensity and for a moment flashed with challenge. Duncan's gaze fixed on his forehead. Boyle had no eyebrows, only black smudges to simulate brows.

The man on the wharf lifted a basket with a questioning gesture, and Boyle pointed toward the column of smoke behind one of the sheds. The man waved, then jumped on the barge and began filling the basket.

"I shall happily escort you to your friends," Boyle offered. "I am aware of their special status, and I assure you the authorities assiduously avoid my little kingdom."

Duncan hesitated. The refinement had slipped back into Boyle's words. He decided to test the Irishman further. "I can never recall, is it the ammonia or the sulfur in the waste that makes the smell so offensive?"

Boyle seemed to welcome the question. "Not much sulfur, not enough. The human body is a veritable chemical factory. Entire industries could be based on its discharges if only—" Boyle shot a glance at Duncan, then collected himself, like an actor who had slipped out of character. "That is to say, 'tis nothing but manure and piss. And the stench protects us as good as a castle wall."

Boyle was making a clumsy attempt to disguise himself. It seemed likely to Duncan that Boyle had after all sold himself into bond, then walked away from his new indenture. Runaway slaves were taking refuge with a runaway bond servant. The bounty men would have a field day, and a rich payoff, if they ever breached the wall of stench.

As Boyle led him toward the stable, Duncan saw that Tobias was now working on the old cart horse, with Pine nowhere in sight. He surveyed the empty stalls. "I thought there would be more," he observed.

"More?" Boyle asked.

"Surely the tanneries take several barrels at a time. A heavy load, too much for these horses."

"Ah. Yes, well. They send their own wagons. And some goes out by barge up the river."

"Tobias," Duncan called out, bringing the former slave out from behind the mare he was brushing. "Miss Ramsey departed without leaving instructions," he said in a friendly tone. "If you are staying here shall we bring bedding, and perhaps some provisions?"

"Nay, nay," Boyle interrupted. "We can manage. I will gladly provide for men with strong backs and weak noses."

Duncan kept his gaze on Tobias, who remained silent, offering only a stiff nod.

When Duncan did not break off, the runaway finally spoke. "Mr. Boyle says the fragrance is our shield. And in the evening he says we can fish off the pier."

Boyle laughed and gave the ex-slave a good-natured pat on the back. As he did so, the hound began barking from somewhere. Boyle stepped out into the open, surveying the grounds, then muttered a curse and without another word sprinted toward the pebble beach, where Pine could be seen disappearing behind a knoll at the tip of the peninsula.

As Tobias resumed brushing the mare, whispering to it in what Duncan took to be his tribal tongue, Duncan wandered toward the little cottage by the water. He lifted the latch and stepped inside.

It took a moment for his eyes to adjust to the darkness. A log smoldered in an ample hearth. On a table beneath the only window a basin stood beside an upright cask with a tap that emptied into the basin. A pipe fashioned of tin extended out of the top of the cask and disappeared into the roof. He was looking at a clever invention, a catchment system to provide running water.

The mantle over the hearth was lined with books of diverse titles, ranging from novels of Defoe, Swift, Richardson, and Fielding to scholarly tomes of Napier, Newton, Harvey, and Linnaeus. The rough-plank table in the center of the room held a pewter plate in need of washing, matching one that lay on the floor, and a dozen more books. Duncan glanced at the door, not daring to linger much longer. He perused the open volume beside the plate and its passage on preparation of potassium salts, then turned to its title page. *The Sceptical Chymist*, authored by Robert Boyle and published in the last century. *Boyle.*

Two small alcoves covered by sailcloth hanging from ceiling beams flanked a disheveled cot. The first held clothing, some of it of fine wool and linen. The second sailcloth released a pungent, fetid odor when he pushed it back. The shelves behind it held jars of what appeared to be decaying excrement.

As he turned to leave, he saw writing on the overhead lintel. Not writing, he realized as he studied it in the dim light, but symbols inscribed with chalk. Or rather one symbol repeated a dozen times, a circle bifurcated down the center with a vertical line. He surveyed the bizarre chamber once more before slipping outside and recalled a term used by one of his Edinburgh professors who taught about the nervous system and mental diseases, including those in which patients shifted between different personalities. Most of the terms were euphemisms. Boyle suffered from what his professor called an overactive mind.

Once outside, he stole back along the shadows of the former fish sheds and was about to emerge onto the path that led off the peninsula, when the whistle of a wood thrush stopped him. Pine was waiting for him in the shadow of the shed nearest the trees.

"You eluded him," Duncan said.

The Oneida simply nodded but then gestured Duncan inside. Owing to a missing section of roof, the interior was well lit. Scattered about the intact part of the shed were dozens of nearly identical slabs of old roof shakes, some propped on the side beams, many others just tossed onto the dirt floor. *127/39*, he read on one, *42/17* on another. Every piece of wood had an inscription, all in the same format, two or three digits, a slash, then two more digits. Some were made in ink, some in tar, others in various mixtures of what he guessed to be lantern black, shoe polish, and paint. All also bore symbols, combinations of circles, squares, triangles, and other geometric shapes above or alongside the numerals.

They didn't speak until they were in the trees, watching Boyle pace back and forth along the top of the knoll by the water, sometimes striking his head with his palm, sometimes raising a palm to shield his eyes as he surveyed the landscape.

"What was it that he didn't want you to see beyond that hill?" Duncan asked.

"Nothing," Pine replied, though his tone was uncertain. "A garden. At least garden beds, raised beds with old planks for sides," he explained and pointed to a shed with two walls stripped to the beams. "Packed with straw and the"—the Oneida searched for a word—"droppings."

"Excrement," Duncan said.

Pine nodded. "But all mixed up, cooked maybe, like a thick stew poured on the straw." He paused as if remembering something. "On the sugar plantations, sometimes they make us—made us—dig out the privies and spread it on the gardens. This Boyle is a poor man. He must grow his own food. Soon he'll be planting there. A gardener."

Duncan was not sure what to call the Irishman to whom Sarah had entrusted two of the runaways. A gardener, perhaps, but also a chemist, a scholar, an inventor, a dung collector, a man with secret compulsive behaviors. He was indeed a man with an overactive mind. Only once had Duncan's professor used another term for the diagnosis. A *lunatic.*

Duncan began sleeping in short spurts, as if he were camped in enemy territory, and yielded to his instincts by walking the grounds during his unpredictable bouts of wakefulness. That night, in the very small hours, he was descending the stairs when he heard whispering and an unexpected smell of singed meat. He advanced to the kitchen on feathered feet and discovered Pine, Henri, and Cuff sitting on the floor in a semicircle around the glowing coals of the hearth. Pine, sensing him, threw up a hand in a ranger signal. *Retreat.* The three men were passing around a red-hot poker, grimacing as they seared the flesh on their forearms. They were burning away their *S* brands, the marks of slavery.

Chapter 7

DUNCAN ENTERED THE THREE CODS in search of John Glover but halted at the sound of a familiar bass voice. The big mulatto was calling out an order to Winifred, who stood inside the corner counter where refreshments were served out.

"No," Duncan corrected. "No more rum punch. Two ales."

Crispus's eyes flashed and he seemed about to protest, then saw who had spoken. "Duncan! Jist rinsing the salt off my tongue."

"Back from Boston so soon," Duncan observed as he guided Crispus toward a quiet table in the corner.

"There and back, quick as a shag bird. Wonder it don't make my head spin."

Duncan, looking at the pewter cup in Crispus's hand, suspected that his companion's head was already spinning. The tavern's rum punch was always served in such cups. Crispus sheepishly set down the cup and pushed it away.

"Miss Sarah?" Duncan asked.

"Safe as houses. Got her back up the hill, and didn't she tell me I should take some leisure, kind soul that she is." Crispus seemed to reconsider his words. "Until I found you, of course, and could make my report. 'Twas just a quick visit to two shops and back off to Hancock Wharf, where we had seen the packet loading."

With danger lurking about them, Sarah had abruptly traveled to Boston, where Major Hastings was laying sinister plans. "What shops?"

"First there was a haberdasher, where she invited me in and asked if I think you would look good in—" Crispus caught himself. "She asked me inside and I waited in a chair by the door," he corrected.

"What did she buy?"

Crispus's brow creased. "Couldn't say. She told me how you and she are getting hitched and such, is all."

"At the second shop?"

"A little place behind Brattle Square, all covered with vines so as I couldn't see inside, and she instructed me to keep watch on the street. Then out with two parcels, tied tight and each placed in an oilskin bag like we use at sea. 'Get it wet,' she said, 'and we'll find ourselves in Hades.'" Crispus shrugged at the nonsensical words, then saw that Duncan was looking at his pewter cup again. "Not my coin, sir," he added as if in apology.

"A stranger bought you a drink?"

"And nigh every soul here." Crispus indicated a well-dressed man at a table by the bar, engaged in energetic conversation with several mariners. "Got an enterprise up New Hampshire way. Looking for strong backs. Logs and such. I told him he'd have better luck in Boston, more men looking for a quick way out of town."

"I don't follow," Duncan said as Winifred arrived with two tankards.

"Spread the word that ye be paying good coin, and infantry deserters will show up. Soldiers are walking away every week, dozens since the troops arrived, folks say. The provosts done executed one but it don't seem to matter. New Hampshire's safe, close enough to reach in a day or two, and plenty of women looking to marry. Last time the army went seeking deserters in New Hampshire, they got chased out by the militia. A man's got a right to choose his freedom, they say up there."

Crispus took a long swallow of ale and wiped his mouth on his sleeve. "Then he says surely there are stout lads who get weary of the sea, or their wives get weary of being without them for months at a time. So he thought he might find a head or two here. He saw me and twisted my arm right hard. 'My dusky Hercules,' he called me, 'come make a new life in his forest primeval. Stay three years and I'll grant you forty acres of bottom land.' 'Don't waste yer breath,' I told 'im. 'The sea is my mistress.'"

"But you waited to say that until after you had his rum in your hand."

As Crispus grinned, a middle-aged mariner with a pipe clenched in his teeth gave a loud guffaw and hurried over to pound him on the back. "As I live and breathe, it's Michael!" he exclaimed. "Last I saw you, you were dancing in an Azores tavern!"

Duncan had almost forgotten that in most of his relationships Crispus used the name Michael Johnson, apparently to obscure something from his past. He inwardly smiled at the thought that, at the moment, John Glover's very proper, very pious wife was also creating names to deceive the authorities.

He rose and wandered toward the rear of the inn, looking for Gabriel, and was about to enter the kitchen when a hand closed around his shoulder.

"You look a well-considered gentleman," came a refined voice. "Prithee, be so kind as to allow me to stand you a punch." It was the gregarious visitor from New Hampshire. When Duncan hesitated, he upped his offer. "Shall we make it a whisky?" he amended and called out to Winifred.

As they settled into their chairs, the stranger began his introduction. "If you permit me, sir, my name is Jeremiah Melville. I am an investor in progress, you might say, for I am opening new supplies of timber for construction of fleets of ships and new abodes and churches for our burgeoning settlements. The colonies advance, sir, and we must advance with them."

The well-spoken man, a few years older than Duncan, had an aristocratic air and wore a green waistcoat faced with satin. He put Duncan in mind of the land hucksters who frequented Boston taverns, but they always offered tales of cheap frontier land, not free whisky.

Melville lowered his voice. "I heard that Marblehead breeds no-nonsense, hardworking men. But I must admit I am hard pressed to find takers of my generous offer. Surely, I tell them, the tasks of felling trees and building my new mill will be but child's play compared to working the Grand Banks, and so much safer. Whatever they are earning a month I will add ten shillings, and still the response is but tepid. I asked if there were charitable societies that might have note of those in need of livelihood, and one of the lads pointed to you and said, 'Mr. McCallum, he knows of such things.'"

Duncan shrugged. "The churches all have charitable committees," he warily offered. "And there's the Scots Charitable Society. They aid Scots coming out of bond, of which there are many." The steady stream of out-of-work Scots was a vestige of the Jacobite rebellions, when hundreds of Scottish prisoners were sent to bonded servitude in America to relieve overcrowded prisons.

Melville lifted his glass toward Duncan. "Promising news. God-fearing Scots such as yourself are a boon to any enterprise. Could you perhaps make an introduction?"

"I have no personal acquaintance there," Duncan lied. "But they are out of Boston, with rooms off of King Street, not difficult to find." He sipped at his whisky as he assessed his companion. "Tell me something, Mr. Melville, where is your tract of land located?"

"Far north in the Merrimack Valley, abutting the grand lake and the mountains."

"And you've had no trouble with the Senecas?"

Melville did not hesitate. "Thank the Lord, no, all peaceful. We gave them a mule packed with blankets and such, told them we will do it every year. And hand out tobacco. They do like their smoke, eh?"

"I'm curious," Duncan continued. "Have you signed up any at all in Marblehead? You will find our mariners a cautious crowd. And most carry debts with local merchants who would be alarmed to see them disappear into the wilderness."

Melville lifted his glass to Duncan again. "Thank you for your wisdom, sir. Tonight is just for making acquaintances, softening them up as it were. If a man expresses any interest, I hand him a plug of good Connecticut tobacco and ask him to find me here tomorrow. We are prepared to be generous, I assure them, with a signing bonus of one pound. Sterling, that is, not any of that flimsy Massachusetts paper. And," he added, query now in his voice, "we pay commission to those who steer a good man to us."

"Generous terms, I'm sure," Duncan said. He drained his dram and pushed back his chair.

Melville offered a genteel smile and extended a small bundle of tobacco. "Perhaps you might later think of some candidates for our adventure."

Duncan accepted the plug with a noncommittal nod. "Enjoy your stay in Marblehead, sir. Perhaps our paths will cross." He rose and lost himself behind the crowd by the bar, then caught the innkeeper's eye. They met in the shadow of the side room, currently unused.

"We caught Vaughn's trail," Gabriel reported. "Glover sent good lads to Salem, Lynn, and Ipswich, as well as the tollgate on the Boston road. Pine's blade did some damage. Your secret soldier wore his arm in a sling, looking to be in great pain, and paid handsomely for passage from Lynn to Boston this morning."

Duncan chewed on the report. The wounded man had not gone to Castle William for succor. "That gentleman buying rounds," he said.

"Melville?"

Duncan nodded. "Keep an eye out."

Gabriel winced. "You saying he might give the slip without making good?"

"I expect he has coin enough. It's only that the gentleman who boasts about his very large tract of timber in New Hampshire does not know that the Seneca lands are hundreds of miles to the west."

"I don't follow."

"I don't either. Just be wary, Gabriel."

The innkeeper shrugged. "As you say. But do you ask me as an innkeeper or as a militia officer?"

"Neither. I ask you as a brother in liberty."

The house was quiet when he returned. A steaming bowl, a spoon, and a small loaf waited at one end of the long kitchen table while Moll sat at the other, reading *The Boston Gazette*. He startled her, and as Cuff entered with an armful of firewood a moment later, he realized that the big African was whom she had expected.

"Pot's still on the fire," she declared and with an oddly urgent action rose to find Duncan a bowl. As she rose, she made a point of covering the paper with the dish towel lying beside her. He filled the bowl with the day's potage and took a chair near the end of the table, gesturing Cuff to the waiting meal. Cuff hesitated and seemed about to slip away, when Moll pointed him to the table, then poured each of them a mug of cider.

"Tell me something," Duncan asked the ex-slave as they began eating. "How long was your servitude in Barbados? Whose plantation?"

"Ain't yer concern."

Duncan took a spoonful of his supper before continuing. "It's just that I need to know why the governor of the colony is so intent on capturing you. He has issued notices with rich rewards for your return. More than I would have expected."

Cuff did not seem surprised. "The others were from a big sugar plantation up in St. Michael Parish. But Henri, Esther, Josiah, and me worked the governor's own fields." Cuff lowered his voice. "I was barracks hump."

"Hump?"

"He housed his slaves in a barracks abandoned long ago by the lobsterbacks. A hump is responsible for getting the others up and out to work and accounting for each at night. Still a slave, just easier work, usually, and a cup of rum on Sundays."

"For how long with the governor?"

"Nigh ten years. The governor had holdings in Jamaica. Eight years there in his tobacco fields. Brought me with him when he got his new appointment in Bridgetown. Seemed to think I would like the promotion. Still a slave, only worse, 'cause the overseers expected me to go rough on my friends. And when a man died from my barracks, it fell on me to dig the grave. Sometimes I dug a grave every week."

"Tobacco," Duncan said pointedly, then extracted the plug given to him by Melville. "Tell me what you make of that," he said and pushed it across the table.

Cuff lifted the plug with a suspicious air then held it under his nose. "West Indies," he declared in his solemn way, then touched it to his tongue and closed his eyes a moment as if to concentrate on the taste. "Jamaican," he confidently announced. "Probably one of the Blue Mountain plantations."

Duncan did not react. "And back to my first question. Why is the governor so upset?"

Cuff shrugged. "He pledged to the planters that he would stop all runaways." He looked down into his mug. "And he was grooming Esther to be one of his fancies," he added in a near whisper.

Another voice broke in. Moll, still at the hearth, had been listening. "Fancies?" she asked.

Cuff cast an embarrassed glance at her.

"An attractive female slave who carries herself well," Duncan explained. "May be put into stylish clothes to perform personal services for the lord of her manor."

Moll seemed genuinely confused. "Personal services?"

Cuff turned to her. "Upstairs services. Like a mare groomed and sent to the stallion."

Moll blushed and went quiet for several breaths. "Then of course they had to flee their oppressors," she declared with a defiant tone.

When they finished their cider, Cuff rose to go sleep by Pine in the stable. Both men claimed to prefer it over the small upstairs quarters given them by the landlady, but Duncan knew that Pine at least was doing so because he would rise every two or three hours to patrol the grounds, sometimes encountering Duncan. "We need to treat the house as a camp in enemy territory," Duncan had told him, and Pine had instantly understood.

As Cuff disappeared out the rear door, Moll hurried to the end of the table, gathered up the paper she had been reading, and stepped to the hearth. Duncan was instantly at her side, restraining her hand as she extended it toward the embers.

"Miss Sarah," Moll protested, "she said don't let you—"

Duncan pried the paper from her grip. "Good night, Moll," he said pointedly, then waited for her to leave before returning to the table.

A column on the front page was again devoted to the fire in Quincy. When a rain had finally cooled the embers enough for the site to be searched, a charred, misshapen body had been found. Duncan was well aware of how an intense fire would shrivel its human victims, often making it impossible to identify them. But, the paper reported, a blackened hand had tightly clutched, and preserved, a locket with miniatures of Bradford's wife and daughter. Despite Sarah's fervent hopes, Bradford had been at his warehouse when the provocateurs burned it.

Duncan and Crispus were on a Boston supply boat before dawn the next morning, which to their good fortune had a friend at the helm. The master agreed to swing close to Quincy and lend them his launch before turning into the dock at Castle William.

"Castle William?" Duncan asked in surprise.

"Aye, half my cargo is for the militia there, the rest bound for the Hancock Wharf. If you can make it back there in time, I'll be leaving on the afternoon ebb."

Duncan hesitated. "I don't follow. Why is there militia at the Castle?"

"Under the law the fortress belongs to the colony, with responsibility for its upkeep lying with the militias. A token detachment is still there, as a matter of form, ye might say. Standing watch, maintaining it as best they can. Some of the fort's guns actually belong to the province, so the lads have to mind them and be sure they get their proper allocation of powder. Before sixty-eight, there was always a full militia company there, with the towns alternating the service. And they will be there when the lobsterbacks depart, God willing. Meanwhile the poor lads suffer the presence of the king's infantry."

"Including Marblehead lads?"

"Aye, but not often. Mostly Boston boys, and those from the close-in towns." The skipper shifted and indicated a point of land. "Quincy," he declared, and barked out orders for his launch before turning back to Duncan and Crispus. "I ain't losing headway, boys, so you'll have to leap for it as we tow her alongside. And mind my brightwork."

There was no need to ask how to find the ruined warehouse. Threads of smoke still rose from the smoldering ruins by the waterfront. The merchant had been successful enough to own a ship and wharf and built his large warehouse alongside. Spectators were still lingering, pausing on the way toward the cluster of buildings that marked the town center, just two hundred paces away. Crispus seemed particularly moved by the ruins, wiping an eye as he walked along the charred remains. Duncan made small talk with onlookers, several of whom, he suspected, were there in the hope of finding something they might salvage out of the ruins. No one he spoke with had been well acquainted with the dead merchant, but then he noticed a man sitting on a set of granite steps that led into the ashes.

The stranger held his head in his hands and seemed to be in deep despair. His waistcoat and breeches were sotted with ash, as if he had been searching among the ruins. Duncan rested a foot on the side of the steps and surveyed the scene more closely, wondering what he might have sought. Only small sections of the brick walls survived, one with the *Death to Smugglers* epitaph in fading chalk. The light covering of snow had melted around the ruins. Apple trees planted along the front of the long warehouse were reduced to charred limbs, likely never to bear fruit again. Misshapen, blackened mounds of what may have been crates, barrels, and bales of cloth or skins rose among the ash. A scent of vinegar hung in the air, no doubt from barrels that burst in the heat. The charred skeletons of a wagon and a coach lay at the far end of the ruined warehouse.

He looked back at the road and tried to reconstruct the disastrous events. A wagon had arrived, bearing barrels of turpentine. Its escort knew exactly where to go and apparently what to look for. He spied a stake with a linen handkerchief tied to it, likely marking where the body was found.

"Ah, thank the Lord."

Duncan turned to find the man on the step looking at him.

"Sir?" Duncan asked.

"It's you. I didn't know what I should do. Such a tragic setback."

"Do I know you?"

"You're Duncan McCallum. The phantom, some call you. Master of secrets for the Sons."

Duncan retreated a step, looking about for signs of trouble.

"Prithee, sir! We've met! At a meeting in Philadelphia city with Mr. Mulligan."

"Mulligan? Hercules Mulligan?"

"Aye, sir. I am what he calls his confidential secretary, though he chuckles when he says it, him being nothing but a haberdasher and all. My name is Kipling. Archibald Kipling."

Mulligan, the Irishman with the unusual name, was a prominent tailor in New York, provider of elegant bespoke uniforms to high-ranking British officers and the secret leader of the Sons of Liberty on Manhattan Island. Duncan had a vague recollection of an aide sitting silently in the back of the chamber at his last meeting with Mulligan, over a year earlier. "What did we discuss at that meeting?" he asked, testing Kipling.

Kipling rose. He was slightly younger than Duncan and slight of build. He cast a wary eye about, as if for eavesdroppers. "Mr. Mulligan had information that day about expanded navy patrols seeking to stop the offloading of cargoes at night along the Delaware and up the Hudson and was helping with your arrangements for a secret cargo being dispatched to Mr. Franklin in London. Old bones, I recall someone saying, no doubt some kind of code."

Duncan released his grip on his knife and stepped closer. "State your business here, Kipling."

"To see Mr. Bradford, of course. Exchange confidential messages."

"Secrets from New York?"

"He was always very careful, said some secrets are worthy of being wrapped in other secrets. If he wasn't here I was to see his man, whom he trusted with his confidences." Kipling surveyed the ruins again and sighed. "Mr. Mulligan will be most distraught."

"His man," Duncan said. "His manager? His apprentice?"

Kipling hesitated. "I'm not entirely sure how to characterize Achilles. I met him only once, when I dined with the family last summer and he sat at Mr. Bradford's right hand. Mr. Bradford was very proud of him, raised him up after inheriting him, taught him to read and do numbers. He was a clerk but highly trusted."

Duncan hesitated. "Inherited him," he repeated. "You mean he was property."

"Well, yes, technically he was a slave, of African origin, but Mr. Bradford had no others, just felt an obligation to his father to keep him. He told me Achilles's parents died long ago, before the inheritance, and he was but a small boy with nowhere to go so Mr. Bradford took responsibility. Raised him, educated him, and on Sundays they'd sit beside each other in church. He's a genteel fellow and treated almost like a partner, with his own rooms here in that corner of the warehouse," Kipling explained, with a gesture toward crumbled beams that marked what had been interior walls. "Close to the water. Achilles told me he likes to lie on the wharf at night and gaze at the stars. Learning to sail, in the little coastal shallop the business uses for trade in the bay." Kipling cast another forlorn gaze over the ruins. "Apparently he wasn't abed when the accident struck."

"And Mrs. Bradford?" Duncan asked.

"Gone with her daughter and their dog. Neighbors say she packed up unexpectedly, left the morning before the fire. No one knows where to, but she does have relatives in Connecticut. She probably received an urgent summons to an ailing mother or such."

"Achilles would not have gone with her?"

"Folks say he was here, unloading the ship with Mr. Bradford the very morning before the conflagration. A runaway now, one of the neighbors suggested, though I find that hard to believe."

"What will you do now, Kipling?"

"Home, I suppose, to report the sad news. Five long days in coaches on bad roads for naught. Now five days back. My poor bones are already aching at the prospect."

Duncan studied the diminutive clerk. If he did secret work for Hercules Mulligan, one of Duncan's most steadfast allies in the Sons of Liberty, then he, too, must be trustworthy. "Or perhaps you could assist me, and if so I will find a berth on a boat to New York for you. A few days easy sail, if the weather holds."

Kipling's expression brightened. "At your service, sir."

"And I shall write a note to Mr. Mulligan. He needs to know this was no accident. There are secret enemies rising against us, calling upon the army for help. Bradford was murdered."

The color drained from Kipling's face, and he collapsed onto the steps. "Murdered!" he gasped. "Dear Lord. Is all lost then?" He stared, unseeing, into the ashes of the warehouse.

By the time Duncan paced once around the ruins and enlisted Crispus in a more specific search, Mulligan's aide had recovered sufficiently to listen to Duncan's plans. Moments later they spread out, Crispus to search the wreckage of the rooms where Achilles lived and Kipling to speak with passersby and the crew of the ship moored below about the missing man. "Say Bradford had a special bequest for Achilles," Duncan suggested, "and we want to be certain he receives it."

Duncan watched the two men step away to their tasks, then entered the expanse of ashes. He walked straight to the fluttering piece of linen, the killing ground. The Deathspeaker had work to do.

Duncan kept his eye on the smoldering ruins as he and Crispus rowed across the edge of the harbor toward Hancock Wharf. He had sensed an evil presence in the ashes and knew Crispus felt the same, for before they cast off the launch he had waded into the water and with near-violent motions scrubbed his face and arms with salt water.

Crispus muttered as he pulled his oar. At first Duncan thought it might be some rowing chant, but then the syllables grew louder.

"Lobsterback, lobsterback, be on your way. In a long black box if I have my say." It was a chant of the Boston waterfront, often heard on the streets near the taverns favored by mariners and laborers, though Duncan increasingly heard it shouted at the soldiers who patrolled Boston's streets. Kipling, sitting on the stern bench, looked about nervously as the words grew louder.

Crispus broke off the refrain and looked back at the threads of smoke. "Their souls to the devil!" he hissed. "Burning a man alive. We'll do for them right enough."

Duncan parsed the words for several strokes of his oar. "Are you saying you know soldiers were at the warehouse?" He had been careful not to share the rumors about soldiers in plain clothes being responsible for the fire.

The big mulatto took another stroke before replying. "Weren't going to speak of it, seeing how you sometimes have business with the army."

"In no measure am I beholden to the army, my friend. Speak plainly."

"Star boots is what folks call them. Grenadiers, the worst of a bad lot. Big brutes looking for trouble. Oxen in petticoats, the boys say to their backs."

"Star boots?"

"First time I saw the pattern was on the cheek of a shipmate lying in the gutter. The bastards just left him there, all bruised and broken. Sometimes they go out at night, looking for a fight." Crispus took a hand off his oar and stabbed out points in the air, in the shape of what might have been a pentagon. "Their boots have extra-heavy soles on account of the grenadiers' always getting rough duty in battle. Those in the Twenty-Ninth put hobnails on their soles, for better traction, and nail them in a star pattern. With every new snowfall you can see them stars all over town. That fire melted the snow around the warehouse, but the mud was full of them. No two stars are identical, since each man nails his own boots. At least five different pairs of boots I saw, maybe more."

It was Kipling who discovered the richest source of information, and Duncan suspected he regretted doing so. After canvassing those on the wharf and the moored ship, eliciting from nervous, untalkative witnesses confirmation only that the fire had been deliberately set, by a "handful" of men or up to a "score of toughs," a youth had approached with a report that Kipling deemed important enough for Duncan to hear firsthand.

Horace was a sturdy youth of perhaps twelve years and, in his words, "something of an apprentice" to Bradford, charged with errands and keeping the warehouse tidy. The fourth son of a Quincy mariner, he declared he knew his way around a ship, especially after having served as cabin boy on a run to the Indies the year before.

"I been teaching Mr. Achilles to sail in the shallop we use on the bay, and he's taking to it real fine, gonna be a supercargo on the next voyage. Mr. Bradford says

I'll have to look after Achilles's rooms while he's gone." The boy looked back at the ruins and his eyes filled with moisture. He was speaking of a future that had been snatched away.

"So you saw the fire, Horace?"

The boy looked down at the ground by his feet. "Like the gates of hell had opened." He pointed to two decrepit wagons sitting side by side a stone's throw away. "I seen the strangers pull up with a team of handsome mules, and I figured Mr. B. and Achilles would need help if a customer wanted goods loaded at such a late hour. But Mr. Bradford saw me running up and he warned me off. So I circled back and hid under the wagons. I heard the voices being raised. Mr. B., he's a good Christian who don't engage in sharp talk, but he did with those soldiers."

"How did you know it was soldiers?" Duncan asked.

"Why, it was all 'yes, sir,' and 'no, sir,' and 'double time' and 'damn your eyes, Private, for being so clumsy.' And the mules had the smell."

"An army smell?"

"I help with the stables down the road sometimes. The stock here eat a lot of salt hay, sometimes with dried seaweed thrown in. Gives 'em, and their droppings, a fishy smell. Army mules get good grain and hay. Ye can smell oats, not fish. Army mules they was, sure as stones."

Horace looked out over the ashes again. "'Leave this instant or I shall summon the watch!' Mr. B. shouted. The man in the cloak—he was the leader, their officer, I reckon—just laughed and slapped him, so hard he fell to his knees. Then the leader kicked him, real hard. They dragged him inside. I ran to the ship, 'cause I got friends there. But they wouldn't help. They were scared, said it wasn't our business. The second mate grabbed on to me and held me tight 'cause he knew I was fixing to run to help Mr. B. 'Leave my fingers, dear God, not my fingers!' Mr. B. cried. And soon after, the screams began. The mate said must be a cat caught in those flames, then he took me below and made me stay with him." Tears streamed down the boy's cheeks. "'Cepting we all knew it was no cat."

The anonymous shop off Brattle Square was locked when Duncan and Crispus arrived, but the apothecary's daughter cracked open the door when Duncan knocked. "No service until lunch is—" she began to announce, then brightened as she recognized Duncan. "Papa!" she called, turning, "'tis Mr. Duncan!" Moments later DeVries appeared, wiping his mouth with a napkin.

"It's but cheddar and cold ham with a rye loaf," he said, "but please join us." He cocked his head at Crispus and introduced himself. "Ah yes, you escorted Miss Ramsey on her last visit."

The adolescent girl straightened her dress, tied back her blond hair, and proudly took on the role of hostess, retrieving plates and cups and slicing ham and bread for the new arrivals. She took delight in serving out seconds to Crispus as Duncan and her father retreated into the workroom. Duncan bided his time, letting DeVries proudly show him a set of glass lenses newly arrived from Bruges before broaching his question.

"When Miss Ramsey was here, what was it you supplied her?"

DeVries paused for a moment, then stepped to a wooden box at the end of the workbench. "And a small batch of bark finally arrived from Peru, though I fear it is but last year's harvest."

Duncan let the Dutchman show him a new box of scalpels from Sweden before pressing. "Miss Ramsey?"

"Prithee, Duncan. The distaff gender will have their secrets. She swore me to confidentiality."

"She will soon be my wife."

"And I can't imagine a better match, for each of you. But she said most particularly not to speak with you about her purchase. Perhaps she plans a surprise for you?"

"She puts herself in danger, my friend, without always knowing the risk."

"Then the sooner you are wed and back on the frontier the better. She did say something about inviting me to a celebration in the Hancock gardens when the tulips bloom," DeVries added. "I arranged that shipment of bulbs to Mr. Hancock from a cousin back home. When I was a boy, I lived near fields where they raised the tulips. You should have seen the endless carpets of red, yellow, and purple! My world was ablaze with color every spring."

Duncan couldn't help but smile at his friend's awkward effort to change the subject. Knowing he would not be able to persuade DeVries to break his word to

Sarah, he looked about, wondering what could have been packed in the two large, heavy parcels wrapped in oilskin that Sarah carried out of the shop. As his gaze wandered, a clock in the shop struck two chimes.

"*Mijn God!* Is it so late?" DeVries exclaimed. "I'm afraid I have obligations elsewhere. Rounds to make." He went to his bench and began adding some bottles to a worn leather doctor's bag.

"Rounds?"

"The Common. The surgeon must shuttle back and forth to the Castle. So twice a week I fill in to administer doses and address minor injuries."

"The Common," Duncan repeated. "You mean the encampment of the Twenty-Ninth Regiment of Foot? Tell me, my friend, do you perhaps have a second bag?"

As a ranger during the French war Duncan once stole into a camp of enemy irregulars to assess their strength. He was confident enough in his language skills and knowledge of the woodland ways to have felt comfortable among the Abenaki and French militia. Climbing the hill with DeVries and Crispus toward the rows of tents, Duncan felt no such confidence. He was walking into the jaws of a beast that would consume him if it divined the truth about him, but here were at least some answers to the questions that plagued him.

They were nearly at the first line of tents when Duncan heard a whispered refrain from his brawny companion.

"Lobsterback, lobsterback, be on your way," Crispus murmured.

Crispus seemed genuinely confused when Duncan stared at him, then caught himself. "Was I singing the song? I did not will it. It's just what my tongue does when I see the bloodybacks."

Duncan slowed, letting DeVries pull ahead. "We are going into the lobsterbacks' lair, my friend. This is not some waterfront alley."

"Yes, sir. No, sir," Crispus replied as he eyed the infantry camp through the light snow that had begun to fall. "I shall hold my tongue." He mouthed the right words, but his eyes were smoldering. His hatred of the occupation troops ran deep.

The Twenty-Ninth had cleverly crafted an infirmary compound by erecting a canopy, and windbreaks, of sailcloth over a dozen smaller tents. The canvas did not banish the cold but did keep out the chill breeze and snow. DeVries led them to the rearmost area, partially walled off by hanging canvas, where patients and orderlies lingered around a small potbelly stove. Along the back wall at a camp desk an orderly opened a ledger that, Duncan suspected, was used to record the diagnosis and treatment of ailing soldiers. Beside the desk two oil lamps were suspended over a portable trestle table, no doubt used for examination and surgery.

A senior orderly reported that the typhus that had swept through the camp was quickly abating, after Castle William ordered the old privies to be covered and new ones opened, with lime spread on them daily. The regimental surgeon also wisely advised that the supply sergeants stop filling drinking water barrels from the millpond behind Beacon Hill.

The abatement of what the soldiers called camp fever seemed to have little impact on the business of the infirmary. The cots were full and the line for sick call long. As DeVries and Duncan finished administering doses to the walking patients, they divided up their examination of the bedridden, each of them taking one row of the tents that flanked the central aisle of the makeshift infirmary. Most patients had broken bones and cuts. When Duncan asked how the injuries had been incurred several soldiers simply recited "Sign of the Ship," "The Mermaid's Rest," and other names of taverns along the waterfront and King Street. One cited an alley near the Long Wharf. "Gave as good as we got," he said with a slight whistling sound, caused by a newly dislodged incisor.

One boyish-looking private thanked Duncan very politely. "It's an odd thing, ain't it, sir, how men just have to fight."

Duncan, perceiving that the young private had a hairline fracture of his ulna, did not look up as he tightly wrapped the forearm with a band of linen. "Odd?"

"Me and my brothers used to pick fights with soldiers back in Bristol, calling 'em names and flinging filth and snowballs and such. Now I'm in the king's uniform and get the filth thrown at me." He shrugged and indicated his injured arm. "But ye gotta protect yer mates. Those boys down by the docks are bullies, same as the scrubs of the rope walks, and the sarge says if we don't defend ourselves, the king will be shamed." He collected his thoughts and shook his head. "I wish we could just go fight the Frogs or Spaniards like proper soldiers do."

Duncan treated two more victims of waterfront skirmishes, learning that most of the civilian antagonists carried makeshift weapons. Many of them brought wouldering sticks, the rods used in the rope walks for twisting fibers, to use as clubs. The last man grinned as he saw Duncan. "'Tis me, sir, Corporal Rhys. From the Castle and Marblehead before." His expression grew more sober. "The vigils, sir."

Duncan recognized the careworn Welsh comrade of Sergeant Briggs who joined the vigil in Marblehead with Briggs, and then days later sang a mournful lullaby as he helplessly watched his old friend die. A grimace wiped Rhys's smile away, and Duncan saw the foot, elevated on rolled blankets, extending from under the bedding. "Gout," Duncan declared as he bent over the hugely swollen toe.

"Aye, comes and goes these past three years. Staying off it for a couple days usually does the trick."

"Congratulations. You have the rich man's disease."

Rhys laughed. "Robbie used to say that, 'cause I told 'im my father was the lord of the manor where my ma worked the kitchen. I never knew him."

"Most often it is triggered by sweet wines and rich foods. But some say too much ale will bring it on."

"Perish the thought, sir."

"I shall see if we can find some angelica root. It often eases the attack."

"Much obliged, sir."

Duncan glanced outside the canvas-walled compartment Rhys lay in. "You can thank me by answering a question or two."

The corporal shrugged. "I ain't got else to do, 'cept read the gospel left by the chaplain."

"The young woman who supplied those meat pies. Was she known as a cook?"

"Not at all. I recollect we went to one of those church suppers, and some of the women were laughing about how they had to keep her out of the kitchens. She was a sport about it, admitted she couldn't be trusted to toast bread. She was one of those who get by on their looks, if ye get my drift. She was clever enough, though. And those pies weren't the first delivery she brought us. I recall there had been apple fritters once, and a fine mince pie at Christmas."

Duncan pulled up a stool close by the cot. He extracted the small flask of whisky he carried and handed it to the corporal. "Good Scotch cures most everything," he said, then leaned closer. "You're saying someone else was doing the cooking."

Rhys took a swallow and gave a grateful nod. "Not like we cared. No need to pry, it was all good eating. Until those pasties," he added grimly.

"And after all, you were used to secrets."

"Sir?"

Duncan motioned for Rhys to take another swallow. "The Marblehead barracks knew Lieutenant Vaughn, who worked in shadows and took members of the Twenty-Ninth for special duties in the night. Like laying an ambush at the St. Michael's cemetery."

Rhys broke off his gaze. "Don't know about that."

"The whole town knows about the other ambush," Duncan suggested, "the one at the boatwright's shed. Vaughn shamed the whole garrison that night. He was wounded. Knife in the shoulder."

"Doubt anyone shed a tear," Rhys said, grimacing as he tried to move his foot. "Just a popinjay sneak thief, if you ask me. He had a uniform sure enough, but it was one of those fancy London uniforms, all lace and brocade. Horse Guards. The king's toy soldiers, some say. Sure, he found volunteers whenever he needed them. Half a crown or more for a night's work. Half a crown goes a long way in a tavern."

"What did your officers say about that? I doubt Lieutenant Hicks cared for it."

"Volunteers were always off duty. And coin passed the officers' palms, to look the other way. But Sergeant Briggs, he was worked up about it. Beneath the dignity of a king's soldier, he groused once to Vaughn. Next day his kit was moved while he was out on patrol, to a drafty garret in the top floor, with no stove or fireplace."

"Who did Vaughn get his orders from?" Duncan asked.

"Like I said, he was one of those London soldiers. One night a hard case did come over from Boston to meet Vaughn, ordered us out of the mess room so they could talk. A man in a lace collar and velvet waistcoat, wearing a cloak with sable trim."

"You mean a gentleman."

"Fine clothes don't make a fine man. Face thin as a blade. A slash of a scar through one eyebrow. If he were in the Twenty-Ninth, I'd say he was a grenadier officer, 'cause they be the cruelest bastards in a cruel company. The kind who'll give you the lash for looking at him the wrong way. Sir. Sorry, sir," Rhys said awkwardly, clearly now afraid he had been too loose with his words.

"Tell me, Corporal, did you know Captain Mallory?"

"Oh, sir, a real pity about him drowning, and him setting to get married to the pretty young widow with the bookshop. Sure, we all knew him, captain of our own company he was for several months, best we ever had. But then he was transferred, to shape up the grenadier company. Real hard cases. I don't know that he ever really got them under harness."

"Where do you suppose his belongings are?"

"Regimental quartermaster, sir. He takes the kits of all who die. If there be no next of kin, then the kit will be held for the Invalids Fund. They have auctions a couple times a year."

Duncan extracted a shilling and pressed it into Rhys's hand. "Find some vegetables to eat, Corporal. Ease off the ale. Simple fare, if you want to keep that toe from swelling again. A good infantryman has to keep his toes in working order. I'll ask the orderly to find you some angelica for the swelling." He rose. "And Corporal," he added, "stay away from the troubles on the waterfront when you're off duty."

DeVries was reluctant to join Duncan in visits to each of the company encampments, despite Duncan's reminder that most soldiers refrained from visiting the infirmary until their conditions impeded their duties. "I am but an apothecary," the Dutchman protested.

"With better knowledge of remedies than most physicians," Duncan rejoined. "And a better inventory of remedies. You well know most people see but small difference between the apothecary and the doctor. I wager half your customers come to you without ever consulting a physician."

DeVries finally agreed when Duncan reminded him the army would pay for all medicines he dispensed, and he summoned the orderly to accompany him, with the infirmary ledger for recording ailments and treatments. Crispus followed along, carrying Duncan's makeshift medical bag. They worked steadily through the camps of each company, dressing a few minor wounds, pulling splinters, prescribing pills and tonics, and speaking whenever they had a pliant patient about the company's experience with the camp fever.

The last camp, a stone's throw from the line of trees that set apart the Hancock estate at the top of the hill, was set farther apart from the others and had a crude gate constructed of bent saplings adorned with an odd assortment of objects. Several well-worn tricorn hats, two sickles, a scythe blade, a marlin spike, and several wouldering sticks and other clubs were jammed into the branches or fastened by twine. One of the clubs was carved with images of sailing ships flanking the words *Wilkes and Liberty*, the popular slogan of protesters in both London and Boston. The snow inside the gate was crisscrossed with star-shaped imprints.

"We know where the infirmary be," said a heavily built slab-faced man standing bare chested in the cold, shaving, as another soldier held a small mirror for him. He lowered his razor as he spotted Crispus, who stared balefully at the trophies on the gate.

"Ain't I seen you making trouble on the Long Wharf?" growled the grenadier.

"And ain't that my friend Eli's stick," Crispus snapped back, "who's laid up with a broken collarbone?" He lifted a hand toward the carved club.

The soldier held his razor out like a sword. "Touch that and ye'll lose yer hand!" he warned.

Crispus's eyes flashed. He was making ready a hot reply as Duncan darted to his side, pushing him back, out of the gateway. More soldiers were taking notice, appearing at the front of their tents.

"Bloodyback!" Crispus spat at the grenadier.

Duncan jerked his companion's arm, pulling him around to face him. "Get on the other side of those trees," he said in a low voice. "I have a more urgent need of you. Go report to John Hancock about what we found at Quincy. To him directly."

"But these are the very bastards!" Crispus protested. "Look at the snow!"

"Go. Now is not the time. Report to Hancock. I will meet you there shortly."

It took several breaths for Crispus to calm and grasp Duncan's words. He gave a reluctant nod and set off at a fast pace toward the mansion beyond the trees. It had been a mistake to bring him, Duncan knew now. He had not sufficiently understood the depth of Crispus's loathing for the soldiers, nor the hair trigger of his temper.

DeVries and the orderly were in the company headquarters tent at the center of the compound when he reached them, checking the ledger. Not one of the grenadiers responded to their sick call. At Duncan's prodding, the orderly stepped to the front of the tent and called out the names of recent fever survivors. "Hartigan,

Stirling, McCauley, Montgomery," the orderly announced. "Present yourselves or be reported to your commander." The bare-chested grenadier, still not donning his shirt despite the falling snow, approached and knocked his heels together. "Private Montgomery, Your Honor, sir!" he declared loudly. His mocking salute to the lowly orderly raised guffaws from his gathering comrades.

Thankfully DeVries maintained his steady demeanor, motioning Montgomery inside the tent. Duncan had heard the questions several times in the prior camps, and as DeVries asked how long it had been since the fever and rash subsided, Duncan paced about the large tent. On a table at the rear, by an unlit potbelly stove, sat an open ledger with the same printed caption on each page: Duty Roster. He glanced at it, scanning the listing of names arranged like a watch list for sailors at sea but recorded in six-hour divisions for patrol duty. He surveyed the tent, confirming that all eyes were elsewhere, and flipped the page to the night of the Quincy fire. Two of the former fever patients the orderly summoned were shown as on duty, but Montgomery and Stirling were not.

He wandered back toward DeVries and the orderly as the third man, McCauley, presented himself. He answered the questions with sullen mutters, confirming that he had burned all his bedding and that he had been free of fever for nearly a week. When DeVries dismissed him, he grumbled, "Don't need no townsfolk prying into army business."

The last man, Private Stirling, was a towering man with a wary but respectful demeanor, who kept his left hand inside his tunic as he answered the usual inquiries. He was the only one of the four to accept the blue pills for "head pain" that DeVries offered. As the apothecary finished, Duncan stepped closer.

"Let's have a look at that hand, Private," Duncan said in his best professional voice.

"It's doing fine, sir. No need for duty restrictions."

"All the same," Duncan pressed and glanced at the ledger book.

Stirling understood the message. If he was listed as infirm in the ledger he would not be permitted on patrols, nor permitted leave in the city. He frowned but removed his hand from his tunic and extended it. "An accident," he explained. "A burn."

The entire hand was wrapped in a band of soiled linen, tied at the wrist. Duncan gestured the soldier into a chair and silently removed the bandage. The hand was bright red and swollen, an ugly row of burst blisters across the knuckles.

"Surgeon laid on oil of witch hazel and said keep it clean," Stirling reported.

DeVries gave a sigh and began rummaging in his kit, producing a clean bandage and a small bottle of oil.

"How long since?" Duncan asked.

"Four or five nights ago," Stirling murmured.

Duncan did a quick calculation. Four nights ago the warehouse in Quincy had burned, with its owner. "It needs cleaning, fresh oil, and a new bandage," Duncan declared and turned to the orderly. "A basin of water," he instructed.

"I'll be fine," the private argued.

"If the flesh mortifies, Private Stirling, you could lose the appendage. How many one-handed grenadiers do you know?"

Stirling muttered something blasphemous but lowered the hand onto the lip of the basin the orderly brought.

"A little sulfur in the water would help," Duncan said to DeVries, who nodded.

"I imagine grenadiers are well acquainted with brimstone," the Dutchman quipped as he sprinkled yellow powder over the basin.

Stirling's resentment faded by the time Duncan sponged off his hand. Duncan made small talk as he worked, then paused as he lifted the witch hazel, glancing about as if for eavesdroppers. DeVries and the orderly were tending to a soldier who presented himself with a two-inch splinter in his forearm. "You need to be more careful with the turpentine next time, Private."

"That lesson's damned well learned," Stirling replied, then hesitated, cocking his head at Duncan.

"Seen this kind of burn before. Men in turpentine mills with lit pipes. And some are sloppy in the way they fill the barrels, leaving puddles on the top. Tell me where you loaded the barrels, and I can see to it they do the job proper next time."

"That old crust Simon by the—" Stirling caught himself. His gaze hardened, then Duncan, feigning absentmindedness, embarked on ruminations about grenadiers he had known in the last war. He knew the old crust Simon, whose warehouse was along the road to Quincy.

As Duncan finished tying the bandage, the orderly closed his ledger and with a suddenly nervous expression looked out of the tent. Men were scrambling, hastily adjusting their uniforms, and donning their bearskin caps.

"Some kind of surprise inspection," the orderly muttered as DeVries closed his bag. "Leave now out the back or we'll be here another hour or two." No one seemed to notice as they hurried out the rear of the camp. Duncan gave his thanks to DeVries and the orderly and excused himself.

Five minutes later he was graciously admitted to the Hancock mansion by a liveried servant and escorted into Hancock's study.

"I could make no sense of Crispus's report," Hancock said, "so I sent him into the kitchen. Where his whalelike appetite will no doubt impoverish me," he added with a grin. "Something about hobnails and stars and bloody-backed demons burning people."

"The Quincy fire," Duncan announced. "It was set by grenadiers of the Twenty-Ninth. I just confirmed it in their very camp."

Hancock stared at him, mouth agape. A loud curse came from the two over-stuffed chairs by the crackling hearth. Samuel Adams and his cousin John were listening.

Duncan barely finished explaining his discoveries about the fire when there was a disturbance at the front door. Hancock leaned into the window. "Dear God, Duncan, what have you done! It is Colonel Dalrymple himself, with a guard of some very coarse-looking soldiers."

Hancock hurried out of the room, mumbling in distress. Angry voices rose in the foyer and moments later an exasperated Hancock reappeared. "He is not here for me," he declared, fixing Duncan with an apologetic expression.

Dalrymple entered a moment later and wasted no time with greetings. He leveled an accusatory finger at Duncan. "You, sir, are appearing all too often in the middle of His Majesty's business! Now you seek to pry into military secrets! Interrogating my men! Examining army records without a by-your-leave! By God, you shall answer!" The colonel barked, his eyes ablaze. Two tall grenadiers appeared behind him, one holding a set of manacles.

"Colonel, prithee!" Hancock pleaded. "Mr. McCallum is a guest in my house. Surely we can speak as gentlemen here."

"Gentlemen be damned!" Dalrymple spat and gestured his grenadiers forward.

Duncan stood motionless, his heart hammering, seized by only one thought. What message could he leave for Sarah?

A low animal-like sound erupted from the direction of the kitchen. A third grenadier, standing guard, rushed forward to intercept Crispus, who was charging toward the colonel, a turkey leg raised as a weapon. The grenadier bent and threw his own massive bulk into Crispus's path, knocking him off-balance, then with a deft hook of his foot, jerked Crispus's legs out from under him. Crispus fell in a heap, his makeshift club flying through the air to land at Hancock's feet.

Duncan recognized the grenadier. It was Montgomery, the gruff soldier who exchanged taunts with Crispus at the encampment. With surprising speed, the grenadier planted his hobnailed boot on Crispus's chest and drew the sword bayonet from his belt. He jammed the point against Crispus's belly. "Shall I spit you now, little pig?" Montgomery sneered.

The unexpected violence caused Dalrymple to hesitate. John Adams stood and broke the stunned silence. "Prithee, Colonel, stand down and we shall give you what you need."

Dalrymple's temper had not cooled. "What I need, Mr. Adams, is irons on this damned traitor! He shall—"

Adams, uncharacteristically, interrupted. "What you need, sir, is the painful truth, which you force us to confess to you." He looked at Duncan and sighed. "Dr. McCallum, I fear, is indeed a clandestine observer. What you might call a secret agent."

Chapter 8

ONE OF THE GRENADIERS BESIDE Dalrymple gave a satisfied grunt at the confirmation of a traitor in their clutches. The other soldier took a step forward, extending the manacles.

The colonel stared at Adams for several breaths before speaking. "Stand down," he growled to his soldiers, then turned to Montgomery, who still hovered over Crispus with his bayonet. "Out. All of you." He fixed Duncan with a malevolent glare. Hancock, his face gone pale, closed the doors behind the soldiers. Crispus scrambled to his feet and disappeared into the kitchen.

"Spies hang," Dalrymple declared in a simmering voice. His hand tightened around the hilt of his sword.

John Adams stepped between the colonel and Duncan. "No, no, nothing like that, Colonel," he said, forcing a laugh. "Purely with the best of intentions." He caught Duncan's eye and gave a barely perceptible shake of his head, signaling Duncan to hold his tongue while the lawyer proceeded with his defense. "A secret Samaritan as it were, all in the interest of preserving the peace." He gestured the colonel toward the overstuffed chair he had vacated. "Prithee, bear with me." Adams turned toward Hancock. "Perhaps some of your excellent port, John?"

Dalrymple did not shift his gaze from Duncan. "I do not take my ease in the presence of a traitor, sir!" he snapped. "I trusted you, McCallum, damn your eyes! You took my gift!"

"Please," Adams implored as Hancock hurried from the sideboard with a nearly overflowing glass. Samuel for once stayed silent, clearly intrigued by the strange drama. Dalrymple frowned but lowered himself into the chair, still glaring at Duncan.

"Domestic tranquility," John Adams declared in his ever-steady voice. "The aspiration of all, citizen and soldier alike. But we are not blind to the discord in our streets. I need not remind you, Colonel, that the poor Seider boy was killed just last week and there are near riots by the rope walks nigh every day. And the populace is especially skittish over the fever that swept through the encampment on the Common. Mothers pull their children away at the first sight of a soldier. Innkeepers are scared to accept a soldier's coin for fear of the dread contagion. If it spreads into the city, what do you think our people will do? What will *you* do, Colonel, when innocent children start dying because of your encampment?"

Dalrymple broke off his gaze at the lawyer's words. "Innocent children, sir? I don't follow."

"The city selectmen and the provincial legislature are terrified of the consequences. Mr. Hancock can so attest as a member of both," Adams added with a glance at the merchant prince that was part warning, part encouragement. Grasping his cue, Hancock solemnly nodded. "If disease spreads, the army will be blamed," the lawyer continued. "Those who are already made restless by the troops will march on the encampment with torches, ready to burn it out. Your soldiers, many of whom seem restless for a fight, will defend themselves. It will be the end of civil order. Blood would run on the streets. So we had to act. And surely you understand, sir, that we could not simply ask the army to confirm that the fever had truly waned, for I fear not all the people trust the army's word. We needed independent confirmation. Secret confirmation, if you will, from a trusted voice, which presented quite a conundrum. Then we realized we were happily acquainted with a physician trained in Edinburgh who is also familiar with the military, indeed fought for the king in the last war."

Dalrymple took a sip of port. "But he spied. Interviewing my men under false pretenses. Prying into medical records. Secretly examining duty rosters, by God!"

"Did not your surgeon expressly request civilian assistance when he could not make his rounds? Did not Dr. McCallum provide the expected healing services?

What was false about a physician treating your sick? And how can a physician perform his duties without questioning his patients? I know the gentleman, sir. He pursues his responsibility to the ailing with great acuity."

Duncan's heart slowly stopped pounding. Adams was talking him off the gallows. "I am prepared, sir," Duncan said to the colonel, "to both praise the army's response to the fever and declare that its measures at sanitation saved civilian lives. I have no doubt the soldiers were none too happy about digging new privies and burning bedding in the winter weather, but their noble sacrifice will be noted."

The portly cousin finally spoke. "As clerk of the assembly," Samuel Adams declared with great gravity, "I shall see to it that the legislature's books so record." He rose to help himself at Hancock's sideboard.

Dalrymple frowned and stared into the fire before speaking. "Your man, your assistant, was badgering my troops."

"I sent him away the moment trouble began," Duncan stated. "And I also spoke with friends of Sergeant Briggs to assure there were no more signs of poisoning among them. I thought you would appreciate further assurance."

The colonel still spoke toward the fire. "General Gage sends frequent inquiries, first about the desertions from the Twenty-Ninth, now about the deaths." He sighed and looked up at Duncan. "I know you stayed with Briggs until the end. That was noble of you. I—I"—the colonel had trouble getting his words out—"I apologize, McCallum. Everyone is on edge these days."

"Accepted, sir," Duncan replied. "As Mr. Adams says, all of us aspire to domestic tranquility."

The colonel set his glass down. "I must gather my men."

"We so infrequently have the pleasure of your company, Colonel," Hancock inserted. "Prithee, pause with us. My kitchen is serving out brandied peaches as we speak. And we shall find some ginger cake and ale for your men as they wait outside." The merchant was inclined to be generous as long as the brutish grenadiers left his house.

They passed the time cordially enough as they consumed Hancock's delicacy, though Duncan was challenged to engage in affable conversation. More than once he paused at the window to study the grenadiers gathered at the foot of the marble steps. He knew for certain that one of their company had committed arson and murder in Quincy and suffered a burn for his role. The surly brute named Montgomery had also been off duty that night.

When Dalrymple finally marched away with his guards, his friends joined him at the window.

"The bastard," Samuel hissed. "Bradford was a good and worthy man. Death by fire, such horror."

"Death after being tortured. I did not share every detail of what I learned. If I had looked more thoroughly, I believe I would have found severed fingers." Samuel gasped. His cousin sank his head into his hands. "But I don't think Colonel Dalrymple knew," Duncan said. "The War Council does not trust its shadow deeds to officers of the line. No, those are reserved for ghosts from London, known only to the major general in New York, I suspect. Ghosts who will haunt all of Boston if we don't stop them soon."

"Gage," the corpulent Adams muttered. "Master of ghosts. The tyrant general who ordered the occupation of our fair city. His is the effigy we should be hanging from Boston trees. His is the contagion we should be most fearful of."

Crispus was uncharacteristically quiet as they walked back to the waterfront. Duncan suspected he had just overindulged in the Hancock kitchen until he finally spoke.

"You know ways, Duncan," Crispus said in a tight voice, "ways to go at them without the blood and thunder. That damned grenadier like to have kilt me. And there was naught I could do but lie there like a piece of meat on his dinner plate. If it's only gonna be about swords and muskets, the bullies like him will always win, 'cause they have the steel. You have ways, Duncan, to come at them quiet like. Teach me. I want to be one of 'em."

Duncan struggled to follow the drift of the words but was loath to disrupt his earnest sentiment. "One of them?"

"One of those freedom men. A fighter in the shadows, like you. Like my brother in London, and that little fella Kipling from New York town. Ye can't love liberty if ye ain't ready to fight for it."

"I thought you were headed back to sea."

"I put my mark on some papers for Carolina is all. But I can find 'em another man."

It takes a quieter demeanor than yours, he was tempted to say, but he heard the pleading behind Crispus's words. He had been deeply shamed by Montgomery, and Duncan sensed that shame was accelerating a transformation that had been building ever since Duncan told Crispus of his London brother. "It takes time," he said instead. "But every man has a role according to his particular talents. There are nights when we have secret voyages along the coast and the need for strong backs to unload boats at remote inlets. Your brother will be proud to hear that you, too, are a secret fighter."

"We could put that in the letter to him?" Crispus asked, referring to the letter he and Duncan started and restarted more than once, because the sailor kept changing the message, and because he was so self-conscious about communicating with his much-better-educated sibling.

"It shall be among our very first words," Duncan replied.

Crispus brightened and nodded pleasant greetings to several passersby hurrying through the dusk. "Let's wait till we find Mr. Bradford's killer, and don't mention today. I know I have a temper. I have to tamp it down. Today I made a fool of myself."

"What I saw at the Hancock house was a brave warrior taking on armed bullies."

Crispus gave a quiet laugh. "You would write that?"

"Of course. And there will be more courageous acts to come, I have no doubt."

Crispus's heart continued to rise. "Fair evening, ain't it ma'am," he cheerfully offered to a woman taking in brooms, baskets, and axe handles on display outside a hard goods shop. As they continued past the shop he broke into a quiet song, not one mocking lobsterbacks, for a change, but a softer ballad of a fisherman wooing a mermaid.

They continued in silence down the darkening street, Duncan lost in unspoken questions about the fate of the Quincy merchant and his slave. He suddenly realized he was alone, and the last two words urgently spoken by his companion reached his consciousness. "Port bow!"

It was a mariner's warning, about trouble ahead and to the left. Duncan slowed and managed to dodge the vicious blow of a club aimed at his head from an alley, deflecting it off his shoulder. A big man with a blackened face swung the club again as Duncan staggered. This time he succeeded. The club met Duncan's spine with such force that Duncan dropped to the packed snow in the alley. He threw up his arms to protect his head as the next blow came.

With a roar Crispus slammed into Duncan's assailant. The swing of the axe handle in his hand sent the man stumbling backward into a brick wall. Crispus knocked the club from the man's hand. Duncan began to rise, reaching for his knife, but then someone behind him kicked the blade from his hand. He spun about to face a second thug with a blackened face, this one wielding a bayonet like a sword. The first man was down, crumpled against the wall and barely conscious. He moaned and held the fingers of one hand, which Crispus had apparently crushed with his axe handle. From somewhere a woman shrieked, "Murder! Foul murder! Call the watch!"

The man with the bayonet grinned, as if he were aware that the sheepish men of the watch, even if on duty, were likely sitting in a cozy tavern somewhere. "Time to see the color of yer guts!" he cackled. "I wonder, can you mend your own sliced belly, Doctor?" He lunged toward Duncan but froze as a gunshot echoed down the alley.

"That," came a high-pitched voice, "was my first pistol." Duncan stepped aside to find Archibald Kipling with a pocket pistol in each hand. "I always load one without a bullet, for a warning shot, and the other with a double shot." He took a step forward, driving the second man deeper into the shadows. "Honestly I forget which one has the bullets," he confessed as he aimed the second pistol at the man's heart. "We can test your fortune or you can toss the blade."

The man cursed and dropped his weapon into the snow. He bent, grabbed his companion by the arm, and dragged him away.

"By Jehovah!" Crispus exclaimed as he pounded Kipling on the back. "Who would have thought this little golliwog had such spirit!"

Kipling grinned. "I've carried these pistols for a year and never drew them." The hand pointing the pistol was shaking, and he seemed unable to move it.

Duncan thrust his thumb under the hammer to prevent a discharge and pried the weapon away. "We are indebted, Kipling. Your boldness saved my life."

They took shelter in the noisy Sign of the Ship tavern at the base of the Long Wharf, with Crispus spending most of the first round of ale praising Kipling, calling him, to Kipling's obvious embarrassment, "the feistiest tomcat freedom fighter I ever did know."

"I have urgent news," Kipling said when he was able to get a word in. "It's why I went looking for you. I did as you asked, made inquiries in waterfront taverns. I found the room of the notorious Vaughn, empty but strewn with bloody linens! Upstairs. Top floor at the rear." Duncan forgot the pain in his shoulder. Tossing coins on the table, he gestured Kipling toward the stairs, then paused. "We must find Naomi, the innkeeper."

"No need," the enterprising clerk said, extracting a key from his pocket. "She already took a shilling for a quick chat and the loan of the key but warned she cannot predict when the occupants will return. Then she gave back the coin when I said, 'The Sons of Liberty thank you.'"

They paused in the landing long enough for Kipling to nervously recharge his pistol, which Duncan took as he shoved the door open. The room was still empty.

Kipling lit a candle from the room off a sconce in the hall and held it high as Duncan studied the scene before them. The bed was disheveled, with blood stains on its sheets and on the linens on the floor beside it. Pine's knife had indeed pierced deep if the wound was still oozing blood.

"When the innkeeper couldn't find him a ready doctor," Kipling reported, "the lieutenant went downstairs and asked if there was a sailmaker who would like to earn a quick half crown. Then he poured himself a stiff gin while an old salt sewed up the gash in his shoulder. A bad wound, they say, deep in the muscle. He was having trouble closing his fingers around his glass."

Vaughn had been crippled, at least temporarily, by the ivory-hilted blade of Jacob Book. "Occupants," Duncan said. "Naomi said *occupants*?"

"Another London gentleman comes sometimes."

"Search everything," Duncan instructed his companions.

Kipling and Crispus were surprisingly thorough, opening the drawers of the small chest, stripping the bed, lifting the mattress from its ropes, looking behind the pieces of framed needlepoint on the walls, even prying back a piece of loose baseboard trim. Crispus uncorked the bottle of gin by the bed, sniffed it with a longing expression, and, feeling Duncan's gaze, set it back without sampling its contents.

"The chimney," Duncan said as Crispus knelt at the hearth, testing for loose bricks.

"Nothing," his friend said as he stared up into the shadows. As he began to crawl out, Duncan handed him the candle and he looked again. With an exclamation of surprise Crispus reached up and produced a leather packet with a strap attached, a correspondence case. "Hanging from a nail by the flue," Crispus explained with a proud grin.

Inside the thin case were a dozen notes and letters in three different hands, two yellow ribbons, a pouch of snuff, and a small, well-used sharpening stone. Duncan tossed the letters and notes on the small table and gestured Kipling toward one of its two chairs.

"Reports on ships," Kipling explained as he scanned the first few notes. "Arrivals in Boston, Marblehead, Portsmouth, Salem, Ipswich, and Quincy, all over the past three months. All those from Britain underlined, those from the wine isles crossed out, but several from Barbados crossed out, then listed again, as if there were renewed interest."

After the shipping reports was a list captioned *Weavers* and another headed *Furnaces*. Kipling lowered his voice as he read aloud from a sheet of random notes: "Bradford warehouse, Quincy. New York messages." He glanced up with a worried expression, then read more: "Where does his boat go in the night? Back by sunrise each time, so within the bay, known to trade with weavers on the North Shore. Why guano?" Kipling looked at Duncan. "Guano? Isn't that bird droppings?" He read on in silence. His voice thickened as he spoke again. "Turpentine," he recited. "How many barrels? How many fit on an army wagon? Find grenadier who can handle a wagon team."

Duncan, at the other side of the table, had taken the letters. They were all short missives with no addressees, no covers at all, each in the same careful, squarish hand that put him in mind of a schoolboy's efforts. The first read like a merchant's order, or warehouse inventory: *Fourteen reels Bilbao, forty boxes snuff, ten indigo, four grindstones, twenty boxes pipes, ten of gloves, and whatever lead you can find.*

The second simply said, *I have reviewed requirements for the weaving factory you suggest and am pleased to report I am willing to accommodate it.*

Duncan spent more time reading, then rereading, the third. *Gage keeps eleven at Fort George, Black Thunder, steel for old ravens. At least six cannon and a dozen horsemen.*

The word *Goat* was inscribed in a different hand at the bottom left corner of each letter. At the right corners were apparent destinations or cities of the address-ees: Boston, Marblehead, and Portsmouth.

Duncan stuffed the second message in his waistcoat, then returned everything else to the packet and had Crispus return it to the chimney, then glanced at his watch. "They started night runs on the Salem coach on the first of the month. It leaves from the front of the tavern at the top of the hour. I will meet you on it." He paused for a moment seeing the uncertain expression on Kipling's face. "And we shall find you passage home from the northern shore," he assured the nervous little man who had rescued them.

Naomi, the well-fed, jocular proprietress of the inn, raised a rolling pin as if ready to evict Duncan from the kitchen when he entered, but upon recognizing him, her face lit up. "Dear boy," she exclaimed and threw her arms around him, the pin jabbing his ribs. "Still scrawny as a scarecrow!" They exchanged small talk before Duncan turned to the matter at hand. Naomi called to one of the scullery maids to bring a serving of fresh potpie and two mugs of winter ale, then pushed him to the table in the corner that served as her office.

"This man with the wound in his shoulder who uses the upstairs room," Duncan said. "What name did he give?"

"Names are cheap on the waterfront, and I nay press a customer when he pays for a month in advance." Nevertheless, she pulled a ledger book from the shelf over her desk. "Three weeks ago." She ran her finger down a column of guest registra-tions. "Mr. Abel Brown," she announced. "Though I put no faith in it from the start since I recall now he stumbled when I asked if that was Abel with an *L-E* or *E-L*. Last time I saw him he was in a bad way. A bit of a dandy in his attire, though this last visit not tending to his clothes. Blood drops on his fancy buff waistcoat. That first night he arrived he kept dropping coins in my hand. 'Quiet room over the alley with access to the back stairs,' he says with the first, then 'a bottle of Lon-don gin to be renewed as needed, clean linens every three or four days, and after supper your best girl.' 'I run no bawdy house, sire,' said I and returned the last coin. Stays here a couple nights a week, his friend sometimes on other nights."

"His friend?"

"Never heard a name. Often used those back stairs when he came. Always wearing a dark cloak with a rich fur collar, maybe sable or mink. Eyes like a hungry hawk. Makes ye think too bad that sword that pierced his brow didn't finish the job. Last time he was here he was waiting at a table and asked if I had seen Mr. Brown.

"'If you mean Mr. Brown wearing the waistcoat stained with little red drops, he be upstairs and in no shape to dine.' Then he snaps something quite blasphemous and stands, flinging his cloak over his arm. It reeked of smoke, and I offered to air it on the line outside, but he just snapped, 'Nosy hag,' and up the stairs he goes. Then five minutes later didn't the chambermaid come down all frightened, saying she had approached their room to tend their fire but didn't dare go in. She was sure murder was afoot, what with all the yelling and bloody linens tossed in the hall. But by the time I got upstairs, escorted by my stable hand with an iron crow, things had quieted. I waited a few minutes. A couple disturbing words, and then some laughter and clinking of glasses, so I retreated to my own business."

"What words?"

"Couldn't make out everything. 'So close and you failed!' says the older one. 'You're exposed! Are you still of use there?' Then Mr. Brown says, 'Those women have become a damned nuisance.' Then the first says, 'Bring me one and I'll make her talk. All I need is an hour and my Italian blade.'"

Naomi paused with a meaningful expression. "Then I couldn't make heads nor tails of them. Is they friend or is they foe? 'Cause the older one finally says, 'Avoid Gage's minions and forget sending anything to the George.' The only Gage I know of is the general whose boot rests on the neck of Boston, and George must be the king. Like maybe it meant send no taxes to the king?"

Duncan nodded but said nothing. General Gage's headquarters were at Fort George, on the New York Harbor. But the words made no sense. Surely not even Hastings would be so bold as to conspire against the major general.

"That was the end of it," Naomi concluded, "for two men with the luck of hard-luck mariners came up the back stairs, and we pretended to be tending the lamps and left."

Duncan chewed on the potpie and her words. He cast an appraising eye over the innkeeper as a cook approached for instructions on the morning meal. Naomi and Duncan had been cordial acquaintances for months. He knew she had met

Sarah while he was in London but always shied away from speaking of her. "The man with the cloak is a major sent from London to sniff out smugglers," he ventured. "The other is named Vaughn, his deputy. Provocateurs."

Naomi hesitated. "I'm not sure I follow."

"That smoke you smelled on his cloak was from the warehouse he burned in Quincy. He killed Mr. Bradford."

The usually talkative innkeeper uttered a low moan and stared into her mug.

"You should let Sarah know about the major. She's weary of warnings from me."

"Sarah. Oh, your fiancée. The auburn-haired beauty who turns every head when she calls at my establishment."

"You should let Sarah know," Duncan repeated. "Most of her nightingales are in Marblehead, but I think there are one or two in Boston who know her song. She needs to hear from one of her own."

Naomi cast a wary eye about the kitchen before giving a small, quick nod. "What would you have me do about my London guests?"

"Just keep a watchful eye. Someone is giving them letters and other secrets. They are using deserters as informers."

The innkeeper raised a hand for Duncan to pause and motioned for one of her young serving girls. "Do I recollect, Sally, that you recently served that haughty Englishman, the one with the slash through his brow?"

"Oh aye, ma'am," the teenaged girl replied, with a shy nod to Duncan, "and not the first time. Always trying to get his paws on me, the scrub."

"He entertained someone I recall."

Sally nodded. "A much more dignified gentleman, of African persuasion. He asked for claret but hardly sipped it. He seemed troubled, kept his head down most of the time. Like he was embarrassed to be with the Englishman."

"What did they speak of?" Naomi asked.

"Hard to say. Talked real low, almost in whispers. The gentleman had papers, I recall, papers he gave to the Englishman."

"Had you seen this gentleman before?" Duncan asked.

"Not that I recollect. He kept his overcoat on, though it was warm enough in here, but underneath I could see his yellow waistcoat. One of those drummers, I supposed."

"Drummers?"

"Of the Twenty-Ninth. All the drummers are Africans and they don't wear the scarlet, only special yellow uniforms. I've seen them parade on the Common. Right sharp they are."

Naomi gazed in confusion as Sally retreated, then shrugged.

Duncan took up his warning again. "Don't press closer. Take note of others who meet with him. Listen especially if they speak more of Gage."

"The tyrant Gage, you mean," Naomi muttered. "The oppressor Gage."

"The major general," Duncan reminded her, "whose word means life or death in these colonies."

The next morning Duncan found Conawago on a bench outside the Three Cods, smoking his pipe and chatting amiably with a youthful mulatto of perhaps twenty years, whom Duncan recalled recently seeing wandering along the Marblehead wharves. The old Nipmuc introduced his companion as "Hugo, the happiest Micmac Cajian I've ever known." Duncan's gaze lingered on his friend. Conawago was still careworn but greatly revived.

The slightly built Hugo acknowledged Duncan with an exaggerated bow of his head and a respectful *monsieur*. The fishing fleet was the source of many new faces and ethnicities, as crews were depleted and renewed in ports as far-flung as Spain, the wine isles, and Newfoundland.

Conawago's choice of words was, as often, rife with meaning. He meant Hugo was a child of the Acadian communities along the Bay of Fundy and its tributaries that were settled in the last century by French farmers, who quickly allied and intermarried with the native Micmac tribe. A happy descendant of that population was rare indeed, for after prevailing in the French war, the British government engaged in clearances of the rich farmlands, brutally dispersing their inhabitants to France, the Caribbean, and even Louisiana. Some escaped to engage in irregular warfare with the British for years, others to disguise themselves with new identities to settle on the Maine coast. Duncan had heard many tragic tales of the diaspora, and if Hugo was a "happy" Cajian it was because he would have been only a young boy at the time.

"Off a boat from St. John and looking to sign on to a long-haul adventure," Conawago added.

Hugo grinned. "Azores! They have volcanoes, mountains that get turned in-side out! Or maybe Valparaíso, where the whales are so thick you can walk across the harbor on their backs!"

Conawago gestured to a plate of fried bread on the bench beside him, and Duncan nodded toward the tavern door. "What do you suppose the kitchen is brewing instead of tea today?"

When Duncan returned with a mug of chicory coffee, Hugo was down by the water, helping an African scullery maid check one of the lobster pots that many waterfront households put out each night. It was early in the season, and the trap yielded only a few small crabs. Hugo upended them onto the planking, then bent to emulate them with a splayed-legs waddle, raising a hearty laugh from the girl.

"John Glover," Conawago said as Duncan lifted a piece of the bread, "took out one of his boats for a couple days. The master's wife was feeling poorly, and they have a newborn. But he told me to tell you there are three new arrivals between here and Salem. That little snow"—Conawago indicated a small two-masted vessel unloading barrels of salt at the wharf in front of them—"and two in Salem Harbor. One bringing in molasses, as soon as they agree on the price for the customs inspector to turn his head. The other a sleek schooner of nearly ninety tons, a craft made for heavy water, he says, but pretty enough to be a private yacht. Gingerbread work on the aft deck rails and polished brass fittings. Unloaded a few barrels of Madeira, though Glover says she would be capable of carrying much greater cargo. And no interest shown in picking up goods in Salem."

Glover would not have provided such detail unless he was suspicious of the vessel. "She have a name?" Duncan asked.

"The *Aphrodite*, Glover named her. Dropped anchor two days ago."

"It's the *Indigo Queen* we need to keep an eye out for," Duncan said.

They watched as Hugo helped an adolescent boy carrying two buckets from one of the town wells. He took a bucket to ease his burden, then broke out in a French ditty that soon had the boy laughing.

"A bit overreaching for Marblehead folk but affable enough," Duncan observed. "Not built to be a whaler."

"Friend to all, it would seem," Conawago said, then puffed on his pipe. "Crispus has been watching too. The Cajian dotes on Boyle's new helpers, walking along with them, giving them apples or a fresh loaf. Yesterday he gave that young African girl from the wigmaker's shop a little bag of rock candy, the bond servant from the cooper's shop a jar of ginger beer."

"Generous," Duncan concluded. "Perhaps he assuages guilt over a recent sin. Or shucks off the loneliness of a long sea voyage. If he was the only Cajian on board his last ship, he might have felt isolated." He had often observed the despondency of solitary mariners at sea.

"No," Conawago said. "His eyes aren't right."

Duncan decided his friend was responding to his prior point. "You mean not good enough to spot whales?"

"His eyes aren't right," Conawago repeated, more emphatically. Duncan watched as Hugo, frolicking with another servant, tiptoed along the edge of the wharf. "He navigates well enough to avoid a dunking."

Conawago, puffing on his pipe, slowly shook his head and sighed. "You have been too long out in this world," the old Nipmuc chastised.

Duncan hesitated as the words sank in. A wave of emotion welled up inside, a surge of sorrow, and love, for the old man. It seemed to wipe his heart clean. He longed not to be in this world, to instead be walking again beside this deep and gentle soul in the wilderness. Duncan's life had drifted too far from the Nipmuc, who was the closest thing to family he had in all the world. Conawago spoke as no one else he had ever known, and once Duncan never had to pause to understand him. His instincts indeed were dulled by the affairs of cities and kings. The old Nipmuc spoke not in terms of simple observed facts but in truths.

"So you and Crispus have been studying him," Duncan said at last.

"Mostly me, since Crispus keeps a close eye on Sarah. No one gives a second thought to a worn-out Indian sitting for a smoke on a bench. Yesterday a kind old lady handed me a halfpence and said she would pray for me. Gabriel says if I stay much longer he might change the name of the tavern to the Old Chieftain," he added with a throaty chuckle. "Sit on this bench long enough and all the world goes by." He turned his gaze down the waterfront, where the Cajian was lending a hand to another servant hauling in a trap. "If he is a friend to just slaves and servants, does that make him a friend to all?" He shrugged. "When I lit my pipe in the kitchen last night, Cuff asked where I found my tobacco." The Nipmuc reached into his belt pouch and dropped a bundle of dried brown leaves on the bench. "'From a young Cajian,' I said."

Duncan lifted it to his nose, wondering why it seemed familiar.

"Cuff leaned into the first fumes after I lit it. Jamaican, he said. Blue Mountain."

A chill rippled down Duncan's spine. It was the same leaf being handed out by the slippery Jeremiah Melville. "Where do you suppose young Hugo lays his head at night?" he asked after a few breaths.

"We know well enough," his friend said. "I suggested to Pine—who now says he is Abishai in town—that he follow Hugo as he departed the waterfront. He crossed out the west side of town, to the water, and rowed a boat out to the fancy schooner."

"Salem Harbor," Duncan said with foreboding. "The *Aphrodite*."

"Peculiar about that. Afterward Pine and I decided to go fishing in the Salem waters. We got close to her, until a crew member warned us off with a raised musket. The *Aphrodite*, it says on her right enough, painted very prettily. Except the name is on a plank tied across the stern, perfectly matched to blend with the hull. Hiding another name underneath. And she flies an odd flag, top half black, bottom red. Like a black cloud over a sea of blood."

Duncan leapt to his feet. "Is everyone accounted for?"

"Moll said all staying at the house were there when I left at dawn."

"Solomon and Tobias?"

Conawago rose, wincing at his arthritic joints, and surveyed the street. "They should be well into their rounds by now. Usually they have all the pots from waterfront houses emptied before breakfast. But no sign of the flower wagon yet," he said, motioning to the two closest homes, where night soil pots waited at curbside. "Shall we take a walk?"

They found the wagon in a salt meadow just north of the town, the old mare happily munching on the salt grass. The night soil barrel was still empty. Solomon and Tobias were nowhere to be seen. Duncan lifted an odd piece of black leather from the back of the cart. It was the well-worn and bloody tip of a whip.

"First Fare festivities," Sarah said and sighed as Moll helped her out of her cloak. "I had no idea of their significance. The pastor says it is as important as Easter to folks here, though with a lot more laughter."

Mrs. Godwin, their usually taciturn landlady, sat with Conawago and Duncan at the hearth, chatting about voyages she had made on her husband's bark to Bilbao and the Azores. "Oh my, yes," she said. "The captain used to lead the parade of boats in the harbor. Just dinghies and launches and a few pinkies trussed up with bunting and such. And the church suppers, the ball, then the dawn blessing of the fleet as they departed on the ebb. Such a carrying-on."

Sarah gave Duncan a quick embrace. "Apparently that little shop by the wigmaker's imported some fireworks before the pact. The militia found out and desperately wanted to buy them, but they have no funds after buying that new brocade for their uniforms. So you and I have donated two guineas to the cause and will be saluted at the ball. And they somehow have in their possession a few naval rockets, so it should be quite the display." She accepted the mug of herbal tea Moll offered and hurried off toward the sitting room. "Have to finish my lists," she explained.

She recently, and most uncharacteristically, had taken to compiling lists: Lists of points to remember for their wedding, lists of Edentown supplies still needed before their overdue departure for the frontier. Perhaps most important of all were her lists for the runaways who would start a new life in Edentown: farrier tools for Solomon, leatherworking tools for Tobias, books and a writing slate for Josiah, and for each a new set of clothes in addition to the one she already provided.

Duncan did not explain that he had returned to the house only to find Pine. As they set out to investigate Boyle's works, Conawago, with surprising vigor, trotted out the door to join them. They captured the mare with little trouble and led her back down the wide path through the grove and toward the Irishman's stable, where Conawago released her from her harness. Duncan and Pine split up to scout the compound. There was no sign of Boyle, no sign of the charcoal barge, no sign of the sturdy riding horse that had been at the stable on their last visit. Could the enigmatic Boyle actually have lured the runaways here just to sell them for the bounty, then fled with the bonemen's silver?

Duncan knocked at the weather-beaten cottage, not expecting an answer. He lifted the latch. The interior had been cleaned and straightened. The bedding on the cot was neatly folded, and a sleeping pallet lay on the floor nearby. Fresh rushes were scattered across the floor. The dishes were all washed and stacked. The books had been cleared from the table and piled on a bench along the wall. Three clay jars with lids sat beside the washbasin. One contained flour, one rice, and one dried beans. A smoked ham hung from an overhead beam.

The floor creaked behind him, and he turned to face Conawago. "The proprietor left."

"But expected two to stay here," Conawago suggested, gesturing toward the beds. "Solomon and Tobias."

"Worth several pounds apiece in bounty," Duncan observed. As Pine stepped in, Conawago bent over the stack of books.

"There's a trail along the shoreline we can follow to the east side of Salem Harbor," Duncan said.

"The harbor?" Pine asked.

"Never raid a stronghold without studying it first," Duncan explained. "We will see you back at the house," he said to Conawago.

"No," the old Nipmuc said as he pulled out one of the books. He set it upright, spine on the table, and let it fall open, then leaned over the passage, marked by a narrow bit of rush.

"You're staying to read?" Duncan asked, feeling uneasy at the thought of Conawago alone in the mysterious compound.

Conawago read for a moment before looking up. "No," he said with a mischievous grin. "Because we have a raid to plan."

After two hours of surveying Salem Harbor from a boulder-strewn point on the side opposite the town, then conferring with Marblehead militia mariners, Duncan, Pine, and Conawago finished an early supper and saw Sarah off to help with First Fare events. They avoided telling Sarah about the captured runaways, but Cuff, sensing that something was afoot, pressed Pine for an explanation. With a reluctant nod from Duncan, the Oneida explained their suspicions about the vessel in Salem Harbor and the fate of the two missing fugitives.

"The bonemen!" Cuff spat. He abruptly disappeared out the rear door and returned moments later with his sharpened sickle.

"The more bloodshed there is, the more likely it is that the authorities take notice," Duncan said. "Eventually you might find a judge who embraces the cause of freedom for all, but you will all be locked up for months while awaiting his verdict. Even if you were freed, by then the bounty hunters will be circling like vultures. What you can do," he added as he saw the defiance burning in Cuff's eyes, "is come and help with the horses and keep watch in our camp on the shore. And now we need to find some grease and some blankets."

The night was cold and the still waters of Salem Harbor reflected the stars like a mirror. They arrived at their launch site, marked by two rock columns at the shoreline. A dinghy provided by their militia friends was waiting. Conawago built a small fire.

"He will betray our presence," Cuff groused.

"His fire is in the lee of the tall boulders, hidden from the boats in the harbor," Duncan explained. "He needs the smoke to call in the spirits," he added as the Nipmuc began a low chant. "That little amulet he touches has his totem inside, his link to his protector animal on the other side." The explanation quieted Cuff, who clearly understood about totems. He watched attentively as Conawago washed his amulet in the column of smoke then turned expectantly to Duncan.

Duncan extracted an amulet from under his tunic and extended it into the smoke. He had not spoken to his protector enough in recent months. He had held it tightly during the ride from town, whispering a Mohawk invocation. If he was to survive the night he would need his protector's help.

Cuff gave a knowing nod. "In my tribe we would pray that we would return washed in the blood of our enemies."

"All we ask for," Duncan said in a near whisper, "is courage. And tonight, help in the frigid waters."

Cuff cocked his head. "But you have the boat," he said, then his eyes went round as Duncan explained his plan. "Suicide! You'll die in this water! It's nearly ice!"

"You have yet to see Duncan when his protector awakens," Conawago interjected.

Pine, the former ranger, directed the launch of the dinghy, examining their two lanterns and making sure their baffles worked. He handed one to Cuff before helping Duncan remove his tunic. "Should be bear grease," the Oneida said as he rubbed the contents of the pail Moll had given them on Duncan's bare back. Duncan coated his arms and chest with the kitchen grease. If the cold penetrated his limbs too deeply, his muscles would fail.

When finished, he pulled on a tight-fitting black linen shirt, to obscure his pale skin, then coated his face with charcoal and tightened the belt that held his knife. Pine and Conawago took their places at the oars, and he stepped into the sturdy little boat.

They were a cable's length from the schooner when he signaled to stop the oars. He touched his totem, draped his legs over the gunwale, and slipped into the water. Timing was critical. He allowed himself five minutes for the swim, then ten minutes on board, but the ebb was stronger than he expected, and after the first minute, he chose to swim underwater, with faster frog-like strokes, surfacing for quick breaths until he was in the shadow of the ship's stern.

Earlier they confirmed that the schooner was rigged with fore and aft anchors to avoid swinging too widely in the often-crowded harbor. Duncan climbed up the stern anchor line, pausing for a moment at the ropes holding the plank that bore the false name. He paused again at the stern rail. Confirming that there was no deck watch, he climbed over. The ship was likely lightly crewed. Some, maybe most, would be onshore for Salem's First Fare festivities.

Duncan moved between shadows as he reconnoitered the deck. He listened for sounds at the chimney pipe for the galley, the likely gathering place for any crew left on board. He considered the layout of the ship. The crew's quarters were likely in the fo'c'sle, the officer quarters at the stern, with cargo stored between and on the deck below. He lifted a heavy belaying pin from the rack at the main mast and slipped down the gangway. He passed the second deck then descended a steeper ship's ladder to reach the deck at waterline, lit only by a dim lantern hanging in the passage between cargo compartments. The air was foul, tinged not only by bilge water but also by the scents of humans. He crept slowly toward the stern, reaching a heavy door that was slightly ajar. It creaked as he opened it into a chamber lit by a solitary candle. A man sat resting at a table in the center of the compartment, his head in his folded arms.

He stirred groggily. "What the hell do you—" he uttered just before Duncan silenced him with a heavy blow. He dropped unconscious.

Lengths of sailcloth hung along either side of the dank chamber. He pulled back the one on the left, exposing a cell of iron bars. Solomon, his face swollen and bleeding, crawled out of the shadows. The fear on his face changed to surprise, and he leaned back, shaking another figure in the darkness. Tobias's eyes went round at the sight of Duncan. Instantly the two men were at the bars, pointing to the ring of keys on the guard's belt.

As soon as Solomon stepped from behind the bars he darted to the opposite side and pulled back the canvas. Another man lay inside, his face also bruised and bloody. "They keep beating him to stop his prayers!" Tobias explained. "But he won't stop! He will die if we don't take him!"

Duncan did not argue. He opened the cell door and let the other two pull the third prisoner out into the light, then he dragged the guard into the cell, locked the door, and threw the keys into the shadows of the opposite cell.

It was too easy, too fast. Pine and Conawago were not due to approach the stern for several more minutes. Now he heard voices above, from the main deck. Men had arrived from shore and were laughing, some even singing. Just as he reached the top of the ladder from the cargo deck, silver-buckled shoes appeared on the stair from the main deck. Duncan leapt up, grabbed the lantern, and shoved it toward the man's face, blinding him for the moment it took for Duncan to swing the belaying pin. Hugo the Cajian collapsed at Duncan's feet.

A second man appeared on the ladder, taking Duncan by surprise. The sailor cursed and reached for the pistol in his belt. The weapon was raised and cocked, too late for Duncan to avert a shot. Suddenly a hand reached out of the darkness and grabbed the weapon, which fired wildly. Cuff emerged from the shadows with a feral growl. He snatched the sailor by the neck and pounded his head into the bulwark. The big African paused to shake water from his sodden clothes, then pointed Duncan to the end of the passage. "Go!" he boomed, then shot up the ladder to the main deck.

Duncan raced down the passage and entered the captain's quarters, lit by moonlight filtering through a row of stern transom windows. Shouts rose from above. A man flew through the air beyond the stern to the sound of a furious roar, his cry extinguished by a loud splash. Duncan grabbed a stool and smashed the center, widest window. "Do all of you swim?" he asked. Tobias and Solomon nodded.

"Never!" groaned the stranger they rescued. "Dear God, no, not a stroke!"

"You're out the window or back in that cell," Duncan said as Solomon climbed through the opening. "Pine and Conawago will be in a dinghy," he explained.

"Just head directly off the stern and you'll find them. And you," he said to the third man as Solomon, then Tobias, leapt into the bay, "when I say jump, you jump!"

Duncan swung himself out, finding a grip on the woodwork above the transom. He stretched with his blade, cutting the ropes that suspended the name plank. As the wide plank slid into the water, he leapt beside it. "Jump!" he cried.

The stranger, suspended in the window, fell rather than jumped. Duncan quickly pulled his head out of the water, shoved him onto the plank and was pushing it away from the ship as a furious shout rose from the window. "Damn yer eyes! You'll ne'er make it away alive, by Jesus!"

A musket cracked and a bullet hit the water a foot from his head with a sharp *zing*. The sound of fighting on the main deck rose to a crescendo, alternating between roars and moans. A second bullet hit the plank, nearly tearing it from his grip. The man on the plank began singing a Wesley hymn, "Soldiers of Christ, Arise and Put Your Armor On," in a surprisingly deep voice. Another bullet hit the water, an arm's length away. A musket flew through the air and splashed in front of them. A louder gun sounded, and a broad patch of water erupted six feet away. Duncan kicked harder. They were firing bird shot now. He tried not to think about the lead ball that might shred the back of his head and instead tried to calculate the time. Were the Marblehead men listening as agreed for the quarter-hour bell from Salem?

A moment later the distant bell rang, and the air above the schooner exploded. Red starbursts and yellow cascades of sparks lit the sky. Two dinghies were launching First Fare fireworks a cable's length from the schooner's bow.

"Damned fools!" someone on the ship shouted. "Too close, too close, veer away!"

The men in the Marblehead dinghies laughed. "For Neptune!" they called and set off more rockets just as Duncan heard a deeper, triumphant laugh and a heavy splash. Cuff surfaced a few feet away and swam to the plank. The Marblehead boats were far enough away that no one could accuse them of targeting the schooner. But there was always a breeze on the harbor, and as savvy mariners, the Marblehead men at the oars knew where to position their boats to assure that the clusters of sparks drifted over the *Indigo Queen*.

"Buckets!" a frantic sailor cried as burning fragments drifted down onto the schooner. "Bring water!"

Another fiery starburst was followed by the fireballs of a navy signal rocket. Cheering rang out from the far side of the harbor.

The plank pulled alongside Conawago's dinghy. "What flotsam have you salvaged now, Duncan?" the Nipmuc asked good-naturedly as he helped the stranger aboard.

"Bless you, sir," the man gasped, taking the offered hand. "My name is Achilles. From Quincy."

Chapter 9

DUNCAN HAD NO TIME TO parse his confusion as they hurried back to the house. He was late for meeting Sarah at the First Fare ball, so he left Achilles in the care of Esther. Drawing a basin of warm water, an insistent Moll wiped the charcoal and grease off his body. She poured him a mug from the kettle as it began to steam on the hearth. He took a hesitant sip and looked up in surprise.

"Aye, 'tis the true leaf from the East," Moll confirmed. "And you'll nay be saying anything to Miss Ramsey, sir. I saved some from back before the no-import pact began, so I'll ne'er be feeling guilty. There's nay restorative like the true leaf," she added as she gripped his chin and vigorously scrubbed at his neck. "And if half of what Solomon and Tobias are saying is to be believed, you be quite the hero, deserving of the nectar."

"We couldn't have made it without Cuff," he said, nodding to the big man who stood before the hearth, still in his sodden clothes, resisting all entreaties to speak of their adventure in Salem Harbor beyond a muttered and repeated "We got 'em, we got 'em."

Half an hour later the Scottish cook had him cleaned and attired in what she called his "number one" woolen waistcoat with Ben Franklin's watch, which she treated like a sacred relic, prominently displayed on the chain draped across his abdomen. She insisted he wait as he stepped to the door, then she disappeared into her room and returned a moment later with two adornments. "I found this ribbon and fashioned little flowers for the two of you." She pinned a little bundle of white ribbon, gathered at the center to resemble a flower, to his lapel and tucked the other into his pocket. "To remind Miss Ramsey," Moll explained, "that First Fare is all about the hope of spring."

Pollard had made the Hancock warehouse, the largest in town, available for the ball by moving most of the stored goods to upper levels and pushing the rest to the outer walls, then covering them with sailcloth. The resulting hall was gaily festooned with lanterns and bunting. A fiddle was played from a platform made of stacked crates that were decorated as an altar to Neptune, to whom the festival was dedicated. As the fiddler wrapped up his tune, a mariner leapt up to play jaunty songs on his hornpipe, which appeared fashioned from a narwhal tusk. From time to time the militia drummer offered his own disjointed contribution. Duncan roamed the perimeter of the crowd, thickest around the bowls of rum punch. After a series of short but polite conversations, he extracted Sarah from a covey of mariners' wives.

"Why, Duncan McCallum, look at you, the proud Jacobite!" Sarah teased as he pinned on her ribbon flower. She might be the only one present who would know that a white rose, popularly recreated as a cockade in white chambray ribbon, was the sign of the lost Stuart throne and its Scottish heir Charlie the Bonnie Prince. "But not a bagpipe in sight, more's the pity," she added with a laugh.

"Moll wanted you to have a harbinger of spring," he replied and led her out onto the dance floor as the fiddle and hornpipe joined in the lively "Fair Sally Loved a Sailor."

"How odd," she murmured as she rested her head on his shoulder. "You smell like bacon."

For most of an hour they danced and conversed with friends about topics as far ranging as the adventurous Captain Cook now exploring in the South Sea, the price of claret and Albany peas, and the best bait for spring cod lines. The ball, like the town, was egalitarian and diversely populated, with native tribesmen, African mariners, and Manx cordwainers sharing good-natured laughter with the town's merchants and captains.

"There's some well-deserved joy," Sarah declared, gesturing toward a well-dressed family by the table of pastries. "You know her, Duncan," she said of the woman by the children. "Amanda Brewster. The older girl, the niece, is wearing the dress we altered for her."

As she spoke, Eldridge Gerry, owner of several merchant ships, approached and lifted his glass to Sarah and Duncan. "Rumor is that Salem started their fireworks early," he observed. "But I hear the two of you saw to it that Marblehead will match their swagger." Duncan prayed that his friends had left enough for a proper show.

His gaze returned to Amanda and her family, and settled on the meaty, blunt-faced man at her side. The joy may be well deserved, but was it well derived? He left Sarah to speak with Gerry about her now famous race with the cutter and found John Glover.

"Tug? Tug Brewster?" Glover asked after Duncan spoke into his ear. Glover studied the nervous man beside Amanda and nodded. "He just bought his boat out of debt," Glover muttered. "And suddenly she's all fitted out for the Banks."

Duncan's gaze went back to the niece. "Would you happen to know, Captain, what Amanda's maiden name was?"

Glover scratched the back of his head as he tried to recollect. "By God, Duncan, it was Yates!" he declared in an excited whisper. "Amanda was a Yates before she got hitched!"

Five minutes later, Glover met Duncan by the town wharf, with Tug Brewster at his side. Brewster halted as he recognized Duncan and seemed about to retreat, until Glover pushed him from behind.

"We were chatting, John and I," Duncan began, "about your newfound wealth. The magistrate was about to impound your boat for debt. But suddenly you paid it off and already have her outfitted to sail with the fleet."

"Bad fortune just be the dues you pay for the good fortune that eventually comes," Tug shot back as he fidgeted with his ill-fitting new coat.

"That older girl with your wife," Duncan said. "She isn't yours."

The abrupt shift brought a scowl to Tug's face. "Of the family."

"You mean of your wife's family. Her brother's motherless child."

"No business of yers," Brewster snapped. Duncan could sense the man's muscles tightening, as if he were coiling for a fight.

Duncan turned to Glover. "What do you suppose, John? What would Amanda do if she discovered her husband's sudden wealth came from selling her secrets to British spies?"

The moon was bright enough for Duncan to see the color drain from the man's face.

"I'm damned well certain what she would do," Glover stated. "She would take the axe she keeps at the woodpile and go sink his boat."

Amanda's husband seemed to have lost his voice. When he finally spoke, it was hoarse. "Bloody Christ, 'tweren't like that!"

"You mean you sold the secrets to your ne'er-do-well brother-in-law, who suddenly had twenty or thirty pounds to give you."

"Boys!" Tug protested. "No one would believe she knows anything worth so much!"

"We would," Duncan replied. "She's a nightingale, Tug, as you well know. And your brother-in-law works for the king's spies. Why wouldn't she just use the axe on you?"

Brewster seemed to stop breathing.

"Maybe she'll let you live, Tug," Glover stated with false gravity. "But don't expect to be making any more children."

Brewster sagged. He stumbled to a crate and collapsed. "I got but a guinea left."

"Not interested in your ill-begotten silver," Glover growled. "We want to know every secret you sold."

Brewster stared out over the harbor, clenching his jaw.

"The longer this takes, Tug," Glover pressed, "the more likely it is that Amanda finds out. I doubt you can hide that axe for long."

"She talks in her bed, in the dark," Brewster murmured. "Sometimes she even answers my questions without recalling doing so."

"Start with how you told them about the meeting at the church, then the loom in the ghost house."

Brewster did not reply.

"The spy whose silver you took beat your wife. She wouldn't talk."

"He never!"

"He did," Duncan insisted, "and she told you she took a bad fall, because she said if you knew he did such a thing, you would kill him and not care if you faced the gallows."

Brewster's face contorted with a new kind of pain. "My Amanda said that? Sweet Jesus, I never . . ."

The confessions came fast. Tug admitted that he had revealed the secret meeting at the church and spoke of a messenger who came across the bay from Quincy in a shallop, always at night. He had told Vaughn he would give no more, but then the magistrate warned that his boat was to be seized.

"Tell us about getting that rich purse," Duncan pressed.

"It was Vaughn and his boss together, after they seized that loom. Yates said I had to go to Boston, and we met in a room at the Sign of the Ship. The boss, the one Vaughn called Major, was in high spirits, told Vaughn to stop whining about his shoulder 'cause finally the prize was in sight. Mustn't scare her away."

"Her?"

Tug wouldn't meet Duncan's gaze. "Ye know. She sleeps in the yellow house. Excepting the major warned Vaughn, 'Hands off for now, I shall take care of this particular filly.' Vaughn seemed put out. The major consoled him, said if we handle her right this goose will lay golden eggs. Then he handed me the purse and offered a toast. 'To the red cock,' he says, 'long may he crow!'"

Brewster sensed that Glover's temper had been building and inched to the far edge of his crate. "And you gave them this filly's name?" Glover demanded.

"Nay, nay! The major had just discovered it that very day. He was in high spirits but struck me as a mite confused, like he had a fish on the line that was too big for his boat. He just wanted to know where she lived."

Duncan reined in his own temper. "Where is Yates tonight?"

"Wouldn't I like to know," Brewster said. "I thought to hire him away from his boat to sail with me, but his captain said he was to report this afternoon and never appeared. Not in any of the taverns."

As Duncan and Glover exchanged a worried glance, Brewster slipped off his crate and darted back to the crowded ball.

Sarah was exhausted by the time they left the makeshift ballroom and leaned on Duncan as they slowly made their way back to the big yellow house. He paused as they reached the door, trying to decide what to tell her about the bounty hunters. "Sarah," he began, but before he could speak further, she put a finger to his lips, then kissed him.

"Have to be up early," she murmured. "I am taking Esther and Josiah to the blessing of the fleet at dawn. Maybe you can take the others up to the roof to watch the fireworks."

To his surprise, most of the house's occupants were gathered around the kitchen table, drinking cider, in a celebratory mood.

"Mr. Duncan rescued us!" Tobias exclaimed to Sarah as she appeared. "Like an angel rising up out the sea!" Conawago looked at Duncan apologetically, rolling his eyes.

"Wouldn't be an angel in the water," Cuff corrected with his customary gruffness. "More like one of those mermen."

"He's a true Neptune!" Solomon added. "Such a prodigious swimmer!"

"More than matched by Mr. Cuff," Duncan pointed out, prompting an awkward toast to the taciturn African.

The announcements seemed to burn away Sarah's fatigue. She fixed Duncan with a chilly gaze. "Rescued, Duncan?"

"There was a schooner at Salem," he began haltingly, then started over. "The governor of Barbados sent . . ." he said. "I didn't want to . . ." He gave up and pulled her toward the sitting room, where they could speak more openly.

By the time they reached the room, Sarah's confusion had melted into anger. She broke away and stood in the center of the room, hands on her hips. "When, exactly, Duncan McCallum, were you going to—"

"Miss Sarah?" The voice was weak and tentative. It came from the long, upholstered bench along the wall. "Is it truly you? Praise the Lord Almighty!" The speaker rose unsteadily and stumbled toward Sarah.

"Achilles!" Sarah cried.

The stranger fell into her arms, sobbing. "Thank God you're alive!" she cried as she tightly embraced him. She looked up at Duncan. Even in the dimness of the room's solitary candle he could see her flush with color. It was her turn to be tongue-tied. "Duncan, I couldn't—" she began. Tears began to flow down her cheeks. "That warehouse was . . . Achilles is one of my . . ."

"Achilles," Duncan observed as he approached and disentangled the sobbing man from her arms, "should lie back down. He has injuries that need more tending and requires a great deal of sleep." He helped Bradford's deputy back to the bench, then joined Sarah at the window, her face in her hands. "What have the times done to us?" she whispered.

He put an arm around her. "The times be damned. As long as we are together, *mo chride*, we can fix anything." As he spoke, the first of the militia's fireworks burst over the harbor.

"They were going to sell me," Achilles explained as Duncan washed the cuts and bruises on his face and hands. Sarah had surrendered to her exhaustion and retired. "They promised me freedom, but all along they meant to sell me to a sugar plantation in Barbados. Those gentlemen in the kitchen," he added awkwardly, "they said that's what they used to be. Sugar slaves." Duncan realized the well-educated Achilles was not entirely at ease with the runaways.

"Perhaps you could start a bit further back," Duncan suggested. "I thought you were already"—he searched for a word—"obligated to Mr. Bradford."

"A slave, you mean? Yes, well, it wasn't like that. I mean, yes, I was technically in servitude, but Mr. Bradford raised me with his daughter, schooled me. Brought me into his church and taught me his business. I have my own home, two rooms in the warehouse, and an allowance. Mr. Bradford is tormented by the notion that a human could be treated as chattel. My twenty-first birthday is coming up, and for it he is going to give me my freedom, start paying me wages, after the papers are drawn up." Achilles quieted for a moment, then spoke in a more tentative, worried voice. "We need to send word to him."

It was more of a question than a statement. Duncan prevaricated for the moment. "You said they offered you freedom. The ones who burned the warehouse. You were about to gain your freedom, in any event."

"And so I told them. But they said it would take an owner's writ of manumission with witnesses and such, that a judge would have to hold a hearing and approve it, and that would take months, even a year. Then they showed me their paper. They had such a writ, already signed by a judge. As I watched, they wrote my name on it and gave it to me. I thought Mr. Bradford would be well pleased, since we could avoid dealing with the courts ourselves. I was that happy and thought they were just God-fearing men who hated servitude, like those we hear from in church. But then they asked questions. Who did Mr. Bradford import for? What names were on the last shipment from England? Had I seen any strange metal shapes in the recent freight from England? Well, I said, I'd have to ask Mr. Bradford, since such things are confidential to his customers.

"They weren't much happy about that, but then their leader just smiled and said in that oily voice of his, 'Of course, we'll just need a quiet conversation with him. Let's fix a meeting time. And my schedule is so very busy, shall we say tomorrow evening, at perhaps eight of the clock? Just say some fellow Whigs want to speak about an urgent matter of common interest.'"

Duncan, cleaning chafed skin around Achilles's wrist, looked up. "You told Mr. Bradford this?"

"He was a bit annoyed. 'Why this business at a pious man's bedtime?' he asked, but we had no way to contact them, to decline. I reminded him that some Whigs have secret affairs. He asked if Samuel Adams sent them. Or our protector."

"Protector?"

"You know," Achilles whispered and gave a meaningful nod toward the second floor. "The keeper of all the pieces, Mr. B. sometimes said. Our guardian angel, he said once. Lives at stake and all. He decided we must meet with these strangers, to get their measures, so we can report back to Marblehead."

Sarah. Sarah was the keeper of all the pieces. "But he was worried?"

"More and more so. He finally woke his wife and daughter and said they must go visit her family in Connecticut, right away."

"Did you get a good look at the strangers, at least?"

"Never saw them before. The mean one who did most of the talking, he had the scars of smallpox on his cheeks, but another was in charge. An Englishman who honed his cruelty in one of those English schools for gentry. When the first man started hitting Mr. B., that one just laughed and said 'more' and 'put your back into it.' Another who stayed close was a brawny man, carried himself like a soldier. He just said 'yes, sir' and 'no, sir' to the other. He was the one who hit me. Mr. Bradford and I were waiting by the warehouse door at the appointed hour. We had just come from inside, where he made me a great gift. I know he had recognized my anxiety, so to ease my mind he told me that he had decided to make me manager of the warehouse and rent the little brick house on the edge of town for me.

"But then those men arrived with their wagon. I asked what's the meaning of this, but the big brute just knocked me down, then when I protested he struck me unconscious. When I came to, I was tied and gagged, inside a big crate with holes drilled in it for air, as if it were made for an animal. What a nightmare. I could see I was on a wagon, but not much more. The crate was sitting in a puddle of turpentine. I heard laughter and then the crackling of fire and a man cursing and another telling him to run to the pier and put his hand in the water, as if he had burned himself. Then came the screams. Screams," Achilles repeated in a hollow voice. "They could have been anybody, I told myself, maybe another of their men got burned. After a while the wagon began to move. We went on for hours. When the crate was finally opened, a young man in flashy clothes was aiming a pistol, while another put manacles on me. Then we got into a dinghy and rowed out to that cursed ship. As they put me in the cell, I said they can't, that the others had a writ that made me a free man. That young one, they called him Hugo, just laughed. 'You ain't a man at all,' he said. 'Nothing but cargo. Sack of bones for sale to the highest bidder.'"

Tears welled in Achilles's eyes. "You haven't said a word about Mr. Bradford. Prithee, tell me he is safe! It's what kept me sane in that terrible cage, telling myself we would be reunited."

"Not in this world, I fear. He was found in the ashes. They had tied him to a post."

The truth Achilles had been trying to deny finally seized him. He burst into sobs. Duncan tried to comfort him, but Achilles shook him off. He just held his head and wept.

Instead of climbing the stairs to his bed, Duncan stepped into the now darkened kitchen and sat on a stool in the warmth of the smoldering hearth. The day and its discoveries seemed endless. It was hard to believe that only hours earlier he and Conawago had enjoyed a few minutes of peace on the bench outside the Triple Fish. Since then he had discovered that bounty hunters had seized runaways under their protection, planned and launched a daring rescue, attended the First Fare ball, and confirmed that his fiancée was keeping secrets that men were dying for. Most disturbing of all was the realization that the bounty men's presence at Quincy to seize Achilles meant they had joined forces with Duncan's enemies from London.

He was so lost in his thoughts that he was unaware that someone else had entered the kitchen until he heard a chair being pulled back from the end of the table. He looked up to see Moll with a glass of what he guessed to be elderberry wine. She had not seen him in the shadows.

She started as he rose. "May I?" he asked, gesturing to the bench at the corner beside her.

"And here I thought all were at last abed," the cook said and nodded to a clay jar on the sideboard below a shelf of cups and glasses.

He poured himself some of the sweet wine and sat. "All these months, Moll, and I've never heard your family name."

"Why, bless your heart for asking. Chisholm. It's Chisholm, Mr. Duncan."

"A bold and daring clan, I recall. *Beannaichte a'Ghaidhealtachd.*"

Moll stared at him blankly. "Sir?"

"Sorry. Blessed by the Highlands. I thought perhaps you might have some of the old tongue."

"My ma and pa had it, I expect. But sorry to say 'tis but gibberish to me."

Duncan noticed the bowl sitting an arm's length away, half-filled with water. He brought it between them. "I'll tell you a secret, Moll. There's a Highland salute to the Stuart throne, you might say, but really it's just a way of keeping the old ways alive. You reach your glass over a bowl of water like this"—he extended his glass—"then draw it back and drink, saying 'To the king across the water.' It's a toast to the true Stuart king."

Moll's eyes went round, and she looked about as if for onlookers. "Scandalous, sir, I'm sure," she whispered with a mischievous grin. "Sounds like one of those Jacobite things. What if the army discovered us?"

"We'd be on the gibbet by noon," Duncan replied, returning the grin. "Try it." He extended his glass again, saying the words, and Moll awkwardly did the same from the opposite side. "To the true king," he said.

She repeated the words, sipped at her wine, and laughed. "We be right proper traitors now. Original traitors," she added with a smile that hinted at a youthful spirit lingering behind her tired features. She was close to, if not past, her fortieth year, he guessed, but in that moment he could see the rugged beauty that had once been hers. "We can teach a thing or two to these American newcomers to the rebel game, eh?" She extended her glass again. "Across the water. The ocean?"

"The true king lives in Rome, yes."

"Now I ken," she said and repeated the toast more solemnly.

"I knew some Chisholms as a lad," Duncan said. "My people were boatwrights and cattle drovers. Sometimes Chisholms would join their herds with ours and we drove them together to market."

"Never in life!" the cook exclaimed. "You must tell me, tell me all!"

He collected memories as she poured them each a pewter mug of cider. "At night the Chisholms would share out whisky," Duncan began, "and always before the first sip they would stand and invoke the clan vow, their slogan as it were. *Feros feria*. I am fierce with the fierce. I remember it well because my brothers and I would shout it when we played at being warriors. It seemed the perfect war cry."

The cook stumbled over the slogan but persisted until she spoke it perfectly. "Prithee, sir, what else?"

Duncan gladly lost himself in the past, offering tales of her Highland clan, and his own, as Moll added logs to the fire and melted cheese on toast. It was a distraction he sorely needed, and the cook seemed genuinely moved by his stories of cow herding, boat building, clan gatherings, and the nightlong fires of the Beltane and Samhain festivals.

When he finally reached his room, he collapsed onto the bed, barely able to remove his shoes before exhaustion overtook him.

He slept late, past dawn, and was downstairs just as Sarah, already in her cloak, was examining the fur-trimmed winter bonnet Moll held out with an expectant expression. She accepted the bonnet, then rolled it up and tied it as a furry band around her temples and ears, mimicking the bands of fur Iroquois women sometimes wore on winter days. For a moment Duncan didn't recognize the attractive woman beside her, then suddenly realized it was Esther, in a fashionable frock and adorned with Sarah's jewelry. Josiah peeked from around his mother, wearing the new clothes Sarah had bought for him. "Away to send off the fleet," Sarah announced. "There's a breakfast first at the church. Josiah claims he is going to consume ten johnnycakes."

"I will meet you at the waterfront in time for the blessing," Duncan promised.

Sarah paused as she reached the door and turned to Duncan. "That young officer who has the revenue cutter, Mr. Oakes, brought a most peculiar invitation, one in which I suspect John Hancock had a hand. I had to indicate it was unlikely

I could comply with the commodore's request, or the general's. Poor boy seemed shocked. 'But people don't decline such invitations,' he said. 'Do I look like an infantryman?' I asked him. 'Or some weepy-nosed ensign at the mast?' He blushed and looked away. 'Most certainly not, ma'am,' he says. 'Then I am not obligated to His Majesty's military, sir,' I told him. He retreated."

"Not before you said, 'Please go back and play with your knots like a good boy,'" Moll added with a grin.

Sarah and Esther laughed. Josiah opened the door, and the three stepped out into the morning chill. Crispus, lingering at the hearth, pulled on an old overcoat and woolen cap and followed a moment later.

Duncan accepted a mug of one of Moll's barely palatable herbal experiments and stepped into the sitting room. The note on the table was in a carefully elegant script and bore the seal of His Majesty's navy. He smiled at Sarah's description of the courier. Oakes was no mister; he was the proud commander of the king's revenue cutter and probably not much younger than Sarah herself. His smile faded as he read the message.

March 5, 1770

Dear Miss Ramsey—I have the honor to convey to you the urgent invitation of the commander of His Majesty's forces in America, Major General Thomas Gage, to meet with him at his New York headquarters for consultations pertaining to harmony with the tribes on the frontier. The general suggests you would be an unparalleled ambassador, as confirmed by the Superintendent of Indian Affairs Sir William Johnson. I sail tonight for New York for my quarterly consultation with the general and can provide the most comfortable of accommodation during the short voyage. Lieutenant Oakes will await your pleasure and convey you to Castle William or explain our arrangements should you wish separate conveyance to the Castle. Weather permitting, we can have you back within a fortnight. With kind regards, I am ever

Your humble servant,
Captain James Lawford
Commodore of His Britannic Majesty's Inshore Squadron

Duncan lowered himself into the chair by the window and read the invitation once more, then still again. Hercules Mulligan had a hand in this. The very clever, very secretive leader of the Sons of Liberty in New York had made a plea the prior year for Sarah to meet with Gage, the most powerful man on the continent, to soften his hard line against colonial patriots and the tribes, with particular regard to the military occupation of Boston. Mulligan had unique access to Gage as his personal haberdasher, and Mulligan was a man of great patience and subtlety. Mulligan was also a friend of William Johnson, who had befriended General Gage during the French war, long before Gage became the much-feared supreme commander.

Consultations pertaining to harmony with the tribes. The Iroquois did remain a potent fighting force and therefore were of constant concern to the royal government, especially the Senecas, who were traditionally aligned with the French and were rumored to be fomenting a new uprising in the Ohio country. But Mulligan played a complex game of chess out of his haberdashery in New York. Sarah, it seemed, had just become a player on his board.

Duncan and Sarah intended to soon sail up the Hudson, newly wedded at last, for their long overdue return to Edentown. They would need to stop in New York for some final supplies. While there, he would speak with Mulligan about the next phase of their Cugnot war machine campaign and discover his real reasons for trying to lure Sarah into the treacherous terrain of the British military's American headquarters.

The Marblehead waterfront was more crowded than Duncan expected. Nearly a quarter of the population worked in the fishing fleet. The other three-quarters, it seemed, turned out to bid them safe sailing on the thousand-mile voyage to the Grand Banks. The crowd was somber and most earnest in singing their hymns as the collected pastors of the town prepared for the blessing. Two years earlier over a score of Marblehead boats had been lost at sea in a terrible storm.

Duncan expected to find Sarah and Esther near the platform from which each vessel was called out and blessed, but they were nowhere to be seen. He was about to send Pine, who accompanied him, to the Three Cods but then spied a group of blue-and-red uniforms. Perhaps the ladies were with their friends in the militia, but not one of the soldiers had seen the women. He was thinking he had forgotten something about their rendezvous, when a hand closed around his arm.

"No time for First Fare," a worried voice said. "The predators are among us already!" Duncan spun about to face Conawago, who had a bloody bruise above his eyebrow.

"I was on my bench at the inn when I saw Sarah and Esther approaching. I began walking toward them and Crispus appeared, roaring like a bull and charging at a big brute of a man coming from the other direction. 'Montgomery, you manburner!' he shouted. Then that Cajian appeared with two more, and they dragged Sarah and Esther away!"

The ivory-hilted knife appeared in Pine's hand. Duncan's hand closed about the hilt of his own blade. "The bounty men! Where?" Duncan cried. "By God! It will be bloody work boarding that schooner a second time!"

The Nipmuc held up a hand. "Esther gave a mighty scream and Sarah cleverly pulled their captors toward the militia. 'To arms!' she called, and Crispus shouted, 'Slavers!' Of course the militia did not come to the ceremony with weapons, but the officers wore their swords and others picked up cordwood for clubs. One grabbed a dead fish, frozen stiff as a board. Those cowards of the *Indigo Queen* were no match for the mariners of Marblehead. They released their prey and faded into the crowd."

"Then where's Sarah?" Duncan asked, his heart still pounding.

"I was threading my way to them when Crispus spied that man he called Montgomery again, as if making ready for another attempt on the women. He pulled Sarah and Esther toward the Hancock packet, just slipping her lines for Boston. Cleared the harbor five minutes ago with the three aboard. Once they arrive, no doubt Sarah will take refuge in the Hancock house."

Josiah broke out of the crowd and ran to Duncan. "My ma and Miss Sarah!"

"They are safe for the present," Duncan said. "But the house is not. Run, Josiah, and warn them. We will be along as soon as I speak to the militia."

Cuff was perched as a guard with an axe by the time they reached the kitchen door. Moments later, the first two militiamen arrived. A dozen more were on the way with their weapons. "We will take the fight to them," Duncan instructed the company. "Find them and arrest them. The charges are kidnapping, torture, and disrupting the blessing of the fleet. Then I will find a later boat for Boston."

They swept the town and found no trace of the bounty men. They swept it again with more militia. By then the sun was sinking, the tide and wind had shifted, and clouds heavy with snow approached on a northeast wind. No one would be sailing to Boston that night.

Duncan comforted Henri and Josiah, assuring them that Sarah and Esther would be relaxing in luxury, in that safest of bastions, the Hancock mansion. Sarah would no doubt take the opportunity to discuss their wedding ceremony with Hancock and his aunt, and perhaps the two women would be the toast of one of Hancock's impromptu dinner parties.

At the yellow clapboard house, however, they did not relax their vigilance. As snow began to fall, Duncan took over the outside patrol, carrying the old bird gun that their landlady produced from her dead husband's wardrobe. He watched as Pine and Cuff disappeared into the curtain of white to see if they might detect any activity on the *Indigo Queen*, then turned toward the harbor, emptied now of the First Fare fleet, hopefully sailing away from the weather. Duncan was more concerned about the storm building around Sarah. "It was snowing like this," came a quiet voice behind him. Rebecca Prescott was on the kitchen step, an overcoat draped over her shoulders. Duncan had not seen much of her since her arrival at the house, for she mostly stayed in her room, watching out the window as if still fearful of ambush. He sat beside her. Only Sarah and Moll had been able to lure her downstairs for late evening chats by the hearth, always punctuated by Rebecca's frequent looks out the window.

"I told him I always loved the swishing sound these soft snows make when they reach the still waters, like the Creator's brush touching his palette. Nathan looked at his watch and laughed, saying let us pretend to be the John Hancock party and be fashionably late for the ball. Plenty of time for a stroll along the Long Wharf." She looked up toward the heavens. "We walked in silence, in the spell of the moment, and he whispered that it was as if the sky had come down for a nighttime embrace of the sea.

"It was so peaceful, just the two of us, speaking of our coming wedding, and how he planned to buy a farm in the Connecticut Valley after four or five more years in the army. Nathan said we would build a grand house, with plenty of room for all our children.

"Then a shadow stepped out of deeper shadow. 'Mallory, you fool,' the man growled. 'You could have been a huntsman for the king.'

"'A viper for the king, you mean, Hastings,' my Nathan replied. I had not met the man who had been undermining his grenadier company, the one the captain called an amoral reptile, but knew it had to be him. 'Run, Rebecca,' Nathan said, just as Hastings drew out a long blade. 'Just run!' I don't think he believed he was in mortal danger. After all, they were both officers in the king's army. I expected there would be sharp words, and afterward Nathan would meet me at the foot of the wharf."

Her voice dropped to a whisper. "I ran but turned in time to see Hastings withdraw the blade from Nathan's back. Hastings searched him for a moment, then kicked him into the water. I screamed. Sailors came running, and Hastings disappeared into the shadows. Every night I am haunted by that image. The dagger being extracted, draining out my Nathan's lifeblood, and that vile man kicking him into the harbor. Often I sleep not at all."

"Searched him for what?" Duncan asked.

"A letter, I think. Nathan was drafting a letter to complain of Hastings. He said he couldn't trust some of his men because they were taking Hastings's silver. They knew my face, because he would sometimes invite me to their encampment. They were the ones . . ." her voice trailed away.

"Who tried to kill you?"

She nodded. "They are monsters, led by a greater monster. Do not think you can defeat them. My Nathan knew best. Just run."

By dawn Duncan was on the waterfront, much quieter now that the fishing fleet had sailed, seeking a boat bound for Boston. He settled for a fat shallop destined for Charlestown. He could hire a ferryman below Breed's Hill to take him across to the North End.

It was midmorning by the time he leapt up the marble steps of the Hancock mansion, still musing over the ferryman's comments about the "terrible doings" of the night before. As he paused to straighten his clothes, suddenly self-conscious of his simple attire, the door opened and one of Hancock's gold-liveried servants gestured him inside with a respectful murmur of "Dr. McCallum, sir." The man ushered him not into the office but to the ornate sitting room, where Hancock's pious aunt sat doing needlepoint.

"Why, Mr. McCallum, always a pleasure," the woman stiffly said as Duncan offered a bow. "But you've missed Johnny. He was off with the selectmen and governor with barely a bite to break his fast. Perfectly awful, isn't it? Blood running in the street. I've told John again and again, don't encourage that firebrand Samuel Adams."

"Ma'am?" Duncan said. "I've just arrived from Marblehead."

"Why, I speak of the riot at the Custom House last night. And more to come. Samuel is down at Faneuil Hall stirring up more mischief this very minute. Next thing you know, we'll be packing up the good porcelain and boarding the windows."

"I actually came to see Miss Ramsey," Duncan said with growing unease.

Lucinda Hancock finally put down her needle. "Dear Sarah? How is the girl? I do so hope you'll prove worthy of her," she added in her usual haughty tone, then eyed his clothing with a disapproving gaze.

"Does she still slumber?"

"Why, Mr. McCallum, you presume too much. I've not seen Sarah for many a day, more's the pity. I think it was that dinner John held for the naval officers."

"But surely . . . perhaps she came without your knowledge?"

The widow was not one to be challenged. "Don't be impertinent! Nothing happens in this house without my knowledge! And if she was in Boston last night, I pray God she had the sense to stay in her quarters."

Duncan murmured his thanks, then his regrets to the tea offered with icy politeness, and bolted out the door. He ran down to the edge of the Common, past soldiers of the Twenty-Ninth Regiment massing in company formation on the open meadow, then leaned against an elm to catch his breath. Down the street at another, larger elm, the one they called the Liberty Tree, a small crowd gathered, watching the troops, some shaking clubs in their direction and calling out all-too-familiar epithets. He was only a block from the house of the more moderate of the Adams cousins. When he knocked, the very pregnant Abigail Adams announced, "I'm sorry, Duncan, John was urgently summoned by the governor, who is quite perplexed over having those soldiers in his jail."

Duncan next stopped at the little ivy-covered shop off Brattle Square. DeVries was shaken. He was gathering up the glass jars from the shelf in his front window. "Oh Duncan, thank God you are safe! Such a night! First all the bells started ringing as if the whole town were in flames. I ran out with my bucket, but there was no fire, just men and boys waving clubs and axes and such. People shouting, people running for shelter, people singing that new liberty song, and drums from the Common mustering the soldiers. I ran back here, locked the door, and sat by the hearth with my daughter in my arms." The girl's head appeared from behind the high-backed chair by the hearth, where she had been hiding. She rushed to the side of her father, who threw an arm around her.

"You haven't seen Sarah?"

"Not since last week." DeVries saw the fear in Duncan's eyes and clutched his daughter more tightly. "Dear God, Duncan, don't tell me she was out in the chaos! There's blood on the street!"

Duncan murmured his goodbye and darted out of the shop, then slowed as the Dutchman's words sank in. *There's blood on the street.* He walked in a daze. Crispus, he decided. Crispus would know, and Crispus was well-known in certain quarters, making him easier to track so long as Duncan used what Crispus called his town name, Michael Johnson. He hurried to the Sign of the Ship and found Naomi at her kitchen worktable. Her eyes were red from weeping.

"So many dead, Duncan," she moaned. "The gates of Hades have surely opened. What is to become of us?"

"My friend Michael Johnson."

"Oh I know, I know," she said, scrubbing at her eyes.

"Where?" he desperately asked.

"Someone said the Royal Exchange Tavern, by the very spot."

Duncan knew the tavern well, just off King Street, and ran. Why would Crispus be sheltering at one of the city's most elite inns and not among friends on the waterfront? One of the rich merchants or officials who knew Sarah must have brought them inside at the early signs of the riot. Slackening his pace as he neared the tavern, he puzzled over the subdued crowd gathered in the plaza in front of the Custom House. There was an open spot at the center of the crowd, as if no one dared tread on that particular patch of packed snow. He squeezed through, close enough to see the edge of the patch. The snow was dirty, but it also held blotches of red. He pushed back through the throng and hurried into the tavern.

The outer room was empty. He followed voices to one of the rear dining chambers. Men were gathered around a table, one of them bent low. Duncan glimpsed surgical instruments arranged along the adjoining table and bloody wads of linen.

"McCallum! Excellent! Another set of trained hands won't go amiss."

Duncan met the gaze of Dr. Benjamin Church, one of Boston's leading physicians. The men standing at the table shifted to admit Duncan. As he stepped forward, his heart shriveled. The indestructible Crispus, the steadfast friend who would lead him to Sarah, lay dead before him.

Chapter 10

"TWO MUSKET BALLS," CHURCH EXPLAINED in a flat voice. "One into the right thorax, entering through the second true rib. The second round entered with great force at the fourth of the false ribs. I suspect the balls were deflected downward by the bones and caused ruin to his organs, though the autopsy will tell us with certainty. Two balls at what range?" Church asked no one in particular, then answered his own question. "Surely no more than a dozen feet."

Duncan, numbed at the sight of his dead friend, barely heard the words. Here was the simple, gentle giant who so wanted to impress his brother by helping in the patriot cause. Here was the muscle-bound drifter who was trying to make more of his life, asking Sarah to teach him to read and write, even hinting that he might remake himself by joining them on the frontier. Here was the only person who could tell him how to retrieve Sarah from her mortal danger.

Duncan realized that Dr. Church was speaking to him. "Sir?" Duncan asked.

"I said, will you assist me with the exam? I mean to open him as soon as my own instruments are delivered. I prefer to use my good German blades."

"I cannot," he murmured in a hoarse voice. "I cannot," he repeated as he backed away, turned, and stumbled out of the tavern.

He wandered, senseless, into the square before the Custom House, lowering himself onto the steps of a boarded-up house. From time to time the crowd shifted, offering a view onto the patch of bloody snow. It looked like an abattoir. Clearly the lifeblood of more than one man had drained out on King Street. He heard distant drums from the encampment of the Twenty-Ninth Regiment but saw no sign of troops. From the direction of Faneuil Hall came the sounds of an angry speaker rousing a crowd. A well-dressed gentleman had taken a seat an arm's length away from him on the steps. The man shook his head in despair.

"I just arrived in the city," Duncan said. "Prithee, what took place here?"

"The soldiers and the radicals have been at each other's throats for weeks," the man said in a moribund voice. "The soldiers have scant pay, so many seek daywork for extra coin and are willing to accept less than what a Boston man needs to support his family. That's the excuse, but the occupation strains us all, with the troops acting as if they are in enemy territory, challenging honest folks on the streets. A couple days ago there was a fracas when a soldier sought a day's work at the big rope walk and the workers assaulted him. And that boy was shot and killed not two weeks ago. Since then, armed gangs of workers and soldiers have been prowling the streets." He paused and sighed as the crowd parted, revealing the bloody swath of snow again.

"When I came by last night the boys were pelting the sentry at the Custom House watch post with snowballs and chunks of ice. The solitary private looked terrified. A handful of troops arrived for his relief, those hulking grenadiers from the Twenty-Ninth, with bayonets fixed. Church bells starting ringing, so naturally people poured out of their houses thinking there was a fire. But it was only to summon reinforcements. More and more men arrived, mostly I'd guess from the waterfront. Sharp words were exchanged, and men gathered around the soldiers, raising clubs."

"What kind of words?"

"The usual. 'Bloody-backed bastards.' 'Lobsterback bullies.' 'Wilkes and Liberty.' I recall the big man who went down first shouting something like 'Man-burner! God rot your soul.' No, no, it was 'God rot your soul, Montgomery.' I guess he knew one of the grenadiers."

Another chill crept down Duncan's spine. Crispus had found Montgomery among the guards and taunted him again. Montgomery loathed Crispus and was no doubt primed to recover his pride following their last encounter, when Montgomery was prepared to run Crispus through with a bayonet until ordered to stand down. This time Montgomery held a loaded musket.

"It was all so confusing. The officer in charge was trying to restrain his men. But then someone shouted 'Fire!' and the muskets discharged."

"You mean the officer ordered the protesters shot."

The man sighed again. "All I know is that the word was shouted and the muskets were fired. The officer called out that he had given no such order. Someone shouted back that he was the only one who could give such an order. But others said there had been a stranger in a dark cloak with a fur collar standing behind the officer, and it was he who shouted the command. No one recognized him and after the smoke of the muskets cleared, he was gone."

A stranger in a dark cloak with a fur collar. Duncan would wager all he owned that Hastings had finally succeeded in sparking hostilities. He looked back toward the Royal Exchange Tavern. Part of him felt compelled to go stand vigil, but he could not bear the thought of watching Church dissect his friend.

He returned to the waterfront, trying to remember the faces of men he had seen with Crispus. He walked the length of the Long Wharf hoping to recognize someone while avoiding as best he could the knots of soldiers, mostly officers, who were hurrying to and from the launches from Castle William and the warships in the harbor. Lowering himself onto a bench, he was seized by a waking nightmare of what Boston might soon become, an inferno of burning buildings and screaming people, punctuated by musket shots. He pushed away his numbness, trying to think of the night before. Crispus would have steered Sarah toward the waterfront, where he had friends who might protect her. With a new desperate hope he realized that Sarah, too, had friends on the harbor.

Naomi stood by the entry to the tavern, staring forlornly at her now-empty tables. "Half our customers are passed out on their beds after storming through the streets all night," the innkeeper wearily declared as she poured Duncan some ale. "And the other half left for Faneuil Hall to be stirred up by the elder Adams, as if they needed more fire under them." She poured some ale for herself and took a long swallow. "My patriot customers say the army has revealed its true intentions in Boston, to eliminate them a few at a time. My Loyalist customers say those who offend the king must pay the cost." She gave a long sigh. "All I know for certain is that a storm has broken upon our city, and who knows what will be left when it stops howling."

"Naomi," Duncan said. "I cannot locate Sarah. She went missing in the chaos of last night."

"Oh dear! And I was praying that the dear woman was safe in Marblehead." She turned and summoned the serving maid who had spoken with Duncan days earlier. "Sally, you said there was a disturbing fellow asking about Sarah Ramsey last evening before the trouble began. Tell Mr. McCallum."

"Yes, ma'am," the nervous teenager said as she dried her hands on her apron. "But as you said to do, if anyone asks, I told him Miss Ramsey no longer resides in Boston, we ain't seen her these past three months or more. He was most persistent. Offered me a half crown and said, 'Let's start over, lass.'

"'I could take your coin,' I told him, 'but it don't make my words less true.' He was a might tipsy, having been celebrating with friends earlier, and most lavish with his coin and leaf."

"Leaf?" Duncan asked.

"Tobacco. He said he was recruiting for a new estate in the north and he kept trying to pull me into his lap, saying if I would join his enterprise he would gladly build a tavern just so he could see me every day. I pushed him away and told him I was a good Christian and had no interest in wild men or the wild country."

"An overdressed gentleman," Duncan said with new foreboding, "named Melville."

"That's the name, but as to being a gentleman I doubt it." Sally leaned closer and lowered her voice. "There's a fine genteel customer who comes in most nights, ever since his ship arrived from the Indies. He invites me to sit with him when it's quiet, and we talk. He's the son of a rich plantation owner, come to arrange his sugar contracts. He was most alarmed at the sight of that man Melville and warned me, 'Stay away from him. Some men may be granted a new life,' he said, 'but never a new soul.'"

"I don't understand," Duncan said.

"I was well convinced to stay away from the blaggard by then so didn't ask more." As she spoke, the door opened, admitting three men with the weathered appearance of mariners. "Why, you can ask him yourself, the one in the plum-colored waistcoat."

Naomi set a pitcher and three tankards in front of Duncan. "Offer them some ale in exchange for a tale."

The three thawed toward Duncan as they imbibed. Their standoffish demeanor disappeared entirely when he revealed he was a physician. By the time he finished explaining the best way to treat the lumbago and rheumatism that were plaguing their captain and first mate, they were chatting like old friends.

"There was a man in here last evening, pestering young Sally. You warned her away," he said to the youngest and best dressed of the three. "She said you seemed to know him."

"Know his face, and that's all, thank God," the stranger said. "Spawn of the devil. I don't know what he calls himself here, but the last I saw him was just weeks ago in Barbados, as he was condemned by the governor to hang for looting boats and killing crews and other dark deeds. Whatever name he uses today doesn't change the fact that he is known in the Indies as Mungo Frye, the most wicked pirate since the last century."

Duncan tried not to show his alarm. That particular spawn of the devil had been asking about Sarah. "Are you suggesting he reached an accommodation with the governor?"

"The governor and Frye are practical men. If Frye caught scent that the governor had a task in mind that required his particular skills, he might have proposed an accommodation, to be sure. The governor let on that Frye had been executed inside the fort, but pirates usually hang on the gibbet in the harbor for a few weeks, and Frye's body never appeared. And his elegant schooner sailed away in the night."

Duncan rose, murmuring his thanks, and found Sally and Naomi in the kitchen. "You said Melville was drinking with friends. Did you hear any words from them?"

"That was upstairs," Sally replied. "Naomi said that trade was slow and I had been working late most nights, so she suggested I take a rest in a third-floor room, one of the quiet ones at the back. I went to the center room, the quietest, forgetting that it was still rented out. That man they call the major was in there, with Melville. They were loading pistols. The major took me for a chambermaid, said don't mind the mess, they would leave a couple extra shillings on the table, but maybe I could tend their fire. Then while I worked at the hearth Melville recognized me and invited me to join them. They was in high spirits. 'A grand night for the king,' the major said as he lifted a glass. 'A grand night for all of us,' says Melville. Then a young man sits up from the bed, a flashy dresser who had been playing with a dagger. 'No blades tonight, Hugo,' Melville says. 'No striking. The major gets his fifty pounds so long as there are no mars on the prize.'

"Then a new man runs up, a big brute with hobnails on his boots and wearing an old overcoat, though I could see the uniform underneath. He was that excited. 'Strolling right along the street!' says he. 'And that damned runaway at her side!' he says. 'Well done, Montgomery!' the major exclaims. 'We'll have you in the Horse Guards yet.' Then they moved fast, belting their pistols and running down the stairs. Half an hour later Melville came back, still excited. Sat and drank until the major and Vaughn came down with a trunk and they all left together."

Duncan stared at Sally, a new dread seizing his heart. He stepped back to the trio and sat by the young man in the plum waistcoat. "Why would Mungo Frye pay fifty pounds for a young woman?"

The man glanced back at Sally. "It's why I warned her away. There's remote, wealthy plantations in the islands run like little kingdoms. I hear tales of how certain of those manor lords will pay handsomely for English beauties. Keep them in luxurious cells, but as prisoners all the same, some wearing silk-covered chains, I hear. Mungo holds auctions when he has such prizes. The bidding starts at a couple hundred pounds but usually goes far higher."

Duncan retreated and collapsed at an empty table. Hastings had found his solution, a way to eliminate Sarah without killing or arresting her, a way that would earn him a rich profit. He meant to sell her to Melville. He looked up to find Naomi and Sally standing over him. "Sarah is in mortal danger!"

Naomi sprang into action. "Fetch my cloak, Sally, and your own. Bring Peg, Constance, and Holly. We'll start at the Hancock warehouse, inquiring of all we meet. Someone must have seen something!"

"The Hancock warehouse?" Duncan asked.

"They were loading goods last night on his coastal sloop, moving back and forth across the street. Many of the Hancock people know her. If Sarah was walking along the waterfront, they would have seen her."

Naomi's small army of observers was well-known in the neighborhood, and most passersby were happy to chat with one of the affable barmaids. Four remembered seeing Sarah or at least, as one said, "a red-haired beauty with a dusky maid at her side." Another asked if they meant the elegant woman with Michael Johnson, then pointed to a man by the warehouse door directing the loading of wine casks on one of the low wagons used for shifting cargo to ships. As he turned Duncan recognized Pollard, the warehouse overseer from Marblehead.

"McCallum? You, too, were stranded in this madness? We were supposed to sail last night but after loading half the cargo my men abandoned me for the riots. Now some say the soldiers are going to start arresting every male, others say the soldiers themselves will be booted out by the governor. Who to believe? Either way we sail within the hour if you need quick passage out of this insanity."

"You were here on the waterfront last night?"

"To my regret, yes. It was as if Lucifer himself had descended upon the city. Bells, bells, bells, with people panicking because they thought a fire was spreading. Then the shouting, and the musket discharge, and the screams. The blood still lies in the snow. I would have thought they would wash it away. Blood in the snow," he repeated. "At least your Sarah had the sense to get away."

Duncan's heart skipped a beat. "You saw her?"

Pollard looked down at Duncan's hand. Duncan had not realized he was tightly gripping the man's arm. He released his hand. "Aye, just before sunset. She was with that exotic friend she brought to the ball, and the bosun who sometimes helps Mr. Hancock, the one called Crispus, or sometimes Michael. They were carrying some parcels tied up with twine. I supposed she must have come to the city for shopping. What miserable timing!"

Duncan hesitated. Sarah had desperately fled Marblehead but once in Boston had decided to call on shops? It made no sense. "Where, Pollard, where did she go?"

"In the safest of hands. It was most peculiar, I grant you. For a moment I actually suspected she was being ambushed. There were four men who ran up behind her, two in dark cloaks, a big one in a shabby overcoat, thought I fancy I glimpsed scarlet underneath. And two others who put me in mind of those fellows who've been wandering around Marblehead passing out tobacco and such. As I watched, they split up, two darting ahead of her and turning back to block her. Johnson cursed at one of them, then grabbed Miss Ramsey most urgently as if he feared she was to be snatched away. The woman with her gasped and shouted something I couldn't entirely make out, though it sounded like 'bonemen!' She clutched Miss Ramsey's other arm tight, like her life depended on it. I was about to offer my assistance when your Sarah called out to several military men making their way to a launch down the wharf. 'Captain,' she calls with great enthusiasm, 'at last! I was so hoping to find you! I happily accept your flattering invitation for New York. I am ready to embark this instant!'

"It was the one they call the commodore, that Captain Lawford, who stepped into the light, surprised but obviously well pleased, and said he was planning to sail from Castle William within the hour. That's when she noticed me. She called me over and asked that I deliver her parcels to Mr. Kipling at her house in Marblehead and tell him nothing is to be altered, then she whispered something to Michael Johnson. 'My man will bring our things later,' she declared to the captain. She wrapped her arm around that of her lady friend and announced, 'What a lovely night for a sail,' and off they went. And after I gathered up her packages, I saw that those devils had taken flight. Mr. Johnson was most upset. 'Murderers pay the price!' he shouted down the alley, as if those stalking Miss Sarah had committed the mortal sin. He waited until she was under way in the navy launch, then he, too, disappeared into the shadows."

As Pollard spoke, the roar of the angry crowd echoed again from the direction of Faneuil Hall, like the rumble of an approaching storm. "If you would be rid of this tormented town, Duncan," Pollard said, motioning toward the waiting sloop, "let us cast off. A beast was loosed last night, and God knows how much blood will flow before it is sated." He had taken only one step down the pier when someone shouted Pollard's name. They turned to see John Hancock climbing out of his carriage.

"Call your men back," Hancock yelled as he hastened toward them. "Everything you can fit on board! I want as much of my inventory out of this Godforsaken town as possible!" As Pollard unhappily complied, Hancock tossed his coat onto a crate. "Enough work for all of us, Duncan." He hesitated when Duncan did not react.

"They tried to take Sarah, John. She barely escaped." He explained what Pollard had witnessed.

Hancock uttered a very uncharacteristic curse and lowered himself onto a crate. "But how, Duncan? No one in her ring would betray her, or even give up her name."

Duncan did not answer. He was staring at Hancock's elegant carriage, or rather the coat of arms painted on its door. "The Red Cock," he said in a heavy voice. "I forgot about the Red Cock."

"The insignia?" Hancock said uncertainly as he followed Duncan's gaze. "My uncle devised it years ago, saying a proper family should have a coat of arms."

Duncan extracted the letter he had been carrying since searching the room used by Hastings and Vaughn, finally giving voice to the suspicion that had been gnawing at him. "You offered to provide funds to Sarah, to pay for the weaving factory to be built for the Hargreaves machines."

Hancock anxiously looked about, then spoke in a whisper. "Yes, but she never accepted."

"At least *she* has the good sense not to use the post for her secrets." He handed the letter to Hancock. "*You* gave them her name, John. They took it from the cover of this letter. The spies had this."

The merchant stared at the paper in stunned disbelief. "No, no, no! This can't be! Yes, these are my words, but not my writing!"

"You wrote to her, used her name and the Marblehead address."

"It was very short and discreet, as you can see."

"About a new weaving factory. A term not used in the colonies. A term that would make sense only to one speaking of the Hargreaves machines."

"It is not my writing," Hancock said again.

"Who handles your post?"

"My footman. A good and loyal man."

"He can read and write?"

"We sent him to school years ago. Just the basics."

"But he is a slave."

"I told you I have no slaves."

"Your aunt's slave."

"Well, technically, I suppose so. Why would that matter?"

"It matters above all. The agents from London are turning slaves against their owners by offering secret writs of manumission. He transcribed your letters before posting them. There was another about Gage. Gage has eleven, it said, and something about cannons and horsemen and black thunder and steel for ravens. Very suspicious."

"My God, Duncan," Hancock said, with a weak laugh. "It was about gifts for Gage's family! Gage has eleven children. I was ordering toy cannons and horsemen for his boys and Black Thunder licorice candy to go with the dolls I already bought for the girls. And for his wife, the one they call the Duchess, who loves her spinet, some of the new steel plectrums to replace the raven-quill ones they used on the old instruments! Surely I cannot be condemned for such noble intentions!"

"They won't arrest you, John," Duncan snapped, unable to hide his bitterness, "because you are too important and such a rich source of information."

"I'm not sure I follow," Hancock said in a choked voice.

"Your servant gave the letters to the spies. What color is his livery?"

"His livery? Gold with burgundy trim. I had it made in London."

"Exactly" was all Duncan said. "He covered it with an overcoat, but it still could be glimpsed." Sally had thought she had seen a drummer of the Twenty-Ninth, but there were other Africans in the town wearing yellowish uniforms.

A sound rose in Hancock's throat that started as a protest but ended as an anguished moan. "But your Sarah," he murmured, "they can't take her, I told you. She is impervious."

"They can't kill her, and they can't arrest her," Duncan agreed. "So they had to find a way to eliminate her without truly eliminating her. They found that way after the spies met the slave hunters from Barbados. They mean to capture her and sell her as a slave. What they call a fancy, sold to some remote plantation in the Indies."

Hancock looked up, stricken. "Dear God, the world collapses!"

Thankfully he had not asked Duncan about the word *Goat* written by Hastings or Vaughn at the bottom of the letter, apparently their nickname for the merchant. Duncan understood now. Huntsmen tied a goat to a stake so it would attract their true quarry.

The wind and tide were fair, the passage swift, but Duncan remembered little of it. For much of the short voyage he sat on the stern hatch cover, sometimes exchanging idle words with the helmsman but mostly watching the receding silhouette of Boston against the dimming sky. A strange sense of finality accompanied him, as if his earth were shifting. He wondered if he would ever see the city again as he had known it. The death of Crispus was a lead weight on his chest, not only because Duncan had grown fond of the strangely sensitive, bullheaded sailor. He had also begun to see how Crispus was evolving, so earnestly trying to make something more of his life.

Crispus died because of the secrets they discovered together. *Murderers will pay the price*, he had shouted after those who stalked Sarah, meaning he had recognized Montgomery, one of the grenadiers who burned the warehouse in Quincy. Crispus already held a deep-seated grudge against the occupying troops and had played a role in past riots, but it was more than a grudge that placed him at the front of bayonets on King Street, waving a club scant feet from the barrels of the Brown Bess muskets. He had gone in search of Montgomery and discovered him among the grenadier troops on King Street. Of the six or seven heavy sixty-nine-caliber balls fired, two had ripped into his flesh. That could only mean that two muskets, one of which was certainly held by Montgomery, were deliberately aimed at him. The second musket was likely held by another grenadier, somebody who witnessed Crispus's outburst at their encampment. The occasion had been too convenient for the grenadiers to resist. They used the melee as a cover to murder Crispus.

Duncan did not recall the last time he felt tears on his cheeks. They flowed not only for the friend he had lost, but for the friend that was to be. The vision he entertained of a new life for Crispus in Edentown had been a rare source of brightness in these dark weeks. More than once he had daydreamed about days when he and Conawago would teach Crispus about life on the frontier. He may have been a misfit in Boston, but he would have fit perfectly among the Iroquois. In his mind's eye Duncan had fashioned a role for Crispus as one of the intermediaries between the tribes and Edentown. He had even awakened one night, grinning, with a vision of Crispus scoring a goal in one of the tribes' lacrosse games. So, too, he had looked forward to the coming day when they would find the hours to compose the long-delayed letter to Crispus's brother in London. It would be a different letter now.

For the first hour he could think of nothing but Crispus. For the rest of the voyage into the moonlit fishing harbor he could think of nothing but Sarah. Their elegant marriage at Hancock mansion, surrounded by DeVries's Dutch flowers, was just one more lost dream now. The ruthless spies following the track of her intrigues were leaving death, destruction, and enslavement in their wake. The runaway slaves she so nobly wanted to help were now in greater danger than ever, and their protectress gone. Duncan would never be able to both help them and save Sarah.

She had recognized the sudden danger on the waterfront and saved herself and Esther but at the cost of surrendering to a journey to New York, into the clutches of the demon of Fort George, the general responsible for the torment in Boston.

Pollard was reluctant to yield Sarah's parcels to Duncan, insisting upon carrying them to the house. He retreated only when they found that Kipling and all the others were already asleep, and only then with a solemn promise from Duncan that he would see them delivered, unopened, to Kipling in the morning.

"Here they rest," Duncan said, pointing to the parcels as they lay on the kitchen table, "where they will greet Mr. Kipling as he arrives for breakfast." But as soon as Pollard left, Duncan took them to his own room, where he stowed them under his bed before opening his musty trunk. He removed the elegant clothing he seldom wore and from the bottom retrieved the pistols and tomahawk he had carried in the war. He was not surprised when Conawago entered. "Another massacre, I hear," the aged Nipmuc said in a weary voice. He once told Duncan he had lost count of the wars and massacres that occurred over his long life.

"The king's huntsmen and the bonemen pursue Sarah together," Duncan announced in a tight voice. "They mean to sell her into slavery in the Indies."

Conawago stared at Duncan, his eyes narrowing. He gave a sober nod, then settled onto the window seat and silently began sharpening his knife. The two of them were at war.

Duncan was waiting in the kitchen when Kipling came down, stretching and looking well rested. He paused and investigated the activity in the normally quiet scullery, where Moll and Henri were packing trunks. "Supplies," he observed, as if

Duncan required an explanation. "Sarah said we must start packing the supplies she gathered for your frontier settlement."

"There aren't many merchants where we live," Duncan said, then gestured to the table. "Let us break our fast together. I have news."

Kipling had heard rumors on the Marblehead waterfront of a shooting in Boston but knew no more. "The Boston papers will probably arrive soon. They will have details."

"I can tell you the details that affect us." Duncan proceeded to explain his tragic discoveries of the day before.

"Crispus?" came a startled voice behind Duncan. "Our Crispus?" It was Solomon, who quickly summoned those working in the scullery.

"Our Crispus," Duncan confirmed and tried to think of how to give meaning to the death. "He died for the truth." He fixed his gaze on Achilles. "He died confronting one of Mr. Bradford's killers."

Moll, to his surprise, crossed herself. She lowered herself into a chair. "Soldiers, you say."

"Grenadiers of the Twenty-Ninth, yes. Tempers had been building on both sides. Six or seven of them, with muskets. Scores of angry citizens pressing all around."

"And those people had guns?" Moll asked in a tight voice.

"They had snowballs and ice balls," Duncan replied. "Four died, and another may yet die, I hear. The soldiers were all arrested."

"Surely it was a horrible accident that English soldiers fired on English citizens," Kipling said.

"Crispus?" Josiah stepped from behind his father, tears in his eyes. "Crispus brought us cake that first night." The boy's voice cracked. "I never had cake before."

"Lobsterbacks will pay," came a deep voice from the hearth. Cuff had been standing in the shadows. "Crispus was my friend. He understood, understood blood was coming. Said no one would take us while he was still alive. Lobsterbacks!" Cuff spat, repeating the word as he pounded a hammer-like fist into his palm.

"We should wait for the papers," Duncan cautioned. "They will have had a day to assemble the facts." As the company decided who should venture to one of the waterfront inns to buy a paper, Duncan took Pine aside and sent him to Salem Harbor, then reported the rest of his news. Josiah had to help his still-frail father to a chair when he learned that his wife had left with Sarah on an uncertain journey to New York. "They had no choice," Duncan emphasized.

"We must get them back!" Henri growled.

"We will get them back," Duncan vowed, though he had no idea how he was to retrieve Sarah and Esther while still keeping the runaways protected.

Breakfast proved a solemn, quiet affair, and the only words spoken were memories of Crispus. When they finished, Duncan rose and bent over Kipling. "I will meet you in your bedroom. I have parcels for you, from Sarah."

Minutes later Kipling stood uneasily by his bed as Duncan closed the door and lowered the mysterious packages onto the comforter. "Open them."

The nervous clerk from New York moved to the other side of the bed, as if to avoid Duncan's reach. "I cannot. Miss Ramsey and Mr. Mulligan said—"

"Miss Ramsey and Mr. Mulligan do not understand the dangers we face. Open them!"

"It is not for me to say," Kipling protested.

"Sarah is in the clutches of the military, the same military who would see her dead if they discovered her secrets." Duncan pulled out his knife. Kipling gasped and backed against the wall. Duncan bent and cut the cord binding the first parcel, then unwrapped the length of duck cloth that covered it.

It held clothing, or more specifically a uniform. The coat was olive in color with buff facing on the lapels, the sleeveless waistcoat and breeches a matching buff color. Duncan looked up in confusion. "This is worn by the New York militia."

Kipling stiffly nodded.

The second package also contained a uniform, this one a blue coat with red facing. It could have been the uniform of a Marblehead militia officer, except for the white leather breeches and checkered shirt. Duncan stretched his memory for several silent breaths. "This is for a Jersey Blue," he finally recalled, referring to one of the more renowned colonial regiments of the last war. The third was another uniform but not one he recognized. The blue broadcloth coat had cream-colored cuffs and lapels, with brass buttons, a cream waistcoat with blue breeches, and a black hat with yellow ribbon edging. "Kipling?"

The slight clerk winced and remained silent.

Duncan's patience was gone. He respected the man's stubborn adherence to his pledge of secrecy, but Sarah's life hung in the balance. "I promised to get you on a boat. The waterfront can be so confusing. The boat you board might be going to New York. Or perhaps I make a mistake. Maybe you go out to the Grand Banks for three or four months, even to Greenland's shores for the seals. Or Bilbao. I recollect there was also talk of a vessel bound for far Constantinople. Most of the captains are friends of mine."

Kipling stared at the floor as he spoke. "The Independent Artillery Company of New London. In Connecticut province."

Duncan held up the Connecticut coat, then compared it to the others. They were all of a similar size, made for a man of his own stature, though broader in the shoulders. "Not for you."

"No, sir," Kipling murmured.

"You work for Hercules Mulligan, the famed bespoke tailor to the military. Why couldn't he make these? Why a Boston tailor?"

When Kipling made no reply, Duncan offered an answer. "Because," he concluded, "the uniforms are for someone here, in Massachusetts. Someone who intends to impersonate officers of three different militia companies."

Kipling glanced up with a wounded expression.

"There is no shame in sharing these things. I have given my life over to Sarah Ramsey and secrets of the patriots. Whose goals seem to increasingly overlap. Tell me, what is it you do exactly for Hercules?"

"I don't know all the details of why he gives me errands like this. I told him I don't want to know, safer for all. In normal days I do his books. He is rather cavalier with his accounts. I had to show him how he sometimes charges less for the sale of his clothing than the cost of the materials, especially when there is expensive lace and gilt-trimmed fabric." Kipling lowered his voice to a near whisper. "And I write things."

Duncan sat on the window seat and gestured Kipling to sit on the bed. "Things?" He considered the nervous, well-spoken man. "What did you do before joining Hercules?"

"I was a scribe. For the general."

Duncan stared at the man in surprise. "General Gage? Thomas Gage?"

Kipling nodded. "I have been blessed with an elegant hand, people say. Orders, decrees, reports to London, official journal entries, letters to field commanders. The general always liked things to be very proper, said such papers would be his legacy, since many would be going into official records and archives."

Duncan studied the diminutive man with new interest. "And you shared the information with Hercules."

"Not at first." Kipling returned Duncan's steady stare, then sighed. "I had a brother, a prosperous merchant who put all his money into a ship. He told me it was just the beginning, that he would soon have a fleet, that with his earnings he meant to endow a church and eventually establish a new college. One night he was caught unloading at a dark harbor on the New Jersey coast. The general was furious about all the smugglers and desired to make an example of him. Seized the ship and cargo and chose to pursue one of those actions against the accused smuggler. If it was just the ship and cargo, that's called *in rem* and only their value is at stake. But when an owner is pursued personally, the damages are tripled and all his assets forfeit, with a one-third share to the governor, who shared generously with the general. My brother was ruined. He was thrown into debtor's prison. They lost their house, their church pew, their best clothing. His wife had to move into a tenement and take on seamstress work to support the children. After my brother caught jail fever and died, I could no longer work for the general. I told him I had to leave so I could support my brother's family, which was true, but I also had to leave because staying would have stained my soul. I had already started sharing information with Mr. Mulligan as my penance, you might say, though soon I willingly embraced the patriot cause." Kipling looked up with a new glint in his eyes. "Four died on the Boston snow yesterday. London has no right to treat us so. Our liberty is given to us by Jehovah, not that George."

"Would the general know of the agents secretly set against us by the War Council?"

"No," Kipling said, then reconsidered. "I don't know. Things are changing. There are new members of the War Council in London, who seem to think their job is to make war. They may not think they need to consult General Gage. But he makes it his business to know everything the government undertakes in the colonies, so perhaps he discovered it. He would not approve. But even the supreme commander has commanders, across the ocean."

"Meaning he would sacrifice Miss Ramsey if need be."

"Surely it would not come to that. Those slavers would never reveal themselves to the general. Mr. Mulligan had met her in Philadelphia, you may recall. He was very impressed with her. The general has a genuine interest in keeping harmony on the frontier, and she is said to have great sway with the tribes."

"But?" Duncan heard the tentativeness in Kipling's voice.

The clerk turned at the sound of someone at the door. Pine entered and fixed Duncan with a worried expression, glancing uneasily at the man on the bed.

"Kipling is one of us," Duncan said.

Pine stepped closer. "She's gone. The *Indigo Queen* sailed this afternoon. Her crew was depleted, at least four men left on shore from injuries from tangling with Cuff that night. Melville and Hugo arrived on the Boston coach then worked the taverns, offering extra silver for sailors to sign on. They found only a couple boys, because the fishing season started. They wanted a dozen, said just a short voyage, but they needed so many because they would be making all sail, day and night, due to urgent business in New York."

Duncan found John Glover on the trim little brig he often used for voyages to the West Indies.

"We need to sail to New York, John," he declared. He couldn't quite understand the amusement that arose on his friend's weathered face. "Today," he stated. "The afternoon tide."

"But Duncan, we be chartered already—"

"I don't care, John. Everything has changed. I will make it up to you somehow. We need to—"

"—for New York," the mariner finished. "Chartered by your Sarah. A quick run, she said, with some of her friends. Though she said you would be staying here."

Duncan took a shuddering breath. "When were you going to tell me this, Captain Glover?"

"She's going to tell you surely. We don't lift anchor for two or three days yet. A couple days' business there, then back, she said. Could return in a week with fair winds."

"Sarah has been taken by the government. To New York. To Gage."

Glover was stunned into silence. "Jesus and his bloody saints!" he muttered, then sat on the stern rail and listened to Duncan's tale of the night before, including the riot by the Custom House and the death of their mutual acquaintance. "Crispus dead! Is it possible? That big bull of a man?"

"I saw him, John. Not even a big bull of a man can survive two musket balls fired at close range. At least three others died. Boston is on the verge of war. And Hastings sparked it. No order to fire came from the soldiers' officer. Hastings caused the incident he wanted and is now off in pursuit of Sarah." He finished by reporting news that the bounty men were now in league with the Horse Guards spies.

"I declare, Duncan, such times we live in. We will pray for Sarah, and for Crispus's immortal soul."

"We will do more than that. We will rescue her. We will stop those who would launch us into war. You have already set your course for New York."

"But I await more cargo. And I don't have a crew, or even all my stores, which alone will take a day to bring on board and stow. First Fare is always the richest haul. Every man with three months to spare sailed with the fleet. I was planning to go to Lynn today, to see who I can pry out of the taverns there."

Duncan gave voice to the idea that had been germinating since he left the house. "The upper Hudson is beautiful, John. A wide river flanked by mountains. Not to be missed."

"Duncan?"

"Suppose we stopped in New York, then sailed north, say up to Kingston, where the road to Edentown starts?"

Glover rubbed the stubble on his chin as he contemplated Duncan's proposal. "So we rescue your Sarah from the bastion of the New York tyrant, then stop a war. And Sarah wouldn't want us to ignore that other business of hers."

Duncan silently eyed Glover. His friend knew more about that business than Duncan did. "So long as we keep Sarah safe," he said with a nod.

"Meaning we take on the British army and navy."

"And the king," Duncan added. "But they never had to tangle with a Marbleheader."

A grin grew on Glover's sturdy countenance. "I've always had a hankering to see the mighty rivers of the midcoast. The Hudson above Manhattan. Maybe even someday the Delaware," he added with whimsy.

Duncan looked toward the big yellow house on the hill. "Then I will finish filling your holds. And I will supply the crew. We sail today."

Chapter 11

IT WAS LATE AFTERNOON, WITH Cape Cod off their starboard bow, before Duncan had a moment to rest, standing by Glover at the helm. He took a deep, satisfying breath. The salt air and scent of tarred rigging was a tonic to his soul. The brig was small but spry, and Glover's touch was that of a seasoned sailing master, keeping her close to the wind now that all her canvas was unfurled.

"I appreciate your not laughing at the performance in the rigging," he said to the Marblehead mariner.

"Your men have spirit, which counts for a lot in my book," Glover replied.

None of the runaways had any experience sailing a ship, and all had seemed reluctant to climb the shrouds. They showed little interest when Glover's first mate scampered up to the maintop and gestured for them to follow. But when Duncan explained that their chances of saving Sarah and Esther might depend on a speedy passage to New York and then started climbing the rigging himself, young Josiah jumped into the shrouds behind him, quickly followed by Pine, Solomon, and To-bias. As Josiah's father, weak but no longer frail, watched anxiously from the deck, his son joined in releasing the mainsail. The new seamen, far from able-bodied, missed stays, released the wrong lines, and argued over how best to climb in and out of the maintop, but after an hour Duncan no longer feared that at any moment one would plunge to his death. He had Henri follow him as he paced the deck, calling orders to the crew in the rigging, telling him that the next day he would assume bosun mate duties, relaying orders to those aloft from either Duncan or Glover at the helm.

"I don't know whether to laugh or cry," Glover added as he watched Tobias slip off a ratline and dangle with his hands on the shrouds, "but they are quick of limb and eager in their work."

"We'll be in trouble if we hit foul weather."

"Which is why I am staying closer to the shore than I would otherwise care to. I know most of the harbors between Boston and Long Island. With luck we can make it into one if we have to ride out a storm."

"Which means staying closer to shoals and revenue patrols," Duncan pointed out.

"All the dangers we face on land, only wetter," Glover said with a grin. "Now steady the wheel so I can light my pipe."

Duncan kept the helm for considerably longer, for Glover was summoned by the first mate to examine a fraying rope, then disappeared belowdecks. He rejoiced at his time in control of the two-masted ship, finding her sharply responsive in spite of the less than perfect set of her sails. She was nimble and would well handle the challenging spring currents of the Hudson if ever they made it so far. If only cargo was shifted slightly to port, he decided, she would be one of the most responsive square-riggers he had ever guided.

He lost track of time as he watched sail and sea and was not aware that his Nipmuc friend approached, only discovered him standing at his side, silhouetted by the setting sun.

"I hated the big ships when I encountered them as a boy," Conawago confided in a contemplative voice. The sea seemed to be renewing him as well. "I was sure they were just misshapen houses that had been set afloat. Man was meant to experience the water in a canoe or dugout, to be one with the water spirits. Only when I was halfway across to France on my first crossing did I begin to appreciate them. In its essence, I realized, a ship is a statement of defiance against the world, an assertion that some men can, and will, go to places they were never meant to be." He fixed Duncan with a meaningful gaze, then lifted his chin, savoring the wind before he spoke again. "It is a place of detachment." He gestured toward Solomon, who was perched halfway up the shrouds, holding on with one hand as he leaned out over the sea. The wind ebbed a moment and Duncan heard his deep laughter. "The Jesuits would say he is having an epiphany," Conawago solemnly concluded. "He has detached from his past and discovered that the life behind a man doesn't have to be the one ahead of him."

Without waiting for a response Conawago spread his arms wide, over his head. The wind freshened, whipping his long silver hair into the air. It almost seemed he was flying. "*Yoyanere! Yoyanere!*" he shouted toward the sky. It was both a joyful laugh and a prayer.

When Glover finally took the helm at the end of the watch, Duncan decided to further investigate the lay of the cargo in the hope he might find a way to adjust the trim. He had not been watching when the new anvil for Edentown had been stowed, and he realized that simply shifting that one object might offer a solution. He climbed down one steep ladder stair and was about to descend another when he was struck by a familiar scent. Duncan knew only one person who flavored her chowder with rosemary. Following the smell to the galley, he leaned against the doorframe until the cook finally turned with a stack of pewter plates.

"Mr. Duncan!" Moll exclaimed. "I ne'er got to speak with you in all the rush!"

"Next I suppose I'll find the widow Godwin in the fo'c'sle doing her knitting."

Moll laughed. "Her seafaring days are behind her. Mr. Glover needed a cook for three or four weeks. And who else is there to look after everyone? Conawago will forget to put on his shoes, and from time to time Cuff needs a rap on his knuckles with my wooden spoon for his coarse language. Not to mention Henri's doses, with Esther gone." She shrugged. "If I had stayed I would have been dragged off to that Methodist church five days a week and fixing dinner for the pastor on the others, and me still working my rosary each night. He be a healthy widower and she a well-off widow. She still has life in her if she would just get out of her rooms, I told her. 'The reverend needs but to sample your own cooking to make an offer,'" she added with another laugh.

As she spoke Achilles appeared in the narrow doorway by the stove, carrying a basket of potatoes.

"You found a way to avoid balancing on the yards," Duncan observed with a grin.

"If I were meant to scrape the sky, I would have been born with wings. Miss

Moll says she has ample work for a pot minder, potato peeler, and all-'round scrubber," Achilles suggested with an uncertain smile.

"Cook's mate on a ship this size is a part-time post," Duncan declared. "There'll be topside duties for you starting tomorrow. We are shorthanded." He saw the worry rising on Achilles's face. "On the deck," he added. "We will keep you out of the sky."

Achilles relaxed and with the flat of his hand against his temple offered what Duncan took to be a salute.

"Moll, dear," came a voice from the pantry. "Might you have a rag to wipe my slates?"

Rebecca Prescott offered a bright smile as Duncan appeared in the entry. "Off to Edentown at last!" she exclaimed. "Our hasty departure caught me off guard. But I managed," she said with a gesture to the wide shelf that normally would have been used for meal preparation. Stacked on it were several small slates, two hornbooks, and several texts. "The lessons we started must not languish, even at sea," the new Edentown schoolteacher stated.

"We are shorthanded as it is," Duncan observed.

"But Tobias is making such great progress with his reading, and Solomon with his addition. Perhaps if I lend a hand on deck, battening hatches and coiling ropes and other such nautical pursuits? Then might I have just half an hour after the morning meal?"

Duncan had no heart to argue with the young widow. "What is life if there is no learning?" he replied with a smile, citing words often used by his mother to cajole him back into his books.

Duncan paced along the compartments of tightly packed crates and bales on the cargo deck. He quickly located the freight bound for Edentown, including the heavy anvil, which he could not budge. Glover had mentioned being under charter for Sarah already but had been coy about her purpose. It had to mean she had already given him cargo for one of her manufacturing schemes.

He retraced his steps with a new eye, reading such labels as existed by lantern. Woolens, shoes, heads for hoes and shovels, crockery, and half a dozen other innocuous items filled the hold. He hesitated at a crate marked *Belgian lace*. Sarah was not fond of lace. Retrieving a small iron crow, he pried off the lid with careful strokes. He grinned. The crate was packed with spindles to be used in looms.

Duncan did not intrude upon the crates marked with the diamond shape Glover used on the flags of his merchant vessels. Glover was a merchant in his own right and still did an active trade with European ports via New York, which was known for not being as fastidious about nonimportation as Boston. The final compartment at the end of the hold, however, was different from the others, with walls and a heavy barred door sealing it off. Many merchant ships had such compartments for more valuable cargo, and in some vessels, captains chose to secure hard liquor in such sealed closets.

He stared at the door, contemplating the maze he found himself in. At every turn in the past weeks the full truth had been hidden from him. Here at least was a barrier he could deal with. He lifted the bar and laid it on the deck. The heavy door groaned so loudly as he opened it that he glanced over his shoulder. A curtain of overlapping oilcloth faced him. He pushed through and discovered that the entire chamber was lined with such cloth, including the ceiling and deck, which was also covered with fresh straw. The cargo rack spanned the entire back wall and held what he took to be casks of wine or liquor, well seated in rows of wooden cradles. Each row was secured with an oak plank mortised at the ends to fit over small wooden eyes, with pegs inserted to hold the planks fast.

Duncan loosened the pegs of the plank at his waist and extracted a cask, shaking it. The contents were not wine or liquor or ale, and to his surprise were not even liquid. Indeed, it was not shaped at all like the casks seen in taverns. He noticed the copper hoops around the container and stared in disbelief and, for a moment, fear. Copper was generally too expensive a material to be used merely for hooping a keg, but it did possess one crucial property. Copper would never spark. Inscribed on the side of the keg, in black paint, were the numerals 14/27, under a row of circles, squares, and triangles inscribed with the same paint. He carefully slipped the keg back into its cradle, replaced the restraining board and its pegs, then left the small, snug compartment exactly as he found it. He reached the deck above, resolved to confront Glover about his secret, dangerous cargo, but then he recognized a raspy laugh coming from a cabin near the one he and Conawago were to share. He lifted the latch, stepped inside, and froze. Conawago was playing chess with the night soil collector.

Conawago seemed not to notice the anger rising on Duncan's face. "You know William, I believe, Duncan," he cheerfully stated.

"We have not exchanged Christian names," Duncan replied in a taut voice. "Apparently William has left the good people of Marblehead in their own filth."

"Not at all, not at all!" Boyle replied, the Irish brogue thick in his voice. "The lads who do my charcoal agreed to take the cart during my absence. I answered all their questions by telling them my mare knows the route and each stop, just let her do the thinking," he added with a laugh.

"I have some questions as well," Duncan said. "Starting with how you allowed Solomon and Tobias to be taken."

Boyle studied Duncan with a cool expression for a moment, then grinned. "I do regret that, but they do tell such a grand tale of their rescue. You are their valiant knight, their brave redeemer." Boyle raised a much-worn silver flask. "I toast you, McCallum." The Irishman took a swallow and extended the flask to Duncan.

Duncan ignored the gesture. He scanned the chamber, noting that a shelf held several of the books he saw at Boyle's cottage. Under the folding bed were three familiar parcels. "Your berth was well prepared. You must have already been on board when we started loading. You were always intending to come."

"We've had a plan, yes."

"You and Sarah."

"Let's say our association of committed patriots."

"Without the knowledge of the Sons of Liberty."

"That would be the Sons led by John Hancock and Samuel Adams? The first is so naive and so taken with impressing senior officials that he may not always even recognize a secret, and the second so fond of ale that he oft loses control of his tongue. The Boston Sons be a leaky vessel. Despite your best efforts, sir," Boyle added. "And no offense intended."

They were on perilous ground. Duncan turned for help to Conawago, who only grinned. "None taken," he stiffly replied. He could not argue the point. He studied the chamber again, attempting to make sense of the man. It was so compact that with one step he was beside the books. He extracted the one that had been open on Boyle's table, the one Conawago examined on their visit. "You were not always a collector of night soil," he observed.

Boyle fixed Duncan with a penetrating, almost challenging gaze. "I've come to see that post as something of a noble calling. A lonely job to be sure, but one with great potential."

Duncan held up the book. "Robert Boyle," he said, reciting the author's name, and then the title. "*The Sceptical Chymist.* I recall the book being used in a class at Edinburgh."

"My extraordinary great-grandfather. One of the most celebrated scholars of his century. Member of the Royal Society. His own father was the wealthy Earl of Cork, but he was only one of fourteen children and the intervening generations were profligate. My dear mother liked to say I inherited his intellect, the greatest treasure of all, though there were times in my youth when I would have gladly surrendered half my gray matter for a handful of potatoes. And there was a trinket from great-grandfather Robert, which I have always valued more than ever she did."

"Trinket?" Conawago asked.

Boyle studied each of them with raised brows, as if deciding whether to bring them into one of his most precious confidences, then pulled a tarnished chain from his neck and with a solemn air laid it out on the nearly empty chessboard. The pendant it held appeared to be two fragments of flat brass hinged with a disc at the top. "The forebear visited Florence in the 1640s and studied with that most venerated of Italian astronomers, who gave him the instrument this survives from."

"Venerated astronomer?" Duncan asked, now genuinely interested. "Surely the old master was not still living by—"

"Oh, but he was! Galileo himself, though he did depart this world not long after. And he gave my grandfather one of his famous compasses for measuring angles and making calculations. Some rascally uncles since then played havoc with it, but I have the one scrap that is left, retrieved from the rubbish bin by my dear mother when she was young." Boyle touched the metal with a fond expression. "I used to hold it for hours as a boy, feeling an odd power in it, like the relic of a saint. Eventually it led me to investigate his old equations. This little scrap inspired my career, ye might say."

Duncan leaned over the metal, examining the numbers inscribed on it.

"Nay be shy, McCallum. Pick it up," Boyle encouraged.

Duncan felt an unexpected thrill as he lifted the tarnished brass that had once been held by Galileo. It certainly had the feel of antiquity. He moved the two fragments of the compass's original arms, each about as long as his thumb, and found that the old disc hinge still functioned perfectly. He recalled a replica of Galileo's famed compass at the University of Edinburgh that was used to transfer angles and calculate trajectories. He saw Conawago's excited anticipation and handed it to his friend, who gave a moan of pleasure as it dropped into his palm.

"Inspired your career?" Duncan asked Boyle.

"As I said, we had no inheritance, just some rocky land in County Munster. Ever wonder why so many Irish lads are in the infantry? We hated the army but hated starvation even more. The bonus paid when I signed up was enough to feed my poor mother for a year. The recruiter asked if I had any particular skills. Numbers, I said. Very well, says he, and shipped me off to the artillery in Cork." Boyle gave a mock salute. "Master Gunnery Sergeant Boyle at your service," he quipped. "I gave them nigh twenty years, supporting my mother and young orphaned nephew nearly all that while."

"But you resigned?"

"In a manner of speaking. My dear mother died of consumption. Then I discovered that a thieving paymaster had begun holding back the money I sent to support my nephew, who had all the ability to finish school and go on to university. A very bright lad, his generation's version of the great-*grandpère*. But he had no support after the neighbors died, and he thought I had abandoned him. He was caught stealing a loaf from an army kitchen. They hanged him on the spot. The day after I heard the news, I was sent to pick up supplies in Limerick. Instead I took ship for Boston."

"You're saying you deserted," Duncan stated.

"I chose to exercise my God-given freedom, ye might say. I was owed two months' back pay and gave the king good value for every shilling I had taken until then. Got to Boston, took day jobs in the rope walks, and sometimes served as tutor for a merchant's children. Miss Sarah visited the shop one day and met me as I was teaching them to count out inventory. She made me an offer a few days later, to take a post as teacher of natural philosophy in her settlement in New York province. But as we got better acquainted and she learned of my background, she had a more intriguing proposition."

Boyle shifted his narrative to sketch out for Conawago what the complete Galileo compass looked like, then explain how a similar device was often used in artillery companies for calculating gun elevations and powder charges. He studiously avoided Duncan's gaze, clearly disinclined to explain Sarah's proposal.

Duncan lifted the seventeenth-century chemistry volume spine upright on the narrow table hinged beneath the bookshelf and let it drop open to what, judging by the dog-eared, worn pages, was its most frequently consulted passage. It was what Conawago glimpsed at Boyle's cottage. "Potassium nitrate," he recited as he scanned the page. He hesitated, suddenly feeling quite foolish for not previously grasping the truth. "The sign on the lintel over your door is from alchemy," he said as he searched his memory. "Potassium nitrate? I am far from a scholar of chemical properties, but I have actually read all three volumes of the *Encyclopedia Britannica*. I recall that it is the most difficult ingredient of gunpowder. Otherwise you just need sulfur and charcoal."

Boyle fixed Duncan with another of his deep gazes, then finally shrugged. "Saltpeter be devilishly tricky," he agreed, using the more common term for the chemical.

"It can be made from human waste," Duncan said.

"Horse manure as well, but that of the two-footed species serves much better, especially when people are eager to daily serve it up. I have often been amused at the thought that all of Marblehead provides my essential ingredient, Loyalist and patriot alike."

"I recall it takes many months," Duncan observed. "The waste has to decompose to release the nitrate."

"Oh aye," Boyle said with a hint of pride in his voice. "Ye got to baby it. It's called the French method, after the clever Frogs who first developed it. Dry it out, though not too much. Add wood ash, keep adding urine over time. It can be done in barrels or laid out in beds of straw."

Duncan recalled Pine's report of strange gardening beds on the hill past Boyle's cottage. "You've done both."

"Aye, though I prefer the beds."

Duncan lowered himself into the remaining chair, his mind racing as he reconsidered the events of recent weeks. "You sell nothing to tanneries then."

"'Twould be a waste of patriotic resources."

Duncan recalled the mystery of the two packages Sarah retrieved from DeVries. She told Crispus that if the parcels were dropped, they'd be in Hades. It made no sense at the time, but now he understood. She had been carrying brimstone. "Sarah Ramsey obtained your sulfur."

"We had difficulty with our lines of supply from the Indies, ye might say, and then with our go-between."

"Bradford in Quincy," Duncan suggested.

"Not his fault. We had a large shipment of guano and casks of sulfur lined up in Barbados, then some damned plantation owner decided to take them for fertilizer and fumigating his barns. Bradford was a good man, rest his soul." He paused, looking at Conawago, who still studied the Galileo pendant. "And yes, Miss Ramsey made other arrangements for sulfur with the Dutch apothecary. I could make do without the guano but not the sulfur. And a sharp job she did of it. I told her once she seemed to have no fear. She replied, 'Mohawks learn to ignore fear.'" Boyle shot a pointed gaze at Duncan. "I didn't pursue that particular assertion, though I must admit I was intrigued."

As he spoke, the door creaked open. "Mr. Boyle," came a high-pitched voice from the other side, "I examined the New York uniform and they forgot the buff at the bottom of the sleeves. But I am certain at Mr. Mulligan's shop we can quickly—" Kipling froze as he saw Duncan, then began to back away.

"No more secrets," Boyle said, gesturing him into the chamber.

"Except," Duncan pointed out, "the secret of twenty kegs of powder stored below. Please tell me you are not planning to explode the headquarters of the British army."

"We have no such intention," Boyle assured him. "Though what a glorious sight that would be, to be sure."

Conawago, too, was intrigued. "You are equipping yourself with costumes," he observed. "As for a theatrical performance. Which perhaps makes those kegs below props for your stage?"

Boyle raised his flask to the Nipmuc. "Your wisdom extends beyond the chessboard." He turned back to Duncan. "Miss Ramsey once called you a juggler of secrets for the Sons of Liberty."

Duncan just returned his steady gaze.

Boyle grinned. "The kind of response I would expect." He raised his flask again and offered it to Duncan. This time Duncan took it, drank, then handed it to Conawago, who likewise took a swallow. He began to return the flask to the Irishman, then paused and handed it to Kipling, who accepted it as he might a communion cup, taking a quick, reverent swallow.

Boyle gave an approving smile. "Here we be. We band of brothers, as the Bard would say." He screwed the cap on the flask and sighed. "The British army has contempt for the provincial militias. They call them Yankee-Doodle clubs and such. In a way it is justified, for the militias have no teeth. Even the few that have a full complement of muskets and a few old cannons from the last war have no gunpowder to speak of. The army only gives them stale or defective powder, and the militias have to accept such leavings since no one makes powder on this side of the Atlantic. The few mills that produced it in the French war shut down years ago, and the Crown sees to it that no one starts anew."

"Until you started producing your pungent source of nitrate," Duncan said.

"Oh aye, we had such grand ambitions at first, but I fear the truth caught up with us. We have neither the equipment nor the excretory capacity to make a meaningful volume. Nor can we attain sufficient quality. Serviceable powder has seven thousand grains to the pound. The best I have achieved is four thousand, too coarse for the military. And weapons have a prodigious appetite. A pound will give less than fifty musket shots. An eighteen-pounder cannon wants six or seven pounds of good powder for each shot. What you saw in the hold is my entire year's effort.

"Which meant our hopes were forfeit. We were lost. I was about to start selling my product to the tanneries, when Miss Ramsey had me join a meeting with a gentleman from Connecticut who happened to be a gunnery sergeant."

"In the New London artillery company," Duncan suggested, recalling the mysterious uniform.

"Exactly. Very knowledgeable gentleman, had served in the British artillery and still in very good stead with the regular army, so much that he is often called upon to teach new artillery recruits in Boston, Newport, and New York. He had been in Boston on such duty when he met Miss Ramsey at one of those Hancock soirees. As you well know she has a way of bringing out confidences. Turns out he had just learned that his younger brother had been illegally impressed and died at sea. 'Never again will I serve the lobsterbacks,' he vowed to us. 'My sole purpose shall be to strengthen the military of the provinces.' That's when she suggested a more private meeting the next day, just the three of us in a room at the Sign of the Ship inn. We went over every detail about the movement of powder, from the way it is shipped from the British mills in carefully marked batches to delivery and shipment by the navy, conveyance to crown arsenals, verification, testing, storage, everything.

"She took great interest in the testing, how each new batch from England is tested before being accepted for the British artillery. If a test fails, we discovered, the entire batch, which might be twenty-five or even fifty kegs, is decommissioned from the arsenal and sent to militia units. The army cares not if militia guns misfire. Turns out the New London artillery company had been taking over much of the testing.

"'So how, prithee,' I ask, 'do we turn a keg or two of defective powder into fifty kegs of number one powder.' 'Don't know,' says he, 'but let's drink on it.' And after a round of punch, your dear Miss Ramsey says maybe we gamble with it, with the odds at fifty to one. The tale of the Trojan horse, she says, only the opposite. We give a gift to the army that we know will be rejected, and in return we receive the real prize. A wagonload of the king's prime powder."

Conawago pounded his fist on the chessboard, upsetting the remaining pieces. "If you could insert a defective keg into a batch and found a way to assure it was the one tested, you could steal fifty good kegs before their very eyes!"

"You've smoked the truth of it," Boyle replied with a satisfied smile.

Duncan was having a more difficult time, "It's been a long day," he said to his companions. "Perhaps we might dissect this grand scheme?"

It was Kipling who answered. "It's simplicity itself. A gunnery expert arrives at the arsenal from Connecticut, seasoned in testing procedures, filling in for the army's own expert whose orders somehow misdirected him to Halifax," he said with a devious grin.

"Only one of your contributions, you clever lad," Boyle declared, pounding the clerk on the back.

"The keg or two of bad powder has to be marked exactly to match the shipping records," Kipling continued, "in which unique numbers are assigned to each British mill. Every keg also bears the mill's identifying symbols, usually geometric shapes set out in a particular order, unique to the shipment, and its batch number. We were able to obtain copies of those records, transmitted to Fort George before the powder was shipped. As the details became available I delivered them to Mr. Bradford, and then Achilles got them to Marblehead."

"Which is why he would sail across the bay to meet Sarah at an old cemetery," Duncan interjected, then paused. "Are you saying you have already done such a switch?"

"There are thirty kegs of prime powder in Portsmouth," Boyle answered with a nod, "another twenty-five in Lexington, from the first exchange at Castle William last November. The New York shipment is bigger. We are hoping for several dozen kegs for arsenals up the Hudson and in Connecticut."

"But how do you get the bad powder in with the good?"

"The arsenal's magazines are full. New powder is stored in empty barracks outside the gate." Kipling paused as if for effect. "And those are guarded, rather lightly, by the New York militia."

"All this assumes the new shipments arrive from England on schedule," Duncan pointed out.

Kipling nodded. "Due this week, on the aptly named *Thunderer*. She is something of a showcase ship, only two years out of the Bristol yard and all spit and polish. General Gage likes to show her off when she's in port. I expect he will escort Miss Ramsey for a visit, with the women of his household."

"Women?" Duncan asked Kipling.

"Well, yes. His American wife, an energetic and valuable woman who stays quite engaged with their eleven children. And there is a servant who is part of the general's household, the household steward, for whom the general has a great fondness. Maiden, I should say," Kipling answered. "A fixture in the fortress, you might say, born to service."

"Born to service?" Conawago asked.

"Her long-departed mother belonged to some Dutch family, her grandparents having been captured in some distant war. And taken many years ago by the government in lieu of taxes."

Duncan leaned toward the man who had been General Gage's clerk. "You're saying that Gage has a slave? And Miss Ramsey does not know this?"

"She's treated most equitably," Kipling said, as if he had to defend Gage. "A very comfortable existence. I am somewhat acquainted with her, since the general often had her come help in his office, especially to serve guests from London. And I can't imagine Miss Ramsey knows, though surely they will meet soon."

Duncan and Conawago exchanged a worried glance. Sarah was being pursued by bounty hunters and spies, and her only chance of surviving lay in remaining amiable with Gage. But her amiability would disappear, and she would turn on the general when she discovered he kept a slave in his household.

When Duncan took over the helm at midnight, Solomon and Tobias were still on deck, despite the end of their watch. Tobias was pointing out constellations to the younger man. After an hour Tobias sought his rest, curling up with a blanket by the mainmast instead of going to his hammock below. Solomon came aft and silently stood at the rail a few feet from Duncan.

"I first started sailing with my grandfather along the Scottish coast," Duncan eventually offered. "I remember telling my grandfather I never wanted to go back to land again, that I wanted to sail forever."

Solomon kept looking out over the moonlit water. "It speaks of a great and quiet power," he said, gesturing to the sea.

"A freedom all its own," Duncan replied. "Here we are severed from all the world, and its troubles fade like a mirage on the horizon. There's only you and the sea and the ship."

"Captain Glover said these waters touch Africa, that my people would have seen them."

"If you wish, you could serve on a Glover ship across the Atlantic. Eventually get home."

The former slave turned toward him with a small, sad smile. "My tribe was farmers, not fighters. The tribe in the mountains were all warriors. When I was a boy they attacked one night, killed many, and took everyone else to sell to the slave ships on the coast. My home is gone. My people are gone."

Neither man spoke for long minutes.

"My own people were lost," Duncan finally said. "Conawago's people were all lost. Sarah calls our settlement on the frontier a refuge for orphans."

"Sometimes it feels like all of this land, all of America, is becoming an orphan."

Duncan recalled the words Conawago had spoken that afternoon. "America is discovering that the life behind it doesn't have to be the life ahead of it."

Solomon nodded. "And here on the sea we are between worlds. Between lives."

"Gathering strength," Duncan said.

"Strength?" Solomon asked.

"Like my grandfather said when I asked to sail forever: take all the strength from the sea that you can, because eventually we always have to go back to the world."

Chapter 12

RETURNING TO THE CITY OF New York had always been inevitable for Duncan, for it was the outpost of the War Council in America, the hub around which all soldiers on the continent orbited, and the nexus of much greater trade and travel than Boston. Duncan believed Colonel Dalrymple when he confessed to having no authority over the Horse Guards operatives, but he doubted that the same could be said of Major General Gage, supreme military commander and the single most powerful man in America. From a distance, in Massachusetts and Philadelphia, Gage maintained a rather mythical appearance, a god only slightly lesser than the deity who ruled in Windsor Castle. Gage had been in his position for many years, revered at first for his victory in the bitter war with Chief Pontiac but now more feared than revered as the surrogate of King George. And Duncan wasn't just venturing into the home terrain of the tyrant. To rescue Sarah, he would have to reach the very lair of the beast.

They arrived in the gray light before dawn, threading their way through the surprising number of anchored vessels, including half a dozen warships, with Glover at the helm and Duncan at the rail with Kipling, who proudly pointed out the landmarks of his burgeoning city. Years earlier, Duncan had disembarked into the New World and entered into his bonded servitude here. This Manhattan was dramatically transformed from the sleepy Dutch town he first encountered. The population had increased to twenty thousand, and even from a distance he sensed an air of prosperity, much more so than in Boston. The streets were mostly cobbled, Kipling reported, and a medical school had been established at King's College, in a great stone edifice overlooking the Hudson. Dutch-style houses with stepped, street-facing gables still dominated the waterfront, but Duncan noted many more traditional English structures beyond them. A surprising number of substantial buildings and steeples punctuated the skyline. The city now had its own police force and several companies of militia, and, Kipling boasted, Vauxhall Gardens on Warren Street was "a pleasure garden said to rival its namesake in London."

Kipling quieted as the four-pointed Fort George came into view at the tip of Manhattan island. The impressive stone structure looming over batteries built along the rocky shoreline served as both the military headquarters and the seat of government.

"Where you once worked, I take it," Duncan observed.

The clerk silently nodded. "First built by the Dutch in the last century," he declared, as if he were more comfortable speaking of the past than the present. "They had a wall that extended across the entire island to protect from the savages." He cast an awkward glance at Pine, standing nearby. "When peace finally came, they tore it down, so you wouldn't know, except its path is now called Wall Street."

"So the fort is where the general conducts his business?" Duncan asked. "And his residence?"

"He has a veritable horde of children, and his wife is from a prominent New Jersey family. An aristocrat, at least in bearing. They call her the Duchess, a formidable woman, as they say. She was reluctant to raise their many children inside the fort so they have a commodious residence nearby." Kipling shifted his gaze to the harbor, then pointed beyond the fort to the wide mouth of the Hudson. "There she lies," he declared, "in all her glory."

Duncan followed his arm toward the biggest of the warships, a ship of the line with three gun decks, "The *Thunderer*," he said with foreboding. "Where will they unload the gunpowder?"

"The arsenal is on the other side of the fort. King's Wharf beyond it is used for government business, but she is too large for the docks so they will off-load into lighters."

"No sign of the *Indigo Queen*," Duncan noted as he scanned the vast harbor again.

"No," Kipling agreed, "but there are many wharves and coves along the rivers we can't see from here."

"They're here," Pine stated, with the confidence of a hunter sensing his prey.

As they approached what Kipling called the Old Slip Wharf on the East River, Duncan assembled his small company. Glover and Boyle agreed to stay with the runaways on board while Kipling led Duncan on an exploratory visit to Hercules Mulligan. The streets they walked were populated mostly by farmers and other vendors taking their wares to market in various conveyances, including carts pulled by sturdy dogs. Unlike in Boston, they were devoid of soldiers. Matrons leaned out windows and called out in Dutch to buy a loaf or jug of milk. A child chased a hoop into an alley.

The sense of normalcy at first brought comfort, but then Duncan realized it would mean Hastings and Vaughn would have a free hand, and he pondered how to find the two men in the sprawling town. Kipling pointed out new streetlights and a sturdy brick building that housed the fire company, with a new pump from Birmingham. Duncan wondered out loud if they should pause at one of the coffee shops they passed since the sun had barely risen, but Kipling explained that Mulligan always opened his establishment early, especially when a new regiment was passing through town. The Twenty-Ninth Regiment, they learned at the wharf, had been relieved of duty in Boston and was arriving in Manhattan as transport permitted. Its soldiers would find a much wider variety of shops in which to drop their coins, not to mention the many taverns and houses of more venal trade, Kipling added. Mulligan was renowned as the haberdasher for officers to call on if they wanted a new uniform or to freshen their old ones with a little brocade or other flash.

Fortunately, there was not yet a line of officers out the door when they arrived at the sturdy three-story brownstone building that served as both his shop and residence. "The Keep," Kipling said as he opened the heavy plank door. "Welcome to Mulligan's Keep."

The large open chamber was lined with shelves holding bolts of cloth and displays of buttons, but no people. Kipling confidently led Duncan through to a closeted set of stairs, which they ascended to the second floor, comprising Mulligan's primary workrooms. If the haberdasher were indeed so busy, Duncan worried, he would have no time to help rescue Sarah. Kipling opened the door to a large

246 | Eliot Pattison

chamber holding several tables covered with heaps of cloth. Mulligan did not look up from the finery he was stitching under a spermaceti lamp.

"Green on the first table, silver ribbon here," the Irishman muttered through the pins held in his mouth. When no one responded, he looked up. His jaw, and the pins, dropped.

"Archibald! Praise God! After that report of Bradford's death I—" his words died away as he caught sight of Kipling's companion. "Do my eyes deceive? Duncan McCallum, as I live and breathe!"

Duncan accepted Mulligan's vigorous handshake, but he had no appetite for small talk. "You met Sarah Ramsey last year in Philadelphia. She has been brought by the military from Boston and is in grave danger. We have to—" Duncan paused, not understanding the grin on the tailor's face.

"Not all the work I do is of a military nature," Mulligan explained. "Though always with the greatest discretion, I assure you." He answered Duncan's obvious confusion by unlatching the door behind his worktable.

Duncan's heart stopped for a moment as he gazed into the bright, sunlit chamber. Sarah had her back to him as two women were fitting the new dress she wore. He held a finger to his lips to silence them as they looked up, then advanced, stopping at arm's length. "Forest green," he softly declared. "Always your best color."

Sarah slowly turned. She stared at him, stunned, then her eyes welled with tears and she threw her arms around him.

"The general can be a most congenial host," Mulligan announced to his back. "We have known each other for many years even though he is from the aristocracy and I a humble Irish tailor. He calls on me for certain favors and grants me some as well. I am, after all, the only one in the city who can supply his favored cashmere stockings. I was happy to agree when he asked if I might accommodate a new friend who had been separated from her baggage. But imagine my surprise when Miss Ramsey appeared!"

"Miss Ramsey," Duncan observed, tightening his embrace, "abounds with surprises."

Sarah finally released him. "But Duncan, what of our friends, where—"

"Josiah and Henri are on the ship," Kipling said, and Duncan saw that he had answered the question forming on the lips of Esther, who had been sitting at the side of the room.

"Everyone from the widow Godwin's house is gone," Duncan added, "except the widow herself, clutching a fat purse to ease her inconvenience. All are on board Glover's brig, which you had conveniently chartered without my knowledge and is now tied up at the Old Slip wharf on the East River." He was not prepared to speak more openly of the runaways. "Also the estimable Mr. Boyle, who has well proven his descent from the fabled chemist."

The announcement brought an uneasy silence and an awkward glance between Sarah and Mulligan.

"I always work for an hour or two before breaking my fast," Mulligan announced. "I believe I smell bacon and fresh bread." He gestured toward a back stairway. "Shall we?"

In the spacious dining chamber at the rear of the house Mulligan waited for his Dutch cook to lay out platters of thick bacon, bread and butter, boiled eggs, cheese, and pickled herring, then closed the door behind her.

"Marblehead's chemist and I have discovered much about one another," Duncan reported. "We shall find a way to see your clever plan through, so long as we can avoid the king's agents and bounty hunters," he added. He turned to Mulligan. "But first you need to understand we have new enemies." He explained what he knew about the clandestine agents who were dogging them.

The Irish haberdasher, much savvier about the workings of the British government than Duncan's friends in Boston, did not question Duncan's conclusions. "My God," Mulligan growled. "They will find New York a fertile hunting ground. I shall warn my people." He had his own network for gathering information. "Be discreet but keep a sharp ear out. As if there weren't tension enough in our streets."

"I read that there was trouble over a liberty pole a few weeks ago," Duncan ventured.

"Many troubles and many liberty poles, but yes, recently we narrowly avoided catastrophe. People are calling it the Battle of Golden Hill." Mulligan proceeded to explain how the Sons of Liberty—what he called the "public" Sons—and the army had been feuding ever since the Stamp Act five years earlier, when the first liberty poles were erected to celebrate repeal of the hated act and the cause of liberty espoused by John Wilkes in England. Three poles had been erected in recent months and each chopped down by soldiers. Iron bands had been placed around the most recent, which had been guarded intermittently by followers of Alexander McDougal, the fiery public face of the Sons in New York. Soldiers had then blown up the pole in the middle of the night with a keg of gunpowder and distributed handbills attacking the Sons as "enemies of the people."

McDougal's men had cornered soldiers posting the handbills, and a struggle had ensued. More citizens, and more soldiers, had arrived, and several of the protesters and as many soldiers had been badly injured.

"Now McDougal is in prison and has become the John Wilkes of New York."

"A Scot, I take it," Duncan suggested as he cracked open an egg.

"Of course. Stubborn, savvy, and silver tongued," Mulligan quickly replied, raising a laugh from Sarah. "And both the soldiers and the citizens feel they have unfinished business. There's talk of arson and blockades of Fort George."

"Arson?" Sarah asked.

"Something of a nefarious New York tradition. There were slave uprisings earlier in the century. An attempt was made to burn down the fort. There were other fires, thought to be deliberate, though no one ever proved it so. Devastating fires. Many lost their homes. Now the protagonists shout 'burn them out' at each other. If the flames start I doubt our new English fire pump will be up to the task. Families are keeping buckets of sand and bed keys at the ready."

"Bed keys?" Duncan inquired.

"To unscrew the bolts that keep a bed together. In many homes the beds are the most expensive pieces of furniture, the first to be rescued in a fire. Bed keys are becoming the bellwether of unrest."

"So General Gage walks a tightrope," Sarah suggested.

"He knows that some on the War Council will be furious when they hear he has withdrawn the Twenty-Ninth from Boston. Too conciliatory by far, they will say, needed to demonstrate backbone, not show his back. If there is provocation here he will have to react ruthlessly to silence those critics in London. There can be no retreat in the city of his headquarters." Mulligan turned to Duncan. "And now you suggest the infamous shooting at Boston's Custom House may have been the work of these provocateurs?"

"The streets were in chaos that night," Duncan explained. "The order to fire was not given from the officer leading the troops. It came from the crowd, from a man matching the description of Major Hastings of the Horse Guards."

A gasp of surprise escaped Mulligan's throat. "Would they truly dare such treachery?" he asked.

"They pride themselves on their daring, in anticipation of great rewards, and some of those very soldiers had been taking coin to act as their bullies. Those on the Council who encourage them will reap vast riches if there is war, supplying the fleets and the army."

"You have a cynical view of those in government, McCallum."

"No. What I have is long and painful experience with certain elements of government. Shared by our electrical friend in London."

"Who tells much the same story of intrigue," Mulligan agreed. Duncan was not the only one who received secret letters from London. "But we are not ready for war. I can barely get militias in different provinces to speak with each other, let alone share munitions or even plans."

"Which is why we have to smoke out what they plan and stop it."

Mulligan frowned. "The general, too, is interested in smoking out plans. He is sending out gallopers."

"Gallopers?" Sarah asked.

Duncan had not heard the term since the last war. "Mounted scouts sent to enemy territory to spy out their opponents."

"Intelligencers, some call them," Mulligan added.

"So Massachusetts is not the only place where the army treats colonists like enemies," she concluded.

"The intelligencers tend to be rather independent spirits," Mulligan continued in a wry tone, "often in civilian clothes, posing as this or that. Some get overly talkative trying to impress the lasses of country taverns, who are often more savvy than they get credit for."

"Who then pass on information to you," Duncan suggested.

There was a hint of pride in Mulligan's grin. "We know the gallopers report directly to the general's headquarters. Urgent messages come from London, urgent gallopers ride out. They seem to have an inordinate interest in metalworking," he added, aiming a meaningful gaze at Duncan. The Irish tailor was the only one in New York who knew of Franklin's war machine scheme. "I could name half a dozen smithies within fifty miles who have had odd visitors, some pretending to be merchants seeking new supplies of metal goods. Asking about shipments from England, about supplies from a firm named Crowley and another from Germany."

Duncan chewed on the words and offered a satisfied smile. Benjamin in London would be pleased with the news that their subterfuge had General Gage worried. "Meanwhile," he said, "we have assassins wandering about New York seeking to foment hostilities and trap Sarah." He took a long swallow of tea. "Why is your house called the Keep?"

Mulligan grinned. "Believe it or not, my stock in trade is more valuable than that of any merchant in Manhattan. So the ground floor has heavy doors and heavy locks, and the windows are sealed with bars and shutters each night."

"Then Sarah stays here."

"With you, Duncan," Sarah interjected.

"Plenty of bedrooms above us," Mulligan offered.

Duncan thoughtfully chewed a piece of cheddar. "Tell me about the new medical faculty at King's College. Kipling and I are most interested."

Kipling looked up from the loaf he was slicing. "We are?"

"Of course. Your talents are underused by the Sons. You are the certificator who opens all doors."

"When convincing observers that an image is true, you must keep the colors so authentic no one notices them," an elderly teacher in Duncan's boyhood boarding school once told him. The gentle old scholar, no doubt long resting in some heavenly library, had been speaking of the techniques of the Dutch Masters, but Duncan long ago realized they applied to the details of any deception, not just that of two-dimensional paintings. The best disguises were subtle, thinly layered over the truth. Thus, when he entered the medical college he carried not certificates and attestations but rather a simple request from Sir William Johnson, the esteemed superintendent of Indian affairs, to allow his valued adviser Dr. McCallum of the University of Edinburgh leave to make inquiries and engage in observations among the faculty for the purpose of establishing some degree of regular medical care in the Mohawk Valley. Kipling, most versatile of clerks, was happy to assist with the forgery and even produced a sample of Johnson's signature. Sir William, if he ever found out, would be highly amused.

"The request is most abrupt," the secretary of the medical school groused when Duncan presented the letter. "You have no appointment."

"Sir William is known for his abruptness," Duncan said with a sigh. "A perquisite of high office, I suppose. I had other business in the city and was about to board my boat for Albany when his messenger intercepted me. We had previously discussed the need to provide physician services in his valley, and he finally found room in his stipend from London. If things go well, we may want to recruit a graduate of your fine establishment."

The secretary nervously adjusted his wig. "Sir William," he repeated.

Duncan straightened the velvet waistcoat on loan from Mulligan and fought the urge to scratch under the powdered wig Sarah had set on his head. He leaned toward the man behind the desk and spoke with a confiding tone. "The hero of Lake George, you no doubt recall. Knighted. He corresponds with King George himself," Duncan added. "But if you find it inconvenient, I shall report the disappointment to Sir William. He does take his responsibility for the welfare of his charges so seriously. If I can just have the correct spelling of your name?"

The secretary's haughty air vanished. "Prithee, no! Surely we can find an accommodation. What exactly do you desire?"

"Advice on practices for obtaining and storing medical supplies. Some discussion about the types of trauma encountered here. We have to anticipate our fair share of violence. It is the Valley of the Mohawks," he reminded the school's clerk. "Have you ever tried to sew the scalp back on the survivor of an Iroquois attack?"

The secretary's face went pale. He seemed unable to speak for a moment, and when he did he had to loudly clear his throat. "No doubt there is a bloody price paid for living among the savages."

"Do you have many assaults with tomahawks still?" Duncan asked in an earnest tone. "Axes? Perhaps the odd angry scythe taking off an arm? Hammer blows to the skull? Trepanning can be problematic without whisky or corn spirits, I can tell you, especially with a carpenter's auger."

The secretary had to collect himself once more. "No doubt the exigencies of the frontier require crude solutions," he stiffly observed.

Duncan leaned closer and lowered his voice. "But imagine the glory, when Sir William mentions to His Majesty how the King's College medical school was instrumental in bringing civilized medicine to his frontier." Duncan paused, scanning the desktop and fixing his gaze on the addressee written on a letter. "And how Mr. Scoville of that school led the noble effort!"

The notion seemed to take the clerk's breath away for a moment. "Sir!" he gasped. "Is it possible? The king himself? Prithee, just tell me what you need!" Scoville hesitated, seeming to recall Duncan's line of questions. "We don't see so many shootings on our streets since we expanded our watch into permanent patrols, but stabbings aplenty. Bar brawls usually. Assaults along the waterfront among the mariner class, that kind of thing."

"Our midwives are accustomed to sewing up the odd slice," Duncan continued, "and are always ready to pack moss and spiderwebs into the usual wounds. It's the more complex injuries that concern me. Opening a wound to reconstruct the muscle and ligature, for example. How to deal with nerve damage, that sort of repair."

The nervous man at the desk considered Duncan's words. "There *was* an interesting case of that nature recently. Dr. Arnett, one of our professors, attended and discussed it in our weekly conference. The wound had been poorly treated, at great risk of contamination. A mishap at sea, it appeared, for it had been sewn up rather crudely with sailmaker's knots. I understand there was an impingement on the nerve."

Duncan tried not to seem too interested. "A naval officer then?" he asked, and was told the man simply gave his name as Vaughn, no rank or affiliation. "Perhaps Dr. Arnett could spare a few minutes when he is next here?"

"Why sir, he is expected this very hour! With that very patient!"

They found Dr. Arnett outside the exam room, waiting for his patient to arrive. The gray-haired physician, retired from naval service, congenially agreed to have Duncan join him and explained that the patient was somewhat cryptic about the origin of his wound, which put the doctor in mind of the deep splinter wounds he had seen in sea battles. "A naval engagement, I would wager, but this man is no sailor. No uniform at all, no voucher to be paid by some purser. Right arrogant cove. Groused that if he were back with Whitehall doctors he'd be healed already, as if to cow me. Refused to explain anything about the circumstances of his injury other than to say it was in the service of the king. And that he would pay handsomely, in good British sterling, none of that provincial paper.

"Some of my colleagues want to believe that he suffered the wound in a duel, probably after alienating the affections of some poor husband's wife. What kind of duel is it, I asked, when a duelist is stabbed in the back?" Arnett said. "Makes no nevermind from the healer's perspective. He'll pay a toll he won't long forget since it will be months before he regains full use of the appendage." The doctor cocked his head at Duncan and gestured to the bench in the exam room. "Now sir, you must repay in kind. Perhaps some tales of wounds from tribal spears. Is it true that if the savages drink the blood of bears they heal more quickly?"

Duncan did not disappoint the surgeon and offered tales of Iroquois healers, then answered questions about the University of Edinburgh. As Arnett inquired about the rumors of body snatchers supplying the school, a gaunt, angry-looking man appeared in the hallway, escorted by Scoville.

"The very patient," Arnett announced under his breath and rose from the bench.

Introduced only as a visiting physician from Scotland, Duncan kept a quiet, professional demeanor as Arnett removed the man's bandage. Only as he peeled away the underlying poultice, causing the man to cast his face up in a grimace, did Duncan get a full look at his features. It was indeed the narrow, poxed countenance he last saw at the Marblehead shed. The wound inflicted by Pine was jagged and deep.

When Duncan finally spoke, he pushed a burr into his voice. "Did ye not ken to administer to the wound when fresh made?" he asked. "Ye might have halted the festering before it started."

Vaughn's eyes flared. "My duties did not permit it," he haughtily replied.

Duncan well knew the man's duties. He had sought to trap Sarah, first at the church cemetery, then at that Marblehead shed, but instead had been trapped himself and fled to avoid arrest by the militia. Then, too, he threw away the life of Jacob Book as if the gentle fisherman were so much rubbish on his path.

"Duties?" Duncan responded. "You're a soldier, then? I am not aware that the king is at war with anyone."

Vaughn silently glared at him. "Just fix my damned shoulder and—" His words were cut off by a gasp of pain as Duncan took his hand and twisted it.

"Loss of motion then," Duncan observed impassively. "It would be helpful to know the circumstances. The nature of the weapon that pierced you. How soon was the wound cleaned? Was it with sulfur water?"

"Circumstances did not permit," Vaughn hissed.

"A misadventure then," Duncan concluded. "I do hope you informed the authorities."

"Circumstances did not permit," Vaughn repeated.

"Ah, well, a fine gentleman like you nay earns his keep with his hands," Duncan ventured absently as he bent over the wound, "so no great consequence, I suppose." Clearly the knife that caused the injury was thrown with great force and was razor sharp, but Duncan knew that already.

"And," Dr. Arnett cut off Duncan, "we'll nay probe into a gentleman's matter of honor."

"Never in life!" Duncan assured them both, then straightened and made a shallow, apologetic bow to Vaughn. "Forgive me, sir, I am a physician assigned to the frontier. More and more it seems I must work among savages."

For a moment Vaughn's gaze held a hint of curiosity, then his customary sneer returned and he snapped at Arnett, announcing that he had an urgent meeting at Government House and to be quick about the new poultice and bandage.

Duncan retreated to a chair at the back of the chamber and remained silent until the Horse Guards officer left, then stepped to the window, joined by Arnett. They watched as Vaughn emerged and hurried down the street where he was met by a square-jawed, compact man. Duncan stared as the man stepped into the sunlight. It was Yates. The Marblehead turncoat had indeed not gone to sea; he joined his new employer in New York.

"That," Arnett pointed out, as the pair turned up an alley, "is not the direction of Government House." He turned to Duncan. "Prithee, McCallum, why did I have the impression that you were somehow acquainted with the man but did not wish to acknowledge it?"

Duncan continued gazing out the window as Pine momentarily appeared between two buildings. Vaughn had no idea that the very man who wounded him in distant Marblehead was again stalking him. Now that they had his scent, they would know his movements in the city. He turned to the professor. "I am from the wilds," he reminded Arnett. "Predators learn to recognize each other if they mean to survive."

Duncan's heart was in his throat as they approached Fort George with Hercules Mulligan at his side. Mulligan had assured him that they would be safe in accepting General Gage's invitation to tea after escorting Miss Ramsey to the *Thunderer*. Duncan had argued about the wisdom of presenting himself directly to the infamous general, but Mulligan pointed out that there could be no better opportunity for assessing the enemy terrain, and Duncan had been invited simply as Sarah's fiancé. Duncan declined to explain that Hastings knew Duncan's face, knew Earl Milbridge had a secret and very lavish price on his head. If he had allied himself with the general, the assassin could be lurking within these very walls.

"Damnation!" Mulligan muttered. The haberdasher had slackened his pace and was staring at the row of barracks along the outer wall. "Empty no longer." The barracks where the Marblehead kegs of powder were to be inserted into the shipment from England were occupied by soldiers.

Duncan recognized the uniforms. "The Twenty-Ninth, from Boston. Recalled after the massacre."

"No one mentioned what quarters were assigned," Mulligan said with chagrin. "Our clever plans have just crumbled to pieces."

The tailor led him past the sentries and into Government House, the largest of the fortress's buildings, then toward the incongruous sound of laughter echoing down a corridor lined with racks of muskets and swords. The chamber they entered was large enough for a small ball, with windows opening toward the vast harbor and overlooking a battery of heavy guns. In a corner furnished with carpet and cushioned chairs for more intimate gatherings, Sarah stood with a man of moderate build in his middle years who wore an infantry uniform far more humble than the brocaded uniforms worn by the covey of younger officers gathered by the hearth.

"Major General Gage," Sarah said, motioning toward Duncan as he approached, "please make the acquaintance of my fiancé, Dr. McCallum."

Duncan tried not to show his surprise. The demon of Fort George, the dreaded tyrant, had a modest, rather plain appearance, though his eyes burned with a deep and questioning intelligence. He appraised Duncan with a stony reserve, then extended his hand.

"Honored, sir," Duncan said as he accepted the greeting. "I am indebted to you for keeping Miss Ramsey safe on her thundering visit." Mulligan had warned Sarah that the general, and the ship's captain, were always eager to impress visitors with a broadside, and they had indeed heard the boom of the guns as they left Mulligan's Keep.

"I must admit that sometimes our distaff visitors faint at the discharge of so many guns," the general replied, "but Miss Ramsey did not flinch. I wish my own troops were so battle hardened," he added with a smile. Gage turned and warmly greeted Mulligan, and the two began chatting about the flood of officers from the Twenty-Ninth Regiment seeking to renew accoutrements and uniforms as they passed through the city on to their new postings. Mulligan mentioned that some had suggested he devise a ribbon or other special adornment to commemorate their service in Boston.

"Most certainly not!" Gage rejoined. "Nothing to be proud of in leaving civilians dead in the street! Why, just today I learned that their comrades still in the Boston jail are facing murder charges!" He sighed. "They are being defended by that lawyer Adams, who exonerated the sailor who harpooned an officer last year. At the time, I considered the man a vile shyster, and now I find I am to pay his fees and pray for his success." The general shook his head. "Such times we live in."

A side door opened and two servants carrying trays of refreshments appeared, led by a striking young woman in a claret-colored dress, her long black tresses tied at the back with a silver ribbon. She exchanged a nod with Gage, who gestured toward a sideboard before engaging Duncan in a conversation about the last French war, having learned from Sarah that he was a veteran of the conflict. To his surprise Duncan discovered that Gage had been an aide to General Braddock and been with the ill-fated general in the infamous Battle of the Monongahela, the worst defeat ever suffered by the British army in its long history of war. Gage was intrigued to learn that Duncan had served with the rangers and been in the final engagements at Montreal, then enthusiastically took up Mulligan's conversation about the current voyage of Captain Cook in the Pacific. As they spoke, the taciturn, graceful woman served them delicacies from the sideboard, then defended herself from overtures from the younger officers with soft-spoken, respectful replies that left them smiling but unfulfilled.

Duncan found Gage surprisingly unassuming, and genuinely interested in world affairs, including the state of tribal relations on the frontier. Having already spent hours with Sarah, the general had insightful inquiries about life in Edentown, ranging from the best varieties of apples for the cold winters to the amount of snowfall and whether they had tried to establish a vineyard. He was intrigued to learn that the Iroquois possessed greater agronomy skills than many European settlers and often maintained large orchards at their communities, then listened attentively as Sarah explained that Edentown's success hinged not on the one-sided proposition that the tribes had to adapt to Europeans but on the premise that Europeans and the tribes had to adapt to each other.

The woman who managed the servants did not retreat when they cleared away the dishes. Duncan suspected the younger officers would have intercepted her had she tried to leave, for they eagerly pressed about her despite her clear lack of interest, until Gage noticed her discomfort. "Hannah," he called out, "do us the honor?"

She offered an apologetic curtsy to the young officers and moved to the general's side.

Gage introduced the woman as "Hannah, the steward of my household. As my wife reminds me, although the king entrusts me with half his empire, I cannot be trusted to manage the family residence. Keeping discipline over a dozen odd regiments scattered over thousands of miles pales by comparison to maintaining order in my hectic abode."

Hannah modestly accepted the praise and, upon hearing of their recent arrival, expressed her hope that their travels had been untroubled. Mulligan, clearly acquainted with the woman, seemed oddly nervous about their interchange with her and steered the conversation to the excellent vintage port served with the cheese, then to a report he had read of the latest fashions in London. "The ladies will soon be trading in their hoops for hip pads I hear."

Expressing his hope for a more extensive discussion later in the week about the state of affairs on the frontier, Gage closed the tea with an invitation for a tour of the fort's grounds, starting with the batteries in the arrowhead-shaped corners of the bastion. As Gage paused with an aide who explained that his signature was required on deployment orders for the Twenty-Ninth, Duncan and Mulligan continued walking.

"If the outer barracks are no longer available, where will the Marblehead kegs have to go?" he whispered.

"The arsenal itself," Mulligan replied, disappointment heavy in his voice. "And we will never get them past the sentries there."

Gage was returning to them, when a voice called out.

"Dr. McCallum, sir? Bless me, I had no idea you had journeyed south."

Duncan turned to face the speaker, a soldier of the Twenty-Ninth who removed his hat. "'Tis me, sir." The soldier pointed to his foot. "Good as new."

"Corporal Rhys!" Duncan exclaimed, then cast a worried gaze over the grounds, wondering who else from Boston may be watching. Seeing no one he recognized, he relaxed. "So the angelica proved—" He hesitated as Rhys abruptly stiffened, his body straight as a musket barrel, his eyes round with fear. Mulligan motioned Sarah to the low wall of the battery and began pointing out the sights of the harbor.

"Corporal," came a voice over Duncan's shoulder, "do you know the good doctor?"

"Sir! Yes, sir!" Rhys replied, looking straight ahead.

The general laughed. "At ease, Corporal. Speak freely, man. Do you know the doctor?"

"Oh aye, sir, General, sir, and more's the good of it. A right prime soul and a right prime healer. Banished the gout out of my foot, sir, when he came to inspect the camp in Boston."

Gage seemed genuinely curious about the words of praise from the obviously well-seasoned veteran. "Inspection, McCallum?" he asked.

"The surgeon of the Twenty-Ninth had duties elsewhere. I assisted with sick call and assured sound practices had been taken to prevent the further spread of camp fever. A spread to the civilian population of Boston would have been most inimical to relations with the army."

Gage grimaced, as if to suggest that relations were inimical enough already. "Cured your gout, you say, Corporal?"

"Cleared up right fast, sir," Rhys said. "His angelica root did the trick. A blessing it was. An infantryman needs two good feet."

Gage assessed Duncan anew. "Major Trent," he said to his nearest aide while keeping his gaze on Duncan, "see that the medical stores of the regiments include angelica, with word to the surgeons to apply it where gout is indicated."

"On orders from Dr. McCallum, sir?" the major asked with an uncertain tone.

"Orders from headquarters. And Major—what is a soldier of the Twenty-Ninth doing inside my fortress?"

"His company's been temporarily assigned to haul stores from the *Thunderer* and replenish the batteries as needed, sir. You signed the order yesterday."

As if to emphasize the point, Rhys snapped to attention again and raised a hand to his temple.

The general sighed. "We have the regiment splitting in so many directions I cannot keep track."

"The withdrawal from Boston was rather abrupt, sir," his aide reminded him.

Duncan looked out over the harbor to hide his reaction. The regiment was being scattered to the winds. Was it to keep it far from the public eye? Or to punish it for the massacre in Boston? And had the grenadier company, the source of Hastings's henchmen, arrived in Manhattan?

Rhys still held his salute. "As you were, Corporal," the general instructed. As Rhys scurried down the tunnel leading to the next battery, Sarah and Mulligan caught up with them.

The general fixed Duncan with another stare, so penetrating that Duncan feared he was seeing not curiosity but suspicion. Gage offered a slight bow to Sarah. "I apologize, Miss Ramsey," he declared with a thin, enigmatic smile, "but I fear I must place Dr. McCallum under my orders."

"Duncan!" Sarah cried. "You must flee! They will seize you again and next time offer no parole! You must leave this very night! We shall go the Hudson docks and find you a boat going north. We shall hire one if need be! We shall buy one if we must!"

He was not sure if he had ever seen Sarah more worked up. After making his cryptic announcement, Gage had assigned an escort for Sarah and Mulligan and required Duncan to accompany him to his office. On his return, she had been sitting with Mulligan in his parlor and had not waited for Duncan's report on the meeting.

"General Gage has put me under orders so I might have authority," he began.

"I hear there's a daily boat to Albany that leaves just after dawn," Sarah pressed. "We can send word to hold a berth for you if—" She paused. "Authority?"

"The general has not been able to spare an army surgeon for duty with the fortress garrison. The surgeon for the Twenty-Ninth is already deployed in New Jersey. But meanwhile, the general has been hearing more details of how camp fever ravaged the Twenty-Ninth encampment in Boston. It suddenly occurred to him that he had seen my name in a report from Colonel Dalrymple, that I was the one who inspected and reassured the civilian authorities that there was no danger due to the aggressive sanitary measures imposed on the camp. He did not reveal until we were alone that Commodore Lawford, already sailing back to Boston, also spoke highly of my efforts with a fatally ill sergeant in his briefings. Now the general earnestly wants to assure the fever does not strike Fort George or his family, especially with so many unfamiliar troops now passing through Manhattan. I am to inspect the fortress and the arsenal and am empowered, with the assistance of one his senior aides, to compel such remedial measures as I see fit."

"But Duncan! It's General Gage!"

"It's General Gage," he agreed. "And I recall an old Mohawk hunter telling me that if you ever find yourself in the cave of an awakening bear it is best to lull him back to sleep." He extracted his watch. "Now we need to find our Irish friend Mr. Boyle and our West Indian troops."

"Troops?" Sarah asked.

"We have a way in now, a way to reset the stage for Boyle, but it means a long night ahead." He turned to Mulligan, who had been listening with avid interest. "I hope you have ample supplies of yellow and red cloth. And see if Kipling is familiar with the papers used by the city constables. Can you find some drums?"

The aide assigned to accompany Duncan on his sanitary inspection was the middle-aged man he met at Gage's tea. Major Trent was a no-nonsense but affable officer who seemed on good terms with the garrison troops. Duncan tried not to glance at his watch too often as they examined latrines, drainage lines to the harbor, and the barracks, at each location accompanied by a noncommissioned officer familiar with the particular subject of inspection. Duncan, supplied with a writing lead and a bound, empty account book, took careful notes, even sketching some of what he saw. The major hesitated only briefly when Duncan asked to see the inner workings of each battery.

"Rats love the same dark dry places that are preferred for gunpowder," Duncan explained. "They are not conducive to military health. And have been known to gnaw into kegs and barrels."

"You must speak of French rats," Trent replied with a laugh, then took him on a tour of the sunken chambers behind each gun emplacement, the ready magazines for quick access to powder and shells, as well as the tunnel that connected the batteries to the adjoining arsenal. The major invited Duncan to join him in that passage, but Duncan, knowing he needed to exhaust another hour, reminded him that they had not yet seen the kitchens or the water closets of the four-story headquarters building. He used up part of the hour interviewing the cooks, looking into pantry stores, and venturing out a seldom-used waterside sally door to examine the water closet outlets. He checked his watch, then decided to sketch the tiled chutes that discharged their waste directly into the harbor to be flushed away with each high tide. Finally he closed his chronicle. "Shall we venture to the arsenal now?" he asked at last.

An artillery sergeant escorted them down a passage lit by carefully shielded lanterns to the complex of dungeon-like chambers where powder was stored and shells were prepared. He stirred up three rat nests and pointed out several unhealthy patches of mold on the walls, which the major ordered to be scrubbed away by nightfall. They had just emerged into the open courtyard of the walled arsenal compound when the major cocked his head. "Are those drums I hear?"

They watched as a strange procession emerged through the gate. Two yellow-clad drummers beat out a loud rhythm as they marched before a wagon driven by a weary-looking infantryman. A mounted man wearing the badge of the city watch rode behind.

"Oh, save us from their thunder," Duncan said with a grin.

"You know these men?"

"Drummers of the Twenty-Ninth. The rattle patrol, folks in Boston called them. Their soldiers wear scarlet but the drummers have these ornate yellow uniforms and grenadier hats."

The major offered a slow nod. "I had heard the Twenty-Ninth drummers were all Africans, but this is the first I've seen of them."

"A regimental tradition, apparently," Duncan explained. "The Twenty-Ninth is very proud of its drummers. Any excuse for a flash of yellow, the people of Boston were saying. Kept many a Bostonian from an honest night's sleep. Up and down the Common where they were camped. They even accompanied the changing of the guard at the government buildings until the citizens complained to the governor. I suspect these two are new recruits, sent on trivial assignments to keep them in practice, which they obviously need."

"So you do know them?"

"Not by name, but certainly by their racket."

"Racket indeed," Trent muttered. "I would have expected more precision in their rhythm."

"We learned in Boston that their officers tended to emphasize the strength of the stroke rather than musical talent." Duncan pretended to study the drummers. "Their faces look familiar. Yes, I saw those two when handling sick call for the Twenty-Ninth."

The major motioned their escorting sergeant closer. "See what they have for us. And remind the sentry that there is a reason we have passwords for entry to the arsenal. We are fortunate Dr. McCallum is here or I might have called out the guard."

Tobias and Solomon looked rather striking in their ornate uniforms, fitted to them perfectly after hours of late-night work by Hercules Mulligan, then broken in during further hours of practice on drums borrowed from the militia hall. The first mate of Glover's brig, an ardent patriot wearing a uniform of the Twenty-Ninth left with Mulligan for alteration, looked appropriately bored as he reined in his team. John Glover, on the horse, had been even easier to equip, for Mulligan had an inventory of the waistcoats and breeches worn by the city's law enforcers. Duncan asked no questions when Mulligan rummaged in a drawer and produced a constable's badge.

"Shall we?" the major asked with a sigh, then approached the wagon. The procession halted but the drummers, their faces expressionless, kept up a ragged beat until the sergeant snapped at them to stop.

Glover ignored the questions aimed at him, just dismounted and produced a paper from inside his waistcoat, carefully crafted by Kipling. He solemnly unfolded it and produced a writing lead. "Sign here to confirm ye got the authority," he declared in a weary voice as he pointed to a signature line behind a paragraph at the top, then motioned to the bottom of the paper. "And here to confirm ye took possession of the stolen goods. Glad to get the nasty stuff off our hands, to be sure."

The sergeant was understandably confused. "Sir?"

"I have been up all night, young man," Glover groused, "deprived of my sleep and my breakfast so let's not draw out the process." He gestured to the driver of the wagon, who twisted and pulled away the sailcloth that covered the contents of the wagon. "Damnable smugglers caught moving up the Hudson last night," Glover explained. "Likely bound for Indian country, judging by all the beads and kettles and blankets they was carrying. One of those boats ferrying your infantrymen across to Jersey intercepted them and decided to bring them to the city's enforcers. Figured ye would want yer goods back. Don't need His Majesty's fine-grained powder winding up in the hands of savages, now do we?" Glover stepped back to let the sergeant finally view the cargo.

"Bloody hell," the sergeant muttered, then stepped closer and examined the marks painted on the kegs before turning back to the major. "Ours sure enough. Some of the units being deployed to New Jersey were given a few kegs of the fresh powder from the *Thunderer*. We are forever cursed by quartermaster sergeants looking for a bit of silver on the side."

Glover shook his paper. "Here and here," he reminded the sergeant, gesturing again to the signature lines.

"Pardon, Doctor," Major Trent said, then stepped to the wagon himself. After a moment he unhappily pointed to the entrance to the magazine tunnel. "Unload them there," he instructed. With a chagrined sigh, the major took the paper and pressed it against the side of the wagon to sign. "We are obliged to the city constables, sir," he declared to Glover.

Ten minutes later the empty wagon was being led by the very loud drummers back out the gate. Duncan continued his inspection, touring through the stable used by the arsenal's heavy horses, then the quarters of the small arsenal garrison and their sanitary appurtenances. He was at the gate, giving his thanks to the major and promising a written report for the general, when two figures appeared in the arched passage connecting to Fort George. General Gage was speaking to a man in civilian clothes. Ice touched his spine as the man turned his face into the sunlight. General Gage was speaking with Jeremiah Melville, ruthless pirate turned slave catcher.

As he approached Mulligan's Keep, Duncan suddenly realized Pine was walking beside him, wearing a brown waistcoat and linen shirt, no doubt borrowed from the tailor's considerable collection of new and used clothing. The Oneida didn't utter a word, just motioned Duncan into an alley.

Kipling and Achilles appeared in the shadows, apparently guarding a patch of ground. Pine gestured to their feet. "They say you have seen this before." Kipling extended a lantern and lifted the baffle that had dimmed its light.

The grenadier company had indeed arrived in New York. The muddy ground showed prints from at least three pairs of boots with studs arranged like five-pointed stars. Their efforts to protect Sarah and the runaways had just grown more difficult, and more dangerous. "Grenadiers of the Twenty-Ninth were watching. Hastings's grenadiers," Kipling declared unnecessarily. "The evil giants of the Twenty-Ninth."

The Oneida's thin, dangerous grin indicated both that he already knew and that he relished the opportunity to engage with the spy's henchmen. "Abishai," he said, reminding Duncan of his invented name. "I am a giant killer. And there are more marks like these near Glover's brig." Without waiting for an acknowledgment, he set off down the alley.

Pine guided Duncan through a maze of winding streets, and finally onto one leading to the wharves along the East River. They halted under one of the elms that lined the street. "Brick house between the wigmaker and the baker," Pine whispered. It was one of the old Dutch houses, its stepped gable facing the street, now serving as a tavern. THE WILD GOOSE, proclaimed a weathered sign over its door. "Vaughn went in, then out a quarter hour later without his sling and wearing a different-colored cloak, a green one. He met with men on a bench by the wharf down here. Four men, meeting each separately. Soldiers, maybe, but in old clothes. The first three he gave purses to as if to buy something. The last one he gave two discs, bigger than coins, like giant bronze coins. That one was Yates."

Kipling instantly recognized the metal discs Pine described. "Tokens of admission to Vauxhall Gardens. They call it a pleasure garden, borrowed the name of the famous one in London. In truth probably a pale shadow of the original but still the most impressive of its kind in the colonies. A popular spot for those seeking distraction. Music, food, jugglers, clowns, and such. Tin discs for Friday. Bronze, that means Saturday. They'll have fireworks."

Duncan, Sarah, and Pine were seated with Kipling in Mulligan's sitting room, a corner of which the tailor used as an office. As Kipling spoke the proprietor entered, pins stuck in a cushion strapped to his forearm and a measuring ribbon around his neck.

"Mr. Mulligan is known to entertain there from time to time," Kipling added and explained to the tailor why they were speaking of the Gardens.

"Tin or bronze?" Mulligan asked as he began exploring a drawer of his desk. "Tonight, then," he said as Pine answered, then held up five of the discs, spread out like playing cards. "We must go!" he announced. "Spy out what the weasels are up to and reap the enchantment of the night!"

Duncan glanced uneasily at Pine. "I doubt we are suitably equipped for—"

"Perish the thought!" Mulligan interrupted with mock indignation. "Do you think I stock my shop with rags, sir?"

"Duncan seldom thinks about his attire," Sarah said with a chastising grin at her fiancé. "But I, for one, would be most appreciative if we could equip our companions in suitable clothing. I believe," she added more slowly, her gaze still on Duncan, "he was expressing concern about our opponents being well armed with daggers and such."

"Ha!" Mulligan said and opened another drawer, then gestured them closer to inspect the objects he laid on the desk. The assortment of weapons included three knives, two pocket pistols, a pepperbox pistol, and a cudgel. "And perhaps with some cajoling," he suggested with a conspiratorial smile, "my warrior clerk will load both his pistols tonight."

Chapter 13

LED BY AN EBULLIENT MULLIGAN and Sarah, who made all the women around her look like drab cabbages, the glow of the procession that filed through the ornate gate of Vauxhall Gardens quickly faded as it progressed onto the grounds. Kipling looked uneasy in the blue velvet waistcoat Mulligan had selected for him. Duncan's nerves were on fire as he watched for danger, and despite the stylish buff waistcoat that Mulligan said looked just like buckskin, Pine fidgeted with the scarf Mulligan used to obscure his neck tattoos.

As they entered the Gardens, Pine studied the overdressed men and women who were filling the plaza. He was so astonished by the European custom of stacked bouffant hair and painted faces that Kipling had to repeatedly push Pine's arm down to keep him from pointing. From one circle of patrons rose a sweet scent reminiscent of the tribes' tobacco, and Pine advanced with interest, then quickly retreated when he saw that the circle was composed of rosy-cheeked Dutch matrons, all smoking delicate porcelain pipes.

When they reached a board posted with upcoming costume events, Pine had Kipling read them all to him. "Mount Olympus," Kipling read from the top. "Become a god for the night." Pine seemed satisfied, perhaps even approving, when Mulligan explained it was a night for honoring the aged gods of a long-ago kingdom. "Highland Fling Night, sponsored by the Saint Andrew's Society. Explorers Night," Kipling read next, "to honor the intrepid souls who opened the planet." He looked up. "Last year when they held this, some women dyed their hair blue and placed tiny ships in it." Pine was clearly still trying to comprehend the description when Kipling read the last event. "Savage under the Moonlight." With an awkward glance at his Oneida friend, he read the subtitle, his voice dropping. "Come as the heathen of your choice. Red-dyed wigs to be provided for those interested in scalping." He clumsily whispered the last words.

"Iroquois are coming?" Pine asked. "Even Tuscarora?"

"It's just pretending the Gardens are a wilderness," the clerk clumsily tried. "They tend to stage such events at the rear of the Gardens, which is more heavily wooded."

Mulligan saved Kipling further discomfort by gesturing toward a vendor at a glowing brazier. "Roasted crab apples!" He reached for his purse. "Dipped in maple syrup!"

They ventured deeper into the pleasure gardens, which were crisscrossed with trails, the widest ones hung with lanterns. At pavilions set at the intersections of the larger trails, musicians performed. One featured a string quartet that played waltzes, but most offered more lively drinking songs or jaunty dancing tunes. All were complemented by booths selling drinks, including a mulled and spiced wine that Mulligan insisted they try. As the others listened to a discussion with some merchants about the unjust imprisonment of the firebrand McDougal, Pine and Duncan retreated to reconnoiter the grounds.

The Gardens were surrounded by a high brick wall. The rear expanse was left natural and dotted with little cleared enclaves populated by couples. London's pleasure gardens were notorious for the tented pavilions and private apartments reserved for the amorous adventures of the wealthy class. Duncan recalled a popular, oft-whispered slogan used by one of the London gardens: *Come lose your identity, and your inhibitions.*

They returned to the main compound, where a large hall served food and drink, and soon spotted Mulligan, Kipling, and Sarah speaking with several naval officers. Duncan was about to join them, when he heard a frantic "Sir! Apologies, sir, I did not see you!"

An army officer spilled his drink as he snapped to attention. Duncan stepped back into the shadows and watched General Gage, wearing a black cloak over his uniform, dismiss the officer with a laugh and wave of his hand. "No harm done, Lieutenant. We are all just weary pilgrims on a quest for relaxation this eve," he added, drawing obsequious laughs.

It was the first time Duncan had seen Gage without an escort. The general moved among the circles of officers, both naval and infantry, buying each a round of drinks before taking his leave. At the last he made a short bow and headed toward the shadowed paths, apparently seeking solitude. He blended almost perfectly with the night and the many other guests drawn to the shadows of the trees.

Duncan gestured to Pine, and they merged into the darkness. Gage had found the perfect cover for meeting with the Horse Guards spies. Ten minutes later, he turned onto a narrow path that led into a dense grove of evergreens. The thick branches reaching to the ground made it impossible for Duncan and Pine to follow inconspicuously, so they sprinted to the far side of the grove and secreted themselves behind a thick oak not far from where the path emerged from the evergreens. Gage did not reappear.

Duncan weighed the possibility of venturing down the narrow, twisting path but knew he would be unable to explain himself if he encountered the general. The path offered no options, no apparent points for escape.

They had nearly reached the main plaza when Pine pulled on Duncan's arm. "The bright coat," he said. "From Marblehead."

His gaze quickly fell on a man in a lemon-colored coat with gold buttons who bent close to an attractive young woman, whispering in her ear. It was Hugo, the Cajian who lured victims into the slave cells of the *Indigo Queen*. Duncan scanned the crowd but saw no sign of Melville.

In Marblehead, Hugo had feigned friendship with slaves and bond servants in the hope of getting leads as to where the runaways were or perhaps even to kidnap and sell his new friends in Barbados. The Cajian whispered something that made the woman blush, then bowed and stepped away to a booth selling wine. Duncan warned Pine, "Stay here. You are worth a sack of silver to that man. Keep out of his sight."

Duncan hurried to the woman waiting for the Cajian. "Beg pardon," he said in a low voice, "but I feel it is my Christian duty. You should know your charming companion fled Boston last month after a husband challenged him to a duel for giving the pox to his wife." Without waiting for a reply, he slipped back into the shadows and with perverse satisfaction watched Hugo return with two cups of wine and look about in confusion for his partner. The woman had taken flight.

When he reached Pine's side the Oneida was watching not the crowd but a figure in another dark cloak making his way along the far edge of the assembled merrymakers. An oversized tricorn, tilted downward at each pool of lantern light, obscured the stranger's face.

"Not here with friends," Pine observed. "Not speaking with anyone."

The figure disappeared between two booths. A moment later another figure filled the gap between the structures. "Him!" Pine spat. It was Vaughn, followed two steps behind by Yates.

"Go back to Sarah and Kipling," Duncan instructed. "Tell them the Cajian and Vaughn are both here. If I don't find you later, I will see you at Mulligan's house. Keep them safe."

The Horse Guards officer showed no interest in concealing himself. Duncan lingered by a booth selling scarves and handkerchiefs, obscured by the crowd, and watched as Vaughn chatted with what Duncan took to be a group of Dutch merchants, bought a cup of mulled wine, then cut off an elderly man walking with a cane to purchase a roasted sausage skewered on a stick. As he ate Yates approached and, receiving instructions, disappeared into the crowd. Vaughn leaned against a barrel, chewing his sausage, and seemed to grow more attentive, as if watching for someone or something. His gaze seemed aimed above the heads of the crowd, but the only things at that height were trees, a flagpole, a raised cupola where musicians played, and a replica castle tower of wood painted to mimic stone blocks. From the top, twenty feet off the ground, two young couples waved to friends. Duncan's gaze lingered on the musicians, suspecting that one may give a signal to Vaughn.

Suddenly Vaughn froze, then smiled, took a final bite of his sausage, and flung the remainder into the bushes behind him. Duncan quickly surveyed the crowd again. When he looked back Vaughn was gone. He cursed himself, then more closely studied the higher reaches that had held the officer's interest. What had changed? Nothing, he thought at first, but then he saw the signal. A blue ribbon was tied around one of the crenulations of the replica tower.

The tower had a narrow set of stairs that allowed guests to climb to the platform. He ascended and found it empty except for a couple who had apparently climbed up not for the view but for a private place to exchange embraces. As he returned to the ground, he spied an adolescent boy sitting on a nearby bench beside a barrel holding brooms and a shovel. The boy was staring with an expression of wonder at something shiny in his palm.

"Am I addressing the keeper of the tower?" Duncan asked.

The boy looked up with an uncertain smile. "If ye mean keeping it clean, then aye, sir." He seemed to realize that Duncan had just come down the stairs. "Oh, sir! Sorry, sir! Did they track mud on the steps again?" He stood and put a hand on one of the brooms.

"Not at all," Duncan replied. "It's just that I fear some maiden lost a fine silk ribbon up there. Perhaps you recall—"

The boy laughed. "No maiden, sir. 'Twas myself."

"I don't understand," Duncan confessed.

In reply the boy held up the tuppence coin he had been holding.

"Someone paid you to tie on the ribbon?"

"Most particular he was. 'The second upright from the left side,' he told me."

"Who did?"

The boy clamped his jaw shut and shook his head. "He said I mustn't speak his name."

Duncan reached into his pocket and extracted a scrap of paper and a writing lead. "A bright boy like you must go to school."

"Oh aye, sir. Four days a week. The new one on Pearl Street."

Duncan produced a shilling from another pocket. "You mustn't speak the name. Just write it down for me," he said, and laid the shilling, the paper, and the lead on the bench.

The boy's eyes went round. He dropped to the bench and began writing, very carefully, in large block letters, then handed the paper to Duncan. *TALBIT*, he read.

"A Mr. Talbot asked you to tie the ribbon. Had you seen him before?"

The boy laughed. "Only about twice a week. It's one of our places."

"Places?"

"After school my friends and I like to watch the taverns, to see the drunks get thrown out and stagger away. He's the proprietor of the Wild Goose, down on Dock Street. He's a mean one, and powerful strong. Sometimes the drunks he tosses out tumble head over heels."

Duncan considered his possibilities as he ventured along the wooded paths again. The tavern keeper set the ribbon to confirm a rendezvous with Vaughn, probably in these very woods. Then he realized there were several men wandering in the Gardens, each a threat in his own way. General Gage, the Cajian, Vaughn, and the tavern keeper were all unaccounted for. He gave up trying to reunite with his friends and pressed his search, walking along every path at least once and lingering in the shadows by the lantern-lit intersections, discovering nothing but more amorous couples.

He returned to the thick grove of evergreens where they had lost General Gage more than an hour earlier. The winding path narrowed, and no lanterns lit it after the first fifteen feet, as if to discourage unwanted visitors. Thirty paces into the grove was a clearing with stored carts, barrels, and wooden silhouettes of forest animals, giving the impression that the grove was used only for storage. But the path continued on the far side of the clearing. Duncan followed it into deeper shadow. He reached what he judged to be the center of the grove when it opened into another clearing, illuminated only by moonlight. It was well groomed, and he caught the scent of early spring flowers planted along the edge. At the back was what at first he took to be a primitive structure, a hunter's cabin with a shallow porch at its front. Venturing closer, he noted that it was skillfully built to resemble such a structure, concealing a more substantial cottage. The door and window, which was obscured with a curtain that leaked light around its edges, were the work of skilled joiners. The supports for the covered entryway were milled posts cleverly covered with thin slabs cut from the edge of timbers to give them the appearance of raw logs. Luxurious pelts of mink and fox hung on the railing between two posts. The hardware on the door was gleaming brass. He was looking at another whimsy of the American pleasure garden, a retreat for wilderness fantasy.

In his mind's eye Duncan revisited the cabin door with the brass lock many times in the days that followed, imagining whom he might have encountered on the other side had he opened it. Behind it, he was convinced, lay the answers to the mysteries that haunted him. It may well have been Gage and Vaughn, possibly even with Hastings, or perhaps the cabin was used by Vaughn to make plans with Talbot the innkeeper and the bounty hunters from the *Indigo Queen*. The more he considered the point, the more he was convinced that Vaughn was indeed using it for that purpose, for the Cajian and his companions were rapidly expanding their role in Vaughn's network. Kipling and Pine had confirmed that the bonemen were meeting daily with three specific men, whom they identified as the servants of prominent merchants.

"Surely there is some mistake," Mulligan said when they explained their discovery and named the merchants. "It's too great a coincidence."

"Why so?" asked Duncan. "And merchants of what?"

"Why, it is like a list of those who are the public face of the Sons of Liberty in New York, second only to McDougal, who now sits in jail for his zealousness. They are merchants of ship's stores and trade goods, with warehouses spread around the harbor."

"No coincidence, then," Duncan replied. "The War Council is convinced the Sons are the root of the evil they seek to exterminate." He turned to Kipling. "You say they are servants. Do you mean bonded indentures?"

"Well, no. These are house servants, well treated but all Africans. Slaves."

"Which means," Duncan grimly explained, "that they will be promised their freedom if they will but spy on their masters, even be shown writs of manumission with their names on them. But they will have nothing of interest to Vaughn because their masters know nothing of our activities. They will run some errands for the king's huntsmen, then when finished the bonemen will collect them." He saw the questioning gazes. "The bonemen," he explained, "help him recruit informers among these servants, something they are adept at, but when Vaughn has no more use for the servants, the bonemen will take them. From the bonemen's perspective, it's a perfect arrangement. Vaughn can't afford any loose ends, and the bonemen can't afford empty cells when the *Queen* sails home. Every one of these informers is destined for the auction block in Barbados."

An urgent message from Fort George informed Dr. McCallum that the general expected his inspection report by the next day at noon. Duncan asked Mulligan for the loan of his desk, paper, and ink. Declining an invitation to a lunch being prepared by Moll on the brig, he spent three hours working and by midafternoon was able to give his completed report to Kipling for delivery to General Gage. Duncan did not expect a reply, and certainly didn't expect Kipling to return with an invitation for Sarah, Duncan, and Mulligan to dine with the general at Fraunces Tavern that very evening.

"The general's a great one for entertaining," Kipling said when Duncan expressed surprise at the invitation. "You saw him at the Gardens. He's there almost every Saturday night. His wife, the Duchess, is none too keen on it and never attends, but he insists it is his duty to keep up the morale of his officers."

Gage brought with him three aides and Hannah, who did not join them at the table but hovered at the door of the second-floor dining chamber, hurrying the waiters and acting as the genteel guardian of their privacy.

"Extraordinary, McCallum!" Gage exclaimed of his report. "I have instructed Major Trent to draw up standing orders based upon your sound advice." He tipped his glass of sherry to Duncan.

Duncan's gaze lingered on Gage. If he was looking at the monster of Fort George, that demon was concealed behind an earnest, often cordial, mask. "I am honored, sir, but most of my points were somewhat obvious."

"And we are ever blind to the obvious. Lime solutions to flush out the inside privies once a week. Lime backfill in every latrine twice a week. Surgeons not to rely solely on sick call to identify problems but to do inspections of living quarters as well. Prohibition on bathing and fishing in sewage discharge areas. We shall comply with it all. Boiling the tableware every week may be a bit over the top, but certainly we can aim for twice a month. And cats. Garrison cats to control rats. We don't need to mention cats in official orders," Gage said in a quick aside to Major Trent, "but we can express the sentiment informally. The children will love it." He turned back to Duncan and spoke in a lower voice. "I wasn't entirely clear about sanitizing the magazines."

"Pull back the first row or two of powder kegs in the magazines and you'll find a festering health hazard, sir. Filth probably left from the days when the Dutch built the fort. Bad for health of the soldiers, bad for the powder. I am surprised you don't find more defective kegs. Do you never test them?"

"There's a munitions expert coming from Connecticut in four days to verify the new shipments," the major pointed out. "A provincial now, but he had long service at an artillery garrison in Ireland."

"Perfect timing to clean the magazines," Duncan offhandedly suggested. "Move the kegs into the tunnels or out into the yard. Scrub down the back walls with lime. Better yet, a new coat of whitewash."

"Perfect indeed!" Gage exclaimed. "And I have just the two men to get the job done. What say you, Major? Can you and the good doctor here get this done before the Connecticut expert arrives? With say a company of foot to assist?"

"I doubt we can find a company on such short notice, sir."

"I have heard," Duncan said, trying to keep disinterest in his voice, "that the fortress technically belongs to the militia."

"By God, you're right!" the general confirmed. "Those called for duty in the militia spend most of their time playing cards at their armory, the sluggards. Make it so, Major. Have the militia do some lifting for a change." He turned and tipped his glass to Duncan once more. "You are a man of versatile talents, I find, Doctor."

The general's unexpected command propelled the supper to a quick conclusion. The major excused himself, saying he would need to urgently contact the militia commanders. Mulligan professed the need to return to his shop or risk disappointing several officers who were deploying to New Jersey the next afternoon. Gage remembered he had promised to join the captain of the *Thunderer* and his officers for drinks in the parlor below.

Duncan and Sarah found themselves alone at the table. "We must get word to the brig," he whispered, recalling how Boyle's kegs from Marblehead had been stacked at the mouth of an arsenal tunnel. "Boyle needs to know we have access to the arsenal, through the militia, to assure his kegs are placed with the batches to be tested." His voice trailed off as he realized Sarah was not listening. She was staring with an oddly troubled expression at Hannah, who in turn was gazing after Gage.

As the general disappeared down the hall, Hannah turned to gather dishes at one end of the table to ease the work of the attendants. Sarah began to help, offering lighthearted conversation. Hannah replied in short, respectful syllables. Duncan did not understand the way Sarah was suddenly hovering over the woman. She seemed to sense something that Duncan was blind to. As Hannah finished and gathered the general's cloak from a peg by the door, Sarah reached out and clamped her hand around the steward's forearm.

Hannah stiffened. "You mustn't!" she cried, then closed her free hand around her exposed forearm and wrenched her arm free from Sarah.

But the forearm had been exposed for a fleeting moment. Duncan at first thought Sarah had been interested in a bracelet or arm ring but now realized it had been a tattoo.

Hannah covered her arm by draping Gage's cloak over it, then resentfully pushed past Sarah, who resisted the woman for a moment. Gage's steward hurried to the door as if desperate to escape.

"You are *kahnyen'kehaka*," Sarah declared to her back.

The words were spoken softly, but Hannah heard. She froze and slowly faced Sarah. *You are Mohawk.*

Sarah opened the top fastening at her neck and pulled out the band of wampum beads that hung there, in the purple-and-white pattern that indicated the Mohawk. "I, too, am *kahnyen'kehaka*," Sarah told the woman.

The turmoil on Hannah's countenance showed anger, then confusion, and finally fear. She turned and fled down the hall.

"Duncan, I really don't know why we can't walk back on such a fine evening," Sarah half-heartedly complained. She had been so preoccupied with her discovery about Hannah that she had not been paying attention until Duncan gestured her into one of the coaches for hire waiting outside the tavern. He chose not to tell her that it was because Pine, on guard outside, had not answered when Duncan, as previously agreed, had given the short whistle for acknowledgment used by rangers.

"We should experience New York in all its grandeur," he said instead, rubbing the luxurious red-dyed leather of their cushioned seat.

Sarah stared back at the tavern as the coach got underway, clearly wondering about Hannah, before answering. "Boston does seem so drab by contrast. Streetlights. Fountains for thirsty horses, why, even some of the alleys are cobbled. And the young women—have you seen all the brightly dressed maidens who stroll the streets in the evening? Some even dance in the street!"

Duncan again chose not to further explain. In boasting of his very modern town, one of the statistics Kipling had recited was that New York claimed nearly five hundred women whose pleasure could be rented, representing one of the community's most thriving industries. "Civic pride, I suppose," he replied as he tied up the leather window flap for an unobstructed view of the street. It was unlike his Oneida friend not to have given a sign of his presence.

Then suddenly Pine was beside him, balancing on the iron step and clutching the edge of the window. "Vaughn and Yates with three men," he reported matter-of-factly. "Opposite side, one block ahead. This tavern," he added with a nod toward the building beside them, "has a back door." As the coach slowed for a crowd gathering on the street, Duncan declared that perhaps a walk would indeed be better and helped Sarah out into Pine's arms. Sarah did not object as the Oneida led her into the tavern.

Duncan stayed in the coach as it inched forward, then touched the purse hanging from his waist and grinned. They hadn't actually intercepted a random crowd, he realized, but rather reached what the locals called the Holy Ground, where much of the after-dark entertainment occurred. He stepped out as they inched toward two women in colorful, low-cut dresses, then extended several shillings and gestured to the coach.

"Sir!" one of the women exclaimed. "Both of us? Such a prodigious appetite!" As the driver was distracted, yelling at boys who had stopped to pet his horse, Duncan helped the two inside and surrendered the coins. "Enjoy the ride, mademoiselles," he said in parting from the confused but giggling women, then found a shadowed perch where he watched as Vaughn and his men began following the slow-moving vehicle.

Kipling was preparing to retire for the night when Duncan and Sarah knocked on the door to his room. He opened the latch, slipped his waistcoat back on and gazed at them quizzically. "Yes?" he asked.

"You never said who the slave was who worked in Gage's household." Duncan's words sounded like an accusation.

"Oh," the clerk uttered with a sigh, and gestured them toward the small bench along the wall, the room's only seating. Sarah sat, Duncan did not. "What I said was that she helped with meals and such."

"Meals and vastly more," Duncan said.

"She did start out as a scullery maid, while her mother served as a cook. She was born into service, as they say."

"It's as if you were trying to obscure the truth, Archibald," Duncan shot back. He realized that Hannah, too, had acted as if she wanted to obscure her truth. "She is a Mohawk."

"Prithee, Duncan, I had no ill intent. Both she and the general long ago asked me not to speak of it. People tend to speak of her as being of Mediterranean stock, either Italian or Spanish, and neither the general nor Hannah dissuade them. At first, I think it was so as not to frighten the children, since the natives are so often depicted in gruesome ways. 'Stay in bed or the Mohawks will scalp you,' some mothers still say at night, that kind of thing. Once when she was younger I caught her reading an account of that terrible raid on Schenectady, where the skulls of mothers and their babies were bashed in with tomahawks. She was crying. I told her that was many years ago, and we never venture so far north in any event, but she was inconsolable, took to her room for hours." Kipling paused and looked out the window for a moment. "Afterward," he added in a contemplative voice, "I wondered about those tears. Was she crying because she thought people would hate her if they knew? Or was she ashamed? Or was she just thinking of her dead mother?" He sighed. "The general himself went in to comfort her and later warned us never to speak of her blood again."

"But Hannah's a slave," Duncan declared.

Kipling looked out into the night sky again. "She's not in chains," he said after several breaths. "She lives better than the average merchant's wife. Never lacks for fine clothes. A leading member of the Gage household. Has the run of the town. The general gives her an allowance, for household expenses and any personal needs."

"She was born to a slave," Duncan said.

"Once it was not unusual for Dutch families to have Indian slaves, captives from the old Indian wars. I've heard that the family that owned her mother gave her to Government House in lieu of taxes. And yes being born to a slave in the eyes of the law makes her a slave."

"You were the general's clerk. You must have seen his personal accounts."

"Of course. He is most fastidious about his finances. Habit from an early age, he says, since he was a second son and could not expect to inherit wealth."

"Income and expense," Duncan said. "Liabilities and assets. Did he list her as an asset?"

Kipling winced and looked down into his hands. "Twenty pounds sterling," he admitted. "Higher than any market price," he said and flushed with color, "if you consider it purely from the financial perspective. Although one evening just before I left his employ, he was sitting alone at his desk, staring at the ledger entries, looking rather lost. Very unusual. I was working at a side table and tried to hide my curiosity. He made an alteration and left. I checked afterward. The change was to Hannah's value. He struck out twenty and wrote in one hundred. But of course he would never sell her. I think maybe it was just his way of assuring she would stay in the household."

"I've been confused about something," Duncan observed. "You left the general's office, but you still obtain information about ship arrivals and gunpowder shipments."

The distant look on Sarah's countenance changed to sudden interest. "That's right," she agreed. "There can't be many with that knowledge. I never asked. Achilles just received the reports from you, then delivered them across the bay."

"We—we've remained good friends, Hannah and I" came Kipling's slow reply.

"She acts against the general's interest?" Duncan asked.

"On occasion it may seem so. But she doesn't see it that way. And she's not the one who . . ." Kipling hesitated and changed his words. "To her, the general is a close friend who happens to be employed by the military. But over the years she became less friendly toward the king. 'He had no right to give away the land of my people,' she told me once. It was the only time she ever acknowledged her tribal roots to me."

In the morning Sarah sent a personal note to General Gage thanking him for the generous banquet and, because Sarah was still a stranger to the city, requesting the personal favor of borrowing Hannah for the day, to introduce her to the best markets and shops. Duncan, ever mindful of Sarah's safety, knew he would not change her mind so just insisted she take Pine as an escort. Mulligan, as she prepared to part, enigmatically declared that he had a meeting at the prison later that day that would assure the safety of all those staying in the Keep.

Duncan was at the door, uneasily watching Sarah and Pine as they walked toward Fort George, when Achilles, breathless, arrived with a message from the brig. Boyle had taken Henri on a reconnaissance, following one of Vaughn's deputies as he left a meeting with the spy at the Wild Goose tavern. "Vaughn's men are buying up barrels of the stuff!" Achilles reported. He spoke in a tight, haunted voice. "Barrels and barrels. Taking them to a storeroom on one of the old docks."

"Stuff?" Duncan asked.

"The killing barrels. Turpentine!"

Duncan arrived at Fort George early the next day, with Conawago walking with unusual energy at his side. The sentry at the gate hesitated upon sight of the Nipmuc, who looked more dapper than Duncan had seen him in months. Mulligan had loaned him a rust-colored waistcoat and new linen shirt. His long gray hair was neatly tied in a braid at his back.

"By order of General Gage," Duncan declared.

The sentry snapped to attention. "Sir!" the soldier barked and stepped aside.

Major Trent greeted Duncan at the wide entrance to the magazine tunnel. He gazed uneasily at Conawago, who waited a step behind Duncan like an eager attendant. As to affirm his role, Conawago withdrew a ledger book from the leather sabretache hanging from his shoulder.

"Dr. McCallum, I wasn't expecting . . . I mean we have procedures for admitting"—he searched for words—"strangers from the north into His Majesty's fortifications."

"No stranger at all," Duncan said. "My amanuensis often assists in my work. We must record the actions taken today. If there is another outbreak, surely the general will want to provide proof to the War Council that responsible precautions were taken."

"Yes, but this—" Trent was having a hard time describing the aged Nipmuc in the elegant attire. As a finishing touch Sarah had tied a russet scarf around his neck, which lent a hint of the gypsy to his appearance.

Conawago acknowledged the major with an impatient bow of his head, then extracted a writing lead and spoke in an earnest, scholarly voice. "Beg your forgiveness, Doctor, but would you perhaps prefer me to inscribe your observations in Latin today? The *medicus lingua?*"

The major's jaw dropped open. Duncan and Conawago left him staring at them as they descended into the tunnel.

The heavy work of moving gunpowder did not commence until the assigned contingent of militia arrived. Boyle had not won his argument that he could slip in undetected with the local soldiers, then appear as a Connecticut artillery officer the next day. They had been at an impasse, for Boyle insisted that their entire scheme would be for naught unless he assured his Marblehead kegs were correctly placed with their assigned batches. Duncan was reviewing for a third time why Boyle's participation could jeopardize the entire plan, and Mulligan was suggesting ways to disguise the Irishman, when someone knocked and Kipling appeared, wearing a New York militia private's uniform. "You forget, sir," he said to Mulligan, "that I am an auxiliary in the militia. Even if I am noticed I will have a perfectly good reason to be in the arsenal. I can identify our marks on the kegs."

"You're the company clerk, for God's sake," Mulligan protested. "This is more like—like a foray into enemy territory."

"I am behind on my required days of service, so no one will question me. In a company of citizen soldiers people come and go. And at the fort many know my face, will be less likely to challenge me if I am found in unexpected places."

"If you are caught—" Mulligan began.

"I will do it," Kipling insisted, now addressing Duncan. "It's like Crispus told me. You can't love liberty if you don't fight for it. I think it means the only liberty worth having is the liberty you earn. I have to do it for Crispus. One of those who died in Boston," he explained to Mulligan. "The first to fall that terrible night. The first to fall for liberty."

"Well, by God, you'd better not fall, Archibald," Mulligan whispered with surprising affection, then collected himself and spoke more loudly. "Or I'll never get my accounts straightened out."

Now Kipling mingled with the uneven ranks of provincial soldiers that marched across the wide yard to follow Duncan and Conawago into the tunnel.

Two hours later they had cleared the first hurdle—with Kipling seeing that Boyle's kegs were mixed in with their marked lots—and were brushing at the walls

"A princess of the *kahnyen'kehaka*," the Oneida declared.

The words wiped the smile from Hannah's face, and she removed the head-piece. "Thomas—I mean, the general—the general doesn't like me to display anything of the tribes. I am supposed to be of what he calls Mediterranean stock."

"But you know some of the Mohawk ways, and the words," Duncan pointed out.

Hannah stared at the feathered headband for several breaths before speaking. "When I was young my mother would take me to a hidden place, usually the attic or down in the rocks below the batteries if the weather was good, to teach me. When she was dying of consumption, she made me promise I would not forget."

She looked away, embarrassed, as she felt again the gaze of Pine.

Mulligan broke the awkward silence. "Well, we shall remedy the dilemma!" he announced, then took the headband and returned to his table, asking Duncan to serve out more wine and apply the poker as he worked. Opening drawers in a cabinet for new materials he quickly applied needle and thread and rose just as Duncan finished his own task. Mulligan triumphantly stretched the headpiece between his hands. He had sewn on a band of golden beads along the bottom and added brocade along the sides. "Now it is the latest fashion from Naples!" he declared. "Or at least that is what we will tell the general," he added. "Only you and ourselves will know it is really Mohawk," he said to Hannah.

Hannah examined it uncertainly, then gradually a smile lit her face. She set it on her head and turned toward the window. "What do you think, Pine?" she asked, but Pine had slipped away.

"I, for one, think it is perfect," Sarah interjected.

Hannah stared at the outer door. "Did I scare him away?"

"Of course not," Sarah said. "He keeps watch. A habit of Iroquois warriors that is hard to break."

Hannah kept staring at the empty doorway. "He said he thinks he played with my cousins when he was young. He said he was of a different clan, a different tribe of the Confederation. He spoke of it again when we were coming into the house. He said he was glad we were of different clans." She turned to Duncan, then Sarah. "Why? Why did he say that?"

Sarah shrugged, feigning ignorance.

"It is getting late," Duncan said. "Let me walk you back."

Duncan felt, rather than saw, the presence of Pine as he escorted Hannah to the fortress. Halfway back to the Keep he sat on a bench in one of the small commons interspersed through the city. Moments later, as expected, Pine sat at his side.

"You let them hide your hair," Duncan said, knowing his friend would take it as a question. Iroquois men were very proud of their hair.

"I had to get closer to them. Vaughn's men were still seeking, still watching, Sarah. I saw Yates, and others from the Wild Goose. And Hannah." There was an odd awkwardness in Pine's voice as he spoke about Gage's steward. "She is Mohawk and not Mohawk. At first, in the morning, she just acted like another fine lady of Manhattan. But your Sarah spoke of growing up with the Mohawk, just little tales. The women singing as they planted maize or taking canoes out at night and drifting with loons as they called to the moon. Hannah grew very interested. By the afternoon she couldn't stop asking questions about the Iroquois."

Pine paused, suddenly self-conscious as he saw Duncan's grin. Duncan had never known him to be so loquacious. He collected himself. "And then others joined. They followed us to Mulligan's Keep. They know much."

"Others. You mean the men of the *Indigo Queen*. The slavers."

"And men they pay. Led by that flash one, the Cajian. Henri has been watching. He makes light with the slave girls in the market and talks with bond servants who work at the shipwrights, close to the docks."

"Why close to the docks?" Duncan asked.

"Maybe they need ship supplies. And cargo."

"Cargo?"

"Maybe they decide the work with Vaughn is too risky. Their ship is anchored close to the docks. Whatever happens they will want to leave with their cells full."

"Where?" Duncan asked in a whisper, more to himself than his companion. "Where is Hastings?"

"Vaughn met him as I was following, met him unexpectedly—I think it was him. Your size, a little older, black hair, well dressed, with an old cut here," Pine ran a finger down his brow toward his left eye.

"That's Hastings."

"He was with that man Melville, of the *Indigo Queen*. Each had a woman on his arm, women with much—" He searched for a word, then made a motion of rubbing his cheek. Duncan supplied the word. "Yes, much rouge," Pine continued. "Vaughn seemed surprised at first, then resentful. Hastings and that Melville live like princes and treat Vaughn like a soldier. Then Hastings had the woman with him take up Vaughn's arm, too, and off they went to a grand house in the neighborhood of the Dutch merchants. It was Hastings's house, for a servant came out and greeted him as the master. Vaughn looked around and seemed to grow angry again, perhaps because he lives at that old Dutch inn. But Hastings laughed and led him inside."

Pine let the words sink in. If there was bad blood between the two huntsmen from London, Duncan could take advantage of it.

"And Solomon followed one of the men Vaughn gave a purse to, to one of those merchants they call a ship's chandler. He took two more barrels of turpentine to that little warehouse by the water."

"Solomon should not take such risks. They know his face. He was to stay on the ship."

"It is not for us to say, *yonkyatennon*." Duncan inwardly grinned. It was the first time Pine had called him friend. "I told him it was safer to stay on the ship and keep learning from Glover about the sails and such. He said he did not lose his chains just to be yoked by fear."

"I want to see that storeroom," Duncan declared.

Half an hour later, after stopping at the brig to ask Henri to guide them, they stood by a ramshackle, darkened storehouse built near the end of one of the old river docks. They lit the lantern hanging by the entrance and opened the door. Pungent vapors wafted out.

"At least a dozen barrels," Henri said. "I saw them just this morning. And a coil of that cord that smolders. The artillery men use it."

"Slow match," Duncan said with a shudder. He lifted the lantern and stepped inside. The storeroom was empty.

"We cannot endure so many enemies," Mulligan warned. They were back in his first-floor parlor, sampling mulled wine with John Glover, Sarah, and Conawago. "The bonemen spread like a plague, offering up coin and false promises of freedom. Soon they will have a spy in every household in Manhattan. And now they have enough turpentine to start a conflagration that could level this town. But," he added after a moment, "we no longer have to worry about the safety of the Keep. I paid a visit to the cell of my friend McDougal today. Every day he has a hundred or more followers gathered outside, with nothing to do but chant his name, and that of Wilkes. McDougal readily agreed to mention to his people that a likely location for a new liberty pole would be the little common just a stone's throw from my front door. He will tell them that those who seek to destroy such poles have already been sighted in this neighborhood. It means," Mulligan explained with a grin, "two or three dozen of McDougal's men will be watching the streets surrounding us and dealing harshly with strangers lurking in nearby alleys.

"But we have to find that turpentine," Mulligan continued. "We need to buy time to search for it. Perhaps," he suggested as he scratched his thick, curly hair, "we could drive wedges between Vaughn and the bonemen, even between the huntsmen themselves."

"I don't follow," Duncan admitted.

"My sense is that those Horse Guards officers are both cruel and cunning but also rabidly ambitious, eager for acts that impress the War Council. It is a high-tension game they play, where the rewards can be staggering. They aspire to knighthood and country estates. Everything is a contest, a battle, to them. They eliminate competitors, they eliminate threats to their mission without remorse, without observing any morality or law of God. Perhaps they already see each other as competitors. It's the way of such men. Vaughn resents Hastings's lavish living."

"Agreed, but—"

"That herring today was like what I used to put in fish traps when I was a boy," Pine abruptly put in.

They stared at him.

"Herring?"

"Bait, he means," Duncan spoke uncertainly but then understood. "We need something to lure in Vaughn, then make an offer that appeals to his ambition."

"That man Hastings killed my friend Crispus," Pine said. "As sure as if he had pulled the trigger. He means to start a war."

Duncan nodded, feeling guilty that he needed a reminder. They had to protect their secret plans, and protect Sarah, but more importantly they had to stop a war. "Hastings wants the hotheads to extract vengeance on the army," Pine continued.

Unbidden, the image of the dead soldier in the cesspit sprang to Duncan's mind. Maybe they had already started.

"But he says you fight a man of shadows from the shadows," Pine declared.

"He?" Sarah asked.

"Crispus," Pine stated. "He walks in my dreams most nights."

Kipling, sipping wine, choked. The color drained from his cheeks.

A chill crept down Duncan's spine. "He visits you, too?"

The clerk gave a silent, sober nod.

"He needs to be settled," Pine declared matter-of-factly. "He will roam in grayness until he is settled."

Kipling, seeming to shiver despite his warm wine, nodded again. "I never see his face," the clerk said in a near whisper, "but that deep voice is unmistakable. He calls to me out of the darkness, out of that grayness, I guess. Only my name. He calls me again and again. At first I thought he was summoning me, like I was going to die. Now"—he cast a glance at Pine—"I think it is something else. Like a summons to battle."

Pine nodded knowingly. Dreams were a fixture of Iroquois life, often discussed, never ignored. His eyes were full of challenge when he turned to Duncan and Mulligan. "You are warriors of the shadows."

Mulligan clenched his jaw, then leaned forward in his chair and nodded. "The shadows are our battleground," the Irish tailor confirmed.

"Maybe we don't need actual proof of what Hastings did that night in Boston." Duncan spoke slowly as the idea congealed. "We only need Vaughn to think we have proof that he caused the massacre, and we are trying to decide what to do with it. Give it to one of the gazettes, in which case London may have to cease all operations of the Black Office in America. Or perhaps give it to the general. Or maybe just to Vaughn."

"Why would we offer that?" Mulligan asked.

"As an exchange. Call off the bonemen, and the evidence can be kept secret. I need him alone for a few minutes, help him understand the risk he faces and the game Hastings is playing with him. Using the slaves is a huge risk. If Vaughn slips up, if the slavers are exposed, or even if Hastings just grows weary of his lieutenant's complaints, Hastings can destroy him. Slavery itself may not yet be a crime, but kidnapping and trafficking in stolen slaves certainly is, a crime worthy of the noose. And we bait the trap by sending a message to one of those merchants whose household now includes a spy, on the pretense that the Sons have to decide what to do with the evidence. Let's say there's a letter that arrived from Boston from an eyewitness to the massacre. A witness who was there and can attest that Hastings ordered the soldiers to fire."

"And then later," Sarah inserted, "I will send a message for Vaughn, left at the Wild Goose. Tell him I am sorry to have disappointed him that night at the harbor cemetery, so he knows whom he deals with. Say I now have something of great interest from Boston, a way for us both to rid ourselves of the noxious major. I will say I will deliver it on the wharf by the brig tomorrow at sunset." She fixed a stubborn gaze on Duncan, sensing his protest. "I've lived among the fishermen of Marblehead long enough to know that live bait is always the best."

Chapter 14

TWO DAYS LATER, AN HOUR after dusk, Sarah was waiting at the brig's wharf when Vaughn arrived. He paused to take in her attire, a sailor's smock fastened with a belt over breeches, then did not resist when she gestured down the pier. Duncan watched from the deeper shadows as Cuff, Glover, and Henri closed in on the two men lurking across the street whom Vaughn had brought as not-too-secret escorts. Duncan's friends quickly disarmed the men and sent them away.

Duncan stepped into Vaughn's path. The officer's protest quickly died away as he saw the pistol in Duncan's hand.

"Your dagger," Sarah said.

Vaughn muttered something quite rude but pulled open his waistcoat, revealing the hilt of his knife. As Sarah began to reach for it, Duncan saw his free hand draw back, ready to grab the knife, or Sarah. "No," he quietly insisted, pressing the pistol against Vaughn's temple and cocking it. Sarah extracted the dagger and melted into the shadows.

"Walk," Duncan instructed, indicating the darker, quieter end of the pier, lit now only by a quarter moon. "To the end, by the Marblehead brig. The one you've had men watching so carefully."

"The letter from Boston," Vaughn snapped. "I want to see it."

"Walk," Duncan said, raising his pistol. "I will tell you what the letter has in it," he said as they reached the end of the pier, adjacent to the silent brig. "The front-page story of every gazette in America. The subject of the most urgent report

General Gage has ever sent to London. There are already tales of a cloaked man giving the order to fire into the Boston crowd on March 5. Now we have a witness who recognized Major Hastings. Interested?"

"I must see it!" Vaughn growled. When Duncan gave no sign of responding, he sighed. "What do you want?"

"The bonemen gone. The *Indigo Queen* sailing away. With empty cells."

"You mistake me for the master of the schooner."

"There's always the other report I could make. How you killed Captain Mallory and Lieutenant Hicks."

"You're daft! I was in Marblehead when Mallory died!"

"You mean Major Hastings did it."

"I hardly know the details. Hastings needed him dead, so he got his morsel of steel."

"Because Mallory was going to expose you."

"Mallory knew Hastings. Mallory was one of those churchgoing fops who disapprove of the Black Office. I was only in one meeting with him. The fool laughed when Hastings told him we are the instruments of the king."

"Because you are only the hounds of a few dark-hearted men on the War Council," Duncan shot back.

Vaughn ignored him. "Hastings said, 'You won't be laughing when I have you transferred to the fever isles.' That's when Mallory said, 'We'll see what the George has to say about that.'" Vaughn's lips curled upward. "That's what got Mallory killed."

Duncan paused, not able to parse the words. "Why did you crucify Hicks?" he demanded. "A lot of trouble for someone skilled in the art of quick assassination. Sewing his mouth, was that supposed to be a message to anyone else who might complain?"

"Either that bastard died or the mission died. But I only killed him the second time. Someone had beat me to the pleasure. When I sliced into his heart it was no longer beating."

"To insert the tokens that would falsely place the blame on Jacob Book. Why Book?" Duncan knew but wanted to hear Vaughn say the words aloud.

"The obvious choice, the deserter whom Hicks was most ravenous about, playing cat and mouse for days with him. Where is the Boston letter?"

Duncan ignored the impatient question. "But the provosts would come. Everyone of interest to you would scatter like deer into deep forest. So Book had to die, to keep away the provosts."

Vaughn shrugged. "The mission above all." He cocked his head at movement by a stack of crates.

To Duncan's surprise, Conawago appeared, with Pine a step behind, holding a small iron camp kettle, one with iron legs for standing over coals. This night the fire was inside, a smoldering bundle of cedar that was giving off fragrant smoke.

Vaughn shook his head in disgust at the two tribesmen. "Let's get on with this, shall we? The letter?"

"I want to hear your agreement, then see the *Indigo Queen* leave. Perhaps I can also go to the gazettes with a report of how the Horse Guards arranged for the imprisonment of Benjamin Franklin in London. He is much beloved in America. Tar and feathers will await you, and worse, if you are exposed. You're familiar with tar and feathers, Lieutenant. Four infantrymen in Marblehead suffered the indignity because of you."

The announcement gave Vaughn pause. "You? That was you? My God!" he added after studying Duncan. "You were at the medical school!" As he spoke, he cast an irate glance at Conawago and Pine, who had set the kettle down only a few feet away. Duncan paused, glancing in confusion at his friends. Their agreed place was as sentinels at the entrance to the pier.

"What nonsense is this?" Vaughn snapped when Pine raised Jacob Book's necklace into the column of smoke.

"*Jiyathontek!*" Pine intoned toward the sky. "*Jiyathontek!*" He was awakening the spirits.

Conawago stepped closer, an arm's length from the officer. "It assures he is watching from the other side," the Nipmuc explained. "Did you kill Jacob Book?"

Vaughn rolled his eyes. "This is getting monotonous. My God, if it will make you go away, yes. The old fish-faced fool thought I—"

The knife in Conawago's hand came up in a blur, expertly angled so that it entered Vaughn's diaphragm and sank into his heart.

A wet, croaking sound escaped the spy's throat.

Conawago twisted the knife, then withdrew it. It was Book's ivory-hilted blade. As Vaughn collapsed, Pine caught him and dragged him to the edge of the wharf. He propped the spy up, beckoned Conawago closer, then took Book's knife and stabbed Vaughn again before dumping him in the swift black waters of the East River.

Duncan stared, stunned, at the swirling river. A bitter protest leapt to his tongue, but he looked at the old Nipmuc and choked it down. This was a debt that Conawago had to pay, the only way to settle Book's spirit on the other side. But Duncan had just lost his leverage against his enemies. "If the authorities ever catch wind, it will go badly," he murmured.

"I killed him," Conawago loudly declared. "I will go confess to the watch this moment if you wish."

"No. I killed Vaughn," Pine said. "My blow took his last breath." His stab into Vaughn's chest had not been out of vengefulness, Duncan realized. He did it to protect Conawago.

Cuff emerged from the shadows holding out one of his blades. His deep voice echoed over the water. "I killed Lieutenant Vaughn!"

"No," Sarah said as she stepped forward with Vaughn's own dagger in her hand. "*I* killed him."

"I, I was the one! A Marbleheader killed the bastard," declared John Glover, incongruously holding a boarding pike as he appeared out of the dark.

Duncan shook his head. "There's not a gallows in New York big enough to hold you all." Conawago, at his side, made a small moaning sound. The aged Nipmuc was trembling. Duncan embraced him for a long silent minute, harnessing his own emotions, then led him into the smoke streaking toward the moon. He reached toward the heavens with an arm, the other still holding Conawago upright, "Jacob!" Duncan called. "Jacob Book, you may rest now. All is good."

"*Yoyanere! Yoyanere!*" Conawago shouted skyward, his voice cracking.

"Now," Cuff solemnly declared, "when I see Crispus tonight, I can tell him that next we will put him to rest."

Duncan had lost track of all the things that could go wrong with Boyle's gunpowder scheme and decided that all he could do was find a way to be present in case he might avert disaster. He therefore sent a message to Major Trent, indicating that since he was soon departing for the north country, he would prefer to close off his engagement with the general by reviewing his report in detail with Trent and, if possible, taking a walking tour so he could demonstrate what senior officers should look for in their future inspections of military installations. It was a gamble, but the major sent his acceptance by return messenger.

He walked with Boyle and Achilles to the militia compound, which consisted primarily of a large hall and a stable, where two heavy wagons and half a dozen bored militiamen waited, then compared watches with Boyle to align their times and set off briskly for Fort George.

Duncan and Major Trent were pacing along the wall above the batteries when they encountered General Gage, watching a group of soldiers gathered by a small gun on a swivel. Duncan counted half a dozen different uniforms, including two of the New London artillery company, for Mulligan had hastily fashioned a second blue and buff uniform when Achilles had insisted that he would join Boyle in the fort. The night before, Boyle had opened a small leather-bound chest to show Duncan the lens he used for initial examination of powder, the delicate jewelers scale he used to compare weights of powder, and the jars and vials of acid he used for various reactions to determine levels of potassium. "All to establish my bona fides," the Irishman said with mischief in his eyes. "Then we place a measured quantity in a small signal gun and ignite it, then finally a full charge in a swivel gun or some such other light cannon aimed at a target."

They watched from the ramparts as the swivel gun was pointed toward a target of floating barrels only fifty yards offshore. It fired not with a roar but a sputter, and the ball, so slow as to be visible in its flight, dropped into the water halfway to the barrels.

Gage groaned. "Another keg!" he shouted. "Test another keg!"

Boyle hesitated only a moment. "Ye heard the general, Private," he said to Achilles, who quickly moved to the first of the kegs grouped in lots at the back of the battery.

"Nay, nay, lad!" Boyle called out. "More random," he instructed and, as they had rehearsed, motioned his assistant toward the back of the collection of kegs.

Achilles heaved up a keg bearing Boyle's secret mark, and another of the militiamen helped him carry it to the front of the battery. It took Boyle only moments to open the keg and charge the gun. Gage watched with rapt attention, as a militiaman touched the firing hole with a slow match. The cannon sputtered and the ball creased the water and sank far short of the target.

"Another lot scratched," Gage muttered, then addressed the major. "Be sure the militia has enough wagons. I fear we have to be generous to them today." He turned back to Duncan. "They say that the long winter voyage from England sometimes sours the powder." Duncan feigned disinterest by pointing with approval at the streaks of lime below the privy discharge ports of the headquarters building.

By the time they reached the arsenal, the second militia wagon was already being loaded with rejected powder kegs. Gage paced silently around them.

"Eighty kegs, sir," a lieutenant reported. "Two lots."

Gage uttered an oath that would have made a regimental sergeant proud, then quickly apologized and turned to the sergeant in the Connecticut artillery uniform. "Is there truly nothing we can do to salvage this powder?" he asked Boyle.

"Ah well, Yer Honor, sir," Boyle replied. "We could open every keg and lay their contents an inch deep over the courtyard," he said in the casual vernacular of a colonial. "We might have just enough room, mind. And of course then we pray it don't rain or get trod on for the next few days. Then we can scoop it up a cup at a time and push it through a sieve, unless ye can find a proper powder sifter, the nearest of which is probably in Halifax or Cork. Then ye repeat and pray even harder. But even if that succeeds, Yer Honor, the potassium value will still be dismal, don't ye see. I suppose it might be bearable to have yer guns cough and gasp when you just be saluting some visiting duke or other brocaded saint, but if your lads are facing a hundred charging Frenchmen with their screaming painted allies and yer grapeshot just sags and drops, it could be downright embarrassing." Boyle raised his brows and grinned at the general. The major, clearly angered by the disrespectful demeanor of the Connecticut sergeant, seemed to brace for an explosion.

Gage, however, just rolled his eyes at his aide, as if to say it might be worth giving up the powder just to be rid of the annoying provincial. "Tell them to carry on, Major," he muttered and retreated a few steps to watch the completion of the loading.

Duncan had just witnessed a miracle. Boyle, with Sarah's help, had transformed barrels of reeking Marblehead waste into eighty kegs of the king's prime gunpowder. As they watched in silence, a young ensign approached and handed the general a slip of paper. Gage read the message and frowned.

"You can inform the governor that I will be able to meet him at ten o'clock tomorrow morn. As if," he continued as the messenger sped away, "I could do anything to solve his problem."

"The governor's problem?" Duncan asked.

"Escaped slaves. Suddenly, starting three days ago we have had an epidemic of runaways. Curiously all from leading citizens, one or two a day. Half a dozen so far. It seems to be a pattern, though no one can cipher it out."

Three days ago, Duncan realized, was when Vaughn met his justice on the East River wharf. The *Indigo Queen* had decided to cut its losses and was preparing to sail. "Odd, sir, that we suffered a similar dilemma in Massachusetts," Duncan stated, exaggerating only slightly. "They were all recovered. They weren't runaways; they were captives. Held in cells on a ship from the Indies."

Gage was only half listening as he watched the first of the wagons roll out the arsenal gate. "Cells?"

Duncan repeated his explanation, then added, "They were bounty hunters. Slavers, capturing new bodies to sell to Indies plantations."

Gage cocked his head. "You astonish me. Slavers? In northern waters? Surely not!"

"I saw their particular boat. A sleek vessel, with much painted bric-a-brac. Two masts, fore and aft rigging for what I believe the mariners call a schooner. I hear they actually tried to conceal the boat's name but were found out. A devilish offense in a maritime town. There was quite an outcry." He could see he had Gage's full attention and lowered his voice. "Now that I recollect, perhaps we could speak somewhere more privately?"

Ten minutes later they were in Gage's office, delayed by the general's need to sign several urgent orders in the outer office and a brief conversation with Hannah, who warmly asked after Sarah and Pine. Gage motioned to a rack on a side table holding several fresh clay pipes, then to a wide jar on his desk. "Virginia leaf," he said, then stepped to the hearth and tossed in a fresh log.

"I am constantly impressed with the scope of your knowledge of the world, Dr. McCallum," Gage said as he offered a smoldering rush to light Duncan's pipe.

"Now you reveal knowledge of events in Massachusetts that may hold lessons for us here."

"I suppose it might be called a new structure of trade," Duncan said after settling into one of the wingback chairs before the hearth. "The Atlantic slave trade is slowly dying, thank God. But the plantations still need replenishment of labor, especially in the Indies, where they lose so many to illness. New enterprises spring up to fill voids."

"You're speaking of a new slave trade within the Americas."

"Sadly I suppose I am. How any good Christian can tolerate the institution is beyond me," Duncan offered as he worked his pipe, not daring a glance at Gage. "Have you perchance encountered a genteel, well-dressed man named Jeremiah Melville?"

Gage went very still. Obviously he had, but he needed to collect his thoughts. "I recall a gentleman by that name looking for workers for his new timber tract up the Hudson. Offering new opportunity for strong healthy men he said, like retiring soldiers or servants finishing their bond term. I recollect grants of land were involved."

Duncan let Gage fret. He settled into a chair by the hearth and worked his pipe. "In Massachusetts," he said, "it was a timber tract in New Hampshire."

"Sir? You suggest he engaged in subterfuge within these very walls? The cad practiced on me?" The general's face reddened. "But surely he can't simply abduct people and put them in chains."

"Surely he can, because he is so charming."

"I don't follow."

"I'm just speaking of the Massachusetts experience, mind. He makes easy conversation, buys rounds in taverns, does small favors, even hands out little pouches of tobacco. He entices people onto his boat with invitations for a meal, a drink, or just a look at his elegant sailing yacht, which has a deck below outfitted like a dungeon. A wolf in sheep's clothing. And existing slaves and bonded servants are a prime target, at least in Massachusetts. He offers freedom. Writs of manumission."

"But their owners would have to sign such writs."

Duncan paused for a moment, nursing his pipe again. Did he dare take the conversation further? "That was the curious part. He had found some secret ally in the government, someone from London with great authority, or perhaps rich bribes, who could get magistrates to sign the writs instead. Some even suggested his secret friend was a senior army officer, so powerful he never had to wear a uniform." Duncan shrugged. "Of course, I would know nothing of such things."

Gage fussed over his pipe, pretending the tobacco was not properly seated. He emptied it in the hearth and stepped to his tobacco jar again. His face clouded with worry. Other pieces fit into the puzzle Duncan had given him.

"There was an amusing riddle in Boston taverns as the rumors flowed," Duncan pressed on in a casual tone, risking a fabrication. "In wartime if a soldier removes his uniform to engage in secret missions against the enemy, he is a spy. But what do you call the officer who takes off his uniform to engage in missions against his own people? I heard different answers. A ferret, a snake, even a mole."

Gage, kneeling at the hearth to light his pipe anew, choked. He stared into the hearth until his coughing ceased, and he did not speak until he returned to his chair. "Doctor, you speak lightly, but if your words are to be credited, they raise grave matters for me."

Duncan waved his pipe in the air. "I do not mean to cause disquiet. I am just a lowly physician sharing curious reports I have heard. Of course, if any of it were true and there are officers secretly working against civilians, you must have a good reason for it." He saw the uncertain gaze his words brought from Gage and shrugged. "I simply mean that surely every officer in America reports to you." He held up a palm. "Prithee, do not respond. I go too far already. You are burdened enough with the obligations of your office. I do not mean to add to your troubles. At least you have a simple answer for the governor."

Gage puffed on his tobacco, fixing Duncan with one of his intense stares. "You've gone this far, Doctor. Prithee, share your suggestion."

"The military has no authority over civil matters, so there is only one thing you can do." Gage cocked his head at Duncan. "Order the navy to search for contraband."

"Contraband?"

"Slaves, after all, are just property in the eyes of the law. So we would be speaking of stolen property meant to be smuggled to the Indies. Maritime smuggling is within the scope of the navy's authority. If the schooner is somewhere in this vast harbor, you could dispatch some marines, perhaps add some grenadiers so the army can share the credit. You will be the hero of the hour, of the week, if indeed you are able to free kidnapped New Yorkers. It would go far to reduce the tension with the townspeople. Everyone hates slavers."

"The navy invades us! Marines in full arms! We are done for!" Achilles's shrill cry interrupted Duncan and Glover in the brig's cabin as they reviewed the cargo list for Edentown. Duncan had never seen Achilles so upset. Before he left the cabin Glover stuffed a pistol in his belt.

Duncan's heart chilled as, standing on the aft deck moments later, he watched four heavy launches being rowed up from the navy's anchorage, steering directly for the brig. Between the sailors laboring at the oars in each launch stood a file of soldiers with muskets.

"Navy officer in the first boat," Glover announced and handed Duncan the pocket telescope he had been using.

Duncan studied each boat in turn before lowering the spyglass. His heart sank. He had pushed too hard, lost his gamble with Gage.

"You can hide in the wall behind the sacks of flour in the stern hold," an anxious voice called behind them. Achilles was pointing the runaways toward the gangway to the lower deck. On their voyage from Boston Duncan helped construct a false wall at the rear of the darkest, most inaccessible hold to create a hiding place for the runaways. Cuff, Tobias, and Solomon all fearfully watched the approaching boats, still on a direct line to the brig.

Glover raised a restraining hand. "No, lad," he said. "It's just the way of this angry river. The currents in the center of the eastern passage are treacherous. The savvy mariner ascends it by hugging the side, which is why they seem to be aimed at us."

"But they *are* aimed at us!" Achilles protested.

"We are moored to a wharf. Why go the trouble of sending boats when they could easily have just marched up Queen Street? Watch and see, they will veer away soon, to cut the current at an angle." Glover pointed to half a dozen ships anchored along the opposite shore, at the western end of Long Island. "The schooner moved yesterday. She is over there, tucked into the shadow of the Brooklyn highlands." As he spoke, there was a flurry of activity along the wharf.

"Clear the way for the ladies, ye sluggards!" the dock boss barked. "Lively now, ye lazy curs!"

Duncan's confused expression changed to a grin as he saw Sarah approaching with Hannah at her side. The wharf workers were pulling ropes and fish traps out of their path.

"We were just walking up from Hanover Square when someone called out the marines are coming," Sarah explained. "We thought you might need reinforcements," she quipped, then introduced Hannah to Duncan's companions, describing her as "my new particular friend."

Hannah, the wind playing with her long black hair, tilted her head to better see the four launches. "He summoned the captains of two ships last night. Very unusual for him. Report immediately, he ordered. Marines to be ready at dawn, strongest oarsmen to be assigned. None of the crews to be told their mission until they board their boats."

Glover watched with the eye of a seasoned mariner and chuckled as a sailor missed his stroke and the leading boat lost headway, the oars tangling. "He'll have his grog withheld tonight," he said with satisfaction, then turned to Hannah. "Beg pardon, ma'am. He? Giving orders to naval captains? Didn't know an admiral was in port."

"The general," Sarah explained. "Hannah serves in the general's household."

Glover blushed and muttered an apology. "You mean *the* general. Major general. Master of all in uniform." He studied Hannah with new interest. "Honored to have ye on board," he said and turned as a small cheer went up from the onlookers. The boats veered away as Glover predicted, indeed heading for the anchorage below the heights on the far side of the water.

Solomon gave a laugh and slapped Tobias on the back. "Not for us, my friend, not for us," he exclaimed in a whisper, then quickly looked away as he felt Hannah's quizzical gaze.

Duncan raised the telescope again, fixing it on the schooner as the advancing sun began to shrink the shadow that obscured it. Sailors were running about her deck as they spied the approaching marines. One of the launches altered course to take up a position behind Melville's vessel. As the lead launch came alongside, there seemed to be an argument, as if the ship's crew were refusing to lower the ladder. They did not seem to notice the launch that took a position under the bowsprit. Two grappling lines were thrown up, and in moments marines were up and onto the deck, met at first by angry resistance. As Duncan watched, two of the *Queen's* crewmen charged at the marines with clubs. They were quickly disarmed, with slams of musket butts. An officer motioned with his sword and the resisters were tossed over the side, to be retrieved by one of the waiting boats. The ladder was thrown over the rail and the schooner was soon crowded with men in uniform, several of whom disappeared belowdecks.

As they waited for the next act in the drama, Glover produced another spyglass and handed it to Sarah.

"One," Sarah said as men began climbing out of the gangway to the lower deck, escorted by soldiers, "two, three, four, five. Six! Six rescued. That's all of them!" she exclaimed, then turned, quieting as she saw that not everyone on the deck shared her enthusiasm.

"Them?" Hannah asked. "Rescued? I thought it was about contraband wine or spirits."

Sarah lowered her glass. "The slaves. The missing slaves. They had been captured for sale in the Indies."

Questions clearly leapt to Hannah's tongue, and she opened and shut her mouth repeatedly, but no words came out. She had seemed somewhat amused as they first began watching the drama, but now something darker overtook her.

"'Rescued' be too big a word," Tobias inserted, staring malevolently at the schooner. He, too, had once been in one of her cells. "Recaptured. Repossessed. Like when a man has his horse stolen and later recovers it. He repossesses it."

Solomon nodded. "Back to being just New York slaves," he said, bitterness in his voice. "Half people, like we was. Can't be a whole person when someone else owns yer body."

Hannah stared, wide-eyed, at Solomon. She held up a hand, palm outward, as if to say she did not want to hear more. Sarah, sensing her discomfort, stepped closer and put a hand on her arm. "The market should be open now. If we hurry we might find some spring greens."

Hannah, however, did not respond. She was studying the Africans on deck.

"You were half people but not now?" she asked Solomon and Tobias. Solomon shot Duncan a worried glance. "Only a figure of speech, ma'am," he said, then touched a finger to his forehead and retreated, followed by Tobias.

"Being banished from the harbor," Glover declared. He had not stopped watching the events across the river. The slaves were in a launch now, being rowed away, and most of the marines had disembarked, leaving a naval officer with a small escort on deck. The officer, clearly in a rage, was pointing emphatically to the mouth of the harbor.

"They should count themselves lucky," Glover continued. "The schooner could be seized for its use in smuggling. Like the ship Hancock lost."

"The general," Duncan mused, "finds himself on difficult terrain. The law may push him to seize it, but politics say otherwise. Seizing it would upset the governor of Barbados, who gave the schooner a commission to recover his runaways. The governor has powerful allies in London. So the general just wants it gone, away from New York."

"With the loss of more of her crew," Glover pointed out. "Those men they picked out of the water are bound for impressment, I have no doubt. The schooner's been stripped practically naked between those lost in Salem and now these."

Hannah, still silent, stepped back to the rail and watched as the launch with the rescued slaves approached. For a moment she seemed to despair, then she turned to Sarah, forcing a smile. "Sing it again, Sarah," she said in a hollow voice, "sing me that song about birds leaving the nest of their mother."

Sarah, surprised at the request, collected herself and began, stumbling at first, then singing a verse in Mohawk of what the tribes would have called a cradle song. It was a lilting, soothing melody about the loving mother who, knowing she will miss her offspring, still encourages them to fly.

Hannah's gaze grew distant. "My mother used to sing that to me. I had forgotten all about it until I heard you speaking in the tribal tongue, and suddenly after all these years it leapt into my mind, like a door had opened up."

"It mimics the songs of the forest birds," Sarah explained. "The thrush, the tanager, and the others, even the owls. My favorite line is 'I weep to see you go, little one, but I owe you a full life. Spread your wings and fly.'"

Hannah gave a sad smile, then breathed deeply, as if to fortify herself, before turning back to the row of launches, now close after crossing the wide river. The rescued passengers were clearly visible in the lead boat. "Look at their smiles," she said in a contemplative voice. "Even a bird with clipped wings still seeks its nest."

Duncan was sitting alone by the hearth in Mulligan's parlor, weighing Mulligan's report that his network had found no trace of the missing turpentine, when Sarah appeared with Rebecca Prescott. They exchanged pleasantries, found refreshment at the always well-stocked sideboard, then sat beside Duncan. Sarah fixed him with a gaze that went from encouraging to chastising when he remained silent. He did not relish the task she had set him.

"We learned more about your captain, Rebecca," he finally said.

Duncan saw the young widow's face tighten. "You mean about his death."

"Confirming that he was killed by Hastings. Your Mallory was offended by what Hastings was doing and threatened to expose him. He indicated he would speak to the George. That's why Hastings stabbed him and threw him into the harbor. He obviously thought that your fiancé could indeed do him harm." Duncan paused as tears welled in Rebecca's eyes.

"The George?" Sarah asked. "Surely not the king?"

"You said he was writing to complain about Hastings," Duncan said to Rebecca. "I think he meant Fort George. Who would he write to at the headquarters in New York?"

Rebecca stared into the fire. "For reasons I never fully fathomed he had a bond of some kind with the major general, said if he could but get a letter in General Gage's hands the general would do the right thing. He had been fussing over the wording. Did several drafts. He warned me he might have to forgo the ball because of the urgent need to send it, but then he declared all the difficult parts done and said to put on my best dress because we were going out to celebrate."

"Urgent," Duncan repeated. "Why so?"

"Because he believed Hastings had subverted some of his own men for dark deeds in Boston and had even darker ones in mind. Some of Nathan's grenadiers were acting most suspiciously and hovering close to his tent as if watching him."

"But the letter was never sent."

"He was planning to finish it and send it the next day. Was it possible, he asked, for me to get it to the post office for him? He didn't feel comfortable just dropping it in the company mailbag."

"Why Gage?" Duncan asked. "What possible bond could he have with the general that made him think Gage would entertain a letter or believe a complaint about a Horse Guards major?" When Rebecca did not reply, he spoke again. "We need to find out. It may be the only leverage left to us."

"Mallory had testimony about Hastings," Sarah mused, "but it's gone now."

Rebecca shrugged. "They wouldn't let me see his kit bag because we were not yet married. Long ago he had sewn a piece of cloth inside it with buttons at the top. His paper safe, he called it. And he would keep his special watch fob there, the one with the intaglio design of a tree with a cross that he was so proud of. He brought it out for the ball."

"But it wasn't on him, not on his—" Duncan began, then caught himself.

"On his body? You saw his body?" Rebecca asked.

"I saw reports," Duncan lied. He had personally searched Mallory's body. There had been no watch, no fob. "And the kit now?"

"Who knows. It went to the regimental quartermaster. They said if there were no next of kin it would be sold for the Invalids Fund in one of the auctions they have from time to time. But in the confusion of the regiment being shifted so quickly out of Boston after the massacre, I don't know." She dabbed at a tear, then choked off a sob. "They didn't take just his life," she murmured toward the flames. "They took mine as well."

Chapter 15

DUNCAN WAS PLEASANTLY SURPRISED AT the attendance for Scottish Night at Vauxhall Gardens. Couples roamed through the grounds wearing plaid sashes provided at the gate. An unexpected number arrived wearing Scottish bonnets and more than a few in kilts and plaid skirts, although some of the kilts were preposterously made of velvet and even silk.

Mulligan had located a bolt of green-and-black plaid and quickly fashioned dresses for Sarah and Rebecca Prescott, who, complaining that she was finished with lurking and hiding, promised to keep her face obscured with a low cap. When Duncan explained what he needed for his own kilt, Mulligan had groused that "Highland tailors must be an impoverished lot," but complied by sending Achilles across town for enough fabric for Duncan to fold around his body in the traditional fashion. Duncan did not have the heart to argue when the tailor produced a large pin mounted with a gaudy bird of cut glass, just rolled his eyes at an amused Sarah and let Mulligan use it to fasten the cloth at his shoulder. He even held his tongue when Sarah placed a wig on his head, then capped it with a Scottish bonnet.

Similarly attired, Pine, Achilles, and a much-recovered Henri fanned out into the crowd. Kipling wore a skirted kilt over his waistcoat, settled high enough on his waist to conceal the pistols tucked into his belt. Duncan expected that they were walking into a trap. Earlier, he noticed that Achilles had been followed while returning to Mulligan's Keep with his armful of plaid. He kept that piece of information to himself for fear of spoiling their festive mood, a rare occurrence in these troubled days. Duncan had been intent on attending to discover at last whom General Gage was meeting with, but now the stakes had risen.

Pine and Henri quickly faded into the shadows as they entered the Gardens, but Achilles and Kipling flanked Sarah and Duncan into the main plaza, where the Saint Andrew's Society was staging something of a Highland concert featuring bagpipes, a bodhran, fiddles, and even a hornpipe. Duncan kept his arm entwined with Sarah's and moved slowly, his instincts telling him that if he did not spot Hastings, it would likely mean that the major had already spotted him.

He tried to recollect who was left of those who had been working for the Horse Guards spies. The men of the *Indigo Queen* were gone, as were probably all those Vaughn recruited from servitude. Vaughn's disappearance had shaken Hastings. Pine had reported an angry encounter between Hastings and the innkeeper Talbot. Talbot had apparently understood the gift that Pine had left on his barroom counter, Vaughn's dagger with a black ribbon tied around its hilt. The innkeeper would have nothing to do with Hastings. But Duncan knew Hastings was resourceful and had ample opportunity to recruit off-duty grenadiers. "Watch for men who look like they belong in a military uniform," he warned his companions in a low voice.

"Like a man who dutifully stood to attention before catching himself when this tune began?" Sarah asked. The musicians were playing a military march. "Now he beats time with his fingers." The man she indicated did indeed have the beefy look of a grenadier. "Or maybe he's just here to protect the general," she suggested.

"But the general isn't yet—" Duncan began, then he followed her gaze. Thomas Gage maneuvered through the crowd toward the stage. He wore rather plain-looking civilian clothes, adorned by one of the plaid sashes and a hat pulled low over his brow. It was the confirmation that Duncan needed. Gage was here for a secret conference, to discuss matters that the general did not want overheard at his headquarters office. Duncan wagered the meeting was with Hastings. The increasingly desperate Hastings may try to persuade the general to seize Glover's brig and its passengers, and if Gage were so convinced, Manhattan would become hopelessly dangerous for them. Their allies would likely be arrested, and the many layers of their secrets slowly stripped away. It could mean the end of the Sons of Liberty in New York, and certainly would mean the end of Sarah and Duncan.

But, Mulligan reminded Duncan, they had yet to find evidence that Gage was indeed directing Hastings. Being blind to that possible connection meant they were blind to their enemy's strategy. The missing turpentine haunted Duncan. If Gage were directing Hastings, then surely the turpentine would not be used to burn the city in which Gage's own family resided. If Gage was not pulling those strings, then the twenty thousand residents of the city were in dire jeopardy.

Pine appeared, hovering in the shadows. As Gage left the plaza and moved into the shadowed woodlands, Duncan signaled for Pine to follow.

Sarah and Rebecca gave all appearances of enjoying themselves. Rebecca laughed when Sarah grabbed Duncan's hand and swung it in time to a particularly lively tune. Between songs, the master of the stage announced that there would be a display of Highland sword dancing in the next hour. Duncan grinned at the thought that New York had become something of a refuge for Scottish tradition, since such dancing, wearing of the plaid, bagpipes, and even swords had been proscribed in the Highlands after the last uprising.

His moment of relaxation vanished as someone behind him tugged at his arm. "Two of Hastings's toughs at the gate," Henri reported. "Beginning to feel like they are spreading a net."

A heartbeat later Duncan saw the unmistakable figure of Hastings. The major had a woman on his arm and appeared to be simply participating in the merriment, but two large, square-shouldered men at his back were keeping a sharp lookout. Another man with a military air leaned against a booth selling roasted potatoes. How many more were there? Duncan couldn't plan a defense without knowing all his enemies.

"You have both pistols?" he asked Kipling. "And reloads?"

"Ye—esss," the clerk nervously replied.

"Go behind that big oak." Duncan indicated a large tree twenty paces off the plaza. "And discharge one into the air. Now," he added as Kipling hesitated.

The clerk collected himself, gave a sober nod, and made his way to the oak.

The loud crack of the discharge instantly brought cries of alarm. In a frenzy of frightened cries and streaming kilts the plaza emptied, except for five men well accustomed to gunfire. They held their positions, watching the shadows and glancing toward Hastings, who had been pulled to the side of the stage by his fearful companion.

A forced laugh came from a man who hurried onto the stage. "Just testing fireworks," he explained and gestured for the musicians to take up their instruments.

Pine reappeared, confirming that Gage had gone into the cabin in the woods.

"Hastings has a defensive line to protect him when he goes to Gage," Duncan suggested. "We have to break it, offer him a distraction, something he has to pursue more urgently, but first, we need to clear the gate." He explained what he wanted Pine and Henri to do, then instructed Achilles and Kipling. Ignoring Sarah's protests, he turned to her companion. "Do you trust me, Rebecca?"

Moments later, having assured that Kipling was escorting Sarah toward the street, he stepped toward the center of the plaza with the young widow on his arm, her cap gone. Rebecca bravely held her chin up so she could be clearly seen as they strolled through the festival. Moments later Duncan watched as Hastings, on the far side of the plaza, froze. His eyes clapped on to the sole witness to his murder of Mallory. With urgent, almost desperate gestures Hastings summoned his men.

Duncan guided Rebecca to the stand selling potatoes and engaged in a whispered exchange with the vendor. He gestured toward a little curtained enclosure behind the stand and slid a shilling across the counter. As the man nodded with a knowing grin, Duncan glanced over his shoulder. Hastings and his men were making their way toward them. He pulled Rebecca into the shadows then into the little enclosure, watching through a gap in the curtains as their pursuers ran past. Instantly Duncan was out. "To the gate, as fast as ever we may go," he urged Rebecca, who gathered up her skirt and set off at a surprising pace.

They reunited with their party under the trees near the gate. Pine pointed into the shadows. Hastings's two guards were bound hand and feet and gagged with linen napkins.

He guided his friends to where Achilles waited with a livery coach. "Don't get in yet," he said. "I need Hastings to see you." Turning to Sarah, he added, "Listen for the call of a nighthawk, then climb in. Straight to Mulligan's." He instructed Pine to stay in the house. "Lock all the doors and don't let Miss Prescott and Sarah out of your sight until I return. Tell Mulligan to be sure his pistols are loaded and primed."

Five minutes later, Hastings appeared by the gate. From the shadows nearby, Duncan gave the sign. As Sarah, Rebecca, and their escort climbed into the coach, he heard Hastings's furious curse, then his sharp orders for his men to pursue their fleeing quarry.

"McCallum!"

Duncan turned at the furious call. Hastings had started back toward the Gardens, then frozen. He had at last recognized his foe. "You're a dead man!" Hastings shouted. Duncan darted into the shadows.

Duncan had nearly reached the plaza when a twig broke behind him. Hastings was ten paces behind him, accompanied by a muscular man who had the look of a grenadier. Duncan sprinted into the plaza, where he expected to lose them in the crowd before exiting into the woods.

A second guard, however, began threading his way through the crowd toward Duncan, cutting him off. Duncan desperately surveyed the scene, then ducked and ran toward the stage, where half the musicians had retired for a rest. As he climbed the stairs onto the platform, he threw off his bonnet and wig, then loosened the braid that bound his long hair, letting it fall to obscure his face in the loose style of the other performers. He picked up a set of bagpipes and launched into the lively "Maggie Lauder," a favorite dance tune of the Highlands. The fiddler and the woman with the bodhran looked up in confusion but gamely joined in. Couples began dancing.

Hastings, gasping from a hard run, entered the plaza, weaving between the dancers, and looked everywhere but to the stage. Duncan watched as the major, clearly frustrated, signaled his men toward the gate. This night Rebecca Prescott was a greater prize than Duncan.

Duncan played one more song, long enough to convince himself that Hastings had taken his pursuit elsewhere, then turned to see the perplexed, though slightly amused, owner of the pipes behind him. "Lovely pipes. Boxwood chanter, is it not?" He returned a grinning nod from the piper and hurried offstage.

The woodland, albeit small, was still substantial enough to stir the feelings of the wilds in Duncan. The events of the past hour excited something in him that had been quiet for too long. He felt the quickening of the warrior as he stole through the moonlit forest. He was back in his element, for after years with his native friends he had come to trust the world of nature far more than the world of men.

He gave couples seeking a romantic interlude a wide berth but slowed to study the few figures who walked alone. Gage had gone unaccompanied to the cabin, which meant he expected to meet someone. He recalled the enigmatic cloaked figure they had seen on their first visit to the Gardens. If Gage wasn't meeting Hastings, Duncan realized it was likely someone bringing a report on the work of Gage's secret gallopers, the general's personal spy force, which had been searching for signs of the war machine conjured by Franklin and Duncan. If he knew what that report said, it would guarantee that he could keep one step ahead of them. When Gage finished in the cabin, Duncan would find a way inside to discover its secrets.

He found a perch among boulders under some maples that allowed a view of where the two paths that led to the spruce grove and the cabin converged. He passed the time trying to banish his foreboding, and for pleasant minutes he settled on memories of sailing with Sarah off the Massachusetts coast, the wind teasing her auburn tresses, every fiber of her being expressing the joy of handling the helm of a fast vessel in a fair-weather wind. She would laugh as the sloop cut the waters of the bay with a high bow spray.

His smile faded as he recalled how that same bay had held the body of the noble Captain Mallory. Rebecca Prescott's story was heart-wrenching, but the gap in her tale gnawed at him. It beckoned like a distant campfire sighted in enemy territory. Gage was an enigma, affable but remote, a man of deep contemplation and deeper secrets. Would his connection with Mallory become the chink in his armor? Why, he asked himself again, would a lowly captain of infantry think the supreme commander would entertain a complaint about a lofty London officer?

A flicker of movement banished his musings. The hooded stranger moved like a phantom, sticking to shadows whenever possible, so deftly Duncan had difficulty following. He was tracking a shadow within shadows. Knowing the brittle branches under the spruces would snap and give him away, he risked all by following on the path itself. The phantom broke into a run at the edge of the clearing, as if the need to reach the cabin had grown more desperate. The cabin door opened before the figure reached the little porch, releasing a pool of soft lamplight. The general reached out to stop the stranger, then gently put his hands on the cloaked shoulders and pushed the cloak to the ground. Gage wrapped his arms around the figure and passionately kissed her. It was Hannah.

"I must see for myself," Sarah insisted.

Duncan had ruminated on his discovery all day as they began preparing for the journey north, not sharing it with anyone. He finally sought Sarah's reaction as they sat alone at dusk in the walled garden behind Mulligan's Keep.

"See what?"

"Their place. The mysterious cabin. I must have the sense of it. Hannah is a friend." The four words spoke volumes. Sarah had recognized the complexity of the terrain Duncan had stumbled onto. Hannah was a grown woman. Hannah was a slave. Hannah was a Mohawk. Hannah was, he suspected, a patriot. Which of these explained what was happening at the cabin?

"The Gardens are closed until the end of the week."

"I was hoping so," Sarah replied with a mischievous glint. "Shall we say in an hour? Not so late as to draw attention from the watch but late enough that there will be few bystanders."

In true Mohawk style Sarah led him on a reconnoiter around the entire Gardens, then returned to a quiet, shadowed place far from the entrance where two oaks on either side extended sturdy limbs over the top of the wall. Without a word of explanation, she dropped the cloak and tricorn hat that had made her one more anonymous figure on the city streets.

A syllable of surprise escaped Duncan's throat. She wore a simple linsey-woolsey tunic of Edentown manufacture, taken from his own trunk. It was tightly bound with a belt of quillwork, made for her by an Iroquois matriarch. The tunic just covered the top of her buckskin leggings. It was her warrior's attire. Duncan grinned. He had not seen her so since leaving Edentown. Without a word she stowed the cloak and hat at the foot of the oak, planted a kiss on his forehead, and leapt onto the tree.

On the other side of the wall they found themselves in one of the Gardens' wooded alcoves furnished with a rustic bench. They reached the main path less than a hundred paces from the dense grove of evergreens that shielded the cabin, walking apart, as if in enemy territory, then froze at the sounds of dogs barking behind them. They had not considered the possibility of guard dogs patrolling the grounds.

"They may just be in someone's yard near the wall," Sarah suggested.

Duncan was not convinced. The barking seemed to be getting closer. He pointed down the path. "Run."

The barking faded by the time they reached the cabin. Duncan extracted two small metal rods, barely thicker than wire, from his pocket. The door was immersed in shadow but his task needed his sense of touch, not his sight. Years earlier a ranger of uncertain background had taught him the skills when they had taken refuge in an old German church for two days during a snowstorm. He inserted the rods, probing and tapping until he heard the satisfying click of the lock. He stood aside and Sarah opened the door.

He hurried to the fireplace in the dimly lit chamber, knelt on the wide hearthstone with his fire kit, and struck a spark. As he lifted the smoking tinder, Sarah bent with a candle.

The chamber had the feel of a rustic parlor, or perhaps a rich merchant's vision of such a parlor. A commodious divan faced the fireplace, the mantle of which bore a row of stuffed birds. Below the divan was a luxurious rug made of three or four bear pelts sewn together. The skins of other forest creatures hung on the log walls. Below the skins on one wall was an elegant sideboard stocked with bottles and glasses. A table with four chairs sat behind the divan. In one corner was tucked a finely crafted secretary's desk with a folding top. In another was the entry to a bedchamber. The bed was large, with expensive linen sheets, down pillows, a down comforter, and a blanket of marten fur.

Sarah paced along the bedroom walls. Silky robes hung from pegs. Cherry-wood candle boxes with sliding tops sat on the nightstands beside the bed. One held little bottles of scented oils, the other feathers. When she sat on the bed with a contemplative expression, Duncan lit another candle and returned to the desk in the parlor. On the top was a large pewter bowl holding ashes and remnants of burned paper. He opened the folding top. Haphazardly arrayed in the working space below rows of pigeonholes were drawings and words. A crude drawing of a deer and the word *ohskennonton*. A sketch of a turtle and *a'nonana*. A canoe and *on-ake*. His heart clenched. Years earlier when he and Sarah were getting acquainted, she had used such images to teach him the Mohawk tongue. On the largest piece of paper in a firm hand that he recognized as Gage's was written *Attonnhets. You are my attonnhets.* He turned the paper over. It was a letter, a short note addressed simply to TG and signed Harrington. It consisted of only two sentences. *Do not yield to these wolves*, it said. *We do not devour our own kind.* He read it again and stared in mute surprise as he finally understood. TG was Thomas Gage, Major General Thomas Gage. Lord Harrington was the most moderate member of the War Council.

He quickly searched the backs of all the other scraps, which yielded only notes on supplies and appointments. His eyes returned to the pewter bowl. The remnants were of the same paper as the letter. Gage was reading letters he did not want revealed at his headquarters office and burning some. He quickly searched the pigeonholes, finding only more scraps with Mohawk words and the printed programs to several theater productions. Three of the four drawers underneath were empty. The fourth held writing paper, ink, and quills. Gage was both reading and writing letters in the cabin.

Sarah appeared and lifted one of the scraps, then another and another. She did not give voice to her recognition of what the papers had been used for, only took his hand and squeezed it, not letting go. He handed her the words written on the back of the London letter and heard her sharp intake of breath.

Sarah seemed disinclined to speak, and he could see in her eyes that she was growing uncomfortable, feeling more like an intruder than a warrior scout. She gave a hand sign to him. *Retreat.*

Moments later they were ready to depart, leaving everything as they had found it and the candles extinguished. As Duncan eased open the door, deep growls rose from the porch. Two large dogs, wolfhounds perhaps, blocked the way, teeth bared. Duncan spoke calming words and extended a hand. The nearest dog lunged. Despite Duncan's instant withdrawal, its fangs came so close they tore his sleeve.

"There is no second door and no meat to distract them."

"We will not hurt them," Sarah said.

"We will not hurt them," Duncan agreed.

They gazed out the window. They sat at the table for long minutes in the futile hope that the guards would tire and wander off. Duncan gradually became aware that Sarah was humming, starting and stopping as if trying to recall a song. Finally she stood. "Dogs are in the clan of *ohkwari*," she whispered, putting a finger to her lips to keep him silent. The Iroquois considered humans to be just another member of the animal family, and according to legend, other species, like humans, belonged to clans. In those tales, dogs belonged to the bear clan.

She positioned herself at the door and began singing, then slowly eased the door open. She did not move at first and just offered up the soft Mohawk melody. It was ancient, some of the words unfamiliar to Duncan. The dogs slowly quieted, then cocked their heads. She took a half step forward, repeating the song. The dogs eased back, and she gestured to Duncan to follow. When they were in the center of the clearing, she knelt and stroked each of the big animals, murmuring into their ears. As they ventured back down the trail, the dogs were at her side.

Duncan remained silent for fear of breaking the spell. When they reached their arboreal passage across the wall, she bent and stroked the animals again, thanking them. He waited until they were over the wall to speak. "It was an old song," he observed. "It sounded like one used by Iroquois spirit speakers when they visited caverns to look at the ancient wall paintings. Something of a charm, I suppose, to put a bear under a spell."

Sarah laughed as she tucked her tresses under her hat again. "That's what many think. But my father, my true father"—she used the term to distinguish the beloved Iroquois sachem who raised her from the aristocratic English ghoul who was her blood father—"told me that was not so. It's not to subdue the bear. It is to ask the bear's forgiveness."

Asking forgiveness. The words stuck with him for hours and were the reason Duncan now perched across from the nondescript building off Broad Street that Mulligan had described as the sole sanctuary for the city's small population of Catholics.

"Priests are officially still banned under some dusty old law," the tailor explained, "but New York is a tolerant town, so they conduct Mass and such without much interference, and all the soldiers from Cork stopping over here have been filling its aisles."

It wasn't an Irish soldier he was interested in but the Welsh corporal who had gone in half an hour earlier. He felt an unexpected tightness in his chest as he entered the surreptitious church. His mother had seen to it that Duncan and his siblings accompanied her most Sundays to what she called the "Roman services," always in out-of-the-way caves or byres, for Catholicism had also been banned in the Highlands of his youth.

He dipped his fingers in the water of the pewter bowl inside the door and awkwardly crossed himself, then stepped into the worship chamber. Ten rows of simple plank benches serving as pews faced an altar, on which tall column candles burned on either side of a large silver crucifix. There were only five others in the sanctuary. Four were gathered together, three dabbing at tears as a gray-haired woman read quietly out of a prayer book. Corporal Rhys sat in the shadows at the back, bent with his elbows on his knees and his head in his hands.

Duncan said nothing as he sat beside the corporal, who took no notice of him. He finally looked up when the mourning party was leaving. "Ah, 'tis you, sir," Rhys murmured.

"When I was young," Duncan said in a near whisper, "most of the priests I met were in caves. To hide from the law, I learned later. For years I thought it was just their natural habitat, that somehow they were related to bats." He gestured about the chamber. "No bats, no priests, no confessionals for absolving sin."

"Ah, well," the Welshman said in a brittle voice. "The stain on us be too great to forgive. I just plead for the young ones, the new blood in the regiment, to be passed over. Their hands are clean. Some weren't even born."

"But you and Sergeant Briggs both served twenty-five years and more." Duncan had already done the painful math. "The last great rebellion."

"Aye," Rhys affirmed, then said nothing for several breaths. "We was held in reserve at Culloden, just sent in later to retrieve our dead and wounded, and later to stack the bodies of the others." Duncan clenched his jaw. *The others*. He meant Scots, mostly Highlanders, including men of Duncan's own clan. "That was at least honorable soldiers' labor," the corporal continued. "But then the Duke of Cumberland sent our company on detached service under General Hawley. The duke, third son of the king. Afterward most just called him Butcher Cumberland.

"'Destroy all Jacobites' was the order, destroy them root and branch. We figured it meant the Jacobite soldiers, the resisters still fighting in the Highlands. But General Hawley said no, the duke meant destroy everything they touched, everything they did. They meant annihilation. At the first village we entered, the major who was seconded to us from Hawley's staff ordered us to line up all the villagers on one side of the road and all their cattle and horses on the other. The major had us shoot all the livestock. When we finished, he said, 'Damn yer eyes, why do you halt, I ordered you to kill the Highland livestock.' He was speaking of women and children. When no man moved, he dismounted and ran his sword through the old woman who was first in line. 'Like this,' he says. 'Use your bayonets, lads, no need to waste good cartridge.'

"It was a waking nightmare, and it only got worse. After the first days the major began staging what he called entertainments. Tying children to trees and offering coin to any man who could sink a knife into them from fifty feet. Herding families into their houses with their animals and firing the house, with bayonets sunk into anyone trying to escape the flames. Oh, the screams." Rhys's words choked away for a long moment. "Women were defiled, then killed. I remember a mother who was handed a pistol and told to shoot her child. She turned and killed the nearest soldier instead. The major laughed and had her drawn and quartered as the child watched. 'Tis a rare night I don't wake up shaking with visions of those days. Nay nightmares, mind. They're memories."

Even if Duncan could have found words, he could not have spoken. His heart was in his throat. The men of his family had mostly died at Culloden or been taken prisoner and hanged. Nearly all of his remaining kin had been at their croft when the Butcher's troops called. Duncan had been a young boy at boarding school in Holland. It was only years later that he learned how soldiers defiled his mother and sisters before killing them and bayoneting his brothers.

"The Butcher casts a long shadow even after all these years," Rhys whispered. "Sins may take a twisted road, my ma used to say, but they will always catch up with a man. My heart was eased a bit when he was taken to an early grave. But it was never gonna be over for the Twenty-Ninth."

"Over?" Duncan managed to ask.

"The curse. The damnation. In this life and the next. Now the angels grow impatient with us, probably even more so after the bloody snow our lads left in Boston."

"You've had misfortunes in the regiment."

"Kind of you to say it that way but nay, nay. 'Tis the hand of God, don't ye see? Sure as I sit and breathe. And who am I to complain?"

Lost in the despair released by the Welshman's words, Duncan did not react at first. "You mean because you were there," he said at last.

"Oh aye, I was there and so, too, Robbie Briggs, though it turned our stomachs and we always volunteered to do elsewise, like watch the mounts whenever we could. But it was us, our company, our regiment. No random misfortunes. 'Tis the angels who've come. Or maybe the ghosts. They would know, you see, they would know and ne'er forget."

"Many know," Duncan observed, not entirely understanding. "It's been nearly twenty-five years. A different world now."

Rhys, staring at the silver crucifix on the altar, seemed not to hear. The flickering of the candles seemed to give movement to the suffering man on the cross. "We inflicted all of it first, don't ye see? Death in a burning barn. Death by blade in the heart. Suffocation in filth. Crucifixion," he added in a whisper, crossing himself.

They sat in silence.

"You'll probably be deployed to New Jersey," Duncan replied after several painful minutes. "I think they allow a few Roman churches there. You can find a real priest."

The corporal nodded. "Sorry to burden you with my confession. I am in yer debt. It eases the burden a bit, gives me a tiny ration of solace, which is all I deserve." He rose to leave. "As they say, sir, peace be with you."

But Duncan could find no peace as he sat alone in the church. He had not known what to expect when seeking out Rhys to understand his torment, and certainly not the new torment he himself felt now. He bent forward as moisture welled in his eyes. The shadow of the Butcher was long.

When he finally stepped back into the sunlight, Duncan felt a strange need to be with Conawago, to sit with the old Nipmuc, whose calm wisdom was like a shelter in a storm. Solomon, training in the rigging with Glover's mate, called down when he boarded the brig. "Tobias found you so soon?"

"Tobias?"

"Captain Glover sent him to fetch you. Urgent-like."

Glover sat in his cabin with an African in his forties, dressed in dark gray livery. "This is Noah," Glover said. "He was in a cell on the *Queen*, certain never to see his home again. Word has spread in the markets that we were responsible for the rescue."

Duncan took a seat at the small table, across from Noah. "We were pleased to help. We learned about the ways of Mr. Melville in Massachusetts."

Noah's voice was deep, his words articulate. "I wish to express my gratitude not merely in words," he declared. "I wish to demonstrate it. I have a wife. We are expecting a child. But for you I never would have seen her or met my child."

Duncan leaned closer. "Demonstrate?"

"Sometimes on that vile schooner they put us in chains and forced us to scrub the deck and repair sails. I saw the *Queen*'s launch leave. It went to another dock and was loaded with barrels. They were taken to Brooklyn, to a warehouse on an old wharf beyond the point, on the harbor."

"The point?"

"I simply mean it is obscured from most of the city. But it has a broad, long view of the bay and harbor."

"How do you know this?" Glover asked.

"My master owns the chandler's shop that sold half those barrels. I work there most days. The young one called Hugo befriended me, or so I thought. I confirmed we had the best-quality turpentine in the city. I helped deliver the barrels to that storeroom on the river. I did not see the barrels leave, but I have many friends who work the lighters that move about the harbor to load and unload ships. They saw the barrels in the *Queen*'s launch being unloaded at one of the old docks below Brooklyn town."

"Why?" Glover asked. "It makes no sense."

"Who can see into the hearts of such devils?" Noah replied, then stood. "I must return to the chandlery."

Duncan repeated the question when Noah had departed. "Why," he asked Glover with new worry, "if your plan is to burn the city, do you take the barrels to the far side of the harbor?"

When he returned to Mulligan's Keep, one of the tables in the upstairs workshop had been cleared of fabric and tailor's tools to accommodate a score of what looked like worn ledger books. Some were stacked at the center of the table.

The rest were being studied by Sarah, Achilles, Kipling, Rebecca Prescott, and Mulligan.

"We have them!" Achilles exclaimed as he spotted Duncan. "Mr. Kipling performed a miracle. The order and minute books for all the years of the general's tenure!"

"Just for the night," Kipling added. "Some of the entries I wrote myself, and I was certain I had never made record of an officer named Mallory, but there was always at least one other clerk, and in the early years the adjutant wrote many entries himself."

Duncan stared, unable to hide his surprise that such important books were so easy for the general's former clerk to come by. They had no malicious intent in their examination of the books, but it still would have been a grievous breach of discipline to remove them. Who, he asked himself, could have smuggled the books out?

"I've looked at the past four years," Achilles reported. "So far no indication of a connection to Captain Mallory." He pulled another volume from the stack. "Or a lieutenant so named," he added, "since Mrs. Prescott states he was promoted just two or three years ago. Nothing in orders, nothing in minutes of meetings, nothing in what they call extracts of correspondence and readiness reports."

If the books contained such information, they would be considered even more secret than Duncan imagined. Civilians caught with them would be suspected of treason.

Sarah looked up, rubbing her eyes. "Show Duncan that peculiar entry you found," she instructed Mulligan.

The tailor turned to a page marked by a piece of ribbon. "A summary by the adjutant of some correspondence received by the general," he reported, then began reading. "Correspondence from the Monongahela brothers indicates that the ten-year commemoration at the grave will be adequately attended. General TG will seek to accommodate on his summer schedule but can make no promise. Colonel W. and a dozen other Virginians confirm attendance, as do officers of both the Forty-Fourth and Forty-Eighth. Unfortunately Mallory will be in Ireland with his regiment." He looked up. "Dated March 1765."

"Our Mallory? He was there?" Duncan asked no one in particular. "With Gage?"

"There?" Mulligan inquired.

"With the Forty-Fourth and the Forty-Eighth. Colonel W. has to be Colonel Washington of the Virginian provincials. It could only mean the tenth anniversary of the Braddock defeat in fifty-five at the hands of the French and their tribes. General Braddock was killed and buried by the Monongahela River."

"Of course!" Kipling put in. "General Gage sometimes speaks of being with the old major general when he died. Said it was his first lesson in American warfare."

"So Mallory was there too, one of the mysterious Monongahela brothers," Mulligan concluded. He looked up at Duncan. "Meaning what?"

"Meaning Mallory indeed had a connection with Gage, a bond forged at that blood-soaked battle. Which would be"—he turned to Rebecca Prescott—"a reason why the lofty major general would entertain a personal letter from a lowly captain of infantry."

"I never saw it," the widow reminded them, "but he told me he had no choice but to make a complaint about the Horse Guards."

"But we have no such letter," Mulligan pointed out. "It was never sent. Gone forever."

"Maybe not," Rebecca said. She raised a sheet of paper, torn at the top where it had been fastened with a tack or peg. "A broadside found by Mr. Achilles, one of many posted around markets today."

The print was so large Duncan could read it across the table. INVALIDS FUND AUCTION AT FORT GEORGE, it said, with the poignant image of a musket resting against a tombstone. Rebecca pointed to finer print at the bottom and explained that in addition to military surplus gear, orphaned kits from four regiments, including the Twenty-Ninth, would be sold to members of the military.

Duncan turned to Kipling. "Who is responsible for the Invalids Fund at Fort George?"

"Why herself," Kipling answered, with an awkward glance at the books on the table. "The Duchess."

"You mean the general's American wife."

Kipling gave a slow nod. Duncan could not make sense of his sudden hesitation.

"The American wife," Duncan continued, "who chooses to raise her children outside the fort, away from the British military. As if she did not want her sons inspired to pursue a military path."

Kipling gave a noncommittal shrug, opened another ledger, and leaned over its pages. "Seventeen sixty-four," he read. "Pontiac would still be waging his war. Correspondence with William Johnson about Fort Niagara."

Duncan, still puzzled by Kipling's discomfort, took a seat and joined in the review of the ledgers. What he read was intriguing, he had to admit, and after reviewing several passages about dispatches of special patrols and receipt of information about the movement of the king's enemies, he switched to reading the most recent journal.

"Already reviewed," Achilles reminded him.

"Another pair of eyes can't hurt," he said, giving no hint that his search had suddenly changed its purpose. He started with entries from six months earlier and soon found the first reference to gallopers being deployed. The mentions were intermittent over the following weeks, just short indications like *four forges, three foundries visited in Jersey. No signs.* And *metal working very primitive, most not able to make steel.* But two brought him a spark of excitement. *Galloper brought back disturbing rumors of iron mines being opened in the Mississippi valley with French advisers,* said one. *Smithies along Connecticut River seem overly acquainted with Crowley offerings.* They were the bits and pieces that he and Franklin were hoping for, confirming that the army was worried about the Cugnot war machine, a puzzle that would gnaw at army strategists, sowing uncertainty, even fear, about patriot capabilities. He touched his Franklin watch and smiled. He looked forward to composing a coded letter to Benjamin on their voyage up the Hudson.

He waited until first Achilles, then soon thereafter Sarah, retired for the night before closing the ledger he was reading and addressing Kipling and Mulligan.

"We never spoke of how we obtained the information about incoming powder shipments. It was quite detailed. A breakdown of lots, manufacturer's codes and delivery dates. A king's secrets. Very closely guarded." He turned to Kipling. "You conveyed the secrets to Bradford, who conveyed them to Sarah through Achilles.

After they were received by your household," he said to Mulligan. "You have a spy in the general's circle."

A sly smile rose on the tailor's countenance. "Define *spy*. We have mutual interests with someone at his table, you might say."

"Someone serving his table, you mean."

"Not dear Hannah, no. She's a good friend who does help us from time to time, but we would not push her to take such a great risk. Not all would face the same risks. Or the same consequences."

Duncan stared at the Irish haberdasher, who offered no further explanation, then realization struck. "My God. The other American in his household, who doesn't want her children to become British soldiers. The Duchess."

Mulligan gave a half nod. "His wife is from a prominent New Jersey family. Thoroughly American, you might say, and willing to do a favor for other Americans from time to time. And rather immune to risk. As well as remarkably cunning. The books were sent out wrapped in dresses she asked me to alter. Some are being worked on by my seamstresses this very night and will be returned tomorrow morning with the books folded inside them and tied into muslin-wrapped bundles. No soldier would dare touch the clothing of the Duchess. Hannah would have helped if we had asked, but we would never put her in such jeopardy." He gestured to the stack of books. "You may have seen that the steward is mentioned from time to time. The genteel hostess. The Mediterranean beauty, one writer said. Practically a second wife," Mulligan added with a chuckle.

Duncan chose not to point out that his words were closer to the mark than he knew. Voices rose in the passage outside the room. He was about to rise and close the door when they stopped.

"Except the one very early passage," Kipling inserted, and picked up a ledger, opening it to a page marked with a strand of yarn. "From the first year of the general's tenure. It seems her mother was gravely ill. Here it is." His finger stopped halfway down the page. He hesitated as he scanned the passage. "The adjutant was sometimes overly precise in his recording. And understand, at the time the general was furious with the provincials over their performance in the Indian war. What it says is 'the Iroquois woman who works in the kitchens is gravely ill, taken to bed with a breathing malady. The regimental surgeon offered to look at her, reported he had a new shipment of respiratory medicines that would help her. General Gage said no, let her fail. One less American stone in my shoe. Better to raise young Hannah in proper British fashion.'"

A gasp rose from behind them. Hannah stood in the doorway, clutching her belly as if she had been kicked.

Chapter 16

T HE NEW DAY WAS JUST a blush in the eastern sky when they pushed
off in the brig's launch with Glover at the helm and Cuff, Tobias, Solomon,
and Duncan on the oars. They had stepped in the little vessel's mast, and by the
time Fort George came into sight they had enough of a breeze to raise the sail. The
fields and orchards of Brooklyn came into view, then the small cove opposite Governor's Island with its collection of wharves and buildings, most of which appeared
to be fish-drying sheds.

"The long structure on the third pier, Noah told me," Cuff explained.

Duncan settled into the bow with his spyglass. The warehouse was ramshackle
but its roof was intact, and two heavy boats were moored alongside, one with scarlet and gold trim.

"The one with the brightwork belonged to the *Indigo Queen*," Glover reported.
"Forced away so quickly by the navy they had no time to recover her."

"Or Hastings simply commandeered it," Duncan suggested.

"Why two boats?" Solomon asked.

Duncan confessed he did not know the answer, then asked Glover to swing
about for another pass, closer to shore. He studied the second boat, a craft wide of
beam, probably used as a lighter for conveying cargoes in the harbor. "The second
one is big enough for a dozen barrels, two rows of six,"

Cuff spoke in a grim tone. "A fireboat then."

"A fireboat," Duncan agreed, "to be towed by the launch toward its target." He turned to study the harbor, then asked his companions to lower the sail and row out into the main current, brisk on the rising tide. They were halfway to Governor's Island, when he asked them to raise their oars. The current grabbed their boat and began pushing it deeper into the harbor with surprising speed.

"So they will tow the fireboat out into this current," Duncan said in a contemplative voice, "when the tide rises like this. They will do it at night with the barrels rigged with slow match, and when they get close enough they only have to release. But toward what?"

"The fort," Tobias suggested.

"No, it would just dash itself on the rocks below the battery," Duncan said. Then realization struck him like a fist.

Glover reached the same conclusion a heartbeat later.

"My God, Duncan," he gasped. "The horror."

There was a closer, and easier, target anchored in line with the fort, a target whose destruction would guarantee a furious response from the king. Hastings meant to burn the *Thunderer*.

The Invalids Fund auction on the parade grounds of Fort George was administered as a public entertainment to encourage civilian bids on surplus military equipment. Vendors crying their wares in Dutch, English, and German sold roasted apples and potatoes, small pastries, cider, and mulled wine. Children crunched on short strings of rock candy. Elderly Dutch matrons hobbled nosily about in wooden shoes, walking sticks in one hand and tobacco pipes in the other, watched with some amusement by the guards who stood at every doorway and tunnel entrance.

The festive air subsided as the Duchess of Fort George, on an elevated platform with her older children sitting behind her, introduced the sale of departed soldiers' belongings with a short but stirring preface about the nobility of any death arising in the course of service. Only members of the military were allowed to bid on the kits, the general's wife reminded the assembly, then struck the proper charitable note by speaking of the great hardships faced by invalid soldiers, often having sacrificed limbs or worse in the cause of their glorious country.

Duncan and Sarah worked their way forward as the first of thirty kits was presented, keeping Rebecca Prescott between them. The young widow had insisted on coming, and they agreed only on the condition that she keep her face hidden under a hood. Pine, too, joined but kept his distance, moving through the crowd with a wary eye.

The bidding progressed quickly, and the crowd thinned as kits were paid for and carried away by new owners. It was Mrs. Prescott who alerted Duncan to the danger. She gave a small moan, seized his arm tightly, and nodded toward the ranks of officers gathered for the bidding. His heart sank. Hastings had outfoxed them again, hiding in plain sight by donning not his ornate Horse Guards uniform but what looked like the tunic and plumed cap of a dragoon officer.

As the last group of kits, those of deceased officers of the Twenty-Ninth, arrived on the platform, Hastings pushed through to the front of the assembled officers. A triumphant gleam was painted on his face and a heavy purse hung from his waist. Hastings no longer needed to attempt murder to acquire the damning evidence against him; he could simply buy it with the king's silver.

"Kit twenty-seven," the Duchess announced, "the earthly goods of our departed Captain Nathan Mallory, much beloved of the Twenty-Ninth Regiment of Foot. Miscellaneous clothing both official and civilian, a worn but very serviceable Solingen saber, a German razor, a Bible, and a workbook of sketches of camp life by the captain. Do I hear one good British pound sterling?"

"One pound six," came Hastings's oily response.

A voice from the other side of the platform joined in. "One seven, if you please, ma'am."

The Duchess leaned forward. "Is that an offer from the enlisted ranks?" she asked in apparent surprise.

Corporal Rhys stepped out of the ranks. "Aye, not graduated to the lace yet, ma'am," he quipped, raising a ripple of laughter. "The lads and I were fond of the captain, ye see. We'd be honored to divide his things among us. As a remembrance, ye might say."

"A rare and eloquent sentiment," the aristocratic wife of the major general warmly declared.

Hastings's interruption was impatient. "Two pounds!"

"Two and two," came Rhys's quick reply.

Duncan felt Mrs. Prescott's grip tighten as the two bidders went back and forth, surpassing any of the bids placed for preceding kits. When the bidding hit three pounds, eight shillings, Duncan's gut twisted. They had thought themselves safe by providing four pounds to Rhys.

Hastings's angry voice cut the Duchess off again. "Four pounds sterling!" he called out.

The Duchess cast a worried glance at Rhys, who seemed at a loss.

"Four good British pounds!" Hastings called again when the Duchess did not acknowledge him.

Rhys dug into his pockets. Companions huddled around him, extending coins. "Four pounds seven and tuppence!" he shouted.

"Sold!" the Duchess declared without a glance toward Hastings.

"Six! By God, six pounds, I say!" Hastings barked. "Damn you, woman, I say six!"

His expletive against the general's wife stunned the crowd and brought instant anger. Officers near him spun about, shoving him out of their ranks. Someone shouted "Satisfaction!" and another declared he would gladly be the Duchess's champion. The eldest Gage son leapt up from his seat on the platform, raising a fist toward the major, and seemed about to leap onto Hastings until his mother laid a restraining hand on his shoulder. Men with walking sticks pummeled the furious Hastings until he stumbled out of their reach. He snapped at them, and reached toward the blade at his side, but then reconsidered. Casting a final furious glare at the Duchess, he retreated.

They spent the rest of the day making preparations for the sail up the Hudson and moving Glover's brig from the East River to a wharf on the western side of Manhattan. Hannah had unexpectedly shown up, looking more careworn than they had ever seen her. She passed the day with Sarah and Pine, even joining in the short transit to the far side of the island, where a dozen of Mulligan's militia friends loaded the gunpowder kegs allocated to the Hudson Valley settlements as well as a small two-pounder field gun destined for the Kingston militia. Sarah and Hannah, her despondent mood fading, efficiently supervised the onboarding of crates of copper teapots—much valued by the Iroquois, spermaceti candles, and barrels and casks of horseshoes, seed, sugar, and even horn for Sarah's button-making enterprise, followed by two millstones and three spinning wheels.

They were enjoying an evening meal at Mulligan's Keep when someone pounded on the door. A soldier stood on the step, casting nervous glances up and down the street.

"He said he had to come," the private blurted out, "but some company wouldn't go amiss. When he said it was for Captain Mallory there was no end of volunteers. He chose six of us and ordered us into a skirmish line." As the private spoke two more soldiers appeared out of the shadows, bracing a battered Corporal Rhys between them.

"You said six of you," Duncan said.

"One be limping back to the fort," the private reported, then gave a sharp whistle and two more soldiers appeared out of alleys on either side of the street. "They came out of the dark, eight of them, leapt on the corporal with clubs. But they didn't know the rest of us were stalking nearby. We gave worse than we got."

"Who were they? Was there an officer with them?"

"Ye mean that scrub who talked rough to the Duchess? No sign of him, except someone stayed in the shadows and was goading the attackers on. Ones we could see looked like waterfront rogues, the kind that can be bought for tuppence and an ale."

Rhys shrugged off the men who kept him upright. He swayed, then collected himself and stepped to Duncan. "Captain Mallory's lost packet, sir, as requested."

Duncan had asked that the letter be brought to him urgently if found in the kit. But he had not expected a melee. Hastings was desperate.

One of Rhys's eyes was swollen shut. Blood trickled out of his hairline. The corporal grinned through a split lip as he extracted a thin oilcloth packet from inside his tunic. Duncan stood aside and gestured the battered corporal through the door, thanking the men who escorted him. In the parlor, he lowered himself into a chair, extending the packet to Sarah as Duncan examined his wounds.

Rebecca Prescott hurried to Rhys's side with a cup of tea, which Rhys eagerly gulped down.

"Two letters," Sarah reported, laying the contents of the package on the table. "Both unfinished. One starts, 'Dearest Rebecca, you stay in my thoughts throughout—'" She abruptly stopped, flushed, and handed the letter to the young widow. "The other," Sarah continued, "goes on for a full page and onto the reverse but is not yet signed. On the outer fold it says, 'Major General Thomas Gage, Fort George, Manhattan Island.'"

She looked up with inquiry to Duncan, who nodded for her to proceed. "'Dear Thomas,' it begins." She continued reading:

It feels rather presumptive to be addressing such an esteemed personage by his Christian name, but I know you insist on it. So please know I offer it in the utmost respect and with my profound gratitude that someone of your sensibilities has assumed the burden of such a difficult command. I think of you and our brothers, as well as our harrowing last day with General Braddock, whenever I touch my watch fob. Thank you again for having them made for our small band of Monongahela brothers. I will treasure it all my life.

Sarah held the letter out for the others to see how Mallory had held the fob to the reverse of the paper and rubbed it with a writing lead so that an obverse of the intaglio image was depicted. The rubbing wasn't perfect, but they could see a tree, flanked by two blurred images. A word was spelled out below the tree, too ill-defined to read.

"*Mementos*," Rebecca Prescott explained. "It means *remember* in Latin. He was so proud of that fob, made special in London on the general's instructions. Only six in existence. An oak tree with a cross in front of it, flanked by a sword and a musket. The fob was his most prized possession."

Sarah continued reading:

I have been heavy of heart in deciding to write you of a miscreant among us, an officer who besmirches us all with his dark deeds. You are aware that I left the Horse Guards to serve in a fighting regiment, but I was in the Horse Guards Palace long enough to make the acquaintance of a vile soul who has risen to the rank of major by winning the favor of the most fractious, bloody-minded members of the War Council. He serves what they call the Black Office, a closely

*guarded secret. I have encountered this Major Hastings in Boston, dressed as
a civilian and sent here, I am convinced, to foment war. He takes his orders
only from the Black Office of the Council and earned a reputation against the
French for secret assassinations and similar unsoldierly deeds. I deeply suspect
that he has one or two associates here and with them is engaging in mischief
repugnant to the morals and integrity of His Majesty's army. I have witnessed
him passing coin, and cudgels, to my own off-duty grenadiers with the entreaty
to teach the protesters a hard lesson. There are rumors that he has practiced
his murderous art in London itself, using the Thames for ready disposal of his
victims.*

*I have confronted the man and suggested he remove himself from the colony.
He laughed and said there is no man in America with the power to remove him.
I said I knew of one. Hence I am writing this missive to give you a chance to respond before we see blood flowing in the streets of Boston, which I am convinced
is his goal.*

*You will no doubt have heard that the Twenty-Ninth has had a battle with
camp fever.*

Here, on the promise of more observations about the regiment's health, the
letter abruptly ended. It was not unusual for military men and mariners to compose correspondence in pieces, in the snippets of time between duties, and as Rebecca had explained earlier, Mallory clearly was intending to add more before he
took a dagger in the spine.

At the other end of the table Rebecca Prescott sat reading the other letter, tears
streaming down her cheeks.

"His name truly is Hercules?" Rhys asked as they walked to Fort George the next
morning. "I thought ye was gibing me. His mother must have had that Irish sense
of humor, eh?"

They had been rehearsing the tale Rhys would relate on his return. He had
been set upon while taking an off-duty stroll in the evening air and Good Samari-
tans took him to the home of Hercules Mulligan, where they heard a physician was
visiting. By happy coincidence the corporal was acquainted with Dr. McCallum,

who insisted that the injury to his head required overnight observation, and the kind doctor also insisted on accompanying him to explain why he had missed morning roll call.

Unknown to Rhys, Pine and Henri followed at a distance, watching for any new assault on the corporal. They had not anticipated encountering a mob. Angry men and boys, more reminiscent of Boston than Manhattan, blocked the gate to the fort. They taunted the sentries, rallying to cries of "Wilkes and Liberty," and threw stones and rotten vegetables. Their air, though, was not vindictive, their shouts not emphatic, and Duncan quickly realized they were just actors in another of Hastings's dramas.

Pine and Henri closed in. Half a dozen of the men in the mob turned, three of them tapping cudgels in their palms. Duncan pointed Rhys to a barrel standing at the side of the street. The corporal leapt onto it and gave a loud two-toned whistle. Once, twice, three times. A man in the colors of the Twenty-Ninth appeared inside the gateway and returned the whistle. "Company B Enlisted Parade!" Rhys shouted in his distinctive singsong voice. The soldier at the gate sprinted away.

Duncan told Rhys to stay on the barrel as he and his two companions put their backs to it, facing the mob. Duncan spied a cask lying in the nearest doorway, darted to it, and as he had seen protesters do in Boston, smashed down with his foot. The cask collapsed and he grabbed staves, tossing two to Pine and Henri, grabbing another for himself. He sensed hubbub inside the fort, men shouting and the rattling of harness. Then he was aware of nothing but the swinging of cudgels, vile curses, and arms reaching for Rhys. He parried one cudgel, thrust against another, then slammed down on an arm with such force he heard the cracking of bone.

Suddenly Rhys's melodious voice broke out into "The Girl I Left Behind Me." It was a popular song of military camps, often sung by the ad hoc choral groups formed in some units. The song was echoed now in multiple deeper voices. Most of the combatants hesitated, looking back toward the gate. An impromptu rescue party was emerging. Two of the tall mules used by army teamsters were mounted by soldiers who leveled long halberds like knights with lances, flanking a double column of two dozen soldiers, some in full uniform, most only in waistcoats, with a drummer in back who had found time to throw on his tall miter cap but not his yellow tunic. The soldiers sang the song with great spirit, emphasizing references to the women of France, Flanders, and Spain with swings of their makeshift clubs and musket butts at every member of the mob within reach. Hastings's hirelings had little stomach for opponents who could give as good as they got. After half a dozen suffered blows that knocked them to the ground, the rest fled. The soldiers, still in rough formation, halted before their corporal, finished their verse on a victorious note, then parted ranks.

"'Tis a fine morning for a stroll, Corporal," the lead soldier observed in an Irish brogue.

"Will miracles never cease?" Rhys quipped as Duncan helped him off the barrel. "The Irish saving the Welsh for a change!"

The fine morning lost its edge when the column reached the parade ground. Two members of the general's staff stood, arms akimbo, at the central flagpole, looking most displeased. The soldiers of the rescue party darted away as General Gage appeared, wiping away breakfast crumbs with a napkin. Pine and Henri followed suit, leaving Duncan standing beside Rhys and two riderless, confused mules.

"The ubiquitous Dr. McCallum," Gage said in a cool voice.

"Feels more like the army has become ubiquitous along my path," Duncan replied good-naturedly.

"My fault entirely, beg pardon, sir," Rhys nervously declared.

"You do not address the general without permission!" one of the staff officers snapped.

Gage frowned but held up a hand to restrain his aide. "You're to blame for this debacle, Corporal?"

"Aye, sir, entirely, sir. I was passing an idle hour on a stroll when some ruffians accosted me. The kind souls who rescued me said there was a renowned physician visiting just down the block and insisted he must treat my wounds. Imagine my surprise when the famed personage turned out to be our old friend Dr. McCallum!"

A young lieutenant ran up and snapped to attention, straight as a board. He looked terrified.

"Duty officer for the Twenty-Ninth?" Gage asked. "This battered corporal belongs to you?"

"Ye—esss, sir," the lieutenant stammered.

"Did the corporal miss his morning muster?" Gage asked, staring accusingly at Rhys, who stared straight ahead.

"Of course he did," came a feminine voice behind Gage. "I am to blame, Thomas. Really, no need for a fuss." The Duchess had a train of young children behind her. "All about the Invalids Fund auction. The noble corporal wanted to keep alive the memory of his dead captain, so he bought Captain Mallory's kit. Inside it he found a letter addressed to Mallory's fiancée, who I knew happened to be staying just down the street. I asked him to deliver it if he had a spare moment. I feel terribly guilty." She reached out and laid a hand on Rhys's arm, examining his injuries, then stepped in front of the corporal and faced her husband, making clear she would protect Rhys. "This man needs to be in the infirmary, Thomas, not under punishment."

"I do hope it wasn't that scrub who tried to outbid you," the Duchess said to Rhys. "So rude." She turned to address her husband. "I declare, if looks could kill you'd be a widower today! You know him, Thomas, that popinjay from London, pretending to be a dragoon officer."

Gage, surrendering to his wife, dismissed his aides and the lieutenant. "To the infirmary with you," he growled, then softened. "Captain Mallory was a good man."

"About that, sir, I—" Rhys was clearly getting tongue-tied.

"Oh, Thomas, see how the poor man shrinks before you!" The general's American wife put a comforting arm around Rhys and pulled him several feet away. They huddled together, then the Duchess turned with the oilskin packet in her hand and stepped to her husband, extending the packet. "How strange. This Captain Mallory was writing a letter to you, Thomas."

Duncan was not entirely sure why the general's wife joined him in seeing Rhys to the infirmary. She made pleasant small talk with the corporal, complimenting both his regiment and the singing she heard "from your unusual collection of comrades," as she put it. They settled Rhys in a cot, and the lavender-scented Duchess left instructions to set aside a portion from the general's lunch to be delivered to the corporal. Then she guided Duncan to an empty rampart.

"I have learned enough to know this man Hastings is a viper who must be excised from our midst," the general's wife abruptly declared. "But I fear, as Mr. Mulligan described to me, that he is one of those color-changing creatures who can disappear before our very eyes." She was, he realized, opening up to him about her patriot sympathies.

"Or appear before our very eyes," Duncan countered. "His arrogance is staggering." He pointed to a figure crossing the parade ground below.

Hastings briskly strode toward the headquarters offices, clad for once in his elegant Horse Guards uniform. The Duchess muttered a surprising syllable under her breath, hooked her arm through Duncan's, and hurried him down the stone steps.

She led him not into the general's office as he expected, but to the corridor that was used by orderlies and attendants, halting at a narrow door. "Servants come and go through here so as not to disturb the work of the office," she whispered. "This time of day the sun's rays through the general's wide window are so bright that this corner is buried in deep shadow. She stands here with the door cracked to listen for cues to serve refreshment. Hannah," she added.

For a moment Duncan wondered about the tightness in her voice when mentioning the house steward, but then the Duchess eased the door open a few inches. Hastings was before them, approaching the general's desk. Gage's two senior aides stood at either side, their faces clenched in outrage. Hastings had interrupted their meeting, walked in without invitation or permission into the inner sanctum of the supreme commander, and had apparently introduced himself without any acknowledgment from the general.

Major Trent, by the general's desk, began a sputtering protest. Gage raised a hand to silence him.

"I am here to right a wrong, sir," Hastings proclaimed. "At the Invalids Auction a grave mistake was made. Your spouse did not hear my higher bid for an item due to the unruly calls of the enlisted men. I most desperately wanted the kit of Captain Mallory, a grand old friend of mine from London."

"Mallory was from the Twenty-Ninth, I recall," Gage stiffly observed.

"Once a dear comrade in the Horse Guards."

"I fear I have no jurisdiction over my wife, sir. And today you are a Horse Guards officer?"

Hastings ignored the question. "I will give ten pounds to the corporal who purchased it and another ten to the Invalids Fund."

"That would be the corporal who was mysteriously accosted last night, then once again outside the gate this very morning."

Hastings hesitated. "I wouldn't know, sir. The Whigs do grow bold."

"Today's mob had an oddly staged tone about it," Gage airily observed, then gestured to Hastings's ornate uniform. "You confuse me, sir. I have yet to receive notice of any Horse Guards being deployed in my American theater. Which means you did not arrive on official transport." Gage nodded to his senior aide. "Major Trent has the tedious duty of reviewing various reports for what might be called loose ends. What was that anomaly you mentioned yesterday, Major? Oh yes, that slave hunter's ship departed here with fewer people than arrived on it, though there is no record of disembarking passengers. A couple of the crew who disrespected the marines were impressed, but that does not fully account for the discrepancy. Do you know the vessel, Major Hastings? It arrived from Massachusetts just after the unfortunate incident of March fifth. But of course a Horse Guards officer would never shame the king by consorting with slave hunters." Gage fixed Hastings with one of his cool, intense stares.

A tiny grin rose on Major Trent's usually stoic countenance. Duncan suspected he had just discovered who on Gage's staff managed his intelligencers. The Horse Guards officer's face flushed with anger, and he appeared to be readying a sharp reply, then reconsidered.

"Your wife, sir?" he asked instead. "Perhaps I could present the funds directly to her? Just let me—"

Gage held up a hand to cut him off, then gestured toward the corner. "The Duchess is quite fond of lavender, which often gives her away. My dear? No need to be shy."

Gage's formidable wife stepped into the brilliant sunlight.

"Odd," she said. "The officer who was bidding on Captain Mallory's kit wore the uniform of the dragoons. Prithee, sir, are you with the dragoons?"

"I am not."

She shrugged. "Then you were bidding under false pretenses, and we have nothing to discuss."

Gage was examining the opened letter on his desk. He did not look up as he said, "Doctor, no need to stand in the drafty hall. Come in and warm yourself."

As Duncan stepped into the pool of sunlight, Hastings's eyes flared and a snarl escaped his throat. "You!" His hand shot into his waistcoat, but then he thought better and withdrew it. "You let this man skulk about the king's North American headquarters?" he accused Gage.

"Dr. McCallum is here at my invitation," the Duchess explained. "He is known to venture into dark places in his steadfast search for contamination." She leveled an icy gaze at Hastings. "Contamination of all kinds. Today he is here to help with the injuries suffered in the attacks last night and this morning. Some of those who assaulted our poor corporal are now in our infirmary, under guard." Duncan glanced at the woman in surprise. They had just been in the infirmary. There were no such patients. "They will be questioned about why they were at our gate, and why at this most unusual hour. And perhaps who paid for their performance?"

Hastings glared at her. His hand inched back toward the blade that Duncan knew was inside his waistcoat.

"Dr. McCallum is also recently arrived from Boston, and also arriving just after the incident on March fifth," Gage put in. "He is the only physician I have ever met who is skilled with both the living and the dead."

Hastings seemed about to erupt. His hand inched closer to the weapon inside his waistcoat.

"Might I see the fob on your watch, Mr. Hastings?" Gage asked.

The fire on Hastings's countenance slackened. "Sir?"

"Your fob. A simple request."

"McCallum is not what he seems!" Hastings barked. "We must detain him, question him."

"Your fob."

"He is allied with the Sons of Liberty!" Hastings declared, stiffening as Major Trent extracted his watch and chain. "He was in London last year. Conspiring with that treacherous rebel Franklin," he added as Trent handed the watch, chain, and fob to the general.

Gage seemed not to hear. He gazed forlornly at the fob, the fob with the intaglio of a wilderness tree and a cross.

"Major Trent," he ordered in a brittle voice, "arrest this man."

Hastings relaxed and fixed Duncan with a victorious sneer. But then the major's hand closed around his own arm. "Unhand me, you ass!" he growled. He pulled away and stepped backward. A second aide closed in from the other side, and he suddenly understood. His dagger materialized in his hand, threatening the two aides as he backed toward the door. He froze at the sound of two muskets being cocked behind him. The sentries from the entry trained their Brown Besses at his back.

"Another wee step and I'll blow your backside through yer belly," came the gruff voice of one of the sentries.

He did not resist when the major removed the dagger from his hand.

"Take Mr. Hastings to a cell," Gage instructed. "I want double guards on him at all times. No visitors, no messages. No conversation of any kind. His words are poison. The *Thunderer* sails for England tomorrow afternoon. He is to be placed on board in the morning in the custody of her marines and confined to his cabin for the voyage. I will so instruct her captain. And Major," Gage continued, "hold the London mail packet boat. I will have reports to send to the War Council and a few other lords."

"Do you have any idea who I am?" Hastings snarled. He quieted for a moment, and Duncan saw the flicker of another sneer. "In the morning," he repeated.

Gage sighed. "If he keeps talking put a gag on him." He watched as Hastings was led out of the room, each of the burly sentries gripping one of his arms, then gazed down at the fob. "I was about to promote Mallory to major," the general declared in a hollow voice, "make him second in command of the regiment." He studied the fob for several silent breaths. "That battle on the Monongahela was where we met. Such a nightmare. Some say it was the beginning of all our current troubles, for it showed that the king's mighty army could be defeated by what were little more than gangs of light infantry. We carried him, the six of us, including Mallory and Mr. Washington of Virginia. When we laid General Braddock down, there was a moment when our arms were still extended, and we just looked at each other. Our hands were covered in his blood."

The general looked up at Duncan. "I don't want another war, McCallum." It wasn't so much a confession as a challenge. Gage knew, he had to know, that fate had not just coincidentally thrown Duncan into his path so frequently, had to recognize by now Duncan's patriot sentiments. What Gage was saying so subtly was that he hoped he did not have to become Duncan's enemy.

Duncan gave a slow bow of his head. "Neither do I, General. Neither do I."

But war seemed closer than ever when he returned to the Keep. No one but Duncan had seen the nascent sneer on Hastings's face, and no one understood why he repeated Gage's words *in the morning*. The reason was clear to Duncan even before Glover reported that the *Thunderer* had been taking on fresh water all day and recalled all her sailors on leave. Hastings may have been dealt with, but he had already set into motion his plan. He did not expect to be boarding the warship in the morning because his hirelings were set to destroy it that night.

Duncan passed restlessly around Mulligan's rear garden, then looked up at the gray sky. He too had had a visit from their dead friend in the night. He had not seen Crispus in his dream the night before, but his deep voice had been unmistakable, echoing from a dark cloud above. "Ye don't deserve liberty," Crispus had reminded him, "if y'er not ready to fight for it."

Duncan stepped inside, grabbed his cloak and hat, and hastened to the brig, where Glover assembled the company.

Duncan did not mince words. "They mean to burn the *Thunderer* tonight." He fixed each man with a solemn gaze. "I may not like what the king's men do but hate war even more. There's over five hundred men on that ship, most of whom will be asleep in their hammocks. Hastings is in custody but has already put the plan in motion. If the ship is lost, the patriots will be blamed and war will not be far behind."

Cuff broke the silence that followed. "Lobsterbacks killed Crispus."

"Lobsterbacks who were being paid by Hastings. Men who will sneak about in the shadows while thousands die. I mean to stop them."

Henri took a deep breath. "Maybe war is what we need," he said. Esther grabbed his arm, as if to restrain him.

"War may come, but we can't win if it comes too soon," Duncan said. "The patriots need arms, need more powder, more fighting men. If it comes, let it be at a time and place of our choosing, not theirs. Hastings and his patrons mean to have the king crush us. I mean to stop them. If it is just me in a dinghy, so be it."

Achilles, the smallest man on the deck, stepped forward. "You're saying we help the patriots by saving a few hundred English sailors."

"I am."

Achilles nodded. "Then I will take an oar," he bravely declared.

"A cruise in the moonlight," Solomon said with a grin as he stepped beside Achilles. "The kind of evening I enjoy."

Cuff muttered under his breath, then joined them. "For Crispus," he said.

Tobias followed. Henri gently removed his wife's hand and stepped forward. Boyle and the first mate, the only other men on deck, completed Duncan's crew.

"No dinghy then," Glover said. "My launch. And may the devil take any man who tries to kill five hundred as they lay sleeping."

"We'll need one of your lanterns," Duncan added.

"Surely we must run dark," Glover said.

"Not for us. For Noah and his friends."

"There it is!" Achilles, in the bow of the launch, called out. The signal from Brooklyn was unmistakable. The bright spermaceti lantern, held by Noah, blinked three times.

"Put yer back into it, lads!" Glover called from the helm.

They moved swiftly into the darkened harbor, following Achilles's whispered directions as he tracked the sail that had set out from the Brooklyn wharf. "Towing the lighter," Achilles confirmed as the half-moon emerged from a cloud. "Just as you said, Duncan."

And just as Duncan said, the two boats were making for the center of the tidal current. Once the fireboat had been set in the right position in this steadiest of tides, it would inexorably strike its target. Not for the first time Duncan shuddered at the thought of the ship ablaze, the men screaming, many trapped by the flames. Once the flames reached the magazines, the ship, and its men, would shower down in fragments over the city. It would be an act of war from which Gage, and the king, could not retreat.

The closer their approach to the towed boat, the more unlikely their success seemed. The wind was freshening from the northeast, pushing against their own vessel while lending more speed to the towboat. Even with Glover, the ablest mariner Duncan knew, at their helm, the odds of intercepting the fireboat seemed desperately low. His friends bent into the oars with superhuman effort, pushing against tide and wind.

"Go, Duncan," Cuff, on the bench beside him, growled. "Get ready."

As Duncan rose to stand in the bow, Achilles called out that the towline had been released. The fireboat was on its own, in the grip of the current, and they were close enough now for him to make out the glow at its stern that indicated its lit fuse.

They were a hundred feet away, then fifty, when a flat crack echoed over the water.

"Muskets!" Achilles cried as another discharge sent a ball zinging overhead.

"Dig deep!" Glover called to his oarsmen. "Now!" he yelled at Duncan.

Duncan leapt just as a wave sent their bow sharply upward. He was in midair when he realized he would not make it. He tucked in his legs, flailed out with his arms, and grabbed the gunwale of the fireboat. More muskets fired as he pulled himself inside, but the towboat was being pushed away by wind and current and soon would be out of range. Ignoring the shots, he leapt onto the first barrel as someone on the darkened *Thunderer* shouted. He had only seconds to reach the fuse. He leapt and fell, slipping in a puddle on the second barrel, then a leg slipped between it and the third. The shouting on the warship grew frantic, followed closely by the screech of a gunport being opened. A drum began beating. Officers frantically called orders.

As Duncan climbed free, he heard a bellow from Glover and realized that against all odds he had turned the launch and was making one more pass. A figure leapt across the open water as, with a great *whoosh*, a barrel burst into flame.

Impossibly, Cuff, a long boarding axe in his hands and balanced on the gunwale, was hacking at the bow. He roared as he chopped down, splintering the thin hull. A second barrel flared, water began pouring in at the bow, slowing the death boat. More lanterns lit a gun crew on the *Thunderer* as they rolled out their loaded cannon to the sound of desperate orders. The rear of the lighter was a wall of flame.

Duncan flung himself at Cuff. The axe flew in one direction, and Duncan, with an arm around Cuff, in the other. He did not bother to surface when they hit the water. He just dove, deeper and deeper as the world above them exploded.

No one spoke of the nightmare in the harbor as they finished preparations for the voyage north. Sarah and Esther had spent the night at the Keep, and Moll wisely chose not to ask questions when the exhausted crew of the launch boarded the brig. She just brought up a cask of revitalizing rum and a basket of her apple fritters and draped sodden clothing over the shrouds. They fell asleep on the deck and woke as the sun reached them, eager to leave the city behind.

It was midmorning when Duncan and Sarah returned with the last load. Josiah and his mother were playing on deck with a calico cat that had taken up residence in Moll's gallery. Solomon and Tobias skittered about the rigging like seasoned mariners, checking the reefing on sails and cleaning the tops of gull leavings with buckets of water hauled up from the deck.

Duncan and Sarah found Glover standing by the helm, studying the running rigging with his first mate. He reached into his waistcoat and produced a letter. "Delivered for Miss Ramsey by a crusty major."

Sarah read the message aloud. "Miss Ramsey, prithee, do not depart before meeting with Major General Gage. He must present your credentials. Signed Trent."

"Credentials?" Duncan asked.

Sarah shrugged. "A message for the tribes, I suppose. I had an errand at the fort in any event. I have my own credentials of a sort to present to him." She paused, contemplating Duncan for a moment, then extracted a piece of paper from the apron she wore and handed it to him. "Kipling helped last night. Quite authentic, just needs two signatures."

Duncan read it and looked up, speechless. "You can't!"

"I will."

———

When they arrived at Fort George, they were immediately ushered into the general's office. Gage sat at his desk with two packets of papers in front of him, one of them already closed with the waxed seal of his office.

"I would call for tea, but we seem to have misplaced Hannah this morning," the general said good-naturedly as he rose. "A hectic few hours here," he added offhandedly, then lifted the unsealed packet. "A duplicate for you, identical to what is under seal for the eyes of Sir William Johnson. I pray you will act together in presenting its contents to the Iroquois Council. I propose to raise a light company of militia among the tribes and settlers of your region. An expression of solidarity, you might say. I will amply supply it from Albany, and we have several former officers thereabouts who might be enticed to take part-time officer commissions. Prithee, Miss Ramsey, your influence as ambassador would make all the difference."

Sarah and Duncan exchanged a surprised glance. She was well aware that such a unit was driven by Gage's interests in keeping French agitators off the frontier. But it was also an important statement of trust in the tribes. Sarah and Duncan had discussed forming just such a unit at Edentown but had shied away after calculating its considerable cost. Now the general, apparently unacquainted with the likelihood that most of the settlers who would heed the call would be ardent patriots, would foot the bill.

"I am honored, General," Sarah replied as she accepted the packet, "and delighted we can find common cause."

Gage led them to the hearth, where for several minutes they exchanged pleasantries. He asked an aide if Hannah had appeared and whether she would be able to offer refreshment, but he was told that she still was apparently delayed. Gage rose and went to the window as if searching for her in the harbor, then returned to his desk. "The tide is on the rise. Good for a northbound sail."

Sarah stepped to the desk, thanking him again for the honor, then laid her own paper on his desk. "It just takes two signatures, General," she declared. "Yours and a magistrate's. Once both are affixed, please send it to me at Edentown."

Gage's smile faded as he read the document. Heat rose in his eyes. "You go too far! Impossible! How dare you—" His angry words died away as the door opened. Hannah stood in the doorway, wearing a very plain, practical dress and her hair in two long braids. At her foot was a bundle made of a shawl tied at the top, the baggage of a penurious traveler.

"No!" Gage shouted. "Not possible!" His sentries drew closer to Hannah.

"Perhaps you aren't familiar with such a document, sir," Sarah calmly explained. "It's a writ of manumission. For Hannah's freedom."

"Never! You can't simply steal her from me! Hannah, cease this charade at once!"

Sarah stayed quite calm, her voice low. "You refer to stealing your property? Or stealing your heart?"

Gage hesitated. "No one makes demands of the king's major general!"

"She will come with me," Sarah said with quiet insistence, "and decide on the life she wishes to lead. Let her go and she will be your best ambassador." As she lifted a quill from the desk and extended it to Gage, there was movement in the outer office. The general's wife appeared. The Duchess said nothing, did not approach, just sat in one of the chairs reserved for those awaiting the general, closely watching. Hannah lifted the bundle to her shoulder.

"Sergeant!" Gage shouted to one of the guards. "She is not to leave! Major!" The sergeant took a hesitant step forward. The major and the other aides retreated.

"Dear God, no," the general said in a much lower voice. "I cannot." His normally stony countenance flooded with emotion.

Tears were streaming down Hannah's cheeks.

"*Atonnhets*," Sarah whispered. "You call her your *atonnhets*. Which is it to be? Is she your slave? Or is she your soul?"

Gage's eyes filled with moisture. "Stand down, Sergeant," he murmured, his voice breaking, then took the quill. He signed and gazed in silence as Hannah smiled through her tears, turned, and walked away, Sarah and Duncan a step behind.

"She knew," Duncan said. He stood with Sarah at the stern rail of the brig, watching the steeples of Manhattan recede. "The Duchess knew about the general and Hannah and found a way to address her problem without the general ever knowing it."

"You mean sending the headquarters record books for us to review."

"Sending the ledgers, yes, but then sending Hannah while she knew we would be reading from them. I never did ask why. What reason did Hannah give for her visit?"

"The Duchess," Sarah confirmed. "She sent Hannah to ask me to see if you had any powdered rhubarb for one of her sons who had a bellyache."

"She could have just asked an orderly in the infirmary," Duncan pointed out. "And she asked for you, not me directly, because Hannah was more likely to linger and chat with you. Not to mention all the times she sent Hannah with you on errands. The Duchess knew you were close to the Mohawks, perhaps learned you had been raised by them. Who better to nurture Hannah's tribal blood? I suspect the Duchess is a formidable chess player."

"A friend to liberty," Sarah reminded him, then twisted about at the sound of new laughter. Pine was leading Hannah on a tour of the ship, explaining the workings of the brig. "He told her they were of different clans," Sarah recalled with a smile. They had both pretended not to know why when Hannah asked. In Iroquois culture only men and women of different clans could marry.

"I believe I have ordered you off the quarterdeck a dozen times, you knave!" Glover, at the helm, barked. Sarah and Duncan turned to see he was addressing the calico cat, who looked up at him and meowed. Sarah laughed and darted away to catch the intruder.

Duncan lingered at the rail, watching the skyline of Manhattan dip below the horizon. They had come so close to being destroyed in the city but also had strengthened ties that would be vital in the future. He had found it difficult to say goodbye to Mulligan, the affable haberdasher who possessed perfect instincts, and contacts, for clandestine work. Kipling had been unexpectedly emotional in saying farewell and promised to always load both his guns in the future. Achilles was pressed by Solomon and Tobias to join them in Edentown but ultimately declared that he would go find Bradford's widow to help her restart her life in Quincy, and would then join Boyle to making more of the "most powerful defective gunpowder in America."

Thomas Gage was a more complicated matter. Duncan had developed a grudging respect for the general. Gage represented so much that was repugnant to Duncan, yet he was a man of honor and had deftly eliminated the threat that Hastings presented to them all. Duncan had no doubt that the cunning Horse Guards officer would escape any meaningful censure in London, for he was protected by friends of the king, but at least he would pose no danger in the colonies for many months. It was slim justice for the horrors he committed but a reckoning all the same.

Hannah's arrival as a new member of their northbound party had excited the runaways, especially after she confessed that she, too, had been a slave. "No longer a half human," she said.

"And sailing to another world like the rest of us," Esther declared and embraced her.

They lived at the intersection of many worlds, Conawago would remind him, and Duncan's particular intersection with Gage's world had ended for now in freedom and honor. He doubted it would be so the next time his world overlapped with that of the supreme commander of British forces.

The deaths of Hicks, Briggs, and the poor private at Fort George still nagged him, for ultimately he could only connect the king's huntsmen to those deaths by surmise, not hard evidence. But that dark world was behind him. Duncan was en route to Edentown at last, where men and women could go about their lives as they saw fit, where they could walk in field and forest without being stalked by assassins. He felt another pang of regret for Crispus and the deaths of Mallory and Book. Their heavy burden also accompanied him north.

Laughter erupted from the waist of the brig. Conawago had found one of the small cannonballs used by the two-pounder gun in the hold, and he and the cat were chasing it as it spun wildly over the deck, changing directions with each slight roll of the ship.

Sarah and Hannah stood at the bow. Sarah pointed toward the northwest where Edentown and, beyond, the Mohawk villages lay. Josiah was motioning his mother to look at the large flag that flew from the top of the mainmast, carefully prepared in Mulligan's shop and depicting a pine tree with a deer on one side, an ox on the other, and a long Iroquois Council pipe underneath. "Miss Sarah says it is the flag of Edentown!" Josiah said to his mother. "It will be our flag! The flag of the free!"

Cuff shouted from the maintop, his Jamaican accent and the rising wind obscuring his words. Something about the bow, it seemed, as if he had spotted a hazard ahead. But then Glover twisted toward the stern and cursed just as the wind eased and the desperate cry became clear.

"Bonemen!" came Cuff's deep voice. "Bonemen coming!"

The *Indigo Queen* was behind them, in pursuit and closing fast.

Chapter 17

"BANISHED FROM NEW YORK BUT not New Jersey!" Glover spat. "She's been hiding in one of the Jersey coves waiting for us to head north."

"We've deprived her of her cargo for the Indies," Duncan observed as he studied the schooner. "She means to rectify that. Our friends who escaped from the islands are worth a small fortune to them. And they will take anyone else they can get their hands on."

"Others?"

"Hannah, Mrs. Prescott, anyone they can drag away. We emptied their cells in Marblehead, and again in Manhattan. They mean to fill their cells by taking the brig. Revenge and a fat profit." He could not bring himself to say that Sarah would be their greatest prize or that those on the brig were ill-equipped to fight.

"She's woefully shorthanded and our lads have been training hard," Glover observed. "And for now the wind favors us," he added with a meaningful gaze. They both knew that on the open sea the schooner could easily overtake the much heavier square-rigged brig, but the loss of many of the *Queen*'s sailing crew and the fair wind blowing upriver would for now offset much of her advantage.

"By Jehovah, they shall not put anyone on my ship in chains!" Glover vowed. "Give me more sail, Duncan," he added, then louder, "Fetch the Irishman!"

Duncan gave a whistle and Tobias, Solomon, and Josiah followed him up the ratlines. The schooner was fast, but she was sailing shorthanded in unfamiliar waters, and with more canvas the brig could make the gap hard to close. Glover had been cautious at the outset of their voyage, half reefing the main and maintop, but now they released the canvas and scampered higher to set the topgallant. By the time they repeated the effort on the foremast, Boyle, Cuff, and Moll were hauling the little field cannon to the stern rail.

"The Kingston militia won't mind if we warm the piece up for them," Boyle declared, patting the gun affectionately.

"It's only an infantry two-pounder," Duncan pointed out. "Her ball will bounce off most hulls."

"Oh aye, just a little belcher, as we used to say, good for making noise on Guy Fawkes night and not much else." A mischievous gleam rose in Boyle's eyes. "Which be why I won't aim her at the hull." He began showing Henri how to secure the cannon with lines to the stanchions. "Not too tight, mind, got to give her room to bounce."

"The sails," Duncan said, understanding now.

"Aye, we'll try some balls with the king's best powder when they get in range. And if they don't do the task, the ladies are fetching an alternative." He gestured toward Rebecca Prescott and Esther, climbing up out of the gangway. They carried a keg of nails between them.

The chase was agonizingly slow, the schooner creeping closer but still nearly a mile away after an hour. Duncan paced along the rail, reconstructing in his mind the winding course of the river ahead. Boyle readied the gun and instructed Josiah and Mrs. Prescott, his makeshift gun crew. Solomon and Tobias stayed in the top; Sarah and Hannah watched for shoals at the bow; and Cuff, Moll, and Conawago readied an assortment of weapons as varied as the inhabitants of the brig. They had unpacked a score of muskets destined for militia, found two sabers, a pike, a harpoon, two new pitchforks bound for the Edentown barns, and a meat cleaver. The muskets gave false promise, Duncan knew, for he doubted that more than four or five of those on board could readily use one. But if the slavers got close enough that they had to use the other weapons, he knew they would be lost. The bonemen would likely have pistols and swords and would not be shy about inflicting wounds to incapacitate their victims long enough to get them in chains.

"There's at least a score of men on that deck," Glover reported and handed Duncan his spyglass before taking the helm from Henri. "Not sailors to be sure, just brutes and bullies hired out of New Jersey taverns."

Duncan's chest tightened as he saw that, if anything, Glover had under-counted the men swarming the schooner's deck. Melville, no doubt enraged by his eviction from Manhattan, had known they would eventually sail up the Hudson and had recruited a small army.

Duncan studied the river ahead of them. "The tributary rivers are at their spring surge," he said to Glover.

"Meaning?"

"We are coming up on one in the next mile, off the western shore. The cross-currents are brutal this time of year. We're much heavier and can absorb more of the blow without skewing about. Steer closer to the western shore. They are dog-gedly following and won't know until they hit the current. It will slam into them. They will lose headway and may be spun about, meaning they will lose time, lose some of the advantage they've gained."

A quarter hour later he watched, with Sarah and Boyle's gun crew, as the *Indigo Queen* hit the runoff from the mountains. His companions cheered as the current seized her, skewing her nearly ninety degrees. Several of her men were knocked to the schooner's deck as the wind slammed into her canvas, shaking her. Several of her lines ripped loose.

"She will have lost half a mile or more by the time she recovers," Duncan reported to Glover. "And the weather's with us," he added, pointing to the dark clouds looming ahead.

Glover stared at the sky for a long moment. "This ain't the wide Atlantic. I can't just steer toward the fog and hide inside a storm. Perhaps ye've noticed the cliffs on either side of us?"

"In another mile we will hit the Tappan Zee," Duncan explained. "The river opens into a bay miles wide. That storm and its mist will hit us about the time we reach the bay, and then we will be lost to her sight. She'll have to follow the shoreline to find the course of the river again. It could buy us another hour or two. And the closer she follows the shore, the greater the chance that she hits the rocky shoals. The Hudson can be merciless, especially to lighter ships like the *Queen*."

"Hopefully," Glover responded, his worried eyes on the thickening clouds, "she's the only one who strikes. And first we'll trim some sail," he added, calling out to Solomon and Tobias, who were waiting in the maintop.

As they entered the Dutch-named Zee, the *Indigo Queen* had closed much of the gap between the two ships, but the storm was nearly on them. Glover veered to the east as if seeking the safety of a cove as they entered the cloud bank descending over the bay. He let Duncan take the helm, with Sarah at the bow watching for the northern channel. The rain was abrupt and intense, slashing at the ship and sending most belowdecks. Josiah laughed as he helped Boyle drape sailcloth over the little cannon, then laughed again when Boyle wrapped his arms around the gun to keep the sailcloth from blowing away. Solomon and Tobias huddled in the maintop, knowing they might be called on to urgently reef more canvas. The bonemen disappeared from sight, and long, soaking minutes later Duncan eased the brig northward.

The passage across the Zee was nerve rattling, and even more so was their entry back into the main channel, with Glover admonishing Duncan for taking too many risks with his brig, though still letting him keep the wheel. An hour later the sun was out, the breeze shifted in their favor, and they were cruising between the high mountains that marked the deepest span of the river. Boyle uncovered the gun and began drying its barrel and touchhole. Glover climbed the ratlines for inspection of the rigging, including the remains of a topgallant sail that had pulled loose and nearly blown away in the storm.

"If the wind stays favorable," Duncan reported, "we can make the cove at Cold Spring by dusk. Deep water where we can take a rest."

"We should keep running," Glover countered. "Our advantage is but temporary."

"I'm too fond of your brig for that. No one sails a ship of any size on the Hudson at night. We'll have a hot meal, Boyle can test the range of his gun, and we can repair the rigging."

Glover gave a reluctant nod. "Sentries," he said.

"Of course. We'll recharge the muskets after all the damp. And I recollect Mr. Boyle has a few kegs in the hold for the Cold Spring militia."

The fishing skiff working the cove as they reached it happened to be manned by three members of that very militia, who upon the news that they were getting some of the king's best powder gave them both a warm welcome and a basket of fish. An hour later, repairs done and muskets recharged, they carried their bowls of Moll's memorable fish stew onto the moonlit deck.

"'Tis a fine handsome land, this New York frontier," Boyle observed. He had taken two ranging shots with his two-pounder in the fading light and declared that "the little belcher has spunk!"

Duncan's instincts kept him on deck as most of the others retired to berths and hammocks below. Cuff, Henri, and Pine stayed with him, implicitly acknowledging the need for vigilance. Cuff retrieved the old harpoon discovered in the hold and lowered himself against the foremast, sharpening its hooked point. Pine leaned four muskets against the quarterdeck rail and another four at the bow rail. Henri fashioned a sling on another and carried it to the maintop. The former slaves all wore fierce, angry expressions. After dinner Cuff had gathered the runaways and proposed a vow, which they all solemnly agreed to. None would be taken by the bonemen so long as any of the others lived.

Duncan slept in brief, restless naps on a pallet Sarah brought from below, but he mostly lay awake, at first trying to convince himself of what he told the others, that the *Indigo Queen* was too light to have made it out of the squall unscathed. His thoughts kept returning to the ruffians he had seen lined up on the schooner's deck. She was a pirate ship at heart, and her pirates would want the brig herself as a prize. Glover would fight to the death to protect his ship, and Duncan would stand at his friend's side.

At midnight he climbed to the maintop and sat with Henri. Duncan had come to highly value the quiet steadfast tribesman whose inner strength, as much as Duncan's medicine, had brought him through his attack of malaria.

"My people would call this a hungry moon," the Ottawa said, pointing to the nearly full moon. "When the creatures awakening from winter sleep go out to slake their hunger."

"Those on the *Queen* may be hungry, but they have yet to discover how sharp our teeth are."

Henri gave a grunt of agreement. They sat in silence, watching the rippling silver of the Hudson.

"She has a knife, razor sharp, that she keeps hidden in her apron," Henri said after several minutes.

"Esther? I suppose she wouldn't hesitate to jab a slaver if she had to."

"She says he has had a good life these past weeks because of you and Miss

Sarah, like years pushed into a short span. Isn't it better if our boy just has that, she says. Our boy," Henri repeated in a choked voice.

"I'm not sure I follow," Duncan confessed.

"The blade. It's for if they break through. I told her that if they do, it will mean I am dead. She said yes, she knew, and the blade was for Josiah and her to join me. She won't let our son be in chains ever again."

It took a moment for the horrible meaning of Henri's words to sink in. "We won't let it come to that," Duncan whispered, his voice gone hoarse.

When he climbed down, Moll was sitting by Cuff. He caught an unexpected scent and smiled. The two had grown fond of each other. She had taken him a cup of her precious India tea.

He stood at the rail, looking toward the sleeping settlement. Earlier, he considered asking them to call out their militia to protect the brig but decided he did not want to bring more innocent souls into their troubles. Now he sensed that had been a mistake.

He did not notice that Glover had joined him until the Marbleheader spoke. "Tell me about your banner, the flag that Mulligan made for you."

"The flag of Edentown. Sarah designed it two or three years ago. A pine tree with a stag on one side, an ox on the other. And under it one of the long pipes smoked by the Iroquois at their council fires."

"You're not a man given to adornment or pride. It's a signal."

"More like a desperate cry for help at this point," Duncan replied, then explained that his instincts had warned him they would likely face danger if they managed to sail up the Hudson with the runaways, so he had dispatched Blue Turtle with messages for two friends in the north. "The superintendent of Indians, who keeps what he calls his guard, a small company of Iroquois warriors who stand ready for emergencies. And a friend, now married to a Mohawk woman, who commanded native rangers in the war and who still responds to my summons. The best fighters I've ever seen."

"So we are going to be rescued from these pirate slavers by coppery knights charging in on white horses," Glover said, skepticism heavy in his voice.

"More likely in birch canoes. And they wouldn't know anything about knights. But yes, I feared trouble and that was the idea."

"That's if your friend Blue Turtle made it over hundreds of miles of some very rough terrain and through towns where the locals may well arrest a strange Indian dashing down their streets. Assuming he didn't just do the rational thing and flee with your horse and coin."

"And then he would have to find my friends, who may be out hunting."

"And they would have to muster a rescue party. And find a way to race down the Hudson. Oh, and pick out our passing ship, which could easily be concealed by fog or night. Not to mention your banner now hangs limp and soaked, not visible from shore. Not much of a plan."

"Not much of a plan," Duncan agreed. He knew he was a fool for placing hope in faraway friends. "But it will mean at least one slave got away."

"Sail round the point!" Henri suddenly shouted from above.

They darted to the other side of the brig. A small boat, a fishing skiff, had rounded the bend in the river, its sail gleaming in the moonlight.

"Some go out at night when the spring moon shines and drag nets for eels," Duncan explained, then called to the maintop. "Just fishing!" He yawned. "Two hours to dawn," he said. "Long day ahead." With luck they would make it to Newburgh, where a grateful, and larger, militia would be ready to help. He felt at last he could sleep and succumbed an instant after his head touched the pallet.

He woke in a gray light that was barely hinting of sunrise. Moll was humming as she heaved a bucket over the side for galley water. They had agreed she would make porridge for breakfast to be served out at duty stations, but he also smelled baking scones, which meant she, too, had had little sleep. The river seemed quiet. The village still slept.

Duncan helped haul up the heavy bucket. "Sir?" she asked, suddenly halting. He followed her gaze to a ghostly shape tucked against the hull. An empty skiff was tied to the anchor line.

An instant later a musket cracked from above. Splinters erupted from the rail near the mainmast. An arm was reaching out of the shadows with a heavy blade, hacking at the thick backstay. Henri appeared, swinging down on a line toward the intruder, who now stood, raising a pistol at him. As Henri landed on the deck an animal-like cry rose from behind him. Cuff charged past Henri, leveling his harpoon. Moll joined in, swinging the now empty bucket on its rope as she advanced on the man.

Duncan grabbed his knife. "Boarders!" he shouted.

Near the bow, Pine grappled with a second man. As Solomon appeared, joining in that fight, Duncan turned to the man with the pistol and paused. It was Yates. The Marblehead turncoat had joined the bonemen. Yates cocked his gun and aimed it at Cuff, who halted two steps away. "You!" Yates spat with an amused snort, as he recognized the man who had once threatened to torture him, then straightened the pistol toward Cuff's heart. Suddenly Moll was on Yates from the side, knocking him to the deck, shouting, "*Mac an diabhuil!*" as she pounded his chest. Cuff was reaching to lift her off when the pistol fired.

Moll rose to her knees, then slumped backward as blood mushroomed over her breast. Cuff roared, lunged, and skewered Yates with the harpoon. Esther, at the gangway, screamed. Cuff lifted the flailing man into the air like a fish on a spear, then threw him, the harpoon still in his belly, over the side. He dropped to his knees and lifted Moll like a child into his arms. "No, no, no!" he sobbed.

The second intruder was thrown to the deck in front of Duncan and Glover. "Trying to slice the anchor cable," Pine reported. "Knife too dull."

"Already cut two braces and some clews," Glover spat and kicked the man. Maiming a Marbleheader's boat was not much different than maiming his child.

"They're trying to delay us," Duncan concluded. "We can't let them do so."

Glover's anger burned away as he grasped Duncan's words. He scanned the rigging. "No real damage, none we can't fix while underway. Tie the rogue to the mast and let's get to work," he announced, then paused and pointed to Moll. "Patch her up, Doctor."

But Duncan quickly saw that patching was unlikely. The ball had ripped through Moll's ribs and was lodged in her lungs. Cuff stood with her cradled in his thick arms. She opened her eyes. "My scones," she murmured through a bloody froth and made as if to climb down. "Can't let my scones burn."

Hannah and Rebecca Prescott took over breakfast preparation as Cuff carried Moll to Duncan's berth. Duncan administered a powerful dose of laudanum, cleaned the ugly wound as best he could, then rose, worried now about the stricken Cuff.

"The ball was meant for me," the big African said as he gazed at the near-comatose woman. His voice trembled. "Why she do that for someone like me?" He looked up, moisture in his eyes, as Duncan took a tentative step to the door. "I'll be here," Cuff murmured and gripped Moll's limp hand.

Duncan paused as he began to climb toward the main deck and looked back at the compartment. *Mac an diabhuil*, the woman who knew no Gaelic had cried. *Son of the devil.*

Once they eased out of the Cold Spring cove, Duncan cut their prisoner from the mast. "Sit," he instructed. The man replied with a defiant gaze, then Pine, Boyle, and Henri, each holding a weapon, joined Duncan. He sat against the mast. Duncan handed him a ladle of water. "Talk," Duncan demanded.

The man swallowed hard. "I was just dragging a net for spring eels out in the Zee when I happened upon this grand schooner run up on a shoal," he started. "'Two shillings for loan of your boat to help pull us off,' their master calls out. They had a dinghy already out with a tow, and another skiff they were offloading stores onto to lighten her, but it weren't getting the job done. I took a line, and four men with extra oars came on board. We got her off when the tide reached her, but she had to limp to shore for repairs and to reload her stores. I took my coin and was about to set off when the skipper says how about another guinea. I didn't like the look of 'im but I ain't seen a guinea in years, so I asked what did he have in mind. 'Easy work for a nimble boy like you,' the master says, 'and I'll give you my best man to help.' Soon Mr. Yates and me was off on the amusing errand, as the master put it."

"The errand?" Duncan asked.

"He said a brig upriver had stolen valuable property of his but his vessel had now lost half a day in her pursuit. So just run up and disable the brig for us, so we can catch up and do our justice. Yates will recognize her, he said. Cut a few lines and off ye go. Easy as pie, he said." The man drained his cup and looked about. "Where's Yates?"

They made their prisoner help repair the broken lines and join in pulling taut the extra reinforcing stay that Glover insisted be added to the mainmast. An hour later they left him on a rocky islet in the middle of the river, keeping his skiff on a towline as compensation for their trouble.

The sun was still high when they reached the long wharf at Newburgh. Half a dozen kegs of powder had been allocated to the militia, and the news brought a dozen grateful men to help with the offloading. "I'll be dogged," said the oldest of the men, a grizzled Dutchman missing two front teeth. "There truly be such a thing."

Duncan followed his gaze toward the top of the mast.

"A pine tree flag, just like he said. Told 'im I never seen one, but now here ye be."

The man instantly had Duncan's attention. "Who? Where is he?"

"Why, a coppery gentleman, gone a day or more. He seemed crestfallen to hear we had seen no such boat. But then I said with the weather turning fair we'll be seeing many more from Manhattan these next days. He chewed on those words, then traded his horse for an old dugout. Took it on the water for a test, and glory be, he could fly in that thing. Told 'im if I was a hare I nay be challenging you to a race."

"I don't follow," Duncan said.

"'Cause of his odd name, ye see. Turtle. Turtle and some color, I recollect. Mayhaps green?"

They left Newburgh with renewed hope and new confidence in their navigation, for the local militiamen had readily accepted the offer of the confiscated skiff in exchange for a seasoned river pilot to guide the brig to Kingston. They departed with three hours of light left and no sign of their pursuers.

"The dose helps considerably," Moll said, wheezing between words, as Duncan checked on her. The red frothing at her mouth had subsided, which only meant the blood in her ruined lung was clotting. She'd had a steady stream of visitors. Josiah was lingering when Duncan arrived.

"Prithee, lad," she said to the boy. "I need something to squeeze when my pain spikes. Might ye fetch one of those wee cannonballs from the hold? I find the smooth cool iron soothing."

As the boy darted away, Cuff appeared with a pewter mug. "Folks at the town gave us a jug of fresh milk."

Moll forced a smile. Despite the tincture of opium Duncan had administered, she was in pain and probably could not swallow much, if at all.

"Such a sweet gesture," she replied in a hoarse voice. "I've nay the thirst this

358 | Eliot Pattison

moment, but save it for by-and-by." She gestured Cuff closer. "What I would dearly love would be some help in getting topside. If I can but get a little sunshine and fresh air, you and I will soon be dancing around the mainmast."

Duncan returned to the quarterdeck and watched a procession rise from the gangway. Cuff carried Moll. Behind them came Rebecca Prescott with a thick pallet. Sarah brought a pillow. Hannah and Solomon supplied a blanket and a straw hat. They made small talk and forced lightness into their voices, though all could see Moll was failing. As they gradually left her side, he saw their moribund expressions. Moll was loved and valued by the entire company and had become something of an anchor for the frail hopes of the runaways. Sarah had even suggested she might run their household when they reached Edentown. She had been indestructible, until the bonemen arrived.

The breeze faded with the sun, and they anchored near a cliff topped by a decrepit windmill. Duncan and Glover climbed the shrouds for an inspection of the rigging while Rebecca and Esther prepared a light dinner of ham and bread, followed, at Moll's insistence, by sweet shortbreads the cook had set by for a special occasion. She insisted that she wanted to sleep on the open deck, if Sarah would just loan her another blanket. Declining all food, she declared she was saving her appetite for the next day, when she vowed she would be back in the galley, making apple fritters, a favorite of Cuff's and Josiah's. Duncan knew, however, that she ingested nothing because she was unable to. He longed to be able to help but knew her wound was beyond mortal aid.

It was close to midnight when he sat on the low stool beside Moll's pallet. He leaned and pinned something to the wide band of her apron, which she had refused to remove. She stirred at his motion.

"Ah, 'tis you, sir," she whispered, and looked down at her apron. "Kind of you." He had fastened a white cockade on her.

"*Slainte mhor*," Duncan said.

She repeated the Gaelic toast to the Jacobite king with a sad smile. "If only we had some good whisky, eh?"

He produced a flask and helped her take a tiny sip as they repeated the toast.

Her Gaelic was perfect. "You must have thought me quite the fool that night in the kitchen when I taught you the toast to the king across the water," he said. "You well knew it already. That was the reason you were there with a bowl of water. Did you do it often?"

"Oh aye, every night before slumber. Prithee, Duncan, might ye speak more of the Chisholms as ye did that night?"

From somewhere close on shore an owl, harbinger of death, hooted.

Duncan took another sip from his flask and launched into stories of Chisholms and McCallums on cattle drives and, in more distant generations, cattle raids. He told of the Chisholm herder who climbed a mountain in a late spring snowstorm in search of a beloved cow and came back stark naked, for he had draped his kilt over the shivering cow and wrapped his linen shirt around her newborn calf. There were tales of dance competitions at clan gatherings and grandmothers who always placed offerings by the houses of newborns so the fairies would not steal the babies. He recalled, too, a Chisholm woman who was a famed swimmer, who everyone knew was a selkie, one of the seals who took human form.

"I recall the brawny Angus Chisholm on a drive when I was a boy," he continued. "He loved to ride his bull, and one of my uncles had his own riding cow. He challenged my uncle to race to a tall tree on the far side of the lake we camped at, winner to take a jar of whisky. He let my uncle speed off on the lake trail and leisurely sipped the last from his flask, then with a great shout of joy charged directly into the lake. Angus and his bull swam across and were waiting when my uncle finally arrived. They laughed all the way back and emptied the jar together."

Though it clearly caused her pain, Moll could not hold back her own laughter.

They went quiet. Duncan silently felt her pulse, which was barely detectable. The owl hooted again.

"How old were you, Moll, when the Butcher's troops came?"

He glimpsed gratitude in the sad smile she offered. It was long minutes before she replied. "Sixteen. Set to be wed in a fortnight."

"I suspected it had to be a seasoned cook who made those special meat pies in Marblehead. But Lieutenant Hicks, such a mystery. Most of those who saw him in the belfry assumed it had to be a mariner, for it took prodigious knowledge of ropes and tackle to string him up so."

Moll's words came between labored gasps. "Been a cook on several ships in my day."

Duncan nodded. "The stitches on his face seemed the work of a sailmaker."

She gazed at the moon for long minutes before she spoke. "We had just come back from the kirk, still in our Sunday clothes. My grandfather, ever a kind Christian spirit, greeted the soldiers warmly and quipped that he could give directions back to the high road since they must have gotten turned all arsy-versy to reach such a remote croft as ours. The officer already had his sword drawn. He just slammed it down, sliced right into my grandfather's skull. 'Wearing a kilt is against the king's law,' he declared as my grandfather dropped dead. We were so shocked we just stared as the soldiers surrounded us. There were six of us left: my parents; my betrothed, Jamie, who had come to church with me; my brother of ten years; my sister; and me. The officer walked about the croft, studying everything. He found a barrel of soupy cow dung my mother saved for the vegetable patch. My brother refused to stop yelling at him, so the officer beat the dear boy to silence, breaking his jaw, then dumped him headfirst into the wet filth, put the lid on, and ordered a soldier to sit on it. They took my father into our byre, tied him to a post, herded in the livestock, and set it ablaze. We had two oak trees, side by side. When Jamie started cursing them as the sons of Lucifer, they took him behind our house so we couldn't see, only heard his screams. They found two planks, spread his feet on one and nailed them, then stretched his arms on the other and nailed them. They hauled him up between the trees like he was nailed to a cross. He kept trying to speak but no words came out. That's when I saw they had sewn his mouth shut and stitched his eyelids up so he had to watch as they stripped my mother and my sister and me. When my mother screamed curses, they held her down and emptied a demijohn of lye down her throat. Then they had their way with my sister and me as Jamie watched.

"They just kept taking us, nearly every man there. Half a day as my ma and Jamie slowly died. After the first hour nothing mattered anymore. I didn't remember much of anything except the brass buttons, since most kept their tunics on. Twenty-nine. All the buttons had the numeral twenty-nine on them. For years the only thing I could remember about that day was the number twenty-nine."

The burning death in the Halifax stable. The crucifixion at Marblehead. The poisoning at Castle William. The suffocation in filth at Fort George. Moll had echoed the killings back onto the Twenty-Ninth a quarter century later.

"They left me and my sister for dead, but we kept breathing. She was broken, never really gained her wits back, and wound up on the streets of Glasgow. Died of the pox."

"Did you seek out the Twenty-Ninth, or was it just happenstance?"

"I was in Halifax working as a cook when they shipped in. When I saw those brass buttons again, I decided it was fate, that the Lord had given me a chance at justice. So I followed them to Massachusetts."

"After burning an officer in his stable."

"After burning an officer in his stable," Moll agreed. "Like you said of the Chisholms, *feros feria*. He screamed. My father didn't scream." She shifted on the pallet. "I just need a moment's help. My apron's a wee bit heavy."

"How did you manage Hicks?"

"I had seen his coarse ways, like those who came to our croft that day. I watched. I followed. He often went by the belfry in the evening, on the way to his barracks. When he approached that day, I made as if to unbutton my blouse and gestured him into the belfry. It was dark. He didn't see the bar I hit him with. Then I went to work. I had been inside before, laid out the ropes and tackle, even the thread and needle. When I was done I sat on the stool and told him what the Twenty-Ninth had done to my family."

"And you had made other dishes for the young Marblehead maiden enamored of an infantryman."

"Oh aye, it was our little conspiracy. I warned her not to be sampling those meat pies for they be too spicy for her."

"And the private at Fort George?"

"Nobody cares about old Moll. I come and go. And watch. He was drunk and no one else was about. They had opened the pits for draining." She shifted again. "Just a little help, sir? My legs don't seem to be working."

"How many cannonballs did you collect?"

"Six." She paused to wipe her mouth. The red frothing had started again. "All I could fit in my apron pockets."

Duncan did not move. He was a doctor, pledged to preserve life.

"I died on that day in forty-six. I've just been in purgatory ever since. But now I've settled accounts, ye see. Now I can join my Jamie, who's been waiting all these years. Just a wee boost, sir."

Duncan knew that even if he chose not to grant her request, she would not last the night.

She gave a long low moan as he lifted her. She had no strength left, barely any breath. As he set her on the rail, she looked up with pleading in her eyes. "Prithee, sir, all that about the Twenty-Ninth, might that be our little secret?"

Duncan slowly nodded. There was no point to sharing his knowledge. "You saved Cuff's life by sacrificing your own. That's the truth, and that's enough."

Moll forced a smile as she cupped his hand in hers. Her touch was cold. "*Ta-padh leat*," she murmured. *Thank you.* She released his hand and shifted her legs over the rail. She straightened her apron, raised her hands toward the moon, and dropped into the deep, dark river.

The owl called one last time.

Chapter 18

DUNCAN LEFT THE EMPTY PALLET for others to discover. Henri, on watch in the maintop, likely saw it all but would know only that Duncan had helped ease a dying woman's suffering.

"We were talking below," Esther said as she stared mournfully at the blood-stained pallet. "She knew. She planned it."

"She knew her wound was fatal," Duncan observed. "Nothing but suffering ahead. She was a woman who lived by her own terms."

"She gave me everything," Cuff said as he stared into the water, his voice twisting with emotion.

"What she gave you," Sarah suggested, "was a new life."

"We should say words," Esther said.

Rebecca Prescott extracted a small silk handkerchief and wiped at her tears, then solemnly dropped it over the side. Conawago withdrew his spare pipe, the one Moll often borrowed, stuffed it with his special tobacco, and dropped it into the river. He fixed Duncan with an inquiring gaze. He knew Duncan, and Moll, too well to assume such a simple explanation for the suicide.

Boyle stepped to the rail beside Cuff, who was scrubbing at his eyes. "Molly darling, may the angels embrace you and welcome you into their ranks." He put a hand on Cuff's shoulder.

"We must catch what little breeze there is," Duncan said. "Moll would not want us overtaken because of her."

Their pace was agonizingly slow. "If the river gives you two good days," their pilot said, "she'll take away another." They added canvas, and added more again, but by late morning they had made no more than three or four miles, with Kingston still far ahead. Glover and Duncan exchanged anxious looks, for they knew the schooner would outpace them in the light breeze.

Boyle, too, seemed to sense the increased danger and stayed close by his gun, calling for more powder and shot to be brought from below. Pine and Hannah, who seemed to be spending most of their time together, freshened the priming in the muskets. Duncan heard the Mohawk woman ask Pine to help her learn the drill of loading and firing one of the weapons, and soon Pine was leading Hannah, Rebecca Prescott, and Esther in musket exercises. The first live round sent Esther careening backward, nearly across the entire waist, but she gamely returned to the ranks and reloaded.

Duncan anxiously paced the deck, watching for shoals and the opportunity to add more sail. Sarah found him standing alone at the bow. She took his hand and remained silent, watching a flight of geese until it vanished over the mountains.

"Glover is the captain of this ship, is he not?" she asked.

"Of course," Duncan absently replied as he stared intensely northward, as if he might make Kingston appear by sheer willpower.

"And he has certain powers," Sarah continued, squeezing his hand.

The words took a moment to sink in. He gently lifted her chin and gazed into her hazel eyes, then embraced her.

"Aye," he said, "he could marry us, *mo chride*." His heart ached as he realized her suggestion was driven by despair. "But it would feel too much like surrender. We have not lost yet."

"They greatly outnumber us," she pointed out.

"Undoubtedly."

"They have better weapons."

"Most likely."

"It breaks my heart to think I have taken our Barbados friends all this way only to have them lose everything. I have given them only a violent end, or new chains."

"Beg pardon, Miss Sarah, but that is what Mr. Boyle would call bloody nonsense."

They turned to see Esther standing nearby, holding a basket. "Excuse, but you two have eaten little more than a few spoonfuls of porridge all day." She extended the basket, which held a small loaf and several apples. "Wasn't meaning to eavesdrop, but here I stand. And it doesn't matter what happens in the next hours. You gave us the joy. The joy of making our own decisions about our lives, the joy of walking freely with our heads up, the joy of being able to embrace those we love whenever we want. And the biggest joy of all, hope."

The words wiped away the strain on Sarah's face. Duncan could see that she was trying to reply but could find no words. Esther pressed an apple into Sarah's hand, handed the basket to Duncan, and hurried back to her son and husband.

"I wager your scout gave up," Glover concluded. He had been chewing on Duncan's news about Blue Turtle. "Headed back north."

"Why would he take to the river in a dugout then?" Duncan asked, trying to understand Blue Turtle's actions but steadily losing hope of reinforcements.

"Tired of his horse, wanted to do some fishing? Who knows?"

"Or the others were waiting at Kingston, and he went to fetch them the fastest way possible. Because he knew if he had not spotted us yet they were certain to find us soon on this stretch of river."

"And the moon will drop out of the sky tonight and crush the schooner," Glover sighed and gripped the pistol in his belt. "It's on our shoulders, Duncan. No one is going to rescue us. So mind yer powder, sharpen yer blade, and find a way to move us faster."

It was late afternoon when Solomon called out the dreaded warning. "Mast over the ridge!"

They had rounded a long tongue of land, and in his spyglass Duncan now made out a thin, tall mast reaching above the land and moving in their direction. He quickly conferred with Glover and Boyle. With the current pushing one way and the wind another, they had a chance of holding their position long enough for Boyle's gun to offer up a surprise as the *Queen* cleared the bend in the river. With luck they might disable her again, giving them time to reach the safety of Kingston. Boyle readied his gun as Glover shouted desperate orders to those in the rigging. They would have to shorten sail, then quickly add more canvas as she turned if they were to avoid the rocky shore. Their pilot muttered in despair, glanced longingly at the skiff, then joined Duncan on the ratlines to help. Boyle elevated his gun, and the brig's distaff marines readied their muskets. Their target would be over three hundred yards away when she first appeared, beyond any accurate firing range, but their fire would surprise, and discourage, the raiders. Pine, meanwhile, had found a good Pennsylvania rifle among the militia supplies. In his hands it had a chance of doing damage.

The schooner rounded the point. The first volley fired. Musket balls ripped up the water short of the vessel, but Boyle's belcher gun left a hole in a sail that instantly widened as the wind caught the edges. Pine waited until the schooner came around, then fired down the length of the ship.

"Hit a man in the shoulder!" Conawago, holding a spyglass, exclaimed. "The others are milling about in disarray! Fire at will, fire at will!" he called out to no one in particular. Boyle's gun answered the call. "And now a piece of their elegant railing has gone missing!" the Nipmuc reported. The muskets fired once again, missing but causing Conawago to cry out, "This apple has thorns, you brigands!"

"The rigging!" Duncan called down. "Fire at the rigging!" So far they had not done enough damage to meaningfully slow the schooner.

He watched as Boyle loaded a double charge and then nails. The belcher leapt up. Its shot perforated more canvas.

He recalled that Boyle had brought some signal charges along. "Guy Fawkes!" he shouted to the Irishman.

Boyle's confusion was only momentary. He would have time for one more shot before the brig had to turn upstream. The *Indigo Queen* was not much more than a cable's length away when he fired. The signal shot hit the already damaged sail and seemed to cling to it without effect, but its many charges had their own short fuses. They burst into their fiery red and yellow display, igniting sail and rigging.

Melville's furious voice echoed over the water as the schooner lost all headway. Men scrambled to cut away the burning rigging as others desperately doused or stomped on the burning fragments that fell on the deck. The thin, gaudy figure of Hugo appeared on the bowsprit, a heavy pistol in his hand. Pine quickly aimed and shot first. The Cajian's red hat flew off and he retreated. Glover brought the brig about and they headed upriver.

The joy they felt from their victory lasted for less than an hour. They had made slow progress and were only three miles from Kingston, their pilot reported, when the wind shifted abruptly, favoring their pursuer. They were on the eastern side of another wide, bay-like stretch of the river with the sun touching the horizon when the *Queen* reappeared. Her damage had been repaired, and with a new jury-rigged sail she was approaching fast.

Boyle groused.

"The skiff!" the pilot called. "We can reach the shore before they are on us!"

"And let them take my ship?" Glover growled. "A Marblehead man never yields his ship. Flee, those who must, but I stay with my brig."

No one fled. The two-pounder was loaded and turned, the muskets readied. The pilot lifted a musket and checked its load.

"On the far shore," Sarah said, pointing to the western bank, deep in shadow, "I thought I saw movement. Small boats maybe, or canoes."

"The light at sunset will play tricks," the pilot said, and tested the heft of his gun.

"They have grappling hooks," Duncan said as he studied the schooner. "They intend to board, and when they do it will be bloody work."

Boyle fired a charge of nails. The muskets fired, all to no avail. The schooner's boarding party was lying prone on her deck.

The wind died to a light uneven breeze and they lost all headway, with no option to maneuver as the schooner closed the gap.

"It's come to this then," Glover declared. He kept one hand on the helm, and raised an axe in the other. "Take my ship over my dead bones!" he roared.

Duncan picked up a musket. *It's come to this.* They had come so far, each in their own particular quest for freedom, only to end on this lonely stretch of the Hudson. They all had the spirit to fight but not enough strength. He cast a regretful eye over his companions. Sarah stood at his right side with two pistols, Conawago at his left with a makeshift spear consisting of a knife tied to a staff. Henri and Esther stood with muskets in front of Josiah, who held a hatchet. Boyle fired the belcher one last time, then stood in the smoke with a huge club, Solomon,

Rebecca, and Tobias at his side. Pine stood beside Hannah, holding the rifle ready for one last shot. Cuff stood apart, two knives in his belt and, in homage to Moll, swinging a heavy bucket. The runaways had chosen death over chains. Daylight was fading, and so was their hope.

They pushed away the first grappling hook, and the second, but then three more flew through the gap between the ships and found purchase. The muskets fired, punching holes in the line of boarders, causing them to hesitate. In the momentary silence an eerie, ululating cry echoed over the water, followed by several more in quick repetition.

"It's—" Sarah began as she twisted to look across the darkened river.

"Just some loons," Duncan said, leveling his musket. He glanced in confusion at Pine, who suddenly thrust his rifle into Hannah's hands, ran to the pile of munitions to grab a naval rocket and slow match, then sprang into the shrouds. As he climbed, he let out the cry of a loon.

Glover stepped before his friends, his eyes wild as he swung his axe, then he hesitated as sparks flared overhead. Pine fired the signal rocket into debris piled in the *Queen's* bow. Melville could be heard over the shouts of his men cursing and yelling for them to run and put out the flames that erupted.

Sarah seized Duncan's arm. Ghostly shapes were climbing over the schooner's stern, then more over their own vessel's stern. Duncan's heart leapt as the figures stole across the deck, silent as smoke, and darted up the shrouds.

The fire out, Melville rallied his men, angrily shoving several toward the rail. They hesitated as Duncan stepped to the rail of the brig and held his musket across his body, not aiming. "You don't have to die," he called out. "But you will if you advance. And if you survive you will be arrested and sent to General Gage, who will hang you as pirates."

"Unless we do so first," came a confident, dangerous voice. A figure stepped out of the shadows, put a hand on the shrouds, and stepped up onto the brig's rail. Duncan's friend Patrick Woolford had donned his old uniform, that of a captain in the king's rangers. He gestured with his sword at the dozen warriors aiming bows and muskets from the stern of the *Queen*, then to the dozen more who had climbed into the rigging and tops, aiming their weapons downward.

Hugo snarled at Woolford and leapt up onto the *Queen's* rail, raising his pistol.

"You can't—" he began, then plummeted backward from the impact of the arrow that embedded in his shoulder.

Hannah, taking refuge at Sarah's side, asked a fearful "Who?"

As the first of the would-be boarders dropped his weapon, Sarah laughed. "Our people, Hannah. Mohawks."

EPILOGUE

THE SMOKE IN THE BARK-WRAPPED lodge was so thick that Duncan could not at first make out all those sitting around the smoldering cedar fire. Conawago motioned him to sit at his side and handed him the long, carved pipe being shared around the circle. Duncan puffed several times, then passed the pipe to the gray-haired woman beside him. Conawago fixed him with an expectant expression. Duncan handed him a piece of paper folded into a fragment of old tartan. The Nipmuc opened the cloth, then studied the paper as Sarah, Hannah, and Pine arrived to fill out the circle. Each in turn took the pipe. Before them were five of the most prominent elders of the Iroquois League, who called out summoning words each time they exhaled the sweet-scented smoke. The three solemn matriarchs and two aged chieftains were gathered not to launch the day's ceremony, Sarah explained earlier, but rather to complete the invitation list.

When Adanahoe, the eldest of the matriarchs and a near saint among her people, had first seen Hannah she gasped, burst into tears, and rushed to embrace her. Long awkward minutes passed before the woman finally collected herself sufficiently to explain that Hannah was the spitting image of the aunt who had cared for Adanahoe in her childhood, during the closing years of the last century, and who had lost her life in the raid in which Hannah's grandparents were taken captive. Tears streamed down Hannah's cheeks as she realized that she had discovered her family.

Now as they sat in the sacred circle, Adanahoe began calling names, first of Hannah's mother and grandparents, then the lost aunt and earlier ancestors, awakening them on the other side, beckoning them to the joy of the day. More names followed as the other elders joined in, raising arms and speaking toward the vent through which the smoke streaked skyward. Duncan recognized some names from tales told around campfires and others of tribal friends fallen in war. He fell into a strange reverie, seeing the lost friends in his mind's eye as he watched the smoke column, where it was said the awakening ghosts sometimes appeared.

He snapped back to attention as first one, then another, of the elders sprang up. "Tashgua! Tashgua!" they shouted in unison, joined by a tearful Sarah. It was the name of the chieftain who had been so fierce in both his defense of his people and his love for his adopted European daughter.

Finally came the turn of the Nipmuc elder. Conawago solemnly extended the tattered swatch of tartan and dropped it into the fire. As its smoke rose, he called out Highland names. "Rory Lawson McCallum! James Alistair McCallum! Lachland Oig McCallum!" His voice cracked, but he pressed on. He had memorized Duncan's list. "Gillian Mary McLaren! Alexander Hugh McDuff! Colin Graham Ogilvie! Rachel Elizabeth McCallum!" They were not Duncan's most renowned ancestors but were the ones he had loved most intensely, the ones he would have wanted to attend had they still walked the earth.

Conawago paused and offered a Scottish name of his own. "Molly Chisholm!" he called into the smoke. "Come be with us, dear Moll!" He fixed Duncan with an inquiring glance, then added one more. "Crispus Attucks, hero of the bloody snow! We need you with us!"

It was midafternoon when they finally descended the hill on which the sacred lodge perched. The lacrosse game that commenced not long after dawn had just concluded, and the settlers and tribal members who played alongside each other were laughing, limping, nursing wounds, and jovially sharing the contents of a cider barrel. Solomon was supporting a lame Tobias on the way to the barrel. They looked more content than Duncan had ever seen them. For the two ex-slaves, this day was also a celebration of the farm and smithy they had started on the outskirts of Edentown. A grinning Cuff, apparently a hero of the game, was surrounded by Iroquois men who were offering drinks and congratulatory slaps on his back.

Long ranks of tables for the coming feast, hosted by Sir William Johnson, both the king's superintendent of tribal affairs and an adopted chieftain of the Mohawks, lay ready at the edge of rolling maize fields. Flanking the tables were slow fires cooking kettles of venison stew and trestles holding barrels of ale, cider, and the flavorful beverage the tribes brewed from sassafras roots. Beyond the tables, guests from Edentown admired the village's fertile orchard and dense plantings of pumpkins.

Duncan heard a shriek of laughter and turned to see Patrick Woolford's daughter riding Blue Turtle like a horse. The girl's father, now head of the new militia company as well as deputy superintendent, was helping a score of excited recruits open trunks delivered by Sir William, packed with the leaf-green coats that would be worn over their new buff waistcoats. A young corporal, wearing a captured red hat that Duncan had first seen in Marblehead, proudly held an oak staff with the militia's new flag, an adaptation of the Edentown flag, with a musket and a bow flanking its solitary tree.

Below the flag was the unit's first trophy, the black-and-crimson flag taken from the *Indigo Queen* in what they proudly called their Battle of the Hudson Pirates. The skirmish had been brief, with most of their opponents abandoning their weapons and fearfully raising hands in surrender as soon as they realized they had been boarded by forest warriors. Woolford's men had stripped the schooner of all weapons and released two slaves taken in New Jersey. To loud curses and vows of vengeance from Melville and the wounded Hugo, they had pried off the cell doors and dropped them into the Hudson. Cuff, Tobias, and Solomon had fashioned nooses, which they placed around the necks of the two bonemen, but Duncan persuaded them that a hanging would attract too much attention and leave the schooner without the officers needed to sail back to the West Indies. Duncan did make it clear that the next time the *Indigo Queen* was seen in the colony—or in Massachusetts, Glover vowed—they would not be dealt with so mercifully. The ex-slaves, not entirely satisfied, scoured the schooner, assembling a pile of manacles and chains, which they also dumped overboard. Afterward Solomon and Tobias held the two bonemen as Cuff carved an *S* into their cheeks.

Duncan had just reached Pine, newly installed as the militia's chief of scouts, when a nervous Mohawk maiden approached and motioned them toward the cluster of tents erected for the Edentown visitors. Rebecca Prescott awaited them.

"I am not to release you until you are both well scrubbed, scented, and attired," the new Edentown schoolmistress declared. "Modesty may not permit me to lend a direct hand, but I shall be waiting outside, ready for final inspection." With a mischievous smile, she directed them into the nearest tent. Inside, four plump matrons, two from Edentown and two from Pine's Oneida clan, awaited with basins of water and pig-bristle brushes. Ignoring the startled protests of their victims, the women began peeling away the two men's clothing.

When Duncan and Pine finally emerged, their hair combed and plaited and smelling of cedar oil, they wore new buckskin leggings and finely worked white doeskin shirts adorned with quillwork patterns. They were led to the nearby hollow, where scores of guests waited under ancient hemlocks. Conawago, wearing his prized velvet waistcoat, stood by Sir William and Adanahoe before a long, flattened boulder that had the appearance of an altar. Arrayed across it were flowers and baskets of fruit. Pine and Duncan stood before the solemn trio, accepting their scrutiny and not reacting when Adanahoe stepped forward for closer inspection. She pulled Duncan's totem pouch out from under his shirt to let it hang over his chest, then produced a jewel-like kingfisher feather, inserted it into Pine's braid, and draped the braid over his shoulder.

As she stepped back beside Sir William and Conawago, Duncan noticed a short, ruddy-faced man behind the superintendent. The stranger wore somber black clothes and appeared extremely nervous about so much Iroquois companionship. He seemed about to flee at any moment, which might explain why Johnson's formidable Mohawk wife, Molly Brandt, and two teenaged sons were standing a few feet behind him.

A low purr of contentment escaped Adanahoe, and a fiddler from Edentown began playing a gentle melody. Duncan and Pine turned to follow her gaze down the path. It wasn't so much a procession that now approached as a throng of joyful faces. Sarah and Hannah, wearing white doeskin dresses decorated with quillwork and bead creatures of forest and field, were surrounded by children of the Iroquois and the settlers, all in their own finery. Several of the girls and boys skipped around the brides, trailing garlands of flowers and colorful ribbons.

Fortunately Duncan knew few words were expected of him in the ceremony, for he was rendered speechless as Sarah approached. She could be one of the fabled princesses of Mohawk, or Highland, legend. Strips of white ermine were braided into her auburn hair. Two narrow bands encircled her neck, one of purple and white beads in the Mohawk pattern, the other a strip of the McCallum tartan. Below them hung a silver chain of semiprecious stones, the gift of Molly Brandt.

He loosened the buckskin strap wrapped around his arm. Sarah gripped his hand, then pressed her forearm against his as Conawago stepped forward. The old Nipmuc carefully wrapped the strap around their joined forearms, tying the ends over their wrists. He then stepped to Pine and Hannah, accepting a second strap from the Oneida groom, and repeated the process, for the two had enthusiastically embraced the Highland tradition when Duncan had explained it.

An Iroquois wedding was nearly all celebration and very little ceremony. Conawago helped Adanahoe extract a wide belt of wampum from a lidded basket on the altar stone, then draped it over her extended hands. The belt, woven with images of tribal tales, had the patina of great age. Adanahoe held the sacred belt, handed down from before memory, as she spoke. The assembly listened as the much-revered matriarch gave thanks to all those in attendance then spoke of the bonds that held a people together and how families built their clans, the clans the tribes, and the tribes the great League itself. When she was done, she lifted the free hands of Hannah and Pine and had them each hold one end of the sacred belt, declaring simply, "You now belong," then repeated the gesture and words with Sarah and Duncan.

Conawago offered a prayer to the earth spirits as he sprinkled salt over their hands and spoke in a low voice, thick with emotion. "My son, my blessing," he said to Duncan. To Sarah, he said, "My daughter, my blessing." Then in a louder voice he declared, "We will hear you."

Duncan took Sarah's free hand and faced her. "I pledge my love, my honor, and my life to you, Sarah Ramsey, and would have all the world know it."

Sarah glowed as she echoed the vow. "I pledge my love, my honor, and my life to you, Duncan McCallum, and would have all the world know it."

They raised their bound arms toward the heavens.

It was the simplest form of the ancient handfast union, with hands and hearts bound before solemn witnesses. Duncan chose not to point out that in the Highlands the witnesses typically included a clergyman, but the point had apparently not been lost on Sir William. After Pine and Hannah recited their own vows, he stepped aside and gestured to the skittish stranger. "If you would but yield us a moment, the Reverend Granger will so attest." Johnson did not wait for a reply, just nudged the reluctant clergyman forward.

The mouselike reverend produced a Bible, which he did not open but clutched as if for protection. "Dearly beloved," he started. His voice cracked, and Duncan and Sarah exchanged an amused glance. He spoke so low and so fast that Duncan doubted many of the onlookers heard him, but then he raised his voice at the critical moment, so that Duncan and Sarah could each offer an energetic *I do.* They had chosen to avoid such formalities of government and church but were content to tolerate them for Sir William's sake.

Hannah, raised in a proper British household, seemed to welcome the Christian ritual. She tightly gripped Pine's arm with her free hand as if fearing he might shy away, then asked Granger to repeat the rites for them. At last the nervous pastor murmured the closing words and the two couples embraced, and more.

The militia, formed into two ranks to create an aisle, broke into a round of repeated cheers as the couples retreated from the altar, with the tribal members shouting "Ka-ya-ya-yay!" rejoined by "Hip-hip-hoo-ray!" from the European members. From the onlookers came hoots, whistles, and war cries.

The feasting, and gift giving, went on long past sunset. Fires, torches, and lanterns were lit. The Edentown fiddler played lively tunes supported occasionally by a tribal drummer, and soon the valley echoed with cheers as tribal members and settlers demonstrated their native dances. The wedding couples glanced often, and expectantly, at the two small lodges set at either side of a huge oak, well furnished with furs and comforters, but dutifully joined in the dances, toasts, and tipsy feats of balance and agility underway at the evening fires.

Children were falling asleep on parents' laps, and the moon was inching over the trees when Patrick Woolford approached and asked if they might spare a few moments for Sir William. Duncan's friend engaged in good-natured banter as they walked, giving no hint of their much more sober dialogue the day before. Ostensibly Duncan and Woolford had slipped away for some trout fishing, but in reality, they had spent most of the afternoon discussing the precarious balance needed to direct a mixed company of Iroquois and settlers. Neither Gage nor Johnson wanted to address the single greatest threat to the peace on the frontier, that of the Europeans stealing across the boundaries of tribal land to snatch up rich valleys and woodland tracts. In his years since leaving the army, moreover, Woolford had become increasingly distrustful of London's politics and a more active supporter of Duncan's work with the Sons of Liberty. They both knew difficult, and probably bloody, years lay ahead. The work of the militia company would not always be directed by General Gage and Sir William.

Sarah and Duncan paused at the entrance to the superintendent's grand pavilion tent, taking in the ever-rich tapestry of Sir William's household. Hunting hounds sprawled, asleep, on the sailcloth underfoot, painted in a checkerboard pattern to resemble a tiled floor. A middle-aged Iroquois woman sat by a brazier, teaching Rebecca Prescott and Esther how to weave dyed quills into a buckskin belt. In a corner lit by several candles Conawago sat playing chess with the clergyman. Josiah and two of Johnson's youngsters played with a top while older Johnson offspring roasted crab apples over a brazier. Sir William, sitting at an elegant camp desk lit by two spermaceti lamps, gestured the three of them to the empty stools before him.

"The Reverend Granger was rather hesitant about venturing into Mohawk lands," the Irishman explained, "but I hold a small mortgage on his wife's father's farm. My ever-charming Molly explained to his spouse that I would tear up the mortgage and present them with the deed if the reverend would but accompany us on a few days of comfortable travel." The superintendent gestured to the chess game. "After an hour with our Nipmuc friend, he declared his amazement that savages could be so civilized."

"Then I suppose we are in your debt," Duncan suggested, perhaps too tentatively.

Sir William smiled. "I know you did not request the European touch, Duncan, but questions will likely be raised from distant quarters. I may be the laird of His Majesty's lands here, but I do not have the authority of even a ship's captain when it comes to matrimony, more's the pity. But"—he indicated a paper on the desk—"Reverend Granger has signed the marriage certificate and"—he lifted a goose quill—"it shall be witnessed by both the superintendent and the deputy superintendent." Woolford took the quill but waited for a nod from Duncan, then dipped it in the desk's inkpot and signed.

"And now for a very fine sherry sent by our friend, the merchant prince of Boston," Sir William declared, rising to retrieve the bottle and glasses from a camp table behind him. "Mr. Hancock has been busy," he continued as he poured. He called for two of the older children to retrieve a small trunk from the back of the tent, which they deposited between Duncan and Sarah. Duncan unlatched the trunk and gestured for Sarah to open it.

On top was a large and lumpy muslin sack with a note from Hancock and DeVries pinned to it: *Although we will not have the pleasure of witnessing it, we will take joy in knowing an English rose will finally stroll among Dutch blossoms next spring.*

"Tulips!" Sarah exclaimed. Inside the sack were several dozen tulip bulbs.

Next, wrapped in red silk, was a gift that took Duncan's breath away. Hancock had sent an entire three-volume set of the *Encyclopedia Britannica*, newly printed in Edinburgh. It would become the centerpiece of the library Duncan and Conawago were building in Edentown.

Underneath the books was a packet of letters with various seals.

"Apparently," Sir William explained, "your former landlady in Marblehead got the notion to forward to the Hancock mansion any mail addressed to you at her house."

"How kind," Sarah observed impassively, then quickly sorted through the letters, scanning the senders. She paused at one, then handed it to Duncan with a knowing gaze. It was from Benjamin Franklin's sister in Boston.

"And"—Sir William continued, a hint of question in his voice—"I had an odd request from General Gage. He instructs me to pay a monthly stipend, a rather generous one, to Hannah, who shall be entered on the militia books as official tribal translator. I take it they must be acquainted somehow? Something of a wedding gift, I suppose? And he further instructs me to consult with the new company's officers to launch a long-range scout down the Ohio to investigate rumors of French activity and, as odd as it may seem, with a particular eye out for new mines and furnaces. I suppose you can find some hearty souls for the adventure, Duncan?"

"We have nothing but hearty souls, Sir William," Duncan earnestly replied, then rose, taking Sarah's hand.

When they reached their wedding lodge, they discovered offerings left on either side of the entrance. A rabbit-fur mitten. A bundle of feathers. An apple pie. Jugs of ale, cider, and maple syrup. Woolford's distinctive silver flask, filled with a fine whisky.

"Go ahead, husband," Sarah said. "Open the letter. Elsewise you'll be sneaking off on our wedding night to read it."

Duncan held the letter into the light of the lantern hanging at the entrance and broke the seal. There was a smaller sealed letter inside the first, which was in Benjamin Franklin's hand and bore a symbol in the corner indicating the code Duncan should use, followed by a question mark. He handed them to Sarah. "Take these. Hide them. Benjamin would agree that I should not spend time deciphering his message on this particular night."

Sarah accepted the message from London, then scanned the cover letter from Franklin's sister. "She sends cordial congratulations and says Benjamin apologizes if he misapplied the code again and for that reason wanted her to convey two essential points." Sarah paused, read silently, then looked up. "Duncan! He reports that a London spy has penetrated the Sons of Liberty in Philadelphia!" When he choked down his response, she shrugged. "Philadelphia is far away. Particularly on this night," she added as if in warning. She folded the small letter into the larger one and slipped them into the new quillwork pouch at her side.

"Two?" Duncan asked. "You said two points."

"Oh," she absently replied as she pushed aside the bear-fur blanket that hung over the entrance. "Benjamin fears we may need to raise alarms about the East India Company and its tea." Before he could react, she pressed a finger to his lips and pulled him inside.

AUTHOR'S NOTE

THE BIRTH OF AMERICA WAS in many ways a miracle wrapped in mystery. It had no antecedents, no deliberate strategies at the outset, no map or plan. Our history books, moreover, generally fail to point out that there existed no institution the patriots could call upon for support. America was built on the backs of remarkable individuals from multiple cultures, economic stations, and religions. The history of the rest of the world can be explained by the dynamics of royal dynasties, military might, ethnic cultures, and religions. The story of America's birth is driven instead by extraordinary people. The challenge of weaving authentic characters into a novel set in the period isn't that of finding compelling characters; it is that of selecting from such a rich cast.

Boston in early 1770 was a town of sixteen thousand, suffocating from the presence of thousands of British troops. As Benjamin Franklin famously warned, if the king were to send occupation troops, "they will not find a rebellion; they may indeed make one." The presence of the troops only fanned the flames of the colonists' defiance. The Crown repeatedly offered concessions with one hand while introducing new oppressive measures with the other. Boston had to endure the highest taxes of any city in the British Empire. London imposed such taxes without consent, dissolved uncooperative legislatures, and ignored petitions for justice. Its severe restrictions on manufacture and trade of vital products such as steel and gunpowder not only injured the colonies economically but also became a deep affront to the self-sufficient spirit of the colonists. The measures turned the

Boston region into a hotbed for sophisticated smuggling, engendering spirited contests between revenue enforcers and defiant free traders.

The disquiet in Boston, heightened by the periodic outbreak of contagious disease in the Twenty-Ninth Regiment's encampment on the Common, tested the tempers, and loyalties, of many who later become prominent in the cause of American independence. These years marked a turning point, the culmination of the identity crisis from which colonists emerged as Americans, British no longer. A poignant example was John Hancock, a complex character known for ostentatious shows of wealth but also great acts of charity, who had difficulty balancing his compulsion to impress the British aristocracy with his role as a leader of the Sons of Liberty. Ultimately, he became one of the most important members of the Continental Congress and dedicated his wealth, and his elegant signature, to the cause of independence.

At the opposite end of Boston's social spectrum were patriots like Crispus Attucks, mariner son of a tribal woman. Little is known about Attucks other than his service as bosun, attesting to his nautical skills, his size—he towered inches over the average British soldier—and his participation in frequent protests against the occupation troops. Attucks's blood was the first to stain the snow in the deadly confrontation of March 5. Although the manipulation of that incident as a means to murder Attucks is a novelist's invention, the role of outside provocateurs is not. London's Black Office, headquarters for the War Council's clandestine affairs, was increasingly active in surveillance of patriots like Benjamin Franklin. The chronicles of the Boston Massacre, moreover, record that a mysterious cloaked stranger was goading those troops at the Custom House. Witnesses reported that it was this civilian who shouted the order to fire, a likelihood supported by evidence that the officer in charge gave no such order.

The massacre raised the stakes, and tensions, for many in Boston. The government was paralyzed by the tragedy, and the Sons of Liberty effectively ran the city for weeks thereafter. The Twenty-Ninth Regiment was indeed dispersed into New York and New Jersey, although not as quickly as posited in this tale. John Adams, who had successfully defended the Marbleheader charged with harpooning a British press gang officer only months before, showed his magnanimity by agreeing to defend the soldiers who had pulled the triggers, including a grenadier named Montgomery. Most of the soldiers were acquitted, but Montgomery and another were found guilty of manslaughter and punished, after invoking "benefit of clergy," by having their thumbs branded. The complex human drama leading up to and following the massacre is examined in fascinating detail in *The Boston Massacre: A Family History* by Serena Zabin and *The Boston Massacre* by Hiller Zobel.

Marblehead was a town whose political and economic significance outweighed its small size. A center of both patriot fervor and smuggling, the fishing port produced many leaders who later gained prominence in the Revolution and the early years of the republic. John Glover, already a sea captain, militia officer, and prominent citizen by 1770, went on to play vital roles in the formation of the American navy, the near-miraculous evacuation of Washington's army after the Battle of Brooklyn, and the famous Christmas crossing of the Delaware. The intriguing tale of Glover and the unique patriots of Marblehead is cogently detailed in Patrick O'Donnell's *The Indispensables*.

Major General Thomas Gage was well entrenched as the long-standing commander of British forces in America, headquartered in New York not just for geographical advantage but also because some of the most aggressive resistance to London's policies had its origins in Manhattan. Confrontations, often violent, over "liberty poles" had been occurring for years, and culminated in the bloody Battle of Golden Hill just weeks before the Boston Massacre. The public faces of the Sons of Liberty in the colony were well known, and targeted for punishment, as evidenced by the imprisonment of Alexander McDougal, later to become one of Washington's most valued generals. The haberdasher Hercules Mulligan served the cause of liberty in more subtle ways, cleverly exploiting his role as tailor to top British officers and eventually running a vital spy network, saving George Washington's life twice from traps planned by the British. Imagination need not be stretched too far to suppose a covert cooperation between Mulligan and Gage's wife, Margaret, known informally as the Duchess. The Duchess, from an old colonial family, had strong patriot leanings, and it is widely believed that she was the secret informant who in 1775 alerted the patriots to her husband's planned march on Lexington and Concord. While there is no direct proof of this, Gage later revealed that he told only his deputy and "one other" of his plans, and shortly after the costly march on the patriot towns he abruptly put his wife on a ship to England.

Although slavery was on the decline in the northeastern colonies by 1770, there were still hundreds of slaves in both Boston and New York, although early in the next decade the institution was outlawed by the courts of Massachusetts, which became the only state reporting zero slaves in the first American census. Our history books seldom speak of the thousands of Native Americans enslaved by colonists, mostly in the seventeenth and early eighteenth centuries, many of whom were sent to servitude on West Indies plantations. It is believed that several mid-Atlantic tribes went extinct as their last survivors died in Caribbean sugar fields. While the conditions of servitude in the North were typically not as severe as on the plantations of the South and the Indies, it was inhuman bondage nonetheless and loathed by most northern supporters of independence. As Duncan discovers in these pages, however, some wealthier patriots had to confront the paradox of advocating freedom for all except those under their own roof.

Runaways were not uncommon, and notices in colonial newspapers offered sometimes rich rewards for their apprehension. Long before northern states outlawed slavery, slaves ran to a different kind of sanctuary in the North: once in Iroquois territory they were safe, for the freedom-loving Iroquois steadfastly refused to surrender runaways who reached their villages.

Historians sometimes contend that the true opening shots of the American Revolution were those fired on that snowy night before Boston's Custom House. Certainly for many, the shooting of unarmed civilians by occupation troops was a defining moment, giving substance to Franklin's warning. The journeys of geographic discovery that had brought Europeans to the continent 150 years before had evolved into journeys of self-discovery, and many of the 2 million colonists were realizing that the path before them was going to be starkly different from the path behind them. As reflected in this tale, the route to freedom was not the same for warrior, slave, merchant, mariner, tailor, or clerk, but by 1770 those routes were quickly converging. For decades the colonists had allowed themselves to be pushed into submission by the British government. Now they were finding a common voice, and a common cause, and they were learning to push back.

Eliot Pattison

© Jed Ferguson

ELIOT PATTISON is the author of the Inspector Shan series, which includes *The Skull Mantra*, winner of an Edgar Award and finalist for the Gold Dagger. Pattison's Bone Rattler series follows Scotsman Duncan McCallum on the road to revolution as he fights to protect the cause of freedom. Pattison resides in rural Pennsylvania. Find out more at eliotpattison.com.